STORM SHADOW

First Published in Great Britain 2016 by Mirador Publishing

First edition: 2016

A copy of this work is available through the British Library.

ISBN: 978-1-911473-10-7

Mirador Publishing
10 Greenbrook Terrace
Taunton
Somerset
TA1 1UT

Storm Shadow

By

Ted Branston

They have sown the wind, and they shall reap the whirlwind

Proverbs. Hosea (8:7)

AUTHOR'S NOTE

We live in troubled times when a clash of different ideologies has tragically manifested itself in violence and bloodshed all too often inflicted upon the young and innocent. This is strictly a work of fiction based on confronting the extremist concept of one such ideology. It is in no way intended to demean or belittle those Muslims in our society who live as part of our nation in harmony with their Christian neighbours, enjoying the freedom to worship an ancient and peace loving religion. For these people, I have all due respect. For those however, who choose to distance themselves from the everyday pattern of life in these Islands, and have perverted the true meaning of Islam to encourage or even actively follow the creed of terrorism, I have nothing but contempt and their barbaric actions defy all rational understanding.

This is the story of an ordinary young man who follows a profession which ultimately requires him to do extraordinary things. I have attempted to portray the impact of this on him and those nearest and dearest to him as realistically as possible, based upon my own experiences of being raised within a close family circle in the heart of the West Country. In this regard some place names are real, others have been fabricated, but Exmoor remains very much for me a place of majesty and beauty that will hopefully never be marred by the events that unfold in these pages.

Similarly all characters depicted herein are entirely fictitious, though some of the organizations they are part of or represent may not be. There is for instance, no Central Counter Terrorist Agency as described, and as we are all aware of the excellent work undertaken by all our existing security agencies, I am not suggesting in any way that these should be supplemented by another, or criticising the role they play in keeping our nation safe.

In conclusion I must offer a word of apology to those men and women who serve in the Yeomanry Regiments of our Army Reserve. In mitigation I would add that I started my long time affiliation with the reserve forces as a Yeoman, being the third generation of a family who served with such Regiments both in Somerset and Dorset. I hope you will accept my portrayal with good humour, influenced as it has been to some degree by the fact that I finished my part time career in the Army as an infantryman, whose view of those who go to war protected by several inches of armour has always been somewhat jaundiced! Having said that however, when we emerge from our holes in the ground to assault an enemy position or are required hold ground when attacked, there is nothing more comforting that having 50 tons of armoured might, packing a 120mm gun to back you up!

Ted Branston,
February 2016.

DEDICATION

To my wife for your unswerving belief that this could happen, to my family and friends for their support and to the men and women of our armed forces who selflessly put themselves in harm's way to ensure our safety.

Chapter One

Farewell to Arms

"Now this is not the end. It is not even the beginning of the end.
But it is perhaps, the end of the beginning."

Winston Churchill, 1942

The first signs of autumn had come early to the South East, and already the leaves were turning colour and drifting down from the trees that lined the avenues of the Military establishments that since Roman times had been the heart of the garrison city of Colchester. The streets shimmered in the morning sunlight from an overnight shower, as chill gusts of wind sent the fallen leaves swirling along the pavements and buffeting the flagpoles which flanked the entrance to the barracks.

The final formalities had not taken long. The paperwork and the return of kit had been dealt with the day before, and the evening spent in the traditional farewell session with his fellow NCOs in the Senior Ranks' Mess. With the long trip ahead of him next day, he had politely avoided over indulging in the endless supply of drinks he was offered and had managed to escape his comrades' generous hospitality, getting to bed not long after midnight.

The final interviews with his Company Commander, the Regimental Sergeant Major and the Battalion Commander that morning had been brief, but the genuine sentiments expressed for his future welfare had left him feeling suddenly alone and vulnerable. He had of course, always known that it would not be easy when the time came for these closing farewells, and when he finally put the comradeship and security of his Regimental family behind him.

At half past ten the taxi was waiting outside the main gate and as the driver loaded his suitcase and kit bag into the boot, he turned to take a last look at the barracks and the sign identifying it as the home of his Battalion. As he lowered himself into the back seat, carefully lifting his prosthetic leg over the sill, the maroon flag emblazoned with the silver winged parachute fluttered boldly from its masthead next to the guardroom, as if paying its own salute to Sergeant Kristian 'KB' Blake, late of the Parachute Regiment.

The taxi turned onto Barrack Street and dropped him off at the Ford dealership, where the salesman he had been dealing with greeted him warmly. The compensation he had received from the MoD for the injuries he had suffered when the IED had taken off his left leg below the knee and torn a chunk out of his arm in Afghanistan, had been paid into his bank account some weeks previously, enabling him to do some hard bargaining at the dealership. As a result he had negotiated a hefty discount on the outright purchase of a brand new Ford Ranger Wildtrak 4 x 4 pick-up truck, now parked on the forecourt in smart black livery. He had chosen the model with the full four door cab and 6 speed automatic gearbox, knowing that the latter would make for easier driving with his artificial left foot.

Stowing his luggage on the rear seats of the cab, he climbed into the driver's seat and after a few minutes briefing from the sales rep and familiarizing himself with the controls, turned the ignition key and after waiting for the seconds needed to warm the air in the cylinders, switched on, and the big three litre diesel burbled into life. Driving an automatic would also be a new experience, but as the Base Transport Warrant Officer had advised him "Just imagine your left foot is screwed to the floor, KB, and you'll soon get used to not having to kick in the clutch". The Warrant had also gone on to suggest that if this proved to be a problem he could supply KB with a screw down version of his prosthetic limb. This was to be repeated when during his farewell party in the Senior Ranks' Mess the night before, much to everyone's amusement, the Warrant had presented him with a tin foot painted in the maroon and sky blue Regimental colours with a four inch bolt drilled through it.

Entering the post code for his destination in the Sat-Nav, he moved the gear selector into drive and eased off the foot brake, accelerating gently to allow the Ranger to pick up momentum. Feeling a surge of excitement behind the wheel of the first new vehicle he had ever owned and with a final wave to the salesman, he nosed out into the traffic and headed for the A12 and Chelmsford.

Half an hour later, and with confidence mounting in his ability to master the unfamiliar experience of allowing his vehicle to take care of the gear changes for him, he pulled into the Chelmsford Service Area and after topping up the tank with fuel, and purchasing a large black coffee to take with him, resumed his journey towards the M25. Even though it was now approaching midday and long past rush hour, the motorway lived up to its reputation as a multi lane parking lot, and it was another two hours before he reached the junction with the M4 and at last was able to pick up some speed as he headed towards Bristol and the South West.

Born and raised on the Somerset Levels and proud of his heritage, he would be spending his first night as a civilian with his parents at The Volunteer, a pub they kept east of Taunton in the small hamlet of Long Lane, close to the small one-time market town of Langport.

In the meantime, and with a long drive in front of him, there was plenty of time for reflection.

Chapter Two

Sniper

"Good results can be obtained with small forces."

Sun Tzu, 'The Art of War'

It had never been his intention to become a Para. Although he had always expected to join the Army, and had followed his years in the Army Cadets with a spell in his local TA unit as part of a Reserve Battalion of The Light infantry, it was a last minute decision that had led him towards the elite regiment, a decision which at times he had come to question during the extreme training that followed his enlistment. Fortunately he had always kept himself reasonably fit, but even this had barely prepared him for the rigours of the six months initial training he had somehow managed to survive.

Of the forty-two recruits that had begun the adventure with him, only a dozen had lasted through the demands of the basic twenty-four weeks infantry training at Aldershot, the mental and physical pressures of Pegasus Company at Catterick and finally the jump course at Brize Norton, where the RAF instructors were almost like genial elder brothers after their Para counterparts. He had emerged from it all with a level of confidence in himself and his abilities he had never thought possible and with his slim six foot frame filled out with a hardness matched only by his mental resolve and commitment to his Regiment.

During those months of training he had relished the time spent in the field and his record showed that he had proved himself not only an expert marksman on the rifle range, but with an aptitude for fieldcraft, endowed as he was with a countryman's natural ability to work in harmony with his surroundings.

Growing up on the Somerset Levels, he had always shared his father's passion for wildlife. Together they had spent hours in his youth tracking the comings and goings of the thousands of migratory geese and ducks that filled the flooded fields around his home during the winter months, and monitoring the progress of wildlife that came and went from the wetlands through the seasons. This not only required patience and the discipline to remain still and silent for long periods of time, but also taught him how to blend into his surroundings so that he became invisible among the reeds and clumps of willow that dotted the marshlands.

With his Basic Training Course Reports highlighting these talents and adding that he had demonstrated 'natural leadership skills', after a relatively brief spell with his Battalion, he was invited to apply for and was granted, a place on a Sniper's course at the Army's Sniper Training Centre at Sennybridge in the Welsh Brecon Beacons, an opportunity which he had welcomed and which would prove to be a cornerstone of the career that lay ahead of him.

At Sennybridge he had quickly learnt that there was a lot more to becoming a sniper than being good with a rifle and having the ability to lie concealed in the reeds by a river bank for a couple of hours. The importance of accurate reconnaissance and observation, concealment and covert movement were drilled into him and his fellow trainees until it consumed their waking hours from dawn to dusk, and then often well into the hours of darkness.

In particular the night-time occupation of an observation post – or OP – and then in the light of day, lying concealed often for hours at a time watching and waiting for a target, tested their patience and self-discipline to the full.

It was during one of these night-time exercises that he had done particularly well. The task was to locate an 'enemy' observation post that the instructors had set up on the fringe of a wooded outcrop perched halfway up a steep slope overlooking a small valley. The trainees were required to locate the OP, select and set up a firing position with a line of sight to their target during the hours of darkness, and then 'eliminate' the OP at first light. Pinpointing the OP was essential, as with the woods effectively screening it from the rear, there were only limited options for finding a firing position that would provide an opportunity for a clear shot.

At their briefing they had each had the opportunity for a detailed examination of the target area on the range maps and with the help of aerial photographs, had weighed up their options for the best line of approach to their objective and the potential sites for their sniping positions.

They were all fully aware that by choosing to access the objective through the scrub and woodland to the rear would be the most dangerous where the snap of a twig or crunch of the undergrowth could quickly betray an intruder, or at worst triggering a trip flare. In spite of these potential hazards KB had chosen this route to his target, rather than across the clearer open ground to the front, reckoning that the 'enemy' would probably be facing away from him as he sought to pinpoint their position.

His gamble had paid off, and after three hours of slow and painstaking stalking through the woods, during which he had safely disarmed two trip flares, he had located the OP and then withdrawn to skirt the copse and set up his firing position approximately 400 metres to the west of his target.

His luck stayed with him when at first light he had confirmed his target without the need for further adjustment to his position, and through his scope was able to identify the location of the hidden observers he had come to dispatch.

A slight movement, as his opposition moved his own rifle into a fire position, provided him with the final confirmation he needed. Cross hairs of the scope on his target, the ball of his finger on the trigger, two gentle deep breaths then a pause in his breathing and he took his shot, the crack of the blank cartridge shattering the peace of the morning.

Within five minutes an instructor appeared and lying by his side, confirmed the 'kill'. A long blast on a whistle then brought all the trainee snipers to their feet, most of them in positions in the valley below their target and some distance from KB.

In the debrief that followed he was expecting some recognition of his success and was therefore somewhat chastened when the senior instructor criticized his method of target location by approaching through the wood.

"What the hell do you think you were doing, Blake?" was the ribald comment, "floating around in woods at night like Casper the freaking ghost?" However, reluctant praise was handed out for his having achieved his objective, albeit with a final comment that in a real situation he might well have been lucky to get away with it, but the 'Casper' label stuck with him for the remainder of the course.

As the course progressed KB found himself paired with a Para from another Battalion. In the field snipers often operated as a two man team, the second member acting as a spotter and observer, with the two alternating sniping duties. KB's partner, Fred Nowakowski, was a third generation Polish Brit, whose grandparents had escaped Poland at the time of the Nazi invasion, and whose grandfather had jumped with the Polish Brigade at Arnhem.

Fred's devotion to all things Para became something of a legend among the trainee snipers, and when one chose to remove Fred's maroon beret from his locker, hiding it as a harmless prank, KB had to forcibly restrain his partner from physically tearing their barrack room apart in his search for the precious headgear.

Once recovered, an uneasy peace was restored, but if Fred had ever discovered the identity of the culprit, KB was convinced that the consequences would have been dire for the mischievous thief.

Fred turned out to be an ideal partner for the West Countryman, although not matching KB's fieldcraft skills Fred compensated with boundless energy and reserves of physical strength that proved to be more than equal to whatever challenge was put to them. Moreover, although inclined to be less patient and meticulous than KB, Fred's ability as a marksman certainly rivalled that of his team mate.

As their term at sniper school ran its course, the two became inseparable and as their skills developed, they began to stand out from the rest of the group. In this, however, they were not entirely on their own, and a friendly but fierce rivalry developed between the two Paras and a pair from the Gurkhas, both teams realizing that they stood a chance of finishing in the coveted first place when the final assessments were made at the end of the course.

In the meantime another special and equally important partnership was developing, this time between the men and their other constant companion, the Accuracy International AW bolt action sniper rifle. Firing a .338 Magnum round from a 10 shot magazine and fitted with the excellent x 25 magnification Schmidt & Bender scope, the rifle had originally been designed for the British Olympic team, but with an effective range of 1,000 to 1,500 metres, it had become arguably the best anti-personnel sniper rifle in the world.

The course instructors had been high in their praise for the accuracy of the rifle, reminding their trainees that it was using this weapon that an NCO of the Household Cavalry had killed two Taliban machine gunners at a range of 2,470 metres in Helmand Province, the feat becoming a legend amongst the sniper fraternity.

With such confidence in their rifle that this instilled in the trainees, coupled with the effectiveness to which they put the supplementary equipment they were issued with, by the time the course ended, they had all become masters of their craft and capable of matching their skills against the best that any other NATO unit could put into the field.

Before returning to their units, however, there was one final exercise which would determine which of the teams would emerge from their training as the best in every part of their hard learnt sniper disciplines.

After the tests in fieldcraft, observation and tactics, KB and Fred Nowakowski were tied with their Gurkha counterparts, with a team from the Rifles hot on their heels. Eventually it was in the live firing exercise and pure marksmanship competitions that the Paras excelled, both scoring the maximum possible at 1,000 metres, and resulting in them emerging as the course leaders.

On returning to his Battalion, KB had barely a chance to settle in properly before he found himself sent on his Junior NCO's course. Once again he entered a world of spit and polish, a stark contrast to his recent experiences in the Brecon Beacons, but he quickly adapted to the new regime and a satisfactory grade on passing out saw him promoted to Lance Corporal. A spell of leave at home was enjoyed and then back to Colchester as the newest member of the Sniper Platoon preparing for his first tour in Afghanistan.

Chapter Three

Afghanistan – First Time Around

"He clasps the crag with crooked hands;
Close to the sun in lonely lands,
Ring'd with the azure world he stands.
The wrinkled desert beneath him crawls;
He watches from his mountain walls,
And like a thunderbolt he falls."

After Alfred Lord Tennyson, 'The Eagle'

The sun rose slowly over the mountains that lay far to the east of their position, leaving the ravines and valleys that scarred the towering walls of rock shrouded in shadow and sending tendrils of sunlight creeping out across the rock strewn escarpment to their front.

They lay concealed at the edge of a large expanse of scrub and waist high tufts of grass on the forward slope of a steep ridge that rose several hundred feet from the valley floor, cut by a glacier of a bygone age and now marked by a shallow river which flowed away to the east, and a barely discernible track which followed its bends and twists. Just below the lip of the escarpment lay a small scattering of stone and wattle dwellings surrounded by a low wall, the home of a handful of families whose livelihood depended on grazing their herds of sheep and goats in the surrounding hillsides.

From the cluster of small houses, wisps of smoke arose into the morning air, suggesting that the occupants were preparing their first meal of the day and occasionally a figure would emerge into the daylight to walk the fifty metres or so down to the riverbank for a quick wash and to draw a pail of water for the homestead.

From their position slightly over six hundred metres to the south, the farmhouses and their surroundings had already been under close observation for over twenty-four hours, and by now the watchers were beginning to wonder whether the intelligence that had brought them here was still holding true.

The team had been chosen carefully. From the Battalion Sniper Platoon, Sergeant Wally McKeegan, a quietly spoken Glaswegian and veteran of Iraq and one previous tour in Afghanistan would co-ordinate the attack, with KB alternating with him as sniper/spotter. Back-up was provided by a second team lead by Corporal Joe Benson, a slightly built Geordie, who with his spotter another Lance Corporal from the Sniper Platoon, now lay no more than six feet to the left of KB and the Sergeant's position, Corporal Benson nursing 'the beast'. Bringing the team up to a total of six, was a young Captain and a Corporal Radio Operator from the Brigade Reconnaissance Force Intelligence Corps detachment.

'The beast' was an American Barrett M82 sniper rifle primarily designed to immobilise and destroy soft skinned and lightly armoured vehicles out to a range of 1,800 to 2,000 metres. Unlike their sniper rifles, the Barrett was semi-automatic and fired a hefty .50 calibre bullet from a 10 round magazine, giving up a marginal degree of accuracy in exchange for the ability to lay down a shattering fusillade of shots much faster than its bolt action counterpart.

Travelling at over 2,500 feet per second, the special armour piercing incendiary round could crack open a cylinder block like a festive walnut or turn a pick-up truck into a ball of fire in seconds. Along with his fellow snipers, KB had developed considerable respect for the Barrett and its capability which shortly would be tested to the full.

For their mission planning they had been called to the Brigade Intelligence Centre at Camp Bastion where they had spent the best part of a day going through a series of briefings. A minute examination of the maps of the area, aerial photographs, logistic and support briefings, plus the latest intelligence on their target, culminated in a four hour planning session jointly led by their own Sniper Platoon Commander, an Intelligence Corps Major and a senior BRF officer.

Based on intelligence gathered by the BRF, their targets were identified as several local leaders of the various Taliban groups operating in their area, plus the individual believed to be the Taliban Area Commander. The indications were that a meeting would take place at the village that they now overlooked, undoubtedly to co-ordinate ongoing insurgency strategy and probably to elect new leaders to replace those lost to the allied forces during a number of successful operations carried out over the preceding weeks.

The unknown factor was the precise timing of the meeting, so rather than attempting to take out the farmhouse complex with a Reaper drone strike, the sniper patrol would be sent in to keep the objective under surveillance for as long as was necessary, and then eliminate their individual targets with the precision that only these marksmen could provide.

It was also expected that the skill of the sniper team in selecting individual targets would limit the collateral damage that would inevitably result from a drone strike.

Photos of the Taliban Commander were circulated and it would be left to the Intelligence Corps Captain to confirm final identification as the Taliban group assembled. It was agreed that action would not be initiated until the last practical opportunity when all the targets were on site and maximum effect could be achieved.

With the objective well inside Taliban dominated territory, the team had been transported by Mastiff Armoured Personnel Carrier to a drop off point at last light several kilometres from the village and from whence they had completed their journey on foot. It was a long trek, necessitating them laying up at daybreak and then continuing their trek the second night guided by GPS to the OP position, where they were well settled in and concealed before sunrise. As no exact timing for the insurgent meeting had been confirmed they had been warned to expect to be in situ for three or four days.

Communications were the responsibility of the Intelligence Corps members of the team, and a link to base via Skynet satellite. Encoded and compressed updates – or sitreps – were being sent at irregular intervals within every twenty-four hour period and by high speed transmissions lasting only a few seconds to minimize any chance of a trace.

Sergeant McKeegan and KB carried their respective sniper weapons with Joe Benson sharing the load of the Barrett and its ammunition with his spotter Lance Corporal Tweedie who, with the Int. Corps members of the team carried standard L85A2 assault rifles. As the senior rank, the Int. Corps Captain was technically in command of the group, but as each member knew and understood the role they had to play, it was considered unlikely to be a situation where there would be occasion or need for re-thinking strategies, and with Sergeant McKeegan in charge of the snipers the Paras had every confidence in their ability to carry out a successful mission. As is normal in the modern British Army when operating in the field, the formalities of rank had been relaxed and the Captain was already being referred to as 'boss'.

In fact the tall, lanky Int. Corps officer, Captain Andrews, turned out to be an affable and easy going character with a wry sense of humour, which was more than could be said for his assistant Corporal Alsop, an irritating young man with an air of self-importance which did little to endear him to the Paras.

Their exit strategy was based on a simple plan. Immediately after the action they would call in a brief sitrep and based upon their assessment of the level of success they would pull back a thousand metres and secure a Landing Zone they had picked off the map for a helicopter lift, or if there was evidence of heavy enemy activity in the area, they would wait until night fall and withdraw on foot, to be picked up by Mastiff at the drop off point close to the one they had used on the way in.

As Captain Andrews had commented, "Let's not bank on being choppered out, guys. With the likelihood of other Taliban groups in the area, the hills will be crawling with the buggers as soon as the first shot is fired and HQ may be unwilling to risk a pick up from a 'hot' LZ.

They had reached their objective without incident, though even for fit men carrying the load of food, water, weapons, ammunition, and night observation kit, the hike from their drop off point had proved to be quite a challenge. Once in position they had confirmed good line of sight to the target, dug themselves into the thin flinty top soil as best they could, and beefed up their overhead cover with the careful deployment of the small camouflage nets they had brought with them.

By sun up they were all in place and the first day passed with each pair taking it in turns to keep the farmstead under observation, but it was not until around dusk was falling that their patience was rewarded when the distant buzz of two-stroke engines alerted the team, and shortly afterwards two motor bikes came up the track by the river and turned into the farm yard.

Both bikes were carrying pillion passengers and all four riders had AK-47 rifles slung over their shoulders. After dismounting they carried out a detailed inspection of all the buildings giving the watchers an opportunity to check out each individual and confirm that their primary target, the Taliban Area Commander was not amongst them.

"This is certainly a recce party set to check out the RV before the meeting," commented the Captain, "so we'll just keep an eye on them and hope their boss shows up tomorrow."

The night had passed agonizingly slowly, two members of the team at a time on watch scanning the farm and the ground immediately surrounding them with their night scopes. Their meal packs had been eaten cold and water drunk sparingly. Other bodily functions were carried out in situ to avoid even the slightest movement which could have betrayed their position.

As the sun rose higher in a sky studded with pure white clouds, activity around the compound increased, two of the recce party had arrived the previous evening emerging to scan their surroundings carefully through binoculars. A few minutes later women and children were seen leaving their homes and gathering in the middle of the farmyard, then to be led away by the other two Taliban to a low building at the far end of the compound. The low half door was flung open and the group shut in, with one of the gunmen squatting down outside. "Something's up," murmured McKeegan. "They're probably keeping the families together as hostages to make sure there's no trouble when the big shot arrives, but I wouldn't like to be in that shed once it starts warming up."

An hour passed and the watchers' patience was rewarded by the sound of approaching vehicles, this time the inevitable Toyota pick-up truck accompanied by yet another motor cycle with pillion rider.

"Can't spot our man in this lot" said the Captain, and the Para snipers agreed that they too were unable to identify him among the half dozen new arrivals now milling about the farm yard and exchanging greetings. These formalities completed, the men dispersed, two entering the largest of the houses while the remainder selected defensive positions behind the walls on the perimeter of the ruins. One in particular seemed to be in charge, checking each man's location to ensure an effective field of fire and scanning the surrounding hills and slopes through binoculars.

The minutes ticked by and once again the sound of approaching vehicles drifted up to the watchers. This time a small convoy of three pick-up trucks was seen coming up the track, and as they came into full view the watchers attention was drawn to the leading vehicle. Instead of carrying more armed guards, it soon became clear that this would require their serious attention.

"What do you make of it, Sergeant?" queried the Captain. "Could provide us with a bit of a challenge!"

"Or a load of grief," replied McKeegan. "There's a Dishka machine gun mounted on that lead truck. I reckon that this is definitely the main party and by the size and strength of the escort, I would say that it's pretty certain our main target has arrived."

At this KB moved his scope from the farm onto the approaching vehicles and saw the ugly snout of the heavy automatic weapon protruding over the cab. This was indeed bad news, as in the right hands the weapon could be highly effective and they were well within its killing range.

"Ok" continued the Sergeant, "listen up. The minute this lot pulls into the farm, we go for it. Benson your priority is to take out the machine gun and gunner first and then immobilize the trucks. Captain Andrews, give us the shout as soon as you have a fix on our man, and meanwhile KB and I will take down as many of them as we can. As soon as I have clear ID from you, Captain, I will concentrate on making the shot, while you Blake will spot for me and provide back-up. Benson, as soon as you are satisfied that the trucks are destroyed switch to any other targets of opportunity in or around the farmhouse. Clear?"

"Clear," came back the replies, and no sooner than the Sergeant had finished giving his orders, the three trucks pulled off the track and drove into the central yard around which the buildings were clustered.

As the driver of the lead truck came to a halt, Benson squeezed off the first shot from the Barrett and split seconds later the armour piercing round ricocheted off the machine gun and knocked the gunner over the side of the truck and out of view. "Fuck it, too high," muttered the sniper, adjusting his sights, switching aim and putting the next round into the cab. The third round hit the chassis mounted fuel tank square on and in an instant flames shot up to engulf the vehicle.

At the same time McKeegan and KB were already engaging their targets and several of the new arrivals had already gone down under the hail of fire that now rained down on them. Benson had now switched his aim to the third in line of the pick-ups which was also dispatched in a ball of fire from its ruptured fuel tank, while a round into the cylinder block had foiled the driver of the middle vehicle's attempts to get it mobile.

In the yard the Taliban were running everywhere, desperately seeking shelter behind the perimeter wall or diving for cover into the farmhouse. "No sight of the main man yet," reported Andrews, as a shot from McKeegan lifted a runner off his feet and threw him backwards from his hastily sought cover to land behind a pile of stones that had once been part of the inner compound.

Benson had switched his attention to the fourth pick-up which was partially shielded behind a broken down outbuilding, and after three further shots a wisp of smoke from under the bonnet indicated that it too was going nowhere.

As the minutes ticked by all movement in the compound ceased as the remaining Taliban crouched behind the walls or sheltered in the farmhouse. "I'm going for the main farmhouse, boss," muttered Benson, and opened fire on the largest of the buildings aiming just below the single window. The effect was almost instantaneous as two figures emerged from the gap that served as an entrance and flung themselves down behind the perimeter wall. The snipers had no time to think about the effect a round piercing the stone and wattle wall and exploding inwards would have had on the occupants, but knew that each hit would be sending shards of flint ricocheting around inside the single room dwelling.

A third Taliban appeared in the doorway and paused briefly in an attempt to establish the direction the shots were coming from. The pause was sufficient for McKeegan to drop him, but before the Scotsman could reload a further figure flung himself out of the building leapfrogging his fallen comrade and sprinting for the farthest wall of the compound over which he tumbled as a shot from KB clipped the stonework missing him by inches.

"That's our man," called out Andrews. "Got a full face as he came through the door, and I'm sure it's him." The fugitive was now fully shielded from the watchers behind his hastily sought refuge, and if by signal the heads of several of the remaining insurgents popped up from behind their cover and sustained fire from their AK-47's crackled through the air.

A moment later it became evident that the fire was not being directed and was aimed haphazardly at the high ground where the snipers lay. The chance of an AK round doing any serious damage at the range the insurgents were firing was minimal, but the characteristic buzz of a heavier calibre round passing overhead alerted the watchers to a different threat. "They must have a sniper down there," said McKeegan. "See if you can spot him, KB."

KB was about to take his aim off the spot where the suspected leader had disappeared over the wall, when a flicker of movement slightly to the left and beyond the wall caught his attention. Just as he adjusted his aim to take a closer look at this disturbance, a Taliban emerged from the surrounding scrub astride a motor cycle, and as the bike slowed the suspect leapt from his cover to vault onto the pillion. KB fired at the same instant, instinctively taking a short lead in front of the bike to allow for its forward movement and the bullet's time of flight to the target.

The .338 magnum round took the man full in the chest, and the bike reared up to flip over backwards trapping the unfortunate rider under it, and throwing its passenger to the ground. An instant later, rounds from McKeegan and Benson both smashed into the targets and a blazing motor bike and a dark stain spreading from beneath it gave testimony to the effectiveness of their strikes.

This caused an eruption of fire from the defenders and with shots from their own sniper kicking up spurts of gravel across the front of their position, it became obvious to the team that although their exact location may not have been spotted, the Taliban had now gained a fairly accurate estimate of where they were hidden.

"Hey guys, we've got company," called out Tweedie. "Insurgents to our east, maybe ten to fifteen spread out and advancing towards us along the line of the track – still maybe two klicks away."

"I'll track them," called back Captain Andrews and as he shifted his position, McKeegan called to the rest of the team to scan the ground beyond the farm to their front and to the west.

With the Barrett ensuring the defenders of the farm kept their heads well down, after a few minutes careful observation, McKeegan confirmed no movement beyond the farm to their front. KB, however, had picked up the glint of sunshine off metal or the windscreen way to the west, and moments later confirmed that there was movement towards them from that direction.

"They probably had standing patrols on the track both sides of us," said the Captain, "and with the sound of the firefight, plus the smoke from the burning trucks they certainly have a good idea of our location and will try to nail us down here." Taking the handset of the radio from his signaller, he then called through to their Headquarters and after a brief conversation, confirmed what they had all guessed would be their next move.

"Time to bug out, guys. We're ordered to pull back to the LZ at best speed and set up a perimeter guard to wait for a lift off. The incoming chopper is being escorted by an Apache, which should give the bad guys out there something to think about, but we need to move now. We'll pull back to the crest using the scrub as cover, so keep low on the ground as far as you can. Benson, you and Tweedie will stay here for five minutes after we've pulled out to keep our friends down there occupied, then RV with us just over the crest. All clear? Okay – let's go!"

As they broke from cover a fusillade of shots greeted their exit and as they had expected it was a short but uncomfortable drag up to the crest of the escarpment on which they had set up their firing position. Led by the Captain and his radio operator, they squirmed their way up the slope to within a couple of metres of the crest, where a narrow plateau stretched along the ridge, before dropping off to a gentle slope to the south and the LZ that was their objective. As they neared the crest, the ground rose sharply and was devoid of scrub, which meant a final desperate drive for cover over the top.

Alsop, the radio operator, had taken the climb up the hill badly and was gasping with exhaustion as he neared the barren patch of shale that marked the end of their climb. The Captain had wriggled over the edge without a problem, but to KB's horror Alsop suddenly staggered to his feet and lunged forward for the few final steps. As he did so, there was the sickening thud of a bullet hitting flesh followed by the distant crack of the Taliban sniper's rifle and Alsop fell forward to be dragged into cover by the Captain.

Almost instantaneously Benson returned fire, and taking the opportunity KB also dived for safety. Leaving the Captain to tend to Alsop, KB manoeuvred himself along the crest until he found a small rocky outcrop from which he could take up a new firing position which overlooked the majority of the farmstead and its surroundings. With their location now known to the enemy and a skilled marksman probably still behind the rifle now being aimed at them from the farmhouse, Benson and Tweedie would now be in need of some accurate fire to cover their escape.

Taking a few moments to regain his breath, KB adjusted his sights for the slight increase in range and elevation and brought the farm back into view through his 'scope. All appeared to be quiet in the farmyard, but his new position had brought the second motor cycle partially into view from behind the wall where it had been concealed. His first shot confirmed the range and the bike toppled over and fell on its side. KB kept up a steady rate of fire on the target area until a shout from his Sergeant called him back to join the others. Alsop was lying on his back, ashen faced with a field dressing strapped to his left shoulder. "It looks as if it missed the bone," the Captain reported to which Benson added, "I think I got their shooter, he moved position after the shot that got Alsop and I'm pretty sure I nailed him."

Slinging his rifle over his shoulder, KB picked up Alsop's rifle and relieved him of the additional magazines he was carrying. Leaning on Tweedie for support, Alsop got shakily to his feet as the party moved off across the open ground that would eventually bring them to the LZ. "Come on, lads," urged the Sergeant. "Those buggers out there are really pissed off and will be busting their guts to get after us, so let's move it."

Even with their walking wounded, they made good time to the LZ where they quickly established a perimeter guard and Captain Andrews radioed that they were in position. "Twenty minutes, guys," called out the Captain as they settled in to wait, the minutes dragging by. From their positions, the snipers anxiously scanned the ground around for any sign of movement and in particular the hills which now lay to their east and which could provide an ideal firing position for a Taliban machine gunner eager to cause problems for their incoming rescuers.

"Bang on time," Tweedie called out, as at last the waiting team picked up the familiar 'whop-whop-whop' of multiple rotor blades and out of the distant haze came the welcome sight of an Apache gunship trailed by a Sea King, skimming over the plain like a brace of giant dragon flies.

The Apache swept over the LZ, broke left and circled to scour the surrounding area, while the Sea King settled down gently in a swirl of choking dust and grit. The door gunner beckoned them forward and they ran towards the now stationary helicopter, half lifting, half dragging Alsop with them. Helping hands hauled them on board and with a thumbs up from their boss, the loadmaster gave the OK for lift off to his pilot and with a surge of power the big bird lifted off and banked towards home.

Chapter Four

Seasoned Warrior

"Regard your soldiers as your children and they will follow you in the deepest valley; look upon them as your beloved sons , and they will stand by you even unto death. If, however, you are indulgent and unable to make your authority felt; kind hearted , but unable to enforce your commands; and incapable moreover, of quelling disorder, then your soldiers will be likened to spoilt children, they are useless for any practical purposes."

Sun Tzu, 'The Art of War'

The debrief from the mission had been thorough, and a few days later it was confirmed that they had achieved their objective. A reconnaissance drone which had flown over and photographed the target area within minutes of their withdrawal had identified one of the bodies lying by the motor cycle as the Taliban area commander, and information which filtered in from local informants suggested that at least two other local group leaders had also been killed in the fire fight. Subsequent flights had indicated that the village had been abandoned by its inhabitants, who had probably fled into the surrounding hills in an attempt to avoid reprisals from the Taliban.

Later on further good news came in via the Sniper Platoon Commander who informed KB that he had been promoted to full Corporal, and that Captain Andrews, Sergeant McKeegan and both he and Benson had been recognized with Mentions in Dispatches.

The remainder of his first tour had been equally action packed. With their Battalion, the Sniper Platoon made up part of the Regional Battle Group South, working in terrain ranging from irrigated farmland to barren desert and from the mountains of Zabul close to the Pakistan border, to the streets of Kandahar City.

From rooftop OP's in Kandahar KB found himself covering street patrols and then within hours, being flown out to accompany fighting patrols and Company assaults on Taliban strongholds across Kandahar Province and southern Helmand. Now leading his own team, he and his spotter also found themselves covering "hearts and minds" operations to win the support of the local populace, and playing their own special role in the successful delivery of a giant hydro-electric turbine to the Kajaki Dam in northern Helmand.

These missions included both long hours of boredom manning OP's covering the convoy route, to "hit and run" patrols creating diversions and attacking the strongholds that the insurgents had reinforced throughout the area – anything to keep the Taliban tied down and away from the convoys to and from the dam site.

As a sniper KB generally was fully aware of how effective his role was in these missions, but unlike many of his colleagues, KB never discussed with them the tally of Taliban that had paid the penalty of challenging his skills as a sniper. He knew, however, that the number was considerable and as his reputation grew amongst his peers, it had also not gone unnoticed by his superiors.

With their tour ended, once back in Colchester the routine of life in barracks was hard to take at first, but a welcome spell of leave with his parents and his sister at the family pub in Somerset helped to soothe the more unpleasant memories that any soldier with wartime experiences carried with them. Like all those who had been in the front line, KB had been warned that sometimes these memories would manifest themselves with flashbacks, violent dreams and more extremely, the debilitating and life changing mental illness caused by post combat related traumatic stress disorder.

To counter these symptoms he had trained himself to separate what he was called upon to do as a fighting soldier and sniper, from what he considered his 'second self' where his energies, both physical and mental were focussed on daily routines, deliberately transferring his thoughts as far from the fire fights as possible. Although he did not realize it, this did have a downside, and his chosen way of controlling his mental processes and the fears and memories that might otherwise have disturbed him, was frequently interpreted by his small circle of friends as being an aloofness that inevitably set him apart.

The popular saying among his peers was that KB was a 'loner' with ice water flowing through his veins, but in the post action reports studied by his superiors it was frequently noted that here was a man who kept a cool head under pressure and displayed the much valued property of remaining calm and controlled in the most dangerous situations.

Had he known this, KB would not have been as surprised as he was to be called in front of his Company Commander shortly after his return, for a session of 'career counselling' which determined that a change in direction would be advisable if he were to achieve his full potential as an NCO.

As a result, shortly afterwards, KB found himself posted out of the Sniper Platoon and sent to Aldershot as a Section Commander and Instructor on a Recruit Course.

Here he was to experience the responsibilities of disciplining and mentoring the raw recruits of whom he had been one not so long before. With his leadership skills developing under the eagle eye of the Platoon Sergeant, instead of adopting the more traditional aggressive and loudly vocal approach of his fellow Section Corporals, KB imprinted his personality on his charges with a quiet but firm resolve that seldom required him to raise his voice more than a few decibels.

His posting to Aldershot was for a year, during which time he was involved with three successive recruit courses. The toughest was the last, for after the first two it became evident that his Sections had a lower attrition rate than the others, so for his final tour he was given a group who had already been earmarked at selection as being only marginally capable of succeeding.

As the course progressed, KB became more and more determined that his flock of 'lame ducks' as they had been nicknamed by his fellow Section Commanders, would at least match the performance of the other sections in the Platoon, and he found himself putting in long hours to give individual tutoring to the most needy. His efforts had paid off, and by the end of the twenty-four weeks the number of drop-outs in his Section numbered no more than those of his colleagues.

Back at Colchester his Battalion was already beginning the long process of work-up to maximum efficiency before another tour in Afghanistan, the highlight of which was intensive field training in Canada at Camp Wainwright in central Alberta, a 600 square kilometre expanse of prairie south east of the city of Edmonton.

Each of the Battalion's Companies was rotated in turn for a two week exercise, being flown out from Brize Norton to Edmonton by RAF Globemaster transports and then transferring to a Canadian FMC Hercules for the jump into Wainwright. Having dropped their Paras, the 'Hercs' then landed on the military airstrip at Wainwright, picked up the outgoing Company and ferried them back to Edmonton for the flight back to the UK.

Apart from a few delays and minor logistical 'fuck-ups', KB's drop had gone well. The Paras had jumped with a full load of backpack, weapons and ammunition. As soon as they had exited the aircraft and made sure their parachutes had deployed properly, they lowered their heavy packs on lines attached to their harness, to hang beneath them as they descended thus reducing the strain on knees and ankles when they landed.

The drop zone – or DZ – was a large relatively flat grassy area covering several acres which had been secured by the Pathfinder Platoon who had jumped in advance of the main body. The entire exercise was to be carried out under tactical conditions to make it as realistic as possible, and as they unclipped their harnesses, got to their feet and rolled up their 'chutes, they could already hear the crackle of blank ammunition in the distance, indicating an early contact with the 'enemy'.

The enemy for this exercise was being provided by the Princess Patricia's Canadian Light Infantry (the PPCLI – nicknamed the 'Picklies', or more known generally as the Princess Pats), a troop of Cougar light armoured vehicles from the Lord Strathcona's Horse (or 'Strats'), supported by signallers and engineers from the Wainwright garrison. Many of these troops had experienced at least one tour in Afghanistan and were well suited to providing the kind of opposition needed to ensure the success of Operation 'Buffalo Jump' as it had been called.

The Paras' tasks had been chosen to replicate those that they might encounter in their forthcoming tour, to seek out and destroy enemy patrol bases and OPs, disrupt his lines of supply and to carry out fighting patrols deep into his territory.

The first task assigned to KB's platoon was to search out and neutralize an enemy sniper team believed to have located themselves close to the western boundary of the training area overlooking the Battle River, and close to a wide gravelled road which provided the main access for vehicles to Camp Wainwright. For KB this was a case of 'poacher turned gamekeeper' and it was hardly surprising that his section was put on the point position, leading the platoon across the ridge that overlooked the river on its eastern boundary.

The PPCLI sniper had chosen a hide in some heavy scrub just below the crest of a hill, and it was not until he fired at a section patrolling the banks of the river below them, that KB was able to pinpoint his location. Moving his team to encircle the marksman from the rear, KB sent a contact report over his radio and ordered a brief burst of fire from the section's Minimi. Almost immediately the 'enemy' rose from their hide, hands raised in the air as it was clearly 'game over'.

There were three of them, the sniper and his spotter, and a young Lieutenant wearing the white armband identifying him as an Umpire, who now greeted KB with a friendly grin and a handshake. "Well done, Corporal, neat job. Sniper position neutralized but no casualties, so these guys are now in your safe keeping. I'm off, so it's over to you." With a cheery wave the umpire took his leave, while KB called in a sitrep.

With darkness approaching, KB was ordered to move his section down close to the roadway and to lie up for the night to await collection of his prisoners who would be taken off for interrogation at first light. For a change, KB found himself out of the main action for a while, so selecting a small copse some fifty metres in from the track as a suitable bivouac site, led his men down the slope and into the trees.

While they laid out their kit and secured their perimeter, KB took the opportunity to question his prisoners, both of whom vowed that they could 'Speek no Ingleesh'. It was inevitable that this was done with a certain amount of humour, although as all of them well knew, in a real scenario proceedings would have taken a more sinister approach, but the search of their kit was thorough and revealed that amongst their personal belongings, both were carrying mobile phones.

Once these formalities were over, the two NCOs agreed to an informal truce 'off the record' and conversation became more relaxed. Knowing any information now exchanged would not be reported as part of the exercise formalities, KB learned the sniper was a Master Corporal from Vancouver Island with four years' service in the PPCLI and his companion was a reservist serving in the Militia, the Canadian Army Reserve. KB was not surprised at this, as he knew Canada's small but well trained Armed Forces relied heavily on the Militia to supplement their numbers both on active service and in major training exercises, and without whom they would otherwise find it difficult to function.

KB also took full advantage of the opportunity to examine the Canadian sniper's rifle, the C14 Timberwolf that fired the same .338 round KB had used to such deadly effect in his own weapon in Afghanistan. This led to an informal discussion on the relative merits of their sniper rifles, both respecting the professionalism of their counterpart.

Their hide perimeter secured and reinforced with carefully placed trip flares, KB ordered his men to break out their rations, realizing that they would also have to feed their prisoners. To his surprise, before the 'boil in the bag' rations were opened, the Master Corporal suggested a better approach.

"Hang on a minute, boss," offered the Canuck. "Would you and your guys prefer a pizza? There are several pizza joints in Wainwright town and we can rustle one if you don't mind waiting for half an hour or so!"

"Sounds great," said KB, noting the murmurs of assent from his Paras, "but I'm not carrying any Canadian dollars."

"No problem" replied the Master Corporal. "They take credit cards, and if you just let me have my cell phone back for a minute, I'll put an order in."

"The marvels of modern warfare," muttered KB, half to himself, as the man rattled off an order for half a dozen extra-large pizzas of different varieties. "In the middle of the Canadian prairies and we're getting pizza for supper!"

The Canadian finished his call by giving the pizza parlour a six figure grid reference for their location, and then hung up. "There are a couple of pizza parlours in Wainwright town who will deliver anywhere in the training area if you give them a grid reference," he explained. "They have been doing it so long, they know these ranges even better than we do!"

"That's all very well," answered KB, "but what happens if they get stopped by any of our patrols or roadblocks?"

"There shouldn't be any hassle," came the reply. "They'll be told they are making a delivery for the exercise control staff, and it's only rarely they get turned back."

Good to his word, within forty minutes a 4 x 4 came down the track and KB and his Canadian captive slipped out of the hide and waved it down. KB produced his credit card and gave it to the driver who printed out the receipt from a hand held card machine which KB signed, after adding on a generous tip. "Thanks, bud," acknowledged his companion, and laden with boxes of pizza, they returned to their hide. "Most of the delivery guys are ex-squaddies or Militia," added the Master Corporal. "And it's certainly not the first time that he's delivered to this area."

Supper dispatched, the section settled down for the night, two at a time staying awake in two hour shifts or 'stags' in case they were bumped by an enemy patrol. Anglo-Canadian relations took a slight dip when KB ordered his charges to be bound hand and foot, and a strip of Gun Tape over their mouths ensured there would be no unwanted sounds to give away their position.

KB took the final stag before first light when the whole section stood to. Breakfast was cold slices of left over pizza from the night before, after which all the tell-tale signs of their unusual field rations were meticulously cleaned up and buried.

They were just finishing their first brew-up of the day when the noise of approaching vehicles sent them back to their allotted firing positions, and a few minutes later two Canadian Army Chevrolet 4 x 4s drove up to their position and their Company Commander Major Fraddon, climbed from the lead vehicle.

Private Thomas, whose position was nearest to the road challenged the officer to halt, and formalities completed, led him to where KB lay. KB jumped up to greet him with a salute which was returned, and the Major suggested he inspect their position. KB led him into the hide, pointing out the location of the trip flares, the defensive firing positions with the Minimi covering the road, and his two bound and gagged prisoners.

KB thanked his lucky stars for insisting that all visible signs of the pizza feast had been cleared up the night before, but his relief soon turned to concern when the Major requested that the men's gags were removed.

"Have you men been looked after properly?" came the first question, to which the PPCLI Master Corporal replied that they had been treated fairly. "Did they feed you?" came the next question, and as the Canadian nodded his assent, the Major turned to KB and added, "well done, Corporal, it seems you have handled things pretty well, but now I must be getting along."

KB followed the Major back to the vehicles and waited while the two prisoners were loaded into the back seats of the second Chevrolet.

"Now, Corporal Blake" said the Major, "let's have your map." With the map spread out on the hood of the vehicle, the Major pointed to a wooded area some three kilometres away. "Your orders are to move out to this position where you will find the rest of your platoon at the Forward Operating Base we have established." KB made a note of the grid reference and the Major continued. "Good job so far, but I will be expecting an extra special effort from you and your lads for the rest of the exercise. You should know I have recommended that you take your Senior NCO's course when you get back to the UK. I want to see you with your Sergeant's stripes up before we return to Helmand, so don't let me down." As the Major climbed into the Chevrolet, a surprised and elated KB saluted him, his thoughts racing ahead to what might lie ahead in the weeks that were to follow.

The rest of the exercise passed with no further incidents, with KB working his section flat out until at last, thoroughly exhausted 'End-Ex' was called and they marched back into Camp for a shower and a few hours' sleep before the flight home.

Back at Colchester KB found himself off on his course within a matter of days, with only the chance of a long weekend's leave. The Senior NCO's course provided him with a whole new set of challenges with renewed emphasis on developing his leadership skills. The course had been far reaching in its scope testing KB and his fellow candidates to the limit of both their mental and practical skills. By the time they reached the end and their final interviews, at which each candidate was informed whether he had passed or failed, KB had become imbued with the belief that the senior NCO's were as often stated, the backbone of the British Army, and it was with considerable pride that he joined the ranks of successful candidates.

As so it was that a few months later, and with training and preparations for their next tour in Afghanistan nearly complete, at the age of twenty-six he gained his promotion and found himself posted as a Platoon Sergeant to his Battalion's C Company.

Chapter Five

Ambush

De fumo in flamman – Out of the smoke into the flames

Latin Proverb

They had left their Patrol Base in the Nahr-e Saraj District of Helmand Province just before first light and were making steady progress towards their objective, a suspected Taliban observation post about six kilometres north-east of the Base overlooking the main road that ran north to link up with the Kandahar – Farah highway.

Signs of Taliban activity in the area had been picked up by a recce drone the day before and the co-ordinates passed down from the Ops Centre in Camp Bastion to KB's Platoon Commander with orders to carry out a 'search and destroy' mission.

KB had been tasked to command a ten man fighting patrol, and in the detailed briefing they had been told that they would have gunship support on call as they carried out a sweep of the area immediately to the north of their Forward Operating Base. Being two months into their tour already, the ground they were covering in the early stages was familiar, a mix of cultivated farmland crisscrossed with irrigation ditches and dense scrubby hedge lines. As they progressed, however, the land gradually rose with any vestige of top soil giving way to sandy grit and rocky outcrops, and it was whilst navigating the crossing of a shallow ravine about five kilometres into their patrol, that they were hit by the Taliban ambush.

The point man, Private 'Tiny' Tibbs had spotted the slightest movement in the rocks above and had shouted a warning a split second before the ambushers opened fire. As the first shots rang out it became clear to KB that the Taliban had chosen their positions well, just below the crest of the ravine and with the sun rising behind them.

In those first few moments the AK rounds rained down on the Paras unchecked, forcing the patrol to go to ground using whatever shelter they could find amongst the scattered rocks. Then the weeks of training and preparation took over, and with a few clear shouts of command KB led a counterattack in a headlong charge up the gently sloping scree towards their hidden assailants.

Just to his left Lance Corporal Fred 'Jacko' Jackson carrying one of the two Minimi light machine guns in the patrol, was racing into the shadow of a boulder to take up a covering fire position when the IED was triggered.

The Lance Corporal took most of the blast full-on, but KB was also knocked sideways and found himself unable to move, with his left leg twisted under his body and a searing hot sensation in his left arm and side.

His recollections of what followed were punctuated by periods of haziness and complete loss of orientation as he drifted in and out of consciousness, but he remembered Jacko's screams and the yells of his patrol as they charged up the slope and drove the insurgents from their ambush positions.

One other paratrooper had been lightly wounded in the fire-fight and he had been told afterwards that two of the Taliban had paid the ultimate price, caught in the withering cross-fire from the rifles and remaining Minimi, whose gunner had calmly shouldered the machine gun and laid down accurate suppressing fire on the enemy positions.

In the post action report his Company Commander's assessment was that the engagement had been a 'quick and effective response' to an ambush situation, but all that seemed of little consequence in the light of what followed for him and Jacko in the long weeks and months ahead.

Under the cover of an Apache gunship, he and his fellow Para had been lifted out by Chinook from the ambush site and were on the operating table at the Camp Bastion field hospital in less than thirty minutes from the time of the incident. The surgical team had worked their miracles on him and his badly wounded comrade, and later the shock of being told he had lost his left leg eight inches below his knee, plus a chunk of muscle from his left arm, seemed to pale in significance when he was told that Jacko had lost an arm at the shoulder and both legs above the knee.

The flight home in the cavernous belly of the RAF's Globemaster was a vague recollection of drifting in and out of a drug induced sleep and the unflagging attention of two RAF nurses who stayed at his and Jacko's side throughout the entire flight to Brize Norton. At Brize they had stayed overnight and after a thorough post-flight examination, were loaded onto an ambulance for the sixty mile journey north to the Royal Centre for Defence Medicine at the Queen Elizabeth Hospital in Birmingham.

During his waking moments on the long trip he had become increasingly concerned about his companion, who seemed to remain in a state of unconsciousness and showed no signs of being even remotely aware of what was going on around him.

Jacko was a relatively new member of his platoon and on his first tour of Afghanistan. Barely out of his teens he had shown an immediate affinity with both the GPMG and Minimi machine guns they were equipped with. During training he had proved himself to be a highly effective machine gunner who had gone to great lengths to understand and operate these weapons calmly and efficiently, when submitted to the pressures imposed on them all during live firing exercises. As a fellow West Countryman, KB had taken the young man under his wing, enjoying his dry sense of humour and respecting his eagerness to learn and his commitment to the platoon.

Jacko had quickly become known in his section for his ability to find a cheery comment to enliven almost any situation they found themselves in, and his ardent support for his hometown Bristol City football club. After leaving school, he had worked for a while at Avonmouth Docks, and having always lived at home, joined his parents when they moved out of the city to enjoy their retirement in the seaside town of Clevedon. Here Jacko had found it tough to find employment, and quickly got bored which even an occasional visit to see The Robins play at Ashton Gate did little to offset. One afternoon, while surfing the internet on his home PC, Jacko had clicked on the Online Recruiting Centre for the Army and had started the process which just over a year later had seen him complete his jump course and join the Battalion as a fully trained Paratrooper.

Jacko had quickly proved himself a good soldier and one KB knew he could rely on. If he had a weakness, however, it was for children and animals. Frequently when on patrol in the outlying villages in their area, Jacko's section commander had to chide him for spending too much time befriending the local children who soon recognized a soft touch for a chocolate bar or a boiled sweet whenever Jacko's section showed up in their neighbourhood.

The situation with the village dogs – who generally avoided the soldiers – could be even more time consuming. Jacko could not resist feeding the skinniest of these unkempt mongrels from his ration packs, or with scraps of food he had scrounged from the patrol base kitchen. The inevitable result was that within minutes of entering a village, Jacko had collected an entourage of small urchins and hungry mutts and his progress resembled something the Pied Piper of Hamelin would have been proud of.

Jacko's love for his canine followers had reached its peak when KB's Platoon had been called in to support the Afghanistan Police with crowd control and anti-terrorist patrols in Lashkar Gah, following a bombing incident in one of the street markets that flourished in the city.

As they were moving down a side alleyway a grenade had been thrown at Jacko's section, which had caused no more damage than momentary disruption to their progress, but as the dust settled Jacko had found himself crouched behind a stack of wooden crates and cardboard boxes, sharing his cover with a small tan coloured pup, shivering with fright and with one of its ears badly torn and bleeding.

How Jacko had smuggled the small canine bundle back to their patrol base was a mystery, and KB and his Platoon Commander had both turned a blind eye when the platoon adopted the new comer as its mascot. The torn ear had been trimmed and bandaged by their medic, which had done little to improve the pup's overall looks, and when one of the squaddies commented that it looked as if he had just gone fifteen rounds in the ring, the dog became known to all as 'Rocky'.

Back in the patrol base Rocky took to following Jacko everywhere, and was soon thriving on the generous supply of scraps that seemed to appear regularly at mealtimes. Rocky had even started to accompany the Paras out on their urban patrols, but always managed to behave impeccably and disappear quietly to a place of hiding known only to Jacko, whenever their CO or Company Commander dropped by on one of their routine visits. In hospital, however, KB had other things on his mind than worrying about what fate had befallen Rocky with the latter's benefactor now lying in the bed next to him.

To KB's concern, in the days following their repatriation it almost seemed as if Jacko had lost the will to fight for recovery. Mr and Mrs Jackson came to visit their son several times, although the trip for the elderly couple was never easy. After spending time by his son's bedside, Mr Jackson would come over to talk to KB, tears welling in his eyes but fighting bravely to keep his emotions in check. He seemed to seek a special affinity with KB who had been next to his son when the IED had detonated, and they talked together about

Jacko for as long as the old man felt he could, while his wife sat by her son's bedside, speaking to him in barely a whisper and gently stroking his forehead.

KB always felt drained when they had left, and in a fit of frustration one afternoon wrote a brief letter to his platoon commander asking if the lads could record a message for Jacko, perhaps including a bark or two from Rocky, which might help their former comrade win his battle. Sometime later he got a letter telling him that the lads were 'working on something' but disappointingly he had heard nothing more.

In contrast to seeing the Jacksons and sharing their sadness, visits from his own parents were always uplifting, both of whom were clearly relieved that their son had survived his injuries and was making steady progress towards recovery. They were full of stories of life in the pub and news of his friends, and encouraged him to start thinking about what the future might hold for him.

The weeks rolled by and after several operations on his stump and some cosmetic surgery to reduce the scarring on his arm, KB was informed that a transfer to the Services rehabilitation centre at Headley Court in Surrey was imminent and one fine early spring morning, he found himself packed up and heading for Leatherhead. Perhaps it was fortunate that there had been no time for a prolonged farewell to Jacko, even if the latter had been aware of his leaving. As it was he was barely able to spend more than a few minutes by his bedside, before he joined two others in the mini-bus for the journey south.

Chapter Six

Headley Court

"He jests at scars, that never felt a wound."
Wm. Shakespeare 'Romeo and Juliet'

Headley Court had been a revelation. Whereas the care and attention lavished on him at the QE had been almost constant, he quickly found out from the start that here he would be encouraged to do as much as possible for himself. At Headley Court he was surrounded by staff who constantly reminded him that he could live and live well with his injuries and provided him with enthusiastic help when needed, particularly when he showed his keenness to try something new or go it alone. Even the physiotherapy sessions were designed to be innovative and challenging rather than purely repetitive. He soon found himself looking forward to the sports activities and he took full advantage of the facilities, all the time becoming more comfortable with his new prosthetic leg until he was walking without the aid of a stick.

As the days turned into weeks the trips to the prosthetic centre for the adjustments to his leg became less frequent, though KB never ceased to marvel at the care that this received from the technicians who worked tirelessly to ensure their patients achieved maximum mobility from their artificial limbs. When comparing himself and his disability with his fellow patients, KB often mentally thanked his guardian angel for allowing him to keep so much of his damaged leg. The fact that the amputation had left him with several inches of the limb below the knee meant that the necessary regime of exercises and trials that would allow him to regain his sense of balance and walk again without the need for a stick, were not nearly as arduous or testing as the gruelling programme of rehabilitation suffered bravely by those less fortunate.

During one of his fitting sessions, the technician in charge asked KB if he would be prepared to act as a guinea pig for a new state of the art prosthetic foot, which duplicated the natural action of the ankle. Assisted by a system of micro hydraulics and mini processors these allowed the wearer to walk and climb or descend stairs with relative ease, almost eliminating the sideways rolling action of those using the conventional and less advanced artificial limbs.

KB willingly agreed to be part of the new limb's trials, and although he found himself spending many more hours than his fellow patients exercising and testing the advanced limb, he found the benefits well worth the extra commitment.

Indeed, thanks to the efforts and minute attention to detail of the technicians, KB soon found himself able to walk at a reasonable pace and even attempt a measured jog. This enabled him to increase his participation in a number of team sports and with his daily work outs in the gym and swimming pool, he was able to regain a comparable level of fitness to that he had achieved during his service with his Regiment.

He also had a running blade fitted which enabled him to increase his performance substantially on the track, but although he surprised himself with the speed he was able to reach over short distances, he preferred to limit his track activities to slower but longer distances as part of his overall fitness and stamina building programme.

There was one sport in particular with which he found himself both intrigued and challenged. Although requiring less pure physical effort than some of the other more strenuous pursuits he enjoyed, it happened to be one of the first sports ever introduced at the rehabilitation unit, so Headley Court was well equipped to provide expert training support and encouragement in promoting the skills of the archer. He also found that in addition to improving his upper body strength, teaching himself to pull the bowstring left handed helped to re-build the muscles in the arm that had been injured in the IED attack. After a week or two of an hour's practice every morning, he found his coordination and accuracy steadily improving and before long he could hold his own in the competitions that featured regularly as part of the centre's programme.

Although recognizing the improved accuracy they provided, he found he preferred the simplicity of the conventional bow to the more complex compound variety. Eventually, after working hard in the gym, plus practice on the archery range as his arm muscles re-built, he found he could manage a bow up to a 45 lb pull. With his bank account steadily building, and little to spend the money on, he decided to purchase a hunting bow and after a morning spent researching his options online, he invested in a Grizzly Field Bow, a supply of arrows and a back quiver. Delivery was made in a matter of days, and continuing practice using his own personal bow soon increased his skill level and accuracy still further.

With his general physical state now well on the way to full recovery, he was encouraged to start thinking about his future and as a result, requested a posting on a short course at the Help for Heroes rehabilitation centre at Tedworth close to the Tidworth garrison in Wiltshire, which ran 'Battle Back' courses to prepare their candidates for a return to civilian life and to assist them in progressing their careers outside the military.

Here he had a wealth of activities to choose from electing to spend as much time as possible in the open air, gradually becoming more and more certain that his future lay in finding employment in the outdoors. Amongst the staff at Tedworth, he quickly established a rapport with Joe Duckworth who ran the forestry side of the Tedworth Estate. He was soon volunteering to spend most of his days working alongside Joe and the Estate workers, and under Joe's tutelage he soon acquired his operator's certificate on a variety of chain saws and became familiar with many of the traditional practices which were the basis of forestry management.

He was only halfway through the course, when news reached him that Jacko had lost his battle and succumbed to his injuries. The funeral with full military honours, was to be held in Clevedon, and on the appointed day, KB was picked up from Tedworth in a mini bus and joined other members of his former platoon for the trip down to Somerset.

It was a fine sunny day as they travelled west, and as they got closer to the town, the banter and conversation between the soldiers tailed off as their thoughts turned to their fallen comrade. The church of St Andrew's was on the western edge of the town, close to the shoreline of the Bristol Channel, and as they drew up close to the gate leading to the grey stone buildings, a large crowd was already gathering. Two flag bearers of the British Legion flanked the entrance, and already a bugler and members of the firing party that would discharge the salute over the grave, stood at ease beside the side path that led to the cemetery.

KB and his group were ushered into the church and took their places in the middle section of the pews, many of which were already filled, amongst them more Legion members and the Mayor and Mayoress, sure proof of the esteem the town held for its lost son.

The church was filling to capacity, and the organist was playing the Eric Coates tune 'The Green Hills O' Somerset' as the coffin entered, the six pallbearers being members of Jacko's section. The hymns 'To be a Pilgrim' and 'Onward Christian Soldiers' were sung, and Jacko's Platoon Commander gave the eulogy. Then, before the final blessing, a young lad in his early teens stepped forward to the lectern and recited the poem 'Epitaph for a Countryman'. KB had not heard it before, and as he glanced along the row of his fellow Paras, he was not surprised to see that more than a few of these war hardened veterans were visibly moved by the words.

Outside a strong breeze was blowing off the Channel, which carried the poignant notes of the 'Last Post' across the churchyard, the crash of the volleys from the firing party flushing the rooks from the surrounding tree tops, sending them wheeling and screeching their rasping cries into the sky above.

Then, in the peace that followed, the mourners stepped forward to pay their final respect at the graveside, each soldier saluting as they bade farewell to their comrade.

Outside, he had but a brief moment to shake the hands of Jacko's parents and offer his condolences, before climbing aboard the bus for the return journey.

Back at Tedworth, his course ended all too soon, and on his return to Headley Court he found himself going through a series of assessments and more fine tuning of his prosthetic leg, and he became even more aware that the time had come to make some serious decisions about his future. Again there was no lack of support from the staff whose responsibility it was to assist in this final stage of his rehabilitation and after several career counselling sessions he elected to pursue the interest in forestry and estate management that had been sparked by his time on his 'Battle Back' course.

With a supporting letter from his counsellor and a reference from Joe Duckworth, he applied for a three month estate management course at Tamar Valley College in Cornwall. With his application accepted, the prospect of life as a student gave him something else to think about as well as his newly acquired civilian status, as he headed west down the M4 towards Bristol and his Somerset home.

Chapter Seven

Home Again

"Home is the sailor, home from the sea,
And the hunter home from the hill."

R.L.Stevenson 'Requiem'

In spite of several delays reaching the motorway, once on the M4 he had made good time and reached the outskirts of Bristol just after 1.00 p.m. With the effects of his 'full English' in the Senior Ranks' Mess now well and truly worn off, he pulled off at the Gordano Services and treated himself to a double Bacon and Cheese Burger from Burger King and a Salted Caramel Mocha from Starbucks.

Lunch over, he now braced himself for the one part of the trip he was not really looking forward to, a visit to see Mr and Mrs Jackson. As he felt guilty that he had not been able to spend more time with them at Jacko's funeral, he had telephoned them and arranged to call in to see them on his way home.

Setting his Sat-Nav to the address they had given him, he was soon at the Clevedon exit from the M5 and shortly afterwards found himself in a quiet suburb of the north Somerset seaside town and parking in front of a pleasant brick built bungalow, set back from the road.

Locking the truck, he opened the wrought iron double gate and walked up the short driveway to ring the front doorbell. From inside a dog was barking and he heard a voice call out, "Just coming." The door opened and the familiar figure of Jacko's dad stood there to greet him. The old man had aged since KB had last seen him, and he was sure the ramrod straight figure he remembered had wilted slightly.

"Come in my boy, I can't tell you how much this means to us, do come in, we have been so looking forward to seeing you." Taking KB by the arm the old man led him through to the living room, where he was greeted with a warm hug by a tearful mum. "There now," she exclaimed, "I am getting all emotional. Arthur, sit the boy down and look after him, while I put the kettle on." Dabbing her eyes with her handkerchief, she hurried off to the kitchen, leaving KB sitting on the settee with Mr Jackson next to him in one of the two armchairs that made up their living room suite.

"Would you prefer something stronger than tea?" Arthur Jackson enquired.

"Thank you, sir, but better not as I'm driving," he replied.

"I quite understand, but please drop the sir and call me Arthur," came the answer, "and as soon as Gladys comes back with our tea, you must tell us how you have been getting on. I must say it does my heart good to see you up and so mobile – and we want to hear all your news."

The words were barely out of his mouth before Gladys came bustling back into the room – with a tray of tea and biscuits. As they sat back in their chairs, KB glanced towards the mantelpiece and noticed in pride of place a framed photo of Jacko in his service dress proudly wearing his maroon beret.

"He was a good lad," commented Arthur, "and it's hit us hard that he won't be coming back to us, but you lads gave him a fine send-off."

"He was a exceptional young soldier, one of the best," said KB, "and I was proud to have served with him. I was sorry not to have been able to spend more time with you at the funeral, which was one I will never forget, particularly the young lad that recited the poem."

"That was Jamie, Fred's nephew," Arthur replied, as KB took a moment to remember that Fred was in fact, the man he had always known as Jacko. "The lad idolized his uncle. He never knew his father who was killed in an accident when Jamie was only a baby, so Fred became something of a father figure to him and they often went to the football together. The lad is really going to miss him, but there, aren't we all?"

This was the cue for the old man to rise from his chair and from a corner cupboard he took the folded Union Flag that had been draped over Jacko's coffin, Jacko's beret and his campaign medals, which he placed on the low table in front of KB.

"It seems so little to remember him by," the old man added, "but I am so glad he did his duty well and was so highly thought of. But now, first of all tell us exactly what you remember of the day of the ambush, and what you have been doing since you left hospital."

With some difficulty KB spent the next half hour answering their questions as best he could and giving them as much detail as he felt was possible of the events leading up to and following the fateful patrol he had led.

Both of Jacko's parents listened attentively to everything KB told them, and bravely managed to keep their emotions in check. Concluding by bringing them up to date with the news that he was due to start his estate management course after a short break at home in the pub, Arthur Jackson stood up from his chair, which KB took as a signal that it was time for him to go, but before he could take his leave, Arthur motioned for him to sit down.

"Stay there a minute Sergeant Blake. There is someone here who I know would like to see you." Leaving the room KB heard the old man open the back door, and seconds later a tan streak of canine lightning bounded into the room. It was Rocky – a sleek, well fed Rocky, far removed from the dust and heat of Helmand Province and now calling a bungalow in a West Country town his home.

Skidding to a halt in front of KB, his one good ear pricked and his scarred ear at half mast, Rocky paused and nose forward, sniffed the hand that KB proffered. At that moment, something stirred in the dog's memory, the tail started wagging furiously and with a sharp bark of recognition KB found himself pushed back into his seat by two strong front paws and a shower of licks lavished on his face. Pushing him gently off his chest, KB tickled the dog's ears and stroked his head, and with an audible sigh Rocky sank onto the carpet at his feet, tail still thumping with sheer pleasure.

All this had proved too much for Gladys Jackson, who was now sobbing into her handkerchief, and Arthur with his hand on her shoulder also had a problem blurting out, "No doubt he knows you, no doubt at all. My son would have been so happy."

"It's just great to see him, but how on earth did he get here?" asked KB.

"It seems that your mates in Afghanistan decided that sending him back to our son might help him recover, so they raised the money needed and an organization called Nowzad took care of the rest of the job. They arranged to have him flown back and put into quarantine, but as you know, our boy died without regaining consciousness, so he never knew that his dog was back in the UK."

"Amazing," KB replied. "I have heard of Nowzad and I know they have brought quite a few dogs back that the lads have befriended, and it's just great to see the old rascal again."

Bending down at his wife's side, the old man took her hand and in a low voice, went on, "Do you want me to ask him?" Gladys nodded her assent, as Arthur stood up and faced KB.

"I know this is a lot to ask, but the truth is that our son was a blessing that came to us quite late in our lives, and we are now both getting on." The old man paused to clear his throat, and KB sensed that there was a lot more to come. "In fact," Arthur continued, "Rocky is a bit of a handful, and neither of us can give him the exercise he really needs, so we were wondering if there was any chance that you might take him on for us?"

KB had half anticipated the question, but it still took him aback and it was a moment or two before he replied. "Tell you what, give me a moment or two to think it over. In fact, let me take him for a walk up the road, and I'll see how we get on."

Without a moment's hesitation the old man went to fetch Rocky's lead and a few minutes later, KB found himself walking up the street with the dog trotting by his side. "Well, old fella," KB addressed his new companion, "I hadn't bargained on this, but I guess I owe it to Jacko and the lads who got you here to see you right." As if agreeing, Rocky wagged his tail enthusiastically, and there and then KB knew that, in spite of some misgivings, Rocky would be coming home with him.

Back at the bungalow, KB informed the Jacksons of his decision which prompted another outburst of tears from Gladys, and shortly afterwards found himself loading a dog bed, drinking and feeding bowls, and a supply of dog food into the back of the pick-up.

Armed with the vet's certificate showing that Rocky had received all his shots and had been neutered while in the care of Nowzad, KB found himself smothered in a motherly hug from Gladys as he said his goodbyes to the Jacksons. With Rocky settled in on the back seat of the Ford, he soon found himself back on the M5 and Junction 25 at Taunton, leading in turn to the A378 that would take him through Langport and then on to the A372 and village of Long Lane and his parents' pub.

Having stayed with the Jacksons a lot longer than he had originally planned, it was nearing four o'clock in the afternoon when he eventually drove into the car park of The Volunteer Inn. Pulling up in front of the long wooden shed that doubled as a garage and work shop, he switched off the diesel and sat for a moment taking in the familiar surroundings. The pub was a hundred yards from a narrow bridge that straddled the River Yeo, and the old stone building fronted on to the only road that ran through the small village that had been his family's home for most of his life.

Behind the pub was a large garden area with a swing and climbing frame for its patrons' children, bordered by the car park on one side, a large pond and the neighbours' fence on the other, and a small paddock at the end in which his sister's horse now grazed.

The garage in front of which KB had parked flanked the other side of the car park together with another long corrugated clad building which housed the pub's skittle alley. Behind this was a wooden stable block with four loose boxes, the end one of which had been fitted out as a tack room. The block had been built on a small concrete apron surrounded by a post and rail fence through which a five bar gate led into a large paddock.

KB's arrival had not gone unnoticed and as he got down from the cab, his mother, father and sister were already crossing the car park to greet him.

His father was the first to engulf him in a bear hug accompanied by a gruff, "Welcome home, son." Jack Blake stood an inch shorter than KB, immaculate as ever in a check shirt, yellow tie embroidered with pheasants, maroon waistcoat, Bedford cords and the highly polished brown market boots that were his trademark. Kathy Blake, his mum, was the next to greet him, a pretty and petite 5 ft. 4 inches, with an aura of femininity that belied a tough streak that KB adored and admired, and had ensured that his childhood never lacked the discipline that had stood him in such good stead during his Army career. Hannah Blake, his sister and junior of four years, matched her dad in height and her mother in looks. Clad in jeans and a well-worn fleecy, her dark brown hair in a page boy cut framed a fresh faced complexion devoid of make-up, from which a pair of strikingly blue eyes scrutinized her brother's new vehicle.

"Nice wheels, Bro'," she greeted him. "Just add a towbar and the horsebox will look great behind it!"

"Dream on, little sister!" he responded with a grin. "I only collected it from the dealer this morning, but I'm pretty impressed so far, loads of power and really easy to handle."

"Thought you might have gone for a Land Rover," was Jack's comment, nodding towards his own pride and joy, a Defender that was parked in one of the bays close by.

"I did consider it, Dad, but to be honest having spent more hours than I care to remember behind the wheel of one or being bounced around in the back, I thought it was time to try something different!"

"Enough talk of your boys toys," interjected Kathy. "Let's get you inside, tea is ready and waiting and you must be starving."

"Sounds great," he replied with a grin, opening the back door of the truck. "But first I have someone here I want you to meet."

Rocky required no bidding to exit, jumping down from the cab and greeting them all with a wagging tail, and singling out Hannah for a few licks of appreciation when she knelt down to give him a hug.

"What kind of a dog is that?" asked Jack.

"A Camp Bastion pure bred!" answered KB with a grin. "But I'll tell you the full story later."

"I'll look forward to that," Jack said, "but right now, I suggest you run your truck into the garage for tonight. We are expecting a few in the bar this evening, and that shiny new paintwork could prove to be too much of a temptation for some of our younger tearaways."

Heeding his father's advice, and with the truck safely garaged and the doors secured under lock and key, KB followed his family back to the pub.

Dog food stowed away in the cupboard next to the sink in the scullery and bags unpacked and clothes put away in his old bedroom next to the en-suite letting rooms leading from the generous living quarters that the family occupied upstairs, KB paused to take in the familiar view overlooking the garden, car park and the fields beyond, then stood the valise containing his archery equipment in a corner of the room next to his wardrobe. Laying out Rocky's bed next to his bedside table and satisfied with his handiwork, he returned downstairs to join his family in their private living room next to the kitchen.

His mother had laid out a high tea on the sideboard, with sandwiches, home-made bacon and egg pie, scones, strawberry jam, clotted cream and one of KB's favourite lemon drizzle sponges.

"You've been busy, Mum," said KB as Kathy handed out the plates. "What a spread!"

"Nothing's too good for the return of our hero," chuckled his dad. "So tuck in, though by the looks of you, you haven't been exactly starving."

"Come on, Dad, not an inch of fat," he replied, thumping his stomach. "Pure muscle!"

"Well you'll have to watch it," Jack continued. "Ten days at home living off your mother's cooking, and that waistline will suffer!"

"Got that covered, Dad – I don't plan on hanging around the bar all day –

lots of walks with Rocky – and a bit of practice with the bow to hone my new-found skills as an archer and to keep building up the arm muscles."

"And you can saddle up Winston and hack him out for me," interjected his sister.

"Hang on, Sis," he hastened to reply. "You know me and what I think of horses – dangerous at both ends and uncomfortable in the middle."

"Didn't stop you before you went off to join the Army," she smiled. "But am I right in thinking that was probably due more to your interest in Alex than the joys of riding?"

The mention of his former girlfriend and the first love of his life, Alexis Baker, brought back a sudden flood of memories. The daughter of Joe and Amy Baker, near neighbours and long- time friends of the Blakes', KB and Alex had grown up and gone to school together. Alex had been his partner at their first dance in the village hall, and to indulge Alex's love of horses, they had ridden out together, though he had stopped short of joining her and his sister when they followed the local Hunt.

In fact the two of them had been what the villagers considered to be 'quite an item' before KB decided to join the Paras. Alex had made it quite clear that there was no way she wanted to be an Army wife, and even an offer from Joe to join him in his builder's business had been unable to dissuade KB from his chosen career path.

"How is Alex?" he asked, noticing the quick glance between his parents.

"I suppose she's all right," Kathy replied. "Still not married, and she's had a series of boyfriends but just recently she has taken up with Isaac Samson, which is certainly worrying Joe and Amy."

"She wants her head seen to" added his father. "That Samson lot never have been any good and life around here would be a lot easier without them."

KB nodded in agreement. The Samsons had originally been travellers who had been settled in the area for many years, but still chose to live in a collection of caravans and mobile homes on land they had bought on the outskirts of a neighbouring village. Ostensibly they made their living by collecting scrap metal from local farmers and businesses, but it was general knowledge that many of their activities were conducted on the wrong side of the law.

Foolish were those locals who failed to secure easily removable and saleable items such as lawnmowers and power tools, and even farmers who owned quad bikes made sure that they were locked away at night.

The Samsons had also established a reputation for being unwelcome patrons at most of the village pubs in the area, and on frequent occasions their heavy drinking had resulted in fights amongst themselves or with the local lads, and in the past Jack Blake had banned several of the family from his pub. Even Jack, however, had to admit that the better behaved of their clan did spend freely when they did visit the pub, and they certainly never seemed short of cash, as was testified by the succession of expensive 4 x 4's they drove.

As was inevitable, KB then found himself the centre of his family's attention, and having explained how he had come by Rocky, their interest then turned to the events leading up to his discharge and his return to physical fitness and the success of his artificial leg.

"It's incredible to see you walking so well, you can't tell at all," said Kathy enthusiastically.

"That's probably due to the fact that I was lucky enough to be fitted with one of the latest designs." he replied, rolling up the leg of his jeans to show them.

"Inside the limb there is a system of mini hydraulics controlled by microprocessors, so the ankle joints are far more flexible, and it also adjusts itself to the ground I am walking over, so it almost duplicates the normal movement of a foot and ankle. The only snag is that the model I have been fitted with is quite new, and the boffins are not sure yet how it will stand up to the wear and tear of normal everyday life. I have to go back to the centre at regular intervals for check-ups and to enable them to make any adjustments necessary."

"Your estate management course at Tamar Valley College should give it a fair work-out then?" said Jack.

"Should do," he replied. "And if I can then land a job in forestry or estate management, we will really find out how well it performs long term."

Their meal finished, Jack left to check the barrels in the cellar and to make sure everything was ready behind the bar for their 5.30 p.m. opening. Meanwhile Kathy and Hannah cleared away the dishes and then went to the kitchen to start prepping for the evening meals they would be serving in the pub's small restaurant.

Calling to Rocky, KB slipped on the dog's lead and leaving the pub, crossed the road to the gateway and footpath that led down to the river bank and the old towpath that ran between Langport and Ilchester. Dusk was falling, and KB knew that his walk would not rival some of the longer treks he was used to, but it was good to get out into the fresh air and as soon as they reached the towpath, he let Rocky off the lead and watched the dog bound away in front of him.

A hundred metres or so down the path, KB noticed that a few sheep had left the flock that was grazing in the field and had scrambled up the embankment in search of richer grazing. Rocky was fast approaching these stragglers, who paused to assess any potential danger from the oncoming interloper, a couple stepping warily backward and then turning to retreat to the safety of the flock.

KB held his breath as the dog reached the spot where the remaining sheep were grazing, and then let out a sigh of relief as Rocky careered through their midst without even pausing in his stride.

"Thank God for that," he muttered to himself, knowing full well the problems associated with owning a dog that was a sheep-chaser. On one occasion in the past, a small pack of rogue pets from the village had played havoc with the flocks that grazed the riverside pastures, savaging several ewes and their lambs, and driving a handful into the river where they had drowned.

Retribution had been swift and effective, and when the same group had attempted a similar foray a few nights later, the farmer who owned the targeted flock had been waiting with two of his farmhands, and a fusillade of shots from well-aimed 12 bores had ended the escapades of the sheep chasers for good.

The subsequent furore in the village led to an upsurge of ill feeling between the farmer involved and the pet owners and for a while the battle lines between the traditional village dwellers and the newcomers to the rural South-West whose dogs had been responsible had been clearly defined, and it was some time before harmony was restored.

Being the only pub in the village, patronised by both sides in what quickly became an ill- tempered spat, the Blakes had found themselves caught in the middle of the feud when trying to be as diplomatic as possible in dealing with both factions.

In the end, rather than lose the much needed custom of the two farmers skittles teams that used the pub as their home alley during the quieter winter months, Jack had little option but to side with these long time locals, but several years later there were some in the village who refused to patronize the pub and rub shoulders with their farming neighbours and their supporters.

Calling to the dog, KB was equally relieved to see Rocky turn and come trotting back to his side, not relishing the thought of pursuing a canine runaway down the river bank in the darkness of an autumn evening.

Back at the pub, the floodlights that illuminated the inn's exterior had been switched on and a warm glow from the lights in the bar shone a cheery welcome into the gathering darkness. From the wisp of smoke from the tall chimney that carried the sparks well away from the pub's thatched roof, KB knew that there would already be a hearty log fire burning in the large open fireplace.

Slipping in through the back door, KB paused at the sink in the scullery to wash his hands, and after drying them, used the towel to rub down the dog and wipe the mud off his paws. Realizing he would not get away with replacing the towel in its muddied state, he opened the door to the washing machine and noticing that a pair of Hannah's equally muddy jodphurs were already there awaiting a wash, he dropped the towel on top, closed the door and taking a clean towel from the drawer in the old Welsh dresser that stood against the back wall, hung it on the hook next to the sink.

Taking a can of dog food out of the cupboard, he filled Rocky's bowl and watched as the dog wolfed down the contents.

"Good to see that today's adventures have not affected your appetite, old fella," he said, as Rocky wagged his tail in appreciation.

By now appetizing smells were beginning to invade the back hallway from the kitchen, but without pausing to investigate and with Rocky at his heels, he went upstairs for a shower and to change for the evening.

Chapter Eight

Old Friends and New Enemies

"I have heard that the ancients used bows and arrows to their advantage."

Sun Tzu, 'The Art of War'

Half an hour later found him fully refreshed and after being chased out of the kitchen by his mother for daring to pause and sample some of the dishes being readied for the evening diners, he joined Jack in the bar.

Although it was still early in the evening, the bar was already filling up, and as he came through the staff door into the working area behind the bar, to his acute embarrassment a cheer and shouts of welcome went up from those patrons who had already come in for their customary pint.

"I told them you would probably be back today," said his dad, obviously pleased with this reaction. "Best you get to the other side of the bar and mingle for a bit, then you can give me a hand if things get busier later on."

The next hour passed in a flurry of greetings from friends and locals, and KB found himself the centre of attention as the bar gradually filled with an increasing number of well-wishers. Seeing that Jack was now beginning to struggle to keep up with the demands of his customers and with the dining room now filled to capacity as well, KB excused himself and returned to help his father out behind the bar.

Rocky had started the evening by circulating amongst the punters quite freely, but as the bar filled up, he retreated to join KB and Jack, finding a space between the soft drink crates under the bar top to curl up and doze off well out of the way of the now noisy and ever increasing throng.

As the evening wore on, KB found himself slipping easily back into the routine of pulling pints and charging glasses from the optics, and he was in the middle of serving a round to a group of his former team-mates from the ruby club in neighbouring Somerton, when the door to the bar opened to admit Joe and Amy Baker accompanied by their daughter Alex.

"Heads up, lad," joked Jack who had joined him at the till and who had also noticed the arrival of the Bakers. "No Isaac Samson in tow, so I guess you will be the centre of attention for the young lady this evening."

"Thanks, Dad," he replied. "But I doubt that. It has been quite a while since I last saw her, and from what you were saying earlier, things have certainly changed."

Turning back to the bar, it was obvious from the broad smiles on the faces of both Joe and Amy that they were delighted to see him, but Alex was looking somewhat less pleased, and KB suspected that the decision to accompany her parents to the pub had not been hers to make.

"Welcome home, Kris," Joe greeted him. "Good to see you back safe and sound, we've all missed you, haven't we?"

Amy was quick to agree, but Alex's response was no more than a slight nod of the head, although KB noticed that this was accompanied by a brief smile. There was no doubt that the tall slim girl that now stood in front of him had changed considerably from the pony-tailed teenage tomboy he had last seen two years ago, before leaving for his first tour of Afghanistan. The jet black hair was now waist length and high cheek bones and full lips were accentuated by carefully applied make-up to a face that had never been even close to the most rudimentary application of cosmetics in her younger years. Her dark brown eyes that now seemed to mock him, were curtained by long false eye lashes, and a tight fitting high necked white blouse and skin black leather trousers with high heeled shoes set off her trim figure to perfection.

"Thanks, Mr Baker, it's really great to be back," he heard himself say. "It will take a while to settle in to civilian life again, but I'm really looking forward to starting a new career."

Perhaps sensing that the latter part of this statement lacked some conviction, Joe continued, "Your dad tells me you are off on an Estate Management course down in Cornwall soon?"

"Yes," KB replied. "I tried my hand at a bit of forestry work during my re-hab training with the Army, and really enjoyed it, so I am doing a three month course at Tamar Valley College, but nothing settled after that at the moment."

"Lots to think about then?" suggested Amy. "But let's get the drinks in, Joe, before I die of thirst."

Nodding assent, Joe ordered two gin and tonics and a pint of draught ale, and he and Amy moved off to sit at a small table at the window, leaving Alex at the bar. After pouring the drinks, KB was surprised when Alex picked up the pint and one of the gins and carried them over to her parents before returning to perch on one of the bar stools.

Rather than being stand-offish as KB had expected, the girl quite clearly wanted to talk and it was not long before he found himself explaining in some detail the events that had so changed his life over the preceding months. As he talked Rocky emerged from his sanctuary beneath the bar as if to add substance to his story, and immediately made another friend as Alex made a fuss of him.

"I really have missed you, Kris," she confided, after he had finished bringing her up to date with all that had befallen him. "And I am sorry now you are back, that you will be leaving us again so soon."

"Well, the course is only for three months," he replied, "after which I'm not sure what will happen. I still have to find a job, so things are pretty much an open book right now. In any case," he went on, "I understand there is a new man in your life, and I gather that the two of you have been quite an item for some time now."

"Oh, you mean Isa?" came the response. "We have certainly had some fun together and he always has plenty of cash to throw around, but I can't see myself settling down with him, if that's what you mean?"

"I hope he understands that," said KB. "And I hope you know what you are doing. Those Samsons are a very strange crowd and they have a rather primitive tendency to regard their womenfolk as possessions, rather than as partners."

"I don't need the 'Beware the Samsons' lecture," she laughed. "I heard that too often from Dad and Mum – but seriously, if you do get stuck for a job and don't fancy pub life, you could always ask Dad if he would take you on. His business seems to be doing pretty well and he isn't getting any younger, so I am pretty certain he would consider it."

"Crikey, she means it," he thought to himself and he was even more surprised when she leant across the bar and placed her hand on his arm, giving it a gentle squeeze.

As if on cue, the door to the bar swung open and the unwelcome figure of Isaac Samson followed by his younger brother Nathan, strode in.

If Isaac had seen Alex's hand now perilously close to holding KB's, he did not show it, and Alex was certainly quick in removing it. As the two made their way to the bar, KB took stock of the newcomers, their thick set frames and well-tanned features offset by heads of wiry tousled hair that was the hallmark of the Samson clan.

"Well, well, if it isn't the one legged wonder come home to roost." came the sneering remark from the older of the two. "Two pints of cider and a gin and tonic for my girl, barman. 'Cos I suppose that's what you are now that you're not flashing your Sergeant's stripes. Quite a let-down for our so-called war hero, innit?"

Ignoring the banter, and knowing full well that any kind of retort would inevitably lead to a further harangue, KB turned away to pour the gin from the optic and draw the pints, noticing that Isaac had taken Alex off to sit at one of the tables, leaving Nathan at the bar.

"That's £9.20, Nathan," said KB, taking the proffered £20 note from Isa's sibling, who was quick to add,

"Wos the matter then peg-leg, cat got your tongue?"

"No trouble here, Nathan," warned KB. "Or you and your brother will find yourself out the door."

"Take more than you and your old man to chuck us out," came the rejoinder, as he pocketed the change and moved to join the couple at their table.

The remainder of the evening passed without incident. Jack, having noticed the exchange between the Samson brothers and his son, made sure he served them their remaining rounds.

By eleven o'clock the bar was emptying and the last of their diners had long gone, and the family set to collecting glasses and wiping down tables while Kathy emptied the till and totalled up the evening's takings.

"Just over £1,000," she reported to the others as they finished off their chores. "A really good evening; you should come home more often, Kris," she added jokingly. "Nice to see so many of your friends here to welcome you back."

"Including Alex!" commented his sister mischievously.

"All over him like a wet shirt, but I don't think Isaac Samson was too impressed," added Jack. "What's more she even went home with Joe and Amy, much to his displeasure. Normally the two of them would have been out the door together as soon as I called 'Last Orders'."

"Well, in fairness he did have his brother with him, and I can't imagine even Alex would appreciate having Nathan playing gooseberry," said KB.

"Don't think that would have been a factor," said Kathy. "If Isaac wanted to take Alex home on his own, he wouldn't have hesitated to tell Nathan to leg it. Anyway, Jack, I can't understand why you allow any of that Samson tribe in the pub," she went on. "They're always looking for trouble and none of our regulars can stand them."

"As long as there is no trouble, it would be hard to ban them," replied Jack, "and as you well know, several of the pubs that have done so around here have suffered the consequences afterwards, which the Police seem to be powerless to do anything about."

They all knew about the incidents that Jack referred to. In the past these had ranged from minor incidents of vandalism to broken windows and break-ins, but since most of the establishments like The Volunteer now boasted motion activated floodlights linked to closed circuit TV in their car parks, these had tended to be on the decrease.

Work done for the night, the family retired to their living room for a night cap. Hannah was the first to excuse herself, being the early riser in the household with her stable to muck out and Winston to exercise.

"I'll just take Rocky out for a run," said KB, rising from his chair. "And then I'll be turning in as well. It's been a long day."

"Well, son," said his dad, "once again, welcome home and thanks for your help this evening. I'll be sorry to see you go when you set out for Cornwall. If you could close the gate to the car park entrance for me and secure it with the padlock and chain that would be fine, and make sure you lock the back door when you come in, then we'll see you in the morning."

"Good night, Mum," said KB, bending down to kiss his mother on the cheek, and calling to the dog he let himself out through the back door and started down the yard, Rocky bounding off towards the paddock.

As he strolled towards the garage, he noticed to his surprise that in addition to Jack's Land Rover another 4 x 4 was still parked in the yard, half hidden by an old plum tree which marked the end of the lawn and the lower part of the car park.

As patrons who had more than the legal limit to drive often left their cars parked overnight to take a taxi home or beg a lift from one of their more sober drinking partners, he thought no more of it, and on reaching the garage, checked the lock on the door and then peered through the window to make sure his truck was still safe and sound within.

Even though all three security floodlights shone out across the yard, the garage was not as well illuminated as the main parking area, and with his back to the latter he did not see the man emerge from the shadows, until an arm was flung round his neck forcing his face forwards into the side of the garage. Taken by surprise, the move caught him off balance and before he could make a counter move, he found himself pinned against the wooden cladding.

"How does that feel, soldier boy?" hissed the familiar voice of Isaac Samson in his ear. "Not so brave now, are we?"

In the distance, the engine of the hidden vehicle roared into life, and the headlights moved slowly towards them.

"Now listen carefully," continued Samson. "If I ever catch you even so much as looking at my girl again I'll take your other fucking leg off and make sure you never walk again, peg leg or no, do you understand me?"

Before KB had a chance to reply, a snarling shape hurled itself out of the gloom, and a loud yelp from his assailant mixed with the sound of ripping cloth indicated that Rocky had found his target.

"Fucking dog, I'll have you," shouted Samson, releasing KB to grab his left buttock where the dog's teeth had sunk home. Turning in an effort to kick the dog away, KB took his chance and caught Isaac a swinging punch in the ribs which pitched him forward onto all fours. Engine running the door opened on the 4 x 4 and a voice from within cried out.

"Get in quick, you silly bugger."

Spluttering and gasping for breath from the effects of KB's blow, Isa scrambled to his feet and staggered towards the safety of the vehicle, but not before Rocky had lunged at him again and, seizing the shard of torn cloth hanging down from his trousers, ripped off a further chunk of the heavy material.

Tires squealing the vehicle lurched forwards and as it hurtled towards the car park entrance, a further threat echoed across the yard.

"I'll get you and your fucking dog," came the cry, and with it the 4 x 4 exited the car park and sped off.

The commotion had roused the occupants of the pub and the back door opened, as Jack, still belting up his trousers, came hurrying across the yard.

"What the hell's going on?" asked his father as KB knelt to pet Rocky who was clearly enjoying being the hero of the hour.

"Isaac Samson," KB replied. "Thought he would come and give me a strong arm warning to keep away from Alex."

The two, with Rocky trotting behind, secured the gate and walked back to the pub where Kathy greeted them with a hug.

"Are you alright, Kris?" she asked anxiously.

"I'm okay" he answered, "just a tad sore around the neck where he grabbed me, but otherwise no harm done, though I doubt if our Samson friend will be sitting comfortably for a day or two." As evidence, he showed the blood stained strip of cloth Rocky had torn from Isaac's trousers, which the dog sniffed with a wagging tail, enjoying even more fuss that was made of him.

"That's it," said Kathy. "No more Samsons in this pub, Jack, or you'll be running it on your own."

"Don't worry, dear," the senior Blake replied. "None of their clan will ever set foot through the door again, as long as I'm the landlord."

That settled they set off upstairs to their rooms, and soon peace descended over the old coaching inn.

After making use of the small en-suite shower and toilet that was a feature of all the rooms at The Volunteer, and half opening his bedroom window, KB had a moment to reflect on the events of the day before unfastening his prosthetic leg and carefully examining the stump for any signs of chaffing. Satisfying himself that all was well, he swung himself into bed and switched out the bedside light, before checking to see that Rocky had settled down on his blanket, apparently quite unruffled by the excitement of the past hour.

A slight breeze blew through the open window and soon the chill of the autumn night pervaded the room. Sleep did not come easily, but eventually he dozed off, his shallow slumber punctuated by visions of Helmand. Someone was shouting at him, but he heard nothing and suddenly there was a white brightness and he woke up to find his bedroom bathed in the light from the floodlights in the yard. As both his parents and his sister's bedrooms were at the front of the pub overlooking the road, he knew that it was unlikely they would have woken up, but his fears that all was not well were confirmed by a low growl from Rocky who had risen from his blanket and was standing by the window, his head raised as he sniffed the air.

Easing himself out of bed, he hopped over to the window and leaning on the wardrobe for support, peered out from the darkness of his room across the car park. As he watched a hooded figure came into view, carrying what looked like a can, and headed in the direction of the garage and stable.

KB did not hesitate, with a hand on the wardrobe to steady himself, he retrieved his valise with his archery equipment and hopped back to the window, where he unzipped the bag and took out his bow and three tungsten tipped arrows. Stringing the bow, he placed two of the arrows on the window sill, and notched the third into the draw string.

The figure in the yard had now reached the garage and was bent over the can unscrewing the cap. Standing up he had started to slosh the contents over the side of the garage when KB took aim at a point above the intruder's head and a metre or so to the right of where he stood.

It was only about thirty metres to the garage and the arrow flew straight and true, smacking into the wooden cladding with a loud thud. Looking about to see the arrow still quivering close to his head, the man turned to seek out its source just as KB released his second arrow, aimed a metre or two short of where the intruder stood. The shaft hit the tarmac and ricocheted towards him causing him to side step quickly out of its way. Before KB had a chance to flight a third, the hooded figure took off across the yard, running as fast as he could for safety and a moment later KB heard an engine rev and a vehicle roar off up the road.

Leaning his bow against the window sill, KB sat on his bed and fastened his prosthetic leg, before slipping on a jacket from his wardrobe. Rocky at his heels, he was crossing the landing when the door opened to his parents' bedroom, and Jack emerged, in the process of fastening up his dressing gown.

"More problems?" he greeted his son.

"I'm afraid so, Dad," came the response. "Somebody was trying to torch the garage, but I managed to scare our visitor off and I think it would be wise to hose down the side as there's probably a couple of gallons of petrol lying around out there."

Leaving the pub together, Jack ran out the hose from the reel by the back door, and in no time they were giving the side of the garage and its surround a good soaking.

"No wonder he took off," commented his father, as KB retrieved his two arrows. "How accurate are you?"

"I've had a lot of practice, Dad," came the reply. "But I've a long way to go yet before I can call myself a true marksman."

"Just as well you didn't wing him, though I suppose we could always argue that if you hadn't scared him off he would certainly have set fire to our garage and we do have that as evidence." Jack added, nodding at the plastic can the arsonist had abandoned as he beat a hasty retreat.

"Best leave it where it is," his son replied. "No doubt the Police will want everything left as we found it."

Hosepipe stowed, the two of them, shadowed by the ever watchful Rocky, returned to the pub, where the lights were now on in the kitchen and they were greeted by Kathy, the kettle already boiling on the stove.

While KB explained to his mother what had happened, Jack fetched the phone from the bar and dialled 999.

"The law should be here within twenty minutes," he said. "They're sending a car out from Yeovil, so they shouldn't be too long."

At that, Hannah appeared at the door and when told of what had happened, accompanied by her father, immediately took off for the stables to check on Winston. It was nearly half an hour later before blue flashing lights in the road outside heralded the arrival of the Police, and Jack unlocked the gate to let them into the car park.

KB joined them in the yard and the two officers lost no time in doing a preliminary examination of the garage. In spite of the thorough job of washing down the garage, the air was till rank with the smell of petrol fumes, and the petrol can was carefully removed and placed in a plastic bag.

"Let's go inside and we can give you our statements there," Jack suggested, as the policemen finished their checks, and they moved into the warmth of the living room, where the officers accepted Kathy's offer of coffee as they settled down, notebooks in hand to record the events of the preceding hour.

"I'll start with you," said the Sergeant, nodding at KB, "as it appears you were first to realise you had an intruder."

"Yes," KB replied, "the security light in the yard came on and it woke me up. I got out of bed and went to the window and saw someone around the garage."

"And what was he up to?" asked the policema.

"Well, I saw him carrying a can, and then he bent down to unscrew the cap. He then started to slosh the contents over the garage, and I got worried."

"And you frightened him off? How did you do that, Mr Blake?"

"Got my bow and loosed off a couple of arrows, one into the side of the garage and one about a couple of metres short of where he was standing."

"I see," said the Sergeant, an unmistakeable note of severity creeping into his response. "And can I see this bow please?"

KB fetched his bow and the arrows from the back hallway where he had left them, and handed them over to the policeman, who examined them carefully before laying them down beside the chair in which he was sitting.

"Why didn't you just shout to warn him off, and then raise the alarm with your father?" he continued. "Surely the two of you confronting him would have been better than risk injuring him seriously?"

"There wasn't time," replied KB calmly, and raising his left trouser leg to show his prosthetic limb, went on, "it was obvious that he was about to torch the garage, and I doubt if a shout from me would have panicked him enough to drop what he was doing and take off, without setting fire to the garage. By the time I had put this on," gesturing to his leg, "and got downstairs he would have had plenty of time to finish the job and make his getaway, and by then the garage would have been well ablaze. Let's be clear about this," he continued, "it would not only have been the garage and its contents, but the garage backs onto the stables and that would almost certainly have gone up as well, to say nothing of the neighbours' fence and the lean-to where my sister keeps her hay and bedding straw."

At this the Sergeant nodded sympathetically, but added, "Nevertheless, you were in possession of a potentially dangerous weapon and it might be argued that it was your intent to inflict bodily harm."

"That's ridiculous," interjected Jack. "My son is an accomplished bowman, and had he intended to injure our visitor he could have easily put an arrow between his shoulder blades. He was quite clearly defending our property and livestock – my daughter's horse – and the consequences of this blatant act of arson could have been very serious indeed."

"Anyway," continued the Sergeant, ignoring the older man's outburst, "can you tell me what might have provoked this attack on your property and have you any idea who might be responsible?"

With some prompting from his family, KB then gave a full account of the events of the preceding evening, including Rocky's part in fending off the assault by Isa Samson in the car park.

At the mention of the Samsons, the Sergeant asked to see Rocky, who trotted in from the back hall and was quite happy to let the young constable make a fuss of him.

"He doesn't appear to be vicious," commented the Sergeant. "Has he ever attacked anybody else?"

"He once went for an Afghan we detained when he was acting suspiciously around the camp perimeter," answered KB "But again, the guy drew a knife on one of my young soldiers while he was carrying out the body search, and Rocky had him by the balls before any damage was done."

"Has he been trained as an attack dog?" queried the Sergeant, "or do you know if he had ever been used for dog fighting, which I believe is a common sport out there?"

"Nope, not to my knowledge, he was only a pup when he was 'adopted' by my platoon, so it's highly unlikely" KB replied. "But he certainly seems to be able to tell the difference between his friends and those who pose a threat to them."

"Did he actually bite Samson?" came the next question.

"Judging by the sound of ripping trouser cloth and the yell Isaac let out, I would say that he probably took a chunk out of his arse," KB answered, causing a chuckle from the younger of the two policemen, and which resulted in a stern glance from his Sergeant.

"Under the circumstances, I would ask you to make sure that your dog is kept under control at all times," the Sergeant continued. "And I must warn you that I will be reporting this, so you may find that we have to remove the dog for a veterinary examination to ensure that he does not have any DNA from a banned breed in him – if so, he may have to be destroyed."

"Hang on a second," came the comment from a clearly agitated Jack Blake. "My son gets assaulted in the car park and could have been badly beaten up if it hadn't been for Rocky here, during the night someone – and no guesses as to who that might be – tries to set fire to our garage with Lord knows what the consequences might have been, and so far all you have done is warn us that the dog may have to be destroyed and that my son could be in trouble for defending our property – it seems to me that there is something wrong here."

"I am only telling you the facts as they seem to me, and may seem to others who could be investigating this case," countered the Sergeant. "But I will be making a full report, and I would like both you and your son to come into Yeovil Police Station tomorrow to make a full statement. I expect our forensic team may be out tomorrow morning to examine the crime scene in greater detail, so please don't go near your garage or touch anything in or around it. In the meantime, my colleague and I will park up outside until first light in case your intruders return, and if I could take the tape from your CCTV camera with me, that would be a help."

Returning with the cassette in hand a couple of minutes later, Jack handed it to the Sergeant and picking up KB's bow and the arrows, the policemen stood up and bid the family a curt, "Thank you, we will see ourselves out."

"What the hell do you make of that?" questioned KB as soon as the back door closed behind them.

"What a waste of bloody time," his father replied. "And I'm afraid that they will do very little about it. None of the local bobbies will go near the Samson's trailer site, as they are afraid of repercussions against their families. In fact, once a year they might bring in a squad from outside the area to conduct a search for stolen property, but apart from recovering the odd quad bike the Samsons have not had time to sell on, nothing else comes of it. Their latest money making scheme is to kidnap family pets and when the owners advertise them as lost in the local paper, they get a phone call offering to 'find' the missing dog or cat for a fairly hefty sum of money. If you call the local Police, they'll tell you that they can only take action if there is proof that a crime has been committed."

"They won't take Rocky away," insisted Hannah. "I'll hide him and tell them he has run off if they come looking for him."

"Let's not worry about that now." said her mother, "but look at the time, it's well past 3 o'clock, so let's get back to bed, things may look a little better in the morning."

"Kris, I'll phone our solicitor first thing, and see if he can come with us when we go in to make our statement," Jack assured his son, and after checking all the downstairs doors and windows to make sure they were secure, the family retired to their rooms to salvage what remained of their night's sleep.

Chapter Nine

The Day After

"If the law supposes that," said Mr Bumble "...the law is an ass."

Charles Dickens, 'Oliver Twist'

It was just after 10.30 a.m. when KB and his father arrived at the Police Station in the neighbouring market town of Yeovil.

Jack had phoned his solicitor earlier, but it was too short notice for him to accompany them although he had briefed them over the phone to keep things simple in their statement and ask for copies.

They were ushered into an interview room, and a young female PC was with them as they wrote and signed their statements. She then left the room and returned five minutes later with the copies they had requested and asked them to accompany her as the Chief Superintendent had asked to see them.

On being ushered into his office, the tall, slim built, uniformed officer rose from behind the desk and gestured for them to take a seat.

"Thank you for coming in this morning," he said. "My name is Chief Superintendent Westwood, and I would appreciate it if we could spend a few minutes going through the events of last evening. I decided to meet you myself instead of having one of my officers interview you, as things from here onwards may not be as straightforward as they would seem. I have your statements here and, subject to the findings of my forensic team, there seems to be no doubt that the incident reported to us was clearly a case of attempted arson, which fortunately failed with no apparent damage done to property or injury to anyone involved.

"I understand we have taken possession of the petrol can which may be the one used by the suspect and also a CCTV recording taken from your security camera. At present these would appear to provide us with the only clear evidence we have, and I will have to wait for further reports before assessing their value if we are to pursue a full investigation into this matter, which I am sure you understand."

"Are you suggesting that a full investigation may not be warranted?" queried Jack.

"Mr Blake," the Superintendent replied, "you must appreciate that in order to bring a successful prosecution in such a case as this, we have to have rock solid evidence, and although that may yet be forthcoming, I have nothing to hand at present which suggests that this is the case. Being a publican, you will also understand what the repercussions might be if we pursued a line of enquiry with the suspect you have identified as being the possible perpetrator, if there is the slightest chance that we could not bring those enquiries to a successful conclusion.

"Speaking to you now off the record and in the strictest of confidence, we both know only too well from past experiences that the Samson family will react aggressively to any steps we take, and the fallout could be both unwelcome and damaging. I do not have the manpower to maintain surveillance on your establishment or any others in your area for any length of time that might be appropriate, and in this case it might be more prudent to let sleeping dogs lie rather than stir up a hornet's nest, unless of course, as I have already said, we have one hundred percent watertight evidence that will stand up in court."

Before Jack or KB could reply, he continued. "And then of course we are bound to take into consideration the manner in which your son chose to react to this intrusion. From my Sergeant's report it does seem likely that this incident could have been the result of earlier events last evening, which provoked this response. I agree that the provocation – if there was such – certainly did not merit the response of an attempted arson attack on your property. Do not forget also that we still have to establish there was a clear link between the incident earlier in the car park between your son and Isaac Samson, but the fact that your son chose to resort to the use of what could be deemed a potentially lethal weapon allegedly to scare off the arsonist, will certainly be a factor that any defence attorney will focus on. In effect, it could be argued tha," nodding at KB, "it was your intent to deliberately inflict bodily harm on an intruder that you believed was a rival to your affections for Miss Baker!"

At this Jack could contain himself no longer.

"That's bloody ridiculous," he burst out. "My son has been away in the Army and has had no contact with Alex Baker for nearly two years, so to suggest he was doing more than just defending our property and livestock is a complete travesty."

"Please believe me, Mr Blake," came the response, "I am entirely sympathetic to your situation, but I have to point out that any loopholes we have in bringing such a case will be exploited by any lawyer worth his salt – and we know that the Samson family can afford the best.

"I am also obviously aware that you have recently left the Army, but my Sergeant's report only provided a very broad outline of your service. It would help me if you could provide a few more details, if you have no objections?"

"None at all," answered KB. "I served with the Paras and did two tours in Helmand. I did my first tour as a member of the Battalion Sniper Platoon. During the second tour as a Platoon Sergeant I was leading a patrol when we ran into an ambush which resulted in my losing one of my men, and the same IED which killed him also took off my leg, hence the reason I am no longer in the Army."

"I understand," replied Westwood. "And I am sorry that your injury cut short your career. You guys did a tremendous job out there and I have the greatest admiration for all you men achieved. What are your plans now?"

"I have a place on an Estate Management course at Tamar Valley College in Cornwall starting next week, and after that I will be looking for a job somewhere."

"Well, I wish you the best of luck," said the Superintendent, the positive note in his voice suggesting that he was pleased that KB would be moving on, "and I hope things work out for you. Now, I have kept you too long already, so many thanks for your time and needless to say, we will keep in touch."

"When can I get my archery equipment back?" asked KB as they were escorted to the door.

"Probably within a week or two." came the response. "And as soon as I am satisfied everything is in order, I will get one of our patrol cars to drop it off for you at The Volunteer."

Formalities over, they left on a handshake and returned to Jack's Land Rover in the station car park.

"Tell you what, Dad," KB said, as he buckled himself into the passenger seat, "they are not going to do anything about it, and they are probably right. The last thing Westwood wants is a small civil war breaking out on his patch, and with all the cuts in Police manpower they're probably hard-pressed to carry out their routine commitments at the moment, let alone contain a family feud between the Blakes and the Samsons."

"It still makes me mad," replied his father, as he steered his vehicle out of the car park. "But it's still going to be interesting to see what happens – if anything. Anyway, we've wasted enough time this morning. I have to call at the Cash and Carry to pick up a few bits and pieces for your mother, anything you need to do?"

"Actually, there is. If there is a phone shop in town, I wouldn't mind stopping by to pick up a mobile. I've never bothered with one up until now, as to be honest, I never had much use for one, but I might find it handy when I leave for college."

Fifteen minutes later, KB left the shop his father recommended with a new I-phone in his pocket and after calling off at the Cash and Carry, made their way homewards to find that Kathy had already opened up for the lunchtime session, with Hannah standing in for her father behind the bar.

"The phone's been ringing off the hook for you," Kathy greeted her son. "A call from a Captain Grayson in Colchester, another from the Admissions Office at Tamar Valley College, and Alex seems desperate to contact you; she's called three times already."

"Thanks, Mum," he replied. "Captain Grayson was our Adjutant, and I can't imagine what he wants, or the college come to that, but if Alex wants me so urgently I'd better call her right away."

"Make your calls in the living room, rather than from the bar," suggested his mother. "Too many long ears to eavesdrop in the bar, and you don't want to set tongues wagging unnecessarily, we've had enough excitement around here to start the rumours flying around the village, without adding fuel to the fire! You'll find the phone numbers they left on the notepad by the phone."

Heeding his mother's advice, and shutting the living room door behind him, KB settled into one of the armchairs and dialled Alex's number.

It was Amy Baker who answered the phone, and it was obvious from the tone in her voice, that all was not well in the Baker household.

"Are you and the family all right?" she asked anxiously. "Isaac Samson was round here just after breakfast this morning, making all kinds of threats about you. It seems he is taking off to Ireland and was demanding that Alex went with him."

"I hope she didn't go," said KB.

"No," Amy continued. "She told him straight that she had no intention of going anywhere with him, which caused another outburst from him and I can tell you, your name came up again and he got quite nasty. Fortunately, Joe and a couple of his men were here having a cup of coffee before they left for the building site, so they saw him off without any trouble, but he was not a happy man when he left. Anyway, tell me what happened last night to cause all this."

"Let me speak to Alex," KB replied "and she can fill you in on the details afterwards."

"Hang on a moment, I'll just fetch her." came the response, and a moment later Alex came on the line.

"Kris, are you okay?" she questioned. "I've been trying to get hold of you. Danny was round here this morning and he's saying you two had some kind of a scrap last night."

"I wouldn't call it a scrap, Alex. After we closed up, I took Rocky for a walk down the car park before turning in and Isa and Nathan were waiting for me. He jumped me and shoved me up against the garage and was warning me to stay away from you when Rocky took exception and tore a chunk out of the seat of his trousers."

A deep chuckle from down the phone line followed, and the comment, "I think Rocky did more than just take a chunk out of his pants, Kris. Isa did tell me he was calling off at the doctor's for a tetanus jab as you had set the dog on him, but I think it's his pride that's been hurt more than anything else. I can't understand why he would be taking off to Ireland at a moment's notice though."

"Probably because in the wee small hours of this morning we had visitors, one of whom tried to torch the garage, and no prizes for guessing who that might have been."

"Wow!" the girl replied. "Was there any damage done?"

"Fortunately no." KB continued. "I woke up when the security lights came on and managed to frighten the intruder off before he could set fire to the petrol he had been spreading around."

"You were a bit of an idiot trying to tackle them weren't you?" queried the girl.

"Never left my bedroom." he answered. "Grabbed my bow and fired a couple of arrows near enough to put the wind up him, and he took off at high speed."

"Didn't realise you had taken up archery!"

"All part of my re-hab programme," he added. "Helps me build up the muscle in my arm, and to be honest, I quite enjoy it, although I may be short on practice for a while, as the Police have confiscated my bow, as well as reading me the riot act on being in possession of what they see as a highly dangerous weapon."

"What are they doing about catching the arsonist?" she asked.

"They say they are investigating the incident, but to be honest I can't see them doing too much about it, probably not enough clear evidence to prosecute anyone, and we both know how they will do anything to avoid an outright confrontation with the Samsons, even if it turns out they are involved. Anyway, I won't be looking for anymore aggro, and with Isa out of the area for a while and me leaving for college next week, things will probably blow over."

"Will I see you before you leave?" came the next question.

"Alex, you know you are always welcome at the pub, but it might be wise to keep our heads below the parapet for a while, as to be seen together in public could be asking for trouble. Apart from anything else, I don't want to leave for Cornwall with you and my family in the middle of a feud with the Samson clan, but I'll be home for weekends from time to time, so maybe we can get together then."

"It really is the shits," was the unladylike reply… "You get home at last after charging around Afghanistan getting blown up, and now you're off again. Will you keep in touch?"

"Of course I will," he answered, and after giving his newly acquired mobile number to her, rang off.

The door to the lounge opened and his mother came in, carrying a mug of tea and a plate of sandwiches.

"I guess that was Alex you were talking to," she said, KB realising that her well timed entrance probably meant she had been eavesdropping on his conversation at the door. "Just a word of advice, I wouldn't be in a rush to get involved with her again. She plays the field, does that young lady, and Isaac Samson wasn't the only young man she got her claws into whilst you were away!"

Knowing from past experience that as close a friend as she was to Amy Baker, Alex would probably not be his mother's first choice as a suitable partner for her son, KB smiled and nodding his assent, assured her that he was not about to march anyone down the aisle at this stage in his life, least of all Alex Baker.

Finishing his sandwiches, he picked up the phone again and dialled the number for the garrison at Colchester, and when the automated switchboard answered, dialled in the extension number for the Adjutant's Office. The duty clerk took his name and he waited as the phone rang through to Captain Grayson's desk.

"Sergeant Blake, thank you for returning my call," came the familiar voice over the line. "Settling into civvie life without any problems, I trust?"

For a moment KB was tempted to suggest to the officer that his homecoming had not been without incident, but instead he assured the Captain that all was well.

"My reason for calling," continued Grayson, "is that I have received a signal from the MoD which might possibly be of some interest to you. As you know, the Regular Forces are in the process of undergoing significant cut-backs in manpower, and the Government is hoping to plug some of the gaps this will create by beefing up the Reserves. I know from your record that you started your Army career in the TA with the Light Infantry and you are probably aware that their successors, The Wessex Rifles, continues to operate in your area. Anyway, I have been requested to contact any former serving members, and in view of your weapons skills, and experience as a Platoon Sergeant, I wondered if there was a chance you might be interested in helping them with their training programme?"

"How would that stand with the fact that I was discharged because of my injuries?" KB asked.

"Well, technically you are not on the Active Reserve which under normal circumstances would ensure your transfer to the Rifles would be virtually automatic, but I know that you are still physically fit and that you did extremely well in your re-hab programme, so we might be able to make some arrangements whereby you were passed fit for limited service with the unit. This would certainly preclude you from any re-call for full time or overseas service, and ensure you were not called upon to carry out any physical activities beyond your capabilities.

"In your favour you have an excellent record, and I am pretty certain the Rifles would welcome having you on board as a Small Arms Instructor, for instance. Right now, however, I only need to know if this might interest you, and if so, I can put the wheels in motion and see what reaction I get."

Unlike many regular soldiers, and having started his Army life as a Territorial, KB did not share the belief held by those who regarded the

Reservists as no more than a bunch of enthusiastic amateurs who were not to be trusted with any tasks that could endanger their lives, or more importantly, the lives of the full time professionals they served alongside.

"Thank you for thinking of me, sir," KB responded. "I might be interested, but I should point out that I start a three month course at Agricultural College in Cornwall next week, after which I will be seeking full time employment hopefully somewhere in the South West, but there is no guarantee that I'll be successful, so I could finish up anywhere."

"I appreciate that, Blake," the Adjutant said, "and we can cross that bridge when we come to it. In the meantime, your – albeit temporary – location in Cornwall should not be a problem as the Rifles Battalion HQ is at Exeter and they have a Company in Truro."

"Not too far to travel then," KB replied. "So I'll wait to hear from you. I'll give you my mobile number in case I'm not at home the next time you call, but there is one thing I would want to be sure of."

"And that is?" asked Grayson.

"I would not be prepared to re-badge, sir. I wouldn't mind serving with the Rifles as a Para on attachment, and that's my only condition."

At this the Adjutant acknowledged that he understood, and after KB gave him his phone number, the officer rang off promising that 'he would see what he could do'.

Making his final call, KB dialled the number for Tamar Valley College and was put through to their Admissions Office.

"Mr Blake," said the woman at the other end, "my name is Sue Warden, and I'm the Admissions Secretary. Thank you for calling back. I was just ringing to confirm that you will be with us next Tuesday. We will be open from 10.00 a.m. until 4.00 p.m. but please try to get here by 3.00 p.m. at the latest, as there is some paperwork we need to complete. When you arrive please come straight to my office, and I will be mailing confirmation to you today. I'll also send you a list of the clothes and other items we recommend you bring with you. I see that you are also a mature student," she added, "may I ask if you have your own transport, and will you be bringing it with you?"

"I do have a pick-up," KB replied. "And I will be bringing it with me. All being well I hope to be at the college at around noon."

"Don't forget to ask for a vehicle pass when you arrive, so that you can access the campus car parks," came the response. "And I note that you will also be requiring accommodation?"

KB confirmed that this would be necessary, as she went on, "I wonder therefore, if you would mind living off campus? We are very short of rooms in the student housing blocks, and I can offer you accommodation in a barn conversion on one of the college's farms, about three miles from the college. You would have to pay a small premium over the usual accommodation fees, but you will certainly have more space there – and more freedom to come and go, would that be acceptable?"

"That sounds great," said KB.

"Fine. I'll reserve rooms in an apartment for you at Tregallis Farm, and we will give you directions when you register next week. Thank you for your time, Mr Blake," she concluded. "We look forward to seeing you next week."

Feeling more than satisfied with the outcome of his phone calls, KB picked up the empty sandwich plate and mug and carried them through to the kitchen, where his mother was busy filling the last of the orders for their lunchtime customers.

"Everything okay?" she enquired.

"Yep, pretty good actually, Mum. Seems the Army may not have entirely finished with me yet, and the college folk have set me up in what sounds like pretty good digs."

"Not joining up again are you?" Kathy asked anxiously.

"Nothing on a full time basis," he replied. "It seems that the Reserves might want to take me on as a Small Arms Instructor, which means a couple of nights a week training, a weekend or two a month and perhaps an annual camp."

"Isn't that rather a lot?" she asked. "How will that fit in with your course at college, and what happens when you find a full time job?"

"Nothing is settled yet, Mum," KB answered, "so I don't have to make up my mind for a while."

"And how did things go with Alex?" she continued.

"Fine. No need for you to start worrying yourself. Alex knows exactly what the score is with me going off to college, and with Isaac apparently hot footing it to Ireland, no doubt to lie low for a while, things should quieten down here."

"Well, if that isn't proof that he was involved with last night's episode, I don't know what is!" concluded his mother. "Good riddance I say, and let's hope he makes the move a permanent one!"

"I doubt that," replied her son. "He'll probably be back in a week or so, particularly when he finds out that the Police aren't going to take any action."

At that his father appeared at the doorway. "Sorry about this, Kath," Jack said. “Just had a bunch of cyclists in looking for bar snacks. I know it’s late, but can you cope?”

With a wry smile Kathy nodded her assent, and KB left with his father to take their orders and help with serving their drinks.

By the time the cyclists had been fed and watered, and the last of the locals had been chased out of the bar, it was approaching 3.30 p.m., so while Kathy and Jack relaxed for a couple of hours in the lounge, KB took Rocky for a walk.

As he crossed the yard, a black van came into the car park and pulled up by the garage. The doors opened and a middle-aged man and a young woman got out, the latter immediately opening the rear doors and removing two sets of white overalls.

“Afternoon,” the man said, taking an ID card out of his wallet and showing it to KB. “I’m Bob Foster and this is my assistant Carla, we’re from Avon and Somerset Police Forensics Unit and are here to check the evidence from the attempted arson attack last evening.”

“Please carry on.” KB replied, indicating an area on the side of the garage. “This is where the intruder was splashing petrol. We did hose it down last night, so I don’t know whether there will be any signs of it still left.”

“More than likely there will be.” Foster remarked. “And in any case we will take a couple of small samples from the timber cladding, and that should confirm what kind of inflammable liquid was used.”

“I can tell you it was definitely petrol,” said KB. “You could smell it last night and I think you’ll find when you get closer to the garage, you may still get a whiff of it.”

“Well, we do have the can and that certainly still had the remains of petrol in it, but no fingerprints at the moment, so it looks as if your arsonist was probably wearing gloves. Anyway, this shouldn’t take too long, so if you have other things to do, don’t let us keep you.”

“If you need anything, you’ll find my father in the pub,” said KB, and leaving them to it, with Rocky trotting at his heels, set off on his walk.

Chapter Ten

Back to School

" 'Tis education forms the common mind,
Just as the twig is bent, the tree's inclined."

Alexander Pope

The rest of the week flew by, and the weekend was taken up with his final preparations before leaving for Cornwall. It came as no surprise to any of his family when the Police called to inform them that they were not taking any further action on the arson incident, due to lack of evidence. They had been told, however, that for the time being 'the file would be kept open should any more information concerning the incident come to light' which they all interpreted as meaning that the whole episode would no longer receive any kind of priority.

Isaac Samson had not shown up again, and although Alex had visited the pub with her parents a couple of times, she and KB had enjoyed no more than a friendly chat, and he had made no move to suggest that for the time being anyway, a closer relationship was in the offing.

The Police had yet seen fit to return KB's bow, so he asked his father to make sure that it was kept somewhere safe when it was eventually delivered back to the pub. He had also agreed with Hannah that she would take care of Rocky during his absence, and the two of them had already established a bond to the point where Rocky would accompany her and Winston on their daily rides around the surrounding country lanes and along the towpath.

Allowing himself two hours for the run down to Launceston and another half hour to reach the college campus, he said his farewells and left the pub just after 9.30 a.m.

Not long after 11 o'clock he reached the outskirts of Launceston, where he pulled off the A30 dual carriageway and turned onto the A388 to take him the remaining six miles or so south of the town to the college. The exit to the campus was clearly signposted, so he had no trouble finding his way to the large car park in the front of the Administration building where the Admissions Office was located.

Already the waiting area in front of the Reception desk was busy, and as KB stood in line to wait his turn, he was conscious of how young his fellow students seemed. Introducing himself to the clerk, he was given a file and asked to take a seat and to read the contents and complete the admissions form it contained.

As he made his way across the foyer towards a vacant seat, the door to the inner office opened and a smartly dressed young woman appeared. Pausing by the Reception desk, KB noticed that the clerk pointed directly at him, and without further hesitation, the woman walked directly over to him and introduced herself.

"Kristian Blake?" she inquired, shaking him by the hand. "I'm Sue Warden, we spoke on the phone last week. Welcome to Tamar Valley College, would you come with me please?"

Without waiting for a response, she turned on her heel, and KB followed her back to the office, aware that the attention he had received had not gone unnoticed from other students in the vicinity, and that he had become the focus of quite a few curious glances.

Closing the door behind them, Sue Warden gestured for him to take a seat opposite her as she sat down behind a desk whose surface was stacked with forms and documents.

"Let me have your file please," she asked, and as KB handed it over, continued, "we'll get this filled out and signed, and then our Principal, Dr Windrush, wants to have a word with you."

"May I ask why?" KB interjected. "I really don't need any special consideration, although I appreciate your help."

"It's not really a case of special consideration," she responded. "In fact we are looking for your help and co-operation as much as anything, but Dr Windrush will explain everything when you meet him. For now let's get these forms completed and then I'll take you across to his office."

Less than twenty minutes later, form filling completed, car park pass in hand and after a briefing from Sue Warden on the facilities the college offered, KB found himself being ushered into the Principal's office.

The portly grey haired and bespectacled man behind the desk rose to his feet as KB entered, and for the second time that morning, KB found himself being warmly shaken by the hand and welcomed to the college.

"A pleasure to meet you, Mr Blake, and may I call you Kristian?" asked the Doctor.

"Please call me Kris," KB replied. "But I must admit I wasn't expecting this, and hope I haven't been singled out for any special treatment, I came here as a student to be treated as any other!"

"The fact that you are, as we say, a mature student, will automatically set you aside from the younger element at the college," continued the Principal. "But that is not the reason why I asked to see you, or that Ms Warden saw to your registration personally. She may have suggested that we are looking for your co-operation in certain matters during your time with us, and as your recent career would suggest that you are no stranger to accepting responsibility, leads me to believe that you can help us.

"We have a situation here in which we have had to give certain undertakings to provide special supervision for one student among our new intake, which is not so much related to his requiring, or in fact needing, extra attention to his tutoring, but more – to putting it bluntly – in keeping an eye on him, both on and off campus. Quite frankly, I do not have the staff available to assign to this, and in any case he already has – how shall I put it – a 'minder' whose primary responsibility that is, but it would certainly put me at ease to know that we have some 'in-house', back-up."

"With due respect, sir," said KB, "I did not come here to act as a wet nurse to any of my fellow students."

"No, no, of course you didn't." answered Windrush. "And I can assure you we are not asking you to undertake any additional tasks that would interfere with your studies. But look, it's approaching one o'clock and I would be most pleased if you would join me for lunch. Normally the staff take their midday meal in the main canteen, but I thought it would be wiser to have something brought in here and I have asked Tom Cousins, our Farm Manager, to join us."

Without waiting for KB's reply, he picked up the phone on his desk, and asked his secretary to find the Farm Manager and also arrange for the food to be brought in.

As they waited, the conversation turned to KB's career in the Paras, with the Doctor expressing particular interest in his experiences at Headley Court.

"I hear they do some splendid work there," the Principal commented, but before KB had a chance to go in to any detail, the door opened and his secretary appeared carrying a plate full of pasties and sausage rolls, followed by a tall, dark complexioned man, who judging by his mud splattered corduroy trousers and Barbour jacket, was certainly the aforementioned Tom Cousins.

Introductions made, and a pasty each in hand, Windrush lost no time in resuming his briefing.

"Kris, Tom here is up to speed on our situation and is aware of why you are here, so let me now fill in the details. Starting on the same course as you today, we have what I suppose might be termed as a 'VIP' in the person of the second son of the Nizam of Surpor. Surpor is one of those hang-overs from the colonial era, and is a small enclave, about the size of the county of Devon, which sits on the border between Pakistan and Afghanistan. When India and Pakistan were partitioned, Surpor became part of the latter, but because, at that time the ruling Nizam and his family had strong political connections with Jinnah, the founder of Pakistan, and later Liaquat Ali Khan who became their first Prime Minister, Surpor was allowed to retain some vestiges of localised independent government, with the Nizam becoming the de-facto governor. In fact they owned most of the land in Surpor anyway, so something of a status-quo was maintained.

"As you can imagine," he continued, "because of its geographic position, in recent years Surpor has become the focus of attention from a number of unwanted quarters, including various factions of the Taliban and Jihadi extremists who have been using the region as a corridor to provide logistics and support to the insurgents in Afghanistan. In the past the present Nizam resisted this as much as he was able, but with only very limited resources he had to rely largely on help from Pakistan. This has been sporadic at best and more recently virtually non-existent, the Pakistani security forces insisting that it was Surpor's responsibility to police its own borders.

"The Nizam therefore requested and is receiving help from our American friends in the form of their Special Forces, and our own security agencies. The result is that activity along these supply routes has certainly been curtailed even if use of them may not yet be entirely denied to the Taliban and their allies.

"The Nizam has two sons, both of whom have been educated in the UK as guests of our Government. The eldest son graduated from Sandhurst eighteen months ago, and is now back in Surpor being helped by the Americans to train an effective local defence force that will shortly take over all responsibility for border security. The second son, Amir Akbar Khan was sent to the Royal

Agricultural College at Cirencester on completing his schooling, which, it was hoped, would eventually provide him with the knowledge to improve farming methods in his own country on his return and manage the family estates.

"Unfortunately, Amir found the social life at Cirencester too much of a distraction and encouraged by some of the less industrious among his fellow students, pursued a path that eventually led to the college requesting his removal. To say that he was something of a hell-raiser would be, apparently, an understatement, but his being sent down from the RAC provided our Foreign Office with something of a problem.

"In due course, we were contacted and asked to find a place for him here at Tamar Valley, on the basis that in a smaller and somewhat isolated West Country college with, shall we say, less privileged and perhaps a rather more down to earth student faculty, the temptation to stray from the straight and narrow would be significantly reduced. Anyway, gentlemen, that is the theory and as I somewhat reluctantly agreed to take young Amir under our wing, it remains to be seen if that premise is valid.

"This brings me to where we are now, and why I have asked you here. As you already know, Kris, we have decided to accommodate you at Tregallis Farm, where we have a barn conversion that provides us with two cottage apartments, both with two bedrooms. Amir and his manservant will be in one, and Amir's minder – or bodyguard is probably a more accurate description, will share the other with yourself. The latter, who incidentally is provided by one of our security agencies, is also an ex-serviceman, so the two of you should be able to get along alright.

"We felt that by accommodating Amir some way off campus, the attraction of our female student quarters would be limited, and he would be easier to keep an eye on. Tom and his family live in the farmhouse, and he will provide further support, should you need it, am I right, Tom?"

"Certainly," replied the Farm Manager. "Any problems, let me know immediately, and between us, we should be able to keep the young man under control."

"Thank you for bringing me into the picture," KB responded, "but perhaps you can also let me know what our security people consider to be the threat to Amir?"

"I gather that there was a suggestion of a potential kidnap attempt during his time at Cirencester," answered the Principal. "But it never materialized or perhaps was nipped in the bud. I suppose that if he were abducted and fell into the wrong hands, he might be considered a useful bargaining chip in influencing the Nizam's policies, but all I have been told is that we are to monitor his moves very carefully and while he is in our charge we share some of the responsibility for his welfare and safety. Anyway, if you have no more questions, I will leave it to Tom to take you out to the Farm. Once again welcome to the college and I hope you find your time here both rewarding and enjoyable. My door is always open to my students, and if I can ever help with advice or counsel, please do not hesitate to come and see me."

At that, the three of them rose from their seats, and KB followed the Farm Manager into the outer office.

"Where are you parked?" asked Cousins.

"In front of the Admin building," KB replied.

"I'll drive round and meet you there, I'm in a Land Rover with the college crest on the door; what are you driving?"

"A black Ford Pick-up."

"Okay, just follow me out to the Farm, and park out front of the Barn. The other party arrived early this morning, so we'll get you introduced and settled in."

With that the Manager left KB to find his way back to the Administration building, and shortly afterwards at the wheel of the Ranger, KB found himself following the Land Rover the three miles to Tregallis Farm.

The Farmhouse and surrounding buildings lay in a small valley surrounded by fields and woodland which rose to meet the skyline on all sides. The final approach to the Farm was a quarter of a mile down a tarmac driveway off the lane they had driven in on from the college. The barn conversion that housed the two cottages was easily identified, with a generous parking area in front, and two front doors flanked by tubs planted out with well-trimmed shrubs. Across from what had once been the working farmyard, the farmhouse itself was situated by a low stone wall, behind which a small lawn and flowers beds flanked the path leading to the front door.

Cousins pulled up in front of the farmhouse, and by the time he had alighted, KB had already parked next to a Nissan Pathfinder outside the cottages. Beckoning for KB to follow him, the Farm Manager knocked briefly on the door of the second cottage, and before there was a response opened it and walked inside.

The front door opened into a small hallway, with a staircase on the left and an open plan living room on the right. The flagstone floors were partly covered by several red and blue patterned rugs and a wood burning stove sat in a large open fireplace on the far wall burning brightly, the reflection of the flames flickering in several brass and copper pots and pans which had been positioned on the hearth.

The room was well furnished with a dining table and four chairs, a low sideboard, a bookcase which stood against the wood panelling of the staircase, and two small sofas with a coffee table at each end and a flat screen TV against the wall. Under the window that overlooked the fields to the rear were two small desks.

"Your roommate is probably with his charge," commented Cousins, "but I see he has the fire lit already and has probably made himself at home. You'll find plenty of firewood in the barn across the yard, and when you run low, give me a shout and I'll lend you my chain saw. There are plenty of fallen trees up in the woods, so you can help yourselves. You can leave the stove burning all night and it heats the radiators upstairs in the two bedrooms and the bathroom. It will also heat the water tank, but there is also an immersion heater you can switch on if you let the fire out. The desks over there have plug-ins for laptops, but you will find your broadband connection fairly slow – one of the penalties of being out in the country. The kitchen is through there," he continued, gesturing towards the door leading off at the far end of the room. "It has everything you need, cooker and fridge etc. Outside at the back there is a linney which has a washer and drier, to be shared with your neighbours.

"What meals you take here is entirely up to you. You'll probably want to do your own breakfast here, and then take lunch and perhaps your evening meal in the college canteen. There's a schedule for the times they open in your file."

Just then the front door opened, and they were joined by a fair haired, stocky, broad shouldered man of medium height who KB judged was probably in his late thirties, casually dressed in jeans and a sweater, who immediately crossed the room to shake KB by the hand.

"Hi, KB isn't it?" the newcomer ventured. "I'm Peter Bowen, your roomie; it's a pleasure meeting you." Taken aback at the familiar greeting, KB found himself looking straight into a face that was well weathered yet fresh and open, and KB immediately noticed the laugh lines which wrinkled the corners of two piercing blue eyes that now scrutinised him. High clipped sideburns and close cropped hair completed the picture and the firmness of the handshake and the muscular frame of the man left KB in no doubt that here was someone who probably led a fairly Spartan life within clearly defined parameters, but who nevertheless possessed a generous sense of humour and would be relatively easy to get along with.

"That's a surprise," he admitted, "I haven't been called KB for a while, but good to meet you too."

Before KB had a chance to ask his new roommate how he had known the nickname by which he had been widely known in the Paras, Tom Cousins broke in. "I'm going to leave you gentlemen to get to know each other and settle in, but again, let me know if there is anything you need. We haven't had any VIPs staying here before, but there shouldn't be too many problems, providing you can keep young Amir Khan under control."

With a nod of his head, the Farm Manager left the two of them.

"Better get my kit unloaded," said KB.

"I'll give you a hand," offered Bowen, and the two of them went outside to offload the Ford.

KB had managed to pack most of his kit in the Bergen rucksack that had already done sterling service as his carry-all during his service with the Paras, and had packed a blazer, grey slacks and a couple of formal shirts in a small suitcase, should an occasion arise when less casual wear was required. A large cardboard box held his laptop computer, a box file, notebooks and some other items of stationery. With KB shouldering the Bergen and Bowen carrying the suitcase and box, moving his gear into the cottage only took a matter of minutes but negotiating the narrow staircase to the first floor did prove more of a challenge, and KB was quite relieved to be able to dump the back pack on the landing at the top of the stairs.

"We have two bedrooms," said Bowen. "One is an en-suite with a shower room, and the other is opposite the full family bathroom. I'm not fussy, either suits me, but you might find the en-suite better for you," he added, nodding knowingly at KB's left leg.

As Bowen disappeared downstairs, KB was left wondering for a second time within the hour, how it was that the man knew so much about him.

KB wasted no time unpacking, pleased with his room furnished as it was with a comfortable double bed, chest of drawers and a cupboard in which he hung his blazer and trousers, also shaking out his shirts and putting them on hangers. The shower room was basic, but well-appointed with a reasonable sized walk in shower, electric razor point, heated towel rail, wash basin and WC. The view from his bedroom window looked out across fields which sloped upwards from the rear of the cottages to meet a line of trees on the skyline, a low hanging mist suggesting that the damp chill of an early autumn afternoon was already beginning to settle over the valley. Pulling the curtains to shut out the encroaching gloom, KB rejoined his companion downstairs.

"Kettle's boiled," Peter Bowen called out as KB reached the bottom of the stairs. "You'll find a couple of mugs with tea bags on the sideboard, milk is in the fridge, and sugar in the jar by the kettle if you take it; I take mine with a dash of milk no sugar."

Tea made KB carried the mugs through the living room, and setting them down on the side tables, settled down in the unoccupied armchair.

"Thanks for your help with my bags," KB said. "And the tea is most welcome. I'll nip into Launceston and find a supermarket in a minute, and stock up with a few essentials."

"Up to you, but there's no hurry," answered Bowen. "I think I've got enough bits and pieces to keep us going for a day or so, and it will probably be easier if we share everything. I don't go too much on keeping things to oneself, and in any case, you are ex-services, so I'm sure you are used to pooling resources."

"No problem – suits me fine," KB replied. "But I'm intrigued – how come you know so much about me?"

The man chuckled. "You have every right to be surprised, but as I'm sure you are aware by now, the young man next door is classified as a fairly high security risk, that's why I'm around to keep an eye on him 24/7 and also why we have been through your service record. Pretty impressive, by the way," he continued. "You seem to have made quite a name for yourself, and by all accounts a promising career was cut short prematurely. How are you getting along with the leg?"

"Well enough," said KB. "It never lets me forget I have got it, but there are not many activities that I wouldn't want to tackle, but am I allowed to ask about your background?"

"Sure," Peter Bowen replied. "Ex Royal Marines; I was with them as a WO2 on Telic 1 in the operation to secure the oil installations in the Al-Faw Peninsula."

"That was quite a show, wasn't it?" asked KB.

"It certainly was," agreed Bowen. "We ran into quite stiff opposition from the Iraqi Army, but the supporting firepower we could call upon was pretty awesome, and the buggers never really stood a chance. Anyway," he went on, "by the time we came back, I had done sixteen years and took the chance to get out. Been divorced for over ten years now, so I didn't have any ties, so after bumming around Canada and the US for a while, I took a job with a Government agency which amongst other things provide bodyguards to foreign VIPs visiting the UK. This particular assignment is fairly typical, and I must admit I shan't be sorry when it's over, young Amir is a real party lad and you need eyes in the back of your head to keep tabs on him.

"In fact, my predecessor got the sack during Amir's time at Cirencester, when the young bugger slipped his lead and finished up in the local nick after being slung out of one of the pubs in town. It seems he got caught shagging the landlord's daughter in her bedroom and I guess her Papa was none too impressed and nearly killed the little sod before heaving him out on the street. Fortunately we alerted the Police as soon as he went missing, and he was picked up soon after. As you can imagine, the shit hit the fan and our guy was out the door. Since then, their Embassy has given him a manservant – Asif – who is also supposed to be helping me, but I don't entirely trust him, so I'm glad to have you around, even if you are not officially on our team."

"I'm surprised he wasn't shipped home," said KB.

"Well, he should have been," replied the other. "But I guess that would have been a massive loss of face for the family, virtually running their own fiefdom in a community where in the upper echelons of local society everybody knows everybody. You can bet your bottom dollar, that there's more than a few among the Surpor elite who would dearly like to see the Khan hierarchy crash and burn, and a son of the Nizam being sent home in disgrace would have played into their hands politically. In any case, our boy next door, while not being the flavour of the month with his dad, is mummy's little darling, in whose eyes he can do no wrong, so unless he does a Guy Fawkes and attempts to blow up the Palace of Westminster, we are stuck with him. By the way, don't worry about supper tonight," he continued. "You are invited to join us for one of Asif's curries. I can't stand the little weasel, but he does wield a mean pan in the galley, and it will give you a chance to meet them both.

"Anyway, if you want to do a shopping run, I'll leave you to it. There's a supermarket on the left just after the roundabout when you get to Launceston. We stopped there on the way in, and it has all the usual stuff."

Thanking Peter for the invitation, KB took his leave and twenty minutes later found himself doing the rounds of the supermarket shelves. When taking the milk out of the fridge to make the tea, he had noticed that there was no cheese, so he made straight to the deli counter where a large block of farmhouse mature Cheddar, and two local cheeses, Cornish Blue and Keltic Gold were added to his shopping basket. KB had a weakness for cheese and was always trying new varieties, even though he had found some of the more pungent goat's milk varieties he had encountered in Afghanistan a little hard to stomach. Some biscuits, a jar of pickle, and a box of muesli, a loaf of rye bread, a jar each of strawberry jam and Marmite, a bottle of Black Grouse Scotch whisky and half a dozen bottles of Skinner's Cornish Ales completed his shopping.

Back at the farm, he stashed his purchases away in the kitchen cupboard and fridge and settled down in front of the TV, whisky in hand, to watch the evening news. Twenty minutes later, Peter Bowen came down from upstairs, in shirtsleeves, jacket in hand and showing quite openly that he was wearing a shoulder holster from which the butt of an automatic pistol protruded.

Aware that this had not gone unnoticed, the ex-Marine was quick to explain. "Glock 17," he said removing the weapon from its holster. Slipping out the magazine and sliding back the action to check that the weapon was clear, he handed it to KB for him to examine. "We all carry them when on 'minder' duties for special VIPs. It's a pain in the arse really, but so far I've never had to pull it for real, so let's hope it stays that way."

"Does the Nizam's son know you are carrying?" asked KB, as he examined the automatic.

"Probably," came the reply. "But he has never said anything, and I haven't raised the subject. Mind you, he is probably so used to seeing people carrying weapons in his own country it may not have occurred to him that there is anything particularly unusual in me being armed."

Nodding his understanding, KB handed back the Glock which Bowen reloaded and after clicking on the safety catch, replaced in its holster.

"While you were out shopping," Bowen continued, "I checked next door and apparently tonight we're having one of Asif's specialities, a lamb curry, and I hope you like your curries hot, as I know from past experience it's likely to be a sizzler."

"No problem – the hotter the better," replied KB.

Accepting KB's invitation to join him with a Scotch, the two sat chatting for a while and after

finishing their drinks KB followed Bowen to the next door cottage, where the spicy aroma of their evening meal greeted them.

Rising from one of the easy chairs, a slender young man dressed casually in jeans and a rugby shirt came forward to greet them, no more than an inch taller than KB, the second son of the Nizam of Surpor was clean shaven, with well-groomed black curly hair crowning a handsome face from which two dark brown eyes with laugh lines at their corners now scrutinised KB. A strong aquiline nose above a mouth which smiled a welcome and displayed perfectly even teeth, completed a picture, which KB had no doubt would have instant appeal to many of the opposite sex.

“May I present his Highness Amir Akbar Ayaz Khan,” Bowen said, handling the introductions. “Amir, this is Kristian Blake, a former serving member of our Parachute Regiment and now a fellow student of yours, and your next door neighbour.”

“A pleasure to meet you, Mr Blake,” the young man responded, shaking KB warmly by the hand. “I expect Peter here has told you all about me,” he quipped, “and I can assure you it’s not all true. In fact I hope over the next few weeks I can impress you with my diligence as a student, and as a model of good behaviour.”

KB found himself smiling at the patently false sincerity with which this was uttered, and joined in the laughter that followed.

“Please call me Kris, Your Highness,” he responded. “And I am sure, all will be revealed in due course!”

“And you must call me Amir, after all, everyone else does, don’t they, Peter?”

“Indeed,” nodded Bowen. “But I sometimes wonder if it would be better if you stuck to a few more formalities, it might frighten off some of the young ladies who seem to swarm around you like bees around honey!”

“Well, I can assure you I do nothing to encourage them,” laughed the young man. “But, come and sit down.” With that he gestured towards the dining table, which KB noticed had been carefully laid for three. As if on cue, a short bearded man appeared in the kitchen doorway, bearing a tray upon which four metal dishes lay.

“This is Asif,” said Amir, by way of introduction. “He looks after me embarrassingly well and is also a great cook.”

Asif nodded assent, without pausing as he laid the dishes on the table. Mumbling something unintelligible and avoiding eye contact with the guests, he completed his task and bowing slightly, returned to the kitchen from whence he reappeared almost immediately with the tray refurbished with two larger bowls, a plate piled high with chapatis and a glass jug containing what KB assumed was orange juice, which he placed before them.

"Thank you, Asif, that will be all," Amir said. "Now let me explain. In the small dishes here we have some cauliflower, spinach, lentils and spicy potatoes. This is plain rice and in this bowl here we have a lamb curry, Karahi Ghosht, which is a recipe based upon your excellent English lamb, cooked with tomatoes, green chillies, ginger, garlic and spices, including of course red chilli powder, so it will be quite hot. Please help yourself."

The rice and curry were ladled into large flat bowls that Asif brought warm from the kitchen, and KB tried a helping of each of the side dishes. Following Peter Bowen's example he poured himself a glass of the fruit juice, and on sipping it realized it was not the orange juice he had expected.

Seeing the look of surprise on KB's face, Amir chuckled and commented, "It's mango juice, Kris. We grow mangoes as one of our main cash crops in Surpor, so I am honour bound to support my home industry."

"It's really pleasant." replied KB. "And the curry is superb."

"Thank you," the young man responded. "Now tell me all about yourself. I understand you served with the NATO forces in Afghanistan?"

Between mouthfuls of the curry – hot enough for KB to feel his scalp prickle – he spent the next half hour recounting his experiences in fairly broad terms, only filling in some of the more colourful details when pressed by his host. In particular he thought it prudent to omit any direct reference to his activities as a sniper, not knowing whether he might be entering an area where some sensitivity might exist. After all, he reasoned, although as yet he had no idea where Amir's personal sympathies might lie, he was certainly a follower of Islam and KB had met plenty who had thought that the British, Americans and their allies, had no business in any Muslim country, let alone being responsible for the demise of a significant number of their fellow believers.

The curry finished, Asif appeared to clear away the dishes, replacing them with a bowl each of a strange looking orange concoction on top of which a scoop of ice cream rested.

"This is Gajraila," explained their host. "It is made with carrots, milk, rice, sugar, dried fruits, almonds, pistachio nuts and coconut. The ice cream is my idea, and I hope you will agree it adds to the dish."

Both KB and Bowen expressed a liking for this unusual pudding, and after coffee and a casual discussion on what was in store for them on the course that lay ahead, the two rose and thanking Amir for his hospitality, took their leave.

As he followed Bowen through the front door of the cottage, KB turned to thank his host again, at which Asif appeared from the kitchen, "And my compliments to the chef." he added nodding in his direction, at which the man bowed slightly in acknowledgement, but the look KB received in return was one of pure venom.

"That was a great meal," KB suggested, as he and Bowen regained the sanctuary of their lodgings. "Young Amir seems a pleasant enough young man, but I can't say the same for Asif. If looks could kill there were a couple of occasions during the evening, when I would have been stone dead!"

"He is a strange bird," agreed Bowen, "and I have a feeling there is more to him than meets the eye. I wouldn't be surprised if he is some kind of agent of the ISI, the Pakistani Inter-Services Intelligence section of their Intelligence Bureau. Anyway, for the time being we must assume that his prime responsibility is to tender to the needs of the Nizam's son, but I am keeping an eye on him."

Wishing each other a good night, they climbed the stairs to their rooms and after reflecting briefly on the day's events, KB soon fell into a deep, and for once untroubled, sleep.

Chapter Eleven

College

There is a friend that sticketh closer than a brother.

Proverbs. 18:24

For the next six weeks KB immersed himself completely in the life of the college and the Estate Management Course he was taking. His fellow students, being on average several years his junior, coupled with his living off campus, his close association with Peter Bowen and his charge, set him apart from much of the day-to-day social activities that invited his participation. In the classroom, however, and during their instruction in the field, he found them a pleasant and easy going group to get on with, the majority of whom were farmers sons and daughters or from rural backgrounds, with whom he could easily identify.

Back at Tregallis Farm, his life fell into an easy routine, breakfast and their evening meal being taken mostly in the cottages and packed lunches they prepared themselves if working outside on the college estate, or taken in the canteen when days were spent in the classroom. His relationship with Peter Bowen developed into a firm friendship based on a mutual respect for each other's past careers in two of the elite units in the British Armed Forces, so with the half term break approaching and a chance for a long weekend off from their studies, KB suggested that he and Amir might like to spend the time with him and his family in Somerset.

"That would make a great change," agreed Bowen. "I'll see what Amir says but it would mean of course, that we would have to shake off Asif for the weekend."

"No reason why he could not hold the fort here," suggested KB, "and we could take my vehicle so that he had the Pathfinder as a run around for the weekend."

"I'll check with my folks and tell them what is going on," said Bowen, "as they may have to get clearance from the Embassy if Amir is going to join us."

With enthusiastic agreement from Amir that he would also welcome a stay with the Blakes, Bowen contacted his superiors and in due course was given permission for the visit with the proviso that he was not to let the Nizam's son out of his sight. Asif, however, seemed less enthusiastic and argued long and hard with Amir before eventually realizing that the young man would not be dissuaded.

It then remained for KB to call his parents and forewarn them of the impending visit, Jack taking it in his stride, but Kathy expressing her concerns at being able to cater adequately to the needs of their VIP visitor.

"We haven't got any visitors booked in for the weekend, so Mr Bowen and your young friend can have a room each and it still leaves us a double for any last minute drop-ins," she confirmed. "But are you sure he won't mind staying with us? – after all, we are only a small country pub and I'm sure he is used to much grander accommodation."

"He's looking forward to it," KB assured her. "Just keep bacon and pork chops off the menu, and he'll be fine!"

"Okay, if you say so," she replied. "We look forward to seeing you, and by the way, you had a phone call yesterday from a Captain Phillips from The Rifles in Exeter. He wants you to call him when you have a moment."

Thanking his mother, KB took a note of the phone number she gave him but before putting the call through, he rang Alex on her mobile. There was no reply, so he left a message letting her know that he would be home the following weekend and bringing some friends with him. He signed off by saying he hoped that she would drop by the pub for a drink, and then called Captain Phillips.

The conversation that followed was brief and to the point. Captain Phillips, the Adjutant for the Army Reserve Battalion, informed him that he had been contacted by his opposite number at KB's former Para Battalion and invited him to visit the Rifles HQ in Exeter for an interview with their commanding officer as soon as it was convenient. As KB was passing through Exeter the following Wednesday afternoon on his way home for the long weekend break, it was agreed that he would be at Wessex Barracks at 1500 hours for the meeting.

After his call, KB told Peter Bowen of the arrangements he had made, which would necessitate a slight diversion and brief stop off in Exeter en route for Somerset, the latter agreeing that this would not be a problem, but commenting, with some amusement at this further development in KB's post regular Army career.

"I'd have thought you would have had enough," he chuckled. "But I must admit I do miss being part of a team, rather than a loner – which is pretty much what I am now. What will you be doing with the Rifles?"

"It hasn't been decided yet," KB replied. "That's if they take me on, but I assume it will be as some kind of instructor."

"Well the best of luck with that," continued his friend. "I never came into contact with many Reservists, but I must admit, you couldn't fault the enthusiasm of those I did come across."

The days passed quickly leading up to their weekend break, KB taking to the books most evenings in preparation for the mid-term exam they would take on the Wednesday morning before they left.

The paper the students would take covered much of what they had learnt in Forestry Estate and Wildlife Management and concentrated on the theoretical aspects of the course, leaving the practical side for ongoing assessments from their field instructors. On the day, KB found the questions straightforward and answered them without too much difficulty, although after they had handed in their papers and as they left the examination room Amir confessed that he had struggled to complete the paper in time.

Back at the cottages they packed their bags, and after a snack lunch in the canteen loaded up the Ranger and headed east on the A30 for Exeter. Asif had already departed earlier in the morning, according to Amir bound for Aston in the suburbs of Birmingham where he was staying with relatives.

"Hardly surprising really," commented Bowen. "Half of Pakistan must have relatives somewhere in the Midlands, so I am sure he won't be without company this weekend."

At precisely fifteen minutes before the time of his appointment they drew up in front of the main entrance to Wessex Barracks where they were greeted by two uniformed security guards. After explaining the nature of his visit and following a quick check of the vehicle, they were asked to wait while one of the guards telephoned for permission to allow them entry.

Instead of being waved through, the security officer beckoned KB to join him in the guardhouse.

"I have Captain Phillips on the line, sir," he said. "He would like a word with you."

KB took the handset as the Adjutant's voice greeted him. "Sergeant Blake, glad you have made it; just one question, who are the gentlemen with you?"

"I have with me his Highness Amir Akbar Khan, the son of the Nizam of Surpor, sir," he responded. "He's on the same course as I am at Tamar Valley College, and with him is Peter Bowen, an ex-Royal Marine. Peter works for a security agency that is currently providing a bodyguard for Amir Khan. We are all travelling together as I'm taking them home with me for our mid-term break."

This news obviously took the Adjutant by surprise, as there was a short pause before he replied.

"You are obviously moving in some pretty impressive circles at your college, Sergeant," came the reply. "Please bring them in with you to the Reception area just inside the main entrance, and I'll meet you there. Now if you would just hand me back to the security guard, I'll see they let you in and show you where to park."

KB thanked the Captain, and handed back the phone, but before they were allowed to enter, the guards asked for personal ID from each of them. KB's driving licence, Peter's agency ID card and Amir's passport satisfied this requirement, and after saluting smartly they were waved through and guided to a bay in the visitors' car park, directly opposite what was clearly signed as the Battalion administration building.

Checking in at Reception, it was scarcely a minute later before the Adjutant came down the stairs into the foyer, and after introductions, asked them to follow him upstairs. To KB's surprise Peter Bowen and the Nizam's son were ushered into the Officers' Mess, and invited to take a seat.

"Please make yourself comfortable – can I offer you a tea or coffee?" the Captain asked. Thanking him, both his guests opted for a coffee, and after asking his secretary to take care of the refreshments, KB followed him down the corridor to the CO's office.

"Come in," was the response to a knock on the door, and KB found himself in a large, spacious room. From behind the desk, a uniformed officer rose to greet them. Walking around the desk, he shook KB warmly by the hand and KB found himself looking into the grey eyes of a man who he guessed was probably in his late thirties. "Welcome to The Wessex Rifles, Sergeant Blake," he said. "I'm Lieutenant Colonel Hazell, and this is Major Denby, who has overall responsibility for the Battalion training programme." At this, an older, grey haired man rose from one of the chairs arranged in front of the desk, and extended a similar welcome.

"Please sit down," continued the Colonel, returning to his chair. "Thank you for coming to see us, and I understand that you might be interested in joining us, possibly as an Instructor?"

"Yes, sir," KB replied. "If you think I might be able to help."

"Well, your application is certainly most timely." continued the CO. "As you probably know the Reserves, or the Territorial Army as we used to be called, are in the process of what we hope will be a major expansion. The concept is that having a well-trained pool of reservists will go some way towards filling the gaps in our Regular Forces that could open up in times of emergency.

"As of now," he continued, "we are struggling to meet recruiting targets, but we are attracting a steady trickle of young men into the Battalion, and our emphasis is on making our training as diversified and as challenging as possible. Our best recruiting tool is our own riflemen, and word of mouth is the best way of bringing new guys through the door, but we still have some way to go yet before we reach our full establishment. If you have any questions, please stop me at any time," he suggested. "Everything clear so far?"

"Yes, sir," KB answered. "I am aware of the expansion programme for the Reserves, and I know from experience that there is nothing like having a friend in the Reserves who is enjoying the experience to encourage you to join!"

"Good, we are on the same track then," Hazell nodded in agreement. "As you will have no doubt guessed, I have your full service record here and I see you started off in the TA with the Light Infantry?"

"Yes, sir," KB acknowledged. "Before joining the Paras, I served with B Company at Yeovil."

"How come you then decided to join the Paras?"

"Thought I'd try something different, sir," KB replied. "And I certainly had no regrets, once the basic training was over!"

"I won't comment on the wisdom of your choice," responded the CO with a smile. "But you certainly have an impressive record and it seems from your last CO's comments, that there was general agreement amongst your superiors that your injury in Helmand cut short a very promising career. On that score, I am bound to ask how you are getting on now, and in particular, do you find your artificial leg restricts any of your current activities?"

"Not really, sir," came the reply. "As you know, I am currently on a course at Tamar Valley College which calls for a considerable amount of physical effort, and to date I have had no trouble keeping up with my fellow students."

"Excellent," said the CO. "I am bound to say that from your background and experience with the Paras we would be happy to have you join us as an Instructor, but you will understand that I will have to get an updated briefing on your medical condition and permission from higher up the line to take you on in that capacity."

"I quite understand, sir," KB answered. "In fact, I'm due back at Headley for a checkup and for them to make any adjustments to my prosthetic in the near future, and I can certainly ask them to forward a copy of their report to you."

"That would be good, and certainly add some weight to my request. To give you some idea of the set-up here, we have a mixture of Regular and Reservists at all levels within the Battalion. We have four Regular officers currently attached, myself as CO, our Training Major here, the Adjutant and our Battalion Quartermaster who is ex-Logistics. Our RSM is also a regular, and we have one WO2 and two staff Sergeants also on strength. Our Admin is taken care of by a team of civilian clerks who work under the eagle eye of a retired RN Lieutenant Commander, but we do have a Regular pay clerk. At the outlying Companies we have additional Regular staff, but other than that, all our officers and NCO's are Reservists. Anyway, enough from me, over to Major Denby here to give you an idea of how we might be able to best use your talents."

Looking up from the notes he had been making, the Major cleared his throat.

"Our thoughts right now, would be to bring you on board as our Small Arms Instructor with special responsibility for training a sniper section and also coaching our small arms team. As this would be part and parcel of our overall training programme, you would report directly to me and any lesson plans would be discussed in full before implementation and would be subject to the approval of the CO and myself. As the CO has outlined, we are fairly well scattered across the West of England, so there will be a fair amount of travel involved although we would probably want to concentrate some specific activities at one location. For instance, if we were to form a sniper section, we would probably base it at one, or at the most two, locations to facilitate training. There would also be a fair amount of preparatory work involved which could mean working in your own time; would you be willing to put in whatever hours would be required?"

"The answer to that at this stage would be a qualified 'yes'" replied KB. "My only slight reservation at the moment is that I don't know what job I am going to land – assuming my job hunting is successful after I finish my course. I have every intention of staying in the West Country but the right jobs are hard to find at the moment, on the other hand I am still single, can live with my parents and help out in the pub to pay my way, and my Reserve pay would certainly help until I was able to find something I really wanted to do."

"I think we can find enough to keep you busy over your weekends," answered the Major. "And although, like all Reserve units, we have to work within a budget, we can certainly employ you gainfully."

"May I make a suggestion, sir?" said KB, turning back to the CO.

"By all means, go ahead," came the response.

"My Estate Management course finishes early in December, so by the end of the month I should have a better idea of what I could be doing job-wise. If nothing comes up, or if I am successful in my hunt for something within a reasonable distance of any of your main locations, I would really like to join you. By that time you'll have had a chance to review my latest medical report, so perhaps we could take it from there?"

"That sounds sensible," agreed the CO. "We stand down over Christmas, so I will leave it with you to contact us after the holiday. Just one further thing, as a bit of a sweetener, if all goes well and you join us in January, I might be able to pull a few strings and get you made up to Staff Sergeant, which is the rank held by most of my regular instructors. I also see, you would prefer not to re-badge, and although that irks me somewhat, I do understand, and I don't believe it would do the Battalion any harm to have a maroon beret within its ranks. If there are no further questions now, I am going to hand you over to Captain Phillips and I know the RSM would also like to meet you, and then you can be on your way."

Thanking the CO for his consideration, after shaking hands with both the senior officers, KB followed the Adjutant down the corridor to another office, where he was greeted by the Battalion's senior NCO, RSM Doble.

The interview with the RSM followed similar lines to the discussions with the CO, the former expressing similar hopes that KB would be able to join then. The RSM then escorted KB back to the Officers' Mess, where he found

Captain Phillips with Peter Bowen and Amir looking at a large picture that hung over the fireplace.

"Hey, Kris," Amir called out. "Take a look at this." Moving across to where they stood he found them examining a depiction of an exhausted man astride an equally exhausted horse approaching the sandstone walls of a fortress town.

"This is actually a print of a painting by Lady Elizabeth Butler done in the nineteenth century, and it shows William Brydon, a surgeon in the Bengal Army, arriving at the gates of Jellalabad in Afghanistan. He was the only survivor to escape a massacre of some 16,000 troops of the British East India Company, following the evacuation of Kabul," explained the Adjutant. "Jellalabad was garrisoned at the time by the 13th Regiment of Foot, the Somerset Light Infantry, and after being besieged for five months, they eventually sallied forth from the fort and defeated the Afghans before returning to the UK. The original is owned by the Tate, but is on permanent loan to the Somerset Military Museum in Taunton, so since the amalgamation of the Rifle Regiments and The Light Infantry, this is now all part of The Rifles' history."

"Jellalabad is not far from the border with Surpor," interjected Amir. "In fact Surpor lies behind those mountains in the background. 16,000 massacred? Some people never learn!" he ended with a mischievous grin.

Thanking their host for his hospitality, they were shown to the front door and once on board the pick-up wasted no time in leaving Exeter behind them as they headed east down the A30 and then onto the A303 across the Blackdown Hills.

"How did things go?" asked Peter Bowen, once they were well on their way.

"Okay, I think," replied KB. "A 'subject to' here and there still to be resolved, but the most important part is that they could definitely use me as a Small Arms Instructor, which would really be great!"

"Good for you, lad," said Peter, clapping him on the shoulder. "Now let's find that pub of yours, I could murder a pint."

Chapter Twelve

Rest and Recreation

A man hath no better thing under the sun
than to eat, and to drink and to be merry.

Ecclesiastes 8:15

It was just after 5.00 p.m. when they pulled into the car park of The Volunteer. The evening was already drawing in and a shower of rain had left puddles on the tarmac surface, adding their dark lustre to the damp chill of a sharp wind which blew in from the surrounding Levels, whistling through the branches of the half dozen leafless trees which surrounded the yard.

Emerging from the warm interior of the cab, they lost no time in unloading their gear before heading for the welcoming lights of the inn. As they approached the back door a dark shape emerged from the shadows and frantic barks greeted them as Rocky came bounding towards them, tail wagging as he recognized KB. Kneeling to make a fuss of the dog, KB noticed that Amir was standing well back with a look of serious apprehension on his face.

"He's okay, Amir," KB called out. "He is a bit protective of the family, but he won't touch you if he knows you are a friend. As a matter of fact, he comes from your part of the world."

"Sorry, Kris," came the response, "dogs are considered unclean in my country, and I can't abide them."

"The truth is, he's shit scared of them," muttered Peter Bowen, as he bent down to stroke Rocky on the head. "But just keep the pup away from the lad, and there shouldn't be a problem"

At that, they continued towards the pub, Rocky trotting at KB's heels, apparently oblivious to the presence of Amir bringing up the rear.

As they approached, the back door opened and Jack Blake came forward to welcome them, shepherding his guests into the living room, where they were joined by an apron clad Kathy who was already busy in the kitchen, and Hannah fresh from bedding down Winston in his stable.

"Sorry there is no red carpet to greet you," quipped Jack, as he shook hands with the Nizam's son. "And I'm afraid we don't stand on ceremony here, so you will have to take us as you find us."

"It's a real pleasure to be here," Amir replied. "I have been looking forward to this visit ever since Kris suggested it, and please treat me like any of your usual guests."

Introductions over, Kathy returned to the kitchen and Jack to the bar, leaving KB to show Peter and Amir to their rooms. Seeing them settled in, KB opened the door to his own bedroom to find Hannah sitting on his bed, a broad grin on her face.

"You didn't tell us you were bringing back a couple of hunks to stay," she said, as he dropped his Bergen in the corner of the room. "Your Prince is quite a dish, and Peter Bowen is certainly worth checking out if you are in to the more rugged type."

"Which you are, little Sis, if your past record in the boyfriend department is anything to go by," he replied. "But a word of warning, Amir has quite a reputation for loving them and leaving them as far as the opposite sex goes, and Peter has gone through one marriage already. My impression is that he is first and foremost wedded to his job, so you could find him quite a challenge."

"I'm up for any challenge," she quipped. "And by the way, I saw Alex yesterday and she told me you had been in touch, so expect to see her in the pub tonight. If I were you, brother dear," she added with a chuckle, "if you are still harbouring any lustful thoughts in that direction, I would strap her into a chastity belt before she sets eyes on his Highness. Knowing Alex, she'll have her knickers off in a flash and waving them in front of him before he's had a chance to finish his first drink!"

"Thanks for the advice, Sis," KB answered, as she left the room. Watching her leave, he reflected that it was time his sister had a real man in her life. Four years his junior, there had been more than one suitor who had sought to impress the bubbly brunette, but then later had discovered that the feminine exterior hid a steely resolve to do things her way with little chance for compromise, and so far she had never felt close enough to any of her boyfriends to soften her approach in the interest of building a long term relationship.

Unpacking his Bergen, he opened the doors of his wardrobe to hang up his clothes and noticed that his bow had been tucked away in the corner. Taking it out, he checked it carefully for any signs of damage, and once satisfied that it had not suffered any harm while in Police custody, returned it to its place of safekeeping, resolving that at the first opportunity that presented itself he would resume his archery practice.

After a quick shower in his small en-suite bathroom, and a change of clothes, he went downstairs to find that his friends had preceded him and had already been seated at a table in the dining room. Peter was already halfway through his first pint, and to his surprise KB noticed that Amir also had a tall glass in front of him, containing what was obviously not an orange juice or coke.

"What have you got there, Amir?" KB asked.

"Apple juice I believe," came the instant response. "And I am finding it surprisingly warming."

At that Jack came up to their table and offered them menus. "Anything you like off the menu tonight, gentlemen," he suggested. "But if you don't mind, for the rest of your stay Kathy will be cooking a special meal for you, and most nights you'll probably be eating early before our customers start arriving."

"Please don't go to any trouble on our part," replied Amir. "I am honoured to be your guest, and in fact, would like the opportunity to take you and your family out for a meal one evening to show my appreciation."

"That's very kind of you," said Jack. "I'll have to check with Kathy, but it might be possible on Sunday. We close the restaurant after lunch and we can get cover for the bar. The hotel in Ilchester does meals on a Sunday evening, and I can give them a call and book a table. It's a long time since Kathy and I have had a meal out, so I am sure she will want to accept your invitation."

As Jack turned to go, KB tapped him on the arm. "By the way, Dad. What did you give Amir to drink?"

"He's got a pint of Thatcher's draught cider," responded his father. "He asked for apple juice, but as I don't have any of the bottled stuff on the shelves at the moment, I thought he would appreciate a pint of one of Somerset's finest."

"No wonder you are finding it warming, Amir," laughed KB. "It's not quite as strong as some of the vintage ciders we sell from time to time, but it's not a low alcohol either and will match some of the strongest ales strength-wise. Just go easy on the stuff is my advice – if you are not used to it, it can creep up on you and the trouble is that it slips down a treat, so it's all too easy to knock back a few pints!"

"I guess I'll just have to ask for forgiveness at my morning prayers," responded the Nizam's son good naturedly. "But don't worry, I did enjoy some of your beers occasionally while I was at Cirencester, and without Asif looking over my shoulder, no one should be the wiser, should they, Peter?"

"My lips are sealed," said his companion. "But KB is right, just go easy on the stuff."

A rib-eye steak apiece and three sticky toffee puddings demolished, the three moved into the bar, which was already beginning to fill with the evening's drinkers. Peter and Amir both selected stools at the bar while KB went behind to give Jack a hand, and it wasn't long before the door from the car park opened and Alex made her entry.

High heeled ankle boots, black tights, matching mini-skirt and a white blouse offset by a bright red waistcoat was the chosen ensemble for the evening, and KB admitted to himself once again, that his childhood sweetheart had blossomed into a stunning beauty that would turn the heads of any hot blooded male in a room.

KB glanced sideways and noticed that her entrance had seized the full attention of the Nizam's son, whose eyes were scrutinising every inch of her as she crossed to the bar. Climbing onto the stool next to Amir, she leant across the bar and offered her cheek to KB for a kiss. The latter duly administered, she sat back on her seat, adjusting her skirt as she did so.

"Welcome home, Kris," she said. "And after you've introduced me to your friends, a large gin and tonic, please."

KB did the honours, this time being sure to give Amir his full title, but if Alex was impressed, she certainly did nothing to show it.

"Please, allow me to pay for that," volunteered Amir, as KB placed the drink in front of her. "And a refill for all three of us," he added.

Peter elected to switch to Scotch, and KB joined him, noting at the same time that this would be the third pint of Thatcher's the young man had downed, but as there were no visible signs of it having any effect on the latter's demeanour, decided not to comment further for the time being.

By the time he turned back to the bar with the fresh round of drinks, Amir was already engaged in a lively conversation and as Hannah had predicted, it was obvious that he was being subjected to the full Alex charm offensive.

Leaving them to get further acquainted and with a knowing wink from

Peter, he took a tray from the shelf beneath the bar and started collecting empty glasses from a number of tables around the lounge area, already vacated by their patrons.

"Quiet night tonight," he remarked to his father as he joined him, already busy stacking the glass washer.

"Mid-week," Jack replied, "always on the quiet side. Mind you, folks just don't have the money to spend these days, and who can blame them for preferring to stay at home when they can pick up a couple of bottles of cheap plonk or a case of lager at a supermarket for what a decent round of drinks would cost in a pub. I tell you, son, if it wasn't for our reputation for good pub food, thanks to your mum, we would be hard-pressed to make a go of things."

As the last of the diners left, and the drinkers in the bar thinned out still further, the door to the kitchen opened and Hannah came through to join them at the bar. KB noticed with amusement that his sister had obviously spent some time tidying herself up before making her appearance, and wasted no time in sitting herself next to Peter.

"Just a coke for me," she replied to Amir's invitation to join them in a drink. "I'm riding tomorrow and will be giving Winston a good workout before the meet on Saturday."

"You have a horse?" Amir was quick to ask. "I have several horses and polo ponies at home and really miss my riding trips into the mountains."

"You ride polo ponies?" asked Alex, for the first time with a note of respect in her tone.

"Oh yes," he replied. "I was riding on my own by the time I was six and was on my first polo pony before I was twelve. Polo is the closest we get to a national sport in Surpor and I have travelled all over the world playing polo, including here in England at your Cowdray Park. The times I enjoy most however, are when I am riding up in the mountains. The scenery is magnificent and the air is so clear you can see for miles, it is hard to realise sometimes that there is so much fighting going on over our border in Afghanistan.

"I also have to be very careful these days, and can no longer go riding without a large escort as there are those who hide out in our foothills who are no friends of my family. But please tell me," he continued, "what is this 'meet' you mentioned?"

"It's a gathering of our local Hunt, the Cotlington. The huntsmen and their followers meet every season at a number of locations in this part of Somerset, and on Saturday they are meeting here," explained Hannah.

"And what do you hunt?"

"It's a long story," continued the girl, "but not so long ago, we used to hunt foxes. That all changed when the Government of the day banned hunting live animals with dogs – or hounds as they should be more properly called, so now we go trail hunting. In our case a team of runners lay a scent trail along a pre-determined route, which the hounds follow. It is quite good fun and gives us a chance to give our horses a good run, but it lacks some of the excitement of hunting a fox which is far less predictable and the outcome is never certain."

"But excuse me," interjected Amir, why would you ban such hunting? In my country we used to hunt the markhor – a large mountain goat – which we do no longer because they have become an endangered species, is the fox similarly endangered?"

"Far from it," laughed Hannah in response. "The fox population was never threatened by traditional hunting, and in fact many now invade our urban areas where they live on what they can forage from discarded food waste and the occasional domestic cat. In rural areas, when they can't find enough rodents, rabbits or ground nesting birds to survive on, they can be a major nuisance taking chicken from poultry farmers."

"So how are they controlled now?"

"In the old days, if an area had a high level of foxes doing damage, the farmer would call in the Hunt and the population was controlled by seeking out the underground dens and culling the fox cubs, or by hunting the mature animals. Nowadays, farmers largely take matters into their own hands so foxes are trapped, shot, gassed or poisoned, and who can blame them? If you have ever seen the carnage wreaked in a hen house by a fox, you would understand. They don't just kill for food, they are a natural killing machine and in that kind of environment they will rip to pieces anything that moves. Ask Dad, we always used to keep a dozen or so laying hens running free in the paddock, but after a while we got fed up with providing free meals for the local fox population."

"So why did the Government ban fox hunting?" Amir asked.

"Pressure from a lot of MP's in urban constituencies, where the fox is seen as a soft cuddly animal persecuted by a bunch of upper class toffs. Then there is the rural lobby, a smaller but equally vociferous group mainly comprised of newcomers to country living who were all too quick to scream 'murderers' at the Hunt and its followers, with whom they are now neighbours. Instead they should have been sitting down and taking a long look at how the balance and wellbeing of wildlife in rural England had been managed successfully for centuries, before they had swapped their townhouses for the village cottage. Quite often it's the same bunch who will complain when a farmer spreads farmyard manure on his land and creates a smell, or their Sunday morning lie-in is disturbed by the church bells ringing. They simply don't understand the countryside and its folk, and think because they have now graced us with their presence, they have a God given right to change everything."

"Wow, I think you have touched a sore spot there!" Peter interjected. "What do you think, KB?"

"One of the problems is that if you were born and brought up in the country, you tend to regards foxes as vermin, not the image of an innocent cuddly animal that the animal rights activists promote," he replied. "Believe me, there's a world of difference between the natural killer the fox is and the image portrayed by a protester clad in a furry suit touting a placard in Parliament Square. I'd have a lot more respect for folks like that if they devoted more of their energies to banning puppy farms and in particular the importation of puppies from Eastern Europe, where many are raised and transported over here in horrific condition. But," KB continued, "that's our Hannah, and you will be able to see the Hunt for yourselves first hand when they meet here on Saturday. There are bound to be a few 'antis' hanging around, and no doubt they will make sure that everything is monitored."

"Does this mean that hunting is dying out?" asked Amir.

"Far from it," answered Hannah. "Most meets are better attended now than they were in the pre-ban days, and support for hunting amongst genuine country folk and those who understand the countryside, is probably at an all-time high."

"I wish I had a horse over here," said Amir, ruefully. "I would really enjoy the chance to join in."

"Well maybe you can," suggested Alex. "I shall be at the meet on Saturday, but my horse Barney could do with some serious exercise before then, and if you would like to try your hand, perhaps you could ride him out with Hannah tomorrow? I can't ride him myself, as I have promised to take Mum down to Taunton in the morning, but if things go well, we could try and find you a mount for Saturday. I am sure Carol Watson who runs the livery stable at Somerton might be able to find something for you."

"I would really like that," replied Amir. "What do you think, Peter?"

"I don't know," said Peter. "I guess it would be okay if you don't go charging off on your own. What do you think, KB?"

"We can keep an eye on the two of them when they are riding out tomorrow, and follow the Hunt on Saturday, but Amir is going to have to find some proper kit to wear. Even though the Cotlington is quite a small Hunt, it wouldn't do to turn up on Saturday wearing a pair of jeans and an anorak!"

"Maybe there is somewhere local where I could purchase whatever I need?" Amir asked.

"There's a very good outfitter – Hardiman & Jacks – in Wells," volunteered Hannah. "If we can find you a horse for Saturday, we could take a trip over there on Friday, but I warn you, if you are looking for a complete outfit, it's going to cost you!"

"That won't be a problem," answered the Nizam's son. "I have had very little expense since I have been at college and have hardly touched my allowance, so as long as your outfitter takes a credit card, I shall look forward to getting kitted out in the style of one of your English 'toffs' perhaps?" – at which they all laughed.

"That's settled then," said Alex. "I'll hack Barney over first thing tomorrow morning, and leave the rest of the arrangements to you."

The door to the bar opened and Joe and Amy Baker joined them at the bar.

"Good to see you again, Kris," said Joe. "Just dropped by to pick up our lass and Amy has been at me all evening to come over and meet your guests!"

Introductions over, Joe bought a round and KB was somewhat relieved to notice that Amir had asked for a coke, as it had become obvious that after his last pint of cider, he had definitely become more talkative and thoroughly engrossed in describing his life back in Surpor to the two girls.

Amy and Joe joined his admiring audience, leaving KB and Peter Bowen to discuss plans for keeping a watch on the riders the following day.

"I'll warn Hannah to stick to a route where we can follow in the pick-up," KB assured his friend, "so there shouldn't be a problem keeping them in sight tomorrow. Saturday could be a different story, however. I'll phone the Hunt Secretary, Major Brennan, in the morning and try and get details of the route they'll be following. Hannah and I know him quite well and he's an ex-Gunner, a good guy, so he might be willing to give us an idea of where they are going as he organises the runners that lay the trail. This should give us an idea in advance of any blind spots we might run into so that we can cut any time we lose contact with them to a minimum."

"That would be a help," Peter agreed. "And I'll lay down the law to him to keep with the main body of the Hunt. As long as he doesn't go charging off on his own, he should be okay."

"He'd better not," KB warned. "Galloping past the Master when the hunt is in full cry is considered a major 'no-no' and Hannah will soon rein him in if he tries anything like that."

"Well if anyone can keep him in check, it's probably your sister. Quite a feisty wee lass, isn't she?"

"That's putting it mildly, a sweet little lady on the outside, but hard as nails on the inside. She would be quite a challenge to anyone taking her on."

"I like a challenge," replied his friend, with a smile.

"Funnily enough, that's exactly what she said about you!" laughed KB.

Chapter Thirteen

Riding for a fall

Pride goeth before destruction, and an haughty spirit before a fall.
Proverbs 16:18

KB was up and had showered by 7.00 a.m. the next morning, and by the time he had taken Rocky out for his morning run down to the paddock and had got back to the house, he found Peter already up and chatting to Kathy in the kitchen.

"Any sign of Amir yet?" he asked.

"No sound from his room," came the reply. "And I'd leave him a while, as I suspect our friend may have a slight hangover this morning. He certainly got very talkative towards the end of the evening, and he was slightly unsteady on his feet going upstairs!"

"He must have knocked back four or five pints of cider," said KB. "Which is about the norm for most of our locals, but if you are not used to drinking, it can certainly have an effect. Anyway, we'd better not leave him too long; Hannah was already down getting Winston ready when I took the dog out, and knowing Alex she will be around with Barney before nine."

"I'll leave him be until eight then," said Peter.

Armed with two cups of coffee, the two moved into the dining room and shortly after Kathy appeared with two cooked breakfasts.

"Two full English for you guys," she said. "But what should I get ready for Amir?"

"Nothing even remotely related to the pig!" replied Peter. "Perhaps some scrambled eggs or a cheese omelette, but don't bother too much, just some toast and cereals would be fine."

After finishing their breakfast, Peter went upstairs to rouse Amir leaving KB to phone the Hunt Secretary. After a few minutes explaining the situation, he made a list of the main landmarks on the route the hunt would be following on Saturday, and after thanking the Major for his help, he followed up with another call to the livery stable owner.

Carol Watson was only too happy to oblige and promised to deliver a suitable mount to the pub the following afternoon, and then to collect it late on Saturday after the hunt. KB agreed a hire fee with her of £150 for the day, which included grooming, delivery and collection.

When Peter returned and while Amir was enjoying his breakfast, KB was able to report on his two successful phone calls.

"No problem with the Hunt Secretary giving you the route for Saturday?" he questioned KB.

"Not once I had explained who I was and the Major had satisfied himself that we weren't hunt saboteurs," he answered. "In fact he seemed quite impressed that they would have a VIP with them on Saturday, and he promised to let the Master know, so that he could also keep an eye on Amir."

"Surely there won't be a problem with saboteurs?" asked Peter. "I mean, the Hunt aren't breaking the law by following a trail, are they?"

"Absolutely not, but there are always a few weirdoes hanging around the fringes, who have caused minor disruptions in the past and who can't bear the thought that there are still plenty of people on horseback out enjoying themselves in spite of the hunting ban! Anyway, you'll be able to see for yourself at the meet. Look out for the dreadlocks, brightly dyed hair colours and Army surplus jackets and you'll spot them easily enough!"

Just then Jack popped his head around the door to the bar, where they had been sitting enjoying their second cup of coffee, to announce that Alex had just ridden in and was down at the stables with Hannah.

Collecting Amir from the dining room, the three of them walked down across the car park to where Barney had been loosely tethered to the paddock railings.

As they arrived, Hannah emerged from one of the two loose boxes leading Winston, with Alex at her side.

"Morning, guys," Hannah greeted them. "All set to go, Amir?"

"I certainly am," replied the Nizam's son. "And thank you, Alex, for lending me your horse, I promise to take good care of him."

"Actually, Barney is more likely to take care of you," she replied with a laugh. "He's not the swiftest but he'll just about keep up with Winston and should give you a good gallop."

"Let me give you a lift home, Alex," KB said. "And you guys just hang on for five minutes or so while I'm gone."

"No panic," replied Hannah. "We'll give Amir a chance to get used to Barney in the paddock here, so no need to rush back," she added, with a knowing wink in her brother's direction.

It was barely a mile to the small holding that was the home to the Baker family, but KB was quick to take the opportunity to put a question to her that had been on his mind since he got home.

"Any news of Isaac Samson?" he asked the girl.

"No," she replied. "Haven't heard a word from him. Still in Ireland as far as I know, and none of the other members of the clan have shown up in the village since you left, but you know what they say about 'bad pennies' so I expect they will be around again sometime. As far as I am concerned," she added, "Isaac is history anyway. But when are you coming home for good? It's been thoroughly boring around here with no one to have fun with, though I must say your dishy Pakistani friend is like a breath of fresh air!"

"Don't get too hung up on Amir," he cautioned, as he pulled into the yard and parked outside the front door of the farmhouse. "He moves in different circles to the likes of you and I, and in any case I can't quite see you converting to Islam and wrapping yourself up in a burqa."

"Not a tad jealous are we?" she chuckled, as she leant across to kiss him on the cheek. "Anyway, have fun," and with that she opened the door and waving him goodbye, disappeared into the house.

Back at the pub, KB found Hannah standing in the centre of the paddock carefully scrutinising Amir's performance on Barney, as he trotted the horse around her.

Joining Peter at the railings the two of them stood and watched until Hannah expressed her satisfaction with Amir's performance.

"He looks okay to me," Peter commented to KB. "But I don't suppose you have a hard hat anywhere you could lend him?"

"I think my hard hat is up in my bedroom," answered KB. "Haven't worn it for years but he's welcome to see if it fits. I also meant to ask if you have any binoculars with you? They would be useful."

"I did bring a pair with me," affirmed Bowen. "They are up in my room with my kit."

"I'll bring along mine also," said KB. "Dad gave me a very nice pair of Zeiss binos back in our bird watching days; let's go get them whilst Hannah is saddling up."

The kit retrieved from their rooms, they rejoined Amir and Hannah, the latter making a last minute adjustment to Barney's girth. KB handed over the hard hat to Amir, who found with some amusement that it was a reasonable fit, though if anything, slightly on the large size.

"We'll follow the towpath down the river to Stodgell's Drove and then onto East Moor," said Hannah. "There we can give the horses a good gallop and you should be able to keep us in view easily enough. We haven't had too much rain recently, so you should be okay in a four wheel drive, just give us plenty of space and don't crowd us."

With that she swung into the saddle and led them out of the car park onto the road. Just as they were about to climb into the pick-up, Rocky ran out of the tack room and when KB opened the door for him, jumped into the back seat.

It was only a hundred yards down to the river, where Hannah and Amir waited for Peter on the track that led up to the towpath. Once on the riverside, Hannah urged Winston forward into a gentle canter which Amir was quick to follow, and with the pick-up some distance behind, it was not long before they reached the entrance to the drove, a narrow track which dropped down from the river bank to level out on the moorland which now stretched in front of them.

On either side of the drove ran deep ditches, which marked the boundaries of a series of chequerboard enclosures. As the weak autumn sunshine warmed the surface of the brackish water that filled the ditches to within a foot of the track, a thin mist rose into the crisp morning air which added an eerie dimension to the levels that now surrounded them on all sides.

"This is like another world," commented Peter as KB guided the Ford cautiously forward in the wake of the two riders. "Quite scenic, but at the same time slightly sinister," he added. "Tell me, KB, is this all pastureland, or can you grow crops here?"

"Nowadays these moors are mainly used as summer grazing by the local dairy farmers, but most of them run sheep here as well," he answered. "Not long ago all this area would have been used for growing osiers, or withies as we call them, which in their time were a very valuable cash crop. The withies were used by a thriving basket and hurdle making industry that also supplied them to fishermen all over the country, and as far north as the Isle of Skye for making lobster and crab pots. The peak demand came during the war, when a lot of airborne supplies were dropped in wicker baskets, as they didn't shatter when they hit the ground. Unfortunately for the growers the post war boom in the use of plastics nearly killed the industry completely, as housewives no longer favoured the traditional hand-made shopping baskets, so a lot of these willow beds were dug up and turned over to pasture."

"I suppose those ditches are for drainage?" questioned his companion.

"They are," agreed KB. "But in the old days they also served another purpose. In wet winters you couldn't even get a horse and cart down these droves to carry out the withies after cutting, so they used to be loaded into punts and the ditches – or reens – as we call them, served as sort of mini canals. They are fairly deep and can be quite dangerous if you happen to fall into one, as I have on more than one occasion. There's usually two or three feet of thick mud in the bottom of them, and the steep banks make it very difficult to scramble out if you don't have any help."

A couple of hundred yards in front of them, Hannah had reined in Winston on the edge of East Moor, where the willow beds had given way to an open expanse of coarse grassland dotted with clumps of reed. A wider track now headed directly across the moor towards the distant tower of Kingsbury church, now clearly visible as the mist slowly dispersed.

Standing up in her stirrups, Hannah waved her arm forward to signal they would be moving off, and KB moved the pick-up forward to park on a slight rise which would give Peter and himself a good vantage point from which they could observe the two riders on their gallop. Opening the rear door to let Rocky out to run loose, the two men climbed into the bed of the pick-up and resting on the roof of the cab, adjusted their binoculars.

Allowing his sniper's instincts to take over, KB automatically did a slow sweep of the ground that lay in front of them before focussing back on the riders who were now moving steadily at a fast canter.

It was about a mile to the end of the track, but as they reached the hard country road that linked the villages of Kingsbury and Hambridge, Hannah slowed to a trot before turning around and heading back towards them. Up until that point, Amir had been content to follow Hannah at a sensible distance, but as they turned he spurred Barney forward and within a few strides was urging the horse into a headlong gallop.

The move had taken Hannah by surprise, who now found herself well behind the flying heels of Barney, and giving Winston a cry of encouragement she charged in pursuit.

"Give the lad his due, he sits a horse well." KB said to his friend. "But Hannah has the better mount and she'll catch him before he reaches us."

As they approached the halfway mark, the track dipped slightly and was covered with a large shallow pool of water which extended either side into the grass. Winston had now closed the gap on Barney to no more than a couple of lengths, and Alex's horse splashed through the water, drenching his pursuer in the spray thrown up by Barney's pounding hooves and splattering Winston in a shower of the black moorland mud.

Unnoticed by the riders, a small flock of Canadian geese had lain concealed in the tall reed grass that dotted the sward to the left of the track, and disturbed by the sound of thundering hoofs from the approaching horses and the oaths pouring forth from Hannah, the lead gander had already started his take-off run which took the skein right across Barney's path as he continued his headlong charge.

Startled by the proximity of the birds as they crossed his line of vision, the big hunter broke his stride with a slight hop and dug in his front legs to come to a spectacular slithering halt. Taken completely by surprise at the sudden halt, Amir described a gentle arc as he sailed over the horse's head to land with a thumping splash in the wettest part of the quagmire that bordered the track on either side.

"Bloody hell, he's come a cropper, let's get down there!" shouted Peter, as the two vaulted over the side of the truck. Rocky following, KB sped off down to the site of Amir's tumble, where they found the young man scrambling to his feet, soaked and muddied, with Barney standing patiently looking on without even a glimmer of panic or concern.

Hannah had dismounted and was doubled up with laughter as she walked forward to join the others already helping a crestfallen but otherwise seemingly unharmed Amir to his feet.

"Oh my God," she exclaimed, "that was quite beautiful, definitely a ten pointer, and I'll give you extra marks for picking possibly the softest spot in the whole of East Moor to land!"

Amir's fall had knocked the wind out him, and he stood, crouched over, coughing and spluttering while Peter and KB checked him over.

"No broken bones as far as I can see," said Peter, the note of relief in his voice quite evident, "Let's get you into the truck and back to the pub to clean you up."

"Oh, no you don't," said Hannah firmly. "It's back up on Barney for Amir, first you can ride him home, and when we get there he is going to need a thorough grooming before we hand him back to Alex!"

"She's quite right," said Amir. "I'm fine now, so let's go." Having recovered his breath and with a leg-up from KB, he swung back into the saddle, adjusted his hard hat and following Hannah, set off for the pub at a sedate walk.

It took them another half an hour before they reached The Volunteer, and while Hannah and Amir rubbed down the horses, Peter and KB washed the pick-up and cleaned the cab of muddy paw marks left by Rocky, who had quietly slipped away to the sanctuary of the bar once he saw the hosepipe in use.

With Amir's wet clothing consigned to the washing machine and their owner showered and changed, the three sat down in the bar for a lunchtime snack.

"Hannah will hack Barney back to Alex's before it gets too dark later on," said KB as they tackled a ploughman's platter apiece, "so I guess we can relax and play a game or two of pool this afternoon. On Thursday evenings we have two of our farmers' skittles teams playing here, so things will get pretty busy and I'll give Dad a hand behind the bar, if you two don't mind amusing yourselves?"

"No problem," replied Peter. "And if I could borrow your truck, I'll give Hannah a lift back from the Bakers',"

"Fine by me," said KB, handing him the keys. "Now let's see how good you are at pool!"

After an hour spent introducing Amir to the game, Hannah joined them to say that she was about to return Barney to Alex.

"I'll follow you to the Bakers' and give you a ride back" said Peter.

"And you and I can take Rocky for a walk," suggested KB to Amir.

At this Peter beckoned to KB and once out of sight and earshot of Amir, he handed him the Glock.

"Just in case," he said. "I'm supposed to keep tabs on the lad 24/7, and I'm probably being over cautious, but better to be safe than sorry."

"I can't imagine any harm coming to him around here," replied KB, "but don't worry, I won't let him out of my sight."

Taking his coat off the pegs in the back hallway, he slipped the automatic into one of the side pockets, and taking down Rocky's lead also collected his father's jacket and returned to the pool room.

"Your jacket is still in the drier, so you'd better slip this on," he said, handing the young man the anorak.

As they crossed the car park, Hannah rode past them followed by Peter at the wheel of the Ford, and as they headed up the main road, KB and Amir turned in the opposite direction and once more climbed the track that led to the river bank and towpath.

The sun that had taken the chill out of the air earlier had now all but disappeared behind a series of menacing grey clouds, which scudded across the sky blown by a stiff breeze coming out of the north east, breaking the dark surface of the river with a procession of wavelets.

Amir shivered despite the quilted protection afforded by Jack's anorak and hood, and even Rocky seemed to have lost his usual energy, staying close by them as he padded quietly along in their footsteps. As they walked, a few drops heralded the beginning of heavier rain to come, quickly turning into a stinging barrage of sleet.

They had only come about half a mile down the towpath, but noticing the discomfort of his two companions, KB turned around and they headed back towards the pub.

As they quickened their pace towards the sanctuary of The Volunteer's lounge and the open fire that KB knew by now would be well ablaze in the grate, he noticed two figures hunched over the bridge which carried the road across the river.

It was almost impossible to make out any more than their shape and outline through the gathering gloom and the storm that was increasing in intensity by the minute, but KB was almost certain that one of them was watching their progress through binoculars.

Just then a gaggle of geese, probably taken as much by surprise as the walkers in the sudden change in the weather, flew overhead honking noisily and then wheeling sharply, settled down in the field to their right.

"Probably twitchers," he thought to himself, but with no hesitation slipped his hand into his pocket to confirm the reassuring presence of the Glock. Nonetheless, he was more than a little relieved when a few minutes later, the two watchers on the bridge left their vantage point and headed off towards the village.

Back in the pub, they joined his parents in the lounge and settled down in front of the TV while Kathy went to the kitchen, returning shortly with mugs of tea and a plate of hot buttered crumpets.

"I am getting to like your English customs far too much," commented Amir, as he sipped on his tea. "But I must say I find your weather not so enjoyable."

"Well, you have certainly come to the right part of England to find the rain," Jack replied. "But this is nothing compared to what we had last year. Just before Christmas we had heavy rainfall for several weeks which flooded most of the land surrounding here, and several villages were cut off completely for weeks."

Leaving Amir and his father comparing the West Country winters with those in Surpor, KB joined his mother in the kitchen.

"No sign of Peter and Hannah yet," he said, peering through the kitchen window towards the car park, still devoid of all vehicles except for Jack's Land Rover.

"I shouldn't worry," replied his mother. "She and Alex are probably boring the ears off Peter talking horses. You know what those two are like when they get together. Oh, by the way, you had better warn your friends that we won't be eating until later this evening. It's skittles night, so I will be feeding the teams after their match, and I have made an extra shepherd's pie for us."

It was another hour before Hannah and Peter returned, by which time KB was already helping Jack bottle-up for the evening.

"You guys took your time," KB commented, as the two of them came into the bar.

"Amy invited us in for a cup of tea," replied his sister almost too quickly, and KB noticed that his sister was blushing slightly. "But if you'll excuse me, I must just check on Winston before changing to help Mum with the prep," she added, as she left the bar.

At this Peter also excused himself, leaving the Blakes to re-stock the shelves and pull the pumps through before opening up.

"Must have been a strong cup of tea," said Jack, with a knowing wink in KB's direction. "It certainly brought the colour to her cheeks."

"I think my tough Royal Marine buddy is quite smitten with my little sister," KB admitted. "But she's in pretty safe hands and quite capable of looking after herself, so best to turn a blind eye and see how things progress, eh, Dad?"

"It wouldn't make a bit of difference what I said anyway," added his father with a chuckle, as their first customers of the evening arrived at the bar.

Within an hour, the bar was filling up as the two skittles teams arrived and KB and Jack were kept busy pulling pints.

"Hello, young Kris," came a greeting from a familiar voice, and KB turned to face one of his favourite local farmers and near neighbour, Obadiah Kernworthy who owned most of the land on the south side of the river for almost a mile from the bridge towards Ilchester. The eldest son of three from a strict Methodist family who had farmed the Levels for generations Obi, as he was known to most, had established himself as one of the village's leading characters.

It was a fact that despite his reputation as a hard man when it came to concluding a deal, he was equally well known for his kindness and generosity in his dealings with his neighbours. Some of the less fortunate villagers had frequently had occasion to be grateful to him, knowing that he could always be relied upon to find them a few hours' work with cash in hand when times were tough. Indeed his tolerance to the pranks of some of the youths in the village also did not go unappreciated.

Many times the lads – KB among them – would raid his orchards on apple scrumping expeditions or go ferreting for rabbits along the hedgerows that bordered his fields, knowing that the most they were likely to receive in the way of a punishment if caught, was a verbal chastising, and the nickname 'Obi' bestowed upon him by the miscreants was a mark of respect, rather than ridicule.

The weather beaten face under an unruly mop of silver hair creased into a welcoming smile, as Obi extended his arm across the bar to shake his hand.

"Good to see 'ee back, my son," continued the farmer in his soft Somerset dialect. "I yer you'm out the Army now, and back to college?"

"That's right, Mr Kernworthy," KB replied. "I'm doing a course at Tamar Valley College down in Cornwall, and hope to find a job in estate and wildlife management once I've finished."

"How be it gwine then?" Obi asked. "Not too much bother for a country lad the likes of you, I'd imagine?"

"It's going pretty well," KB answered, pulling the farmer his usual pint of cask ale. "Bit of a change from Army life, but I am enjoying it."

"Tha's alright then," came the response. "I yerd tell you 'ad a spot of bother with they Samsons last time you was 'ome?"

"Unfortunately true, Mr Kernworthy, but I understand Isaac Samson – who was the cause of the trouble – is over in Ireland now, and Dad hasn't seen any other members of his family in the pub since he left."

"Bleddy gud job too, I say," said the farmer. "They buggers be a load of trouble and I've had me fair share of 'em. Whilst you was gone, one of my best dogs went missin', and they had the neck to phone I up and zaid they'd found 'im wanderin' over to Langport, and if I wanted 'im back they like a reward of dree hundred quid! I told 'em to bugger orf, and if the dog weren't back in me yard straight away, I'd be down to zee 'um wi' me shotgun under me arm. T'wer bleddy magical, the dog showed up on me doorstep within dree 'ours! Mind you, 'ad a couple of sheep stole the followin' week, and cudn't prove 'twer they wot took 'em, so I 'spect they had their own back on I."

Just then Peter and Amir joined them at the bar, and as KB poured them their drinks, Obi introduced himself.

"Friends of yorn?" he asked, as they returned to the pool room.

"Yes, staying with me over the mid-term break. Amir, the tall lad is over here from Pakistan studying at the college, and Peter Bowen is keeping an eye on him."

"Do the Pakistani lad have any mates along with 'im?" came the next question. "Reason for my askin', is that I zeed a couple of 'em parked up in the gateway to the school yesterday afternoon, and this mornin' they was drivin' through the village again, proper slow, as if they was lookin' out for zummat."

"Nothing goes unnoticed in a village," thought KB to himself. "Did you notice what kind of car they were driving?" he asked.

"Light coloured job it 'twer," was the response. "A sort of silver, and I think it 'twer one of they flashy German makes. Twern't a Merc, I knows what they buggers looks like, could 'av bin a BM whotsit or a Ordi."

"Well, thanks for the info, Mr Kernworthy," said KB. "They certainly aren't friends of Amir's as far as I know, but we'll keep an eye open for them."

Leaving the farmer to join his friends in the skittle alley, KB busied himself collecting empty glasses and helping Hannah clear the tables in the dining room. With one of their cask ales dry, KB went out to the cellar to change the barrel, and on his return found his father sitting down on the customers' side of the bar enjoying a well-earned rest.

"You don't know what a difference it makes having you home and giving me a hand," Jack commented. "I've been talking it over with your mum and wondered if there was any chance at all you might consider joining me in the business as a partner?"

"I'd have to think about that, Dad," KB replied, taken by surprise at the suggestion. "I appreciate the offer, but I wouldn't want to be an added strain on the pub's cash flow, and in any case, would that really be fair to Hannah?

She helps out a lot, and I wouldn't want her to feel that she was being pushed out."

"Hopefully she'll get married one of these days," came the answer. "But anyway, take your time and give it some serious thought, and as it could be a while before you find a job after you have finished college, I would welcome any help you can give us in the meantime."

It was gone ten o'clock by the time the teams finished their match and returned to the bar for their food and nearly another hour passed before the farmers were on their way, leaving the family to clean up and then settle down in the living room, a plate of Kathy's shepherd's pie on their laps.

With their late supper over, Peter and Amir left for their rooms and once KB had taken Rocky out for his walk down to the paddock and checked that all outside was secure, KB also climbed the stairs and in no time was settling down for the night.

Half an hour passed as he lay awake with his thoughts running over the day's events. The watchers on the bridge and Obadiah Kernworthy's observations on the two men seen in the village could be coincidental, but certainly had aroused his suspicions, and Peter had been equally concerned when KB had confided in him.

As he turned on to his side, willing sleep to engulf him, Rocky gave a low and scarcely audible growl from his bed in the corner of the room, and KB heard the unmistakable creak of a loose floorboard on the landing outside. Swinging his leg out of bed, he grabbed the crutch he always kept by his bedside, and hopped over to the door. As he gently opened it and peered out, he noticed that further down the passageway the fire door to the guest rooms was closing silently.

Moving as quietly as he could, he made it to the door just in time to see through its' small reinforced glass window, the unmistakable figure of his sister entering Peter Bowen's bedroom. It was quite obvious that Peter and Hannah's night was far from over, and deciding that discretion was the better part of indulging a brother's natural instinct protecting a younger sister, he returned quietly to his room.

Chapter Fourteen

Fit for a Prince

"Give thee clothing of delight,
Softest clothing, woolly, bright."

William Blake 'The Lamb'

Breakfast the next morning was a somewhat subdued affair, lacking some of the easy conversation between the three men that usually marked this morning ritual. Peter seemed particularly quiet, lost in his own thoughts and no doubt mulling over the events of the preceding evening. Refraining from making any comments which might indicate to his friend that he was fully aware of the former's late night tryst, KB finished his plate of bacon and eggs and leaving Amir and Peter to prepare for the morning's excursion to the outfitters in Wells, paused in the kitchen to give his mother a hug and then ventured out into the car park to find his sister.

It was a grey, overcast morning and a slight drizzle was falling as he walked down the yard to the loose boxes where Hannah was already rubbing down Winston after her morning ride out.

As he neared the stables, Rocky came around the corner to greet him and it was obvious from his mud flecked coat that he had accompanied Hannah on her hack around the lanes which crisscrossed this part of the Levels. The light was on in Winston's box, and he paused to lean over the stable door while his sister busied herself brushing the caked mud out of the horse's thick winter coat.

"Morning, Sis," he greeted her. "Good ride this morning?"

"Not bad," came the response. "Took him down Bailey's Lane and then cut back up onto the river bank. Quite muddy up there," she admitted, ruefully.

"And he got really plastered – so I guess I should have had more sense and stuck to the roads."

"How long are you going to be?" asked KB. "We should head over to Wells fairly early so that we are back in plenty of time to be here when Amir's horse is delivered from the livery stable."

"Give me twenty minutes or so and I'll be with you," replied the girl. "And in the meantime you might want to give that dog of yours a good rub down. Mum will have a fit if he goes near the living room in that state."

Calling to the dog, he retraced his steps to the pub and spent the next ten minutes giving Rocky a vigorous towelling. No sooner had he finished and consigned the muddy cloth to the washing machine, than Hannah joined him.

"I'll just pop upstairs and make myself respectable," she said. "So we should be ready to roll in about ten minutes or so."

With that, KB joined his two friends in the pool room, where Peter and Amir were honing their skills with the cue.

"He's getting too good for me," commented Peter. "Seems to have an eye for angles and he's taken a couple of games off me already."

"At a pound a game, I'm making a fortune!" laughed Amir. "But I have a feeling it's just beginner's luck."

"We are about ready to leave, guys," said KB and at that the two players replaced their cues in the rack and followed him out to the yard.

As KB started up the pick-up and drove it out of the garage, Hannah joined them and taking a seat in the back, where she was joined by Amir, Peter climbed into the front passenger seat and turning left onto the road, headed towards Wells.

The fine intermittent drizzle which had fallen earlier, now turned into a steady downpour as they headed out of Somerton. On the outskirts of the ancient market town, they joined the main Glastonbury – Wells highway, and as KB slowed to a halt at the road junction, he instinctively glanced in his mirror. About a quarter of a mile behind him a silver grey BMW came into his view, and as KB pulled away from the junction, it turned left to follow him.

For the next three miles, KB said nothing, but the BMW stayed on station well behind them but making no attempt to close the gap or overtake, even when he dropped his speed slightly to see if the driver would close up.

"Nothing to worry about yet," KB said to Peter, mindful of Obi Kernworthy's comments, "but we might have company. Silver grey BMW about half a mile or so behind and he's been tailing us since Somerton. I'll adjust your mirror so that you can keep tabs on him."

"I have him in sight," confirmed Bowen. "Perhaps we should pull over and see if he reacts?"

"I need to get some diesel soon," KB responded. "There's a filling station just the other side of Street, and I'll pull in there. If he picks us up again once we are back on route, it seems pretty likely he is following us." The conversation had drawn no comment from Amir, but Hannah leant over into the front, her hand on Peter's shoulder.

"Do you really think we are being followed?" she asked, the tone of her voice betraying her concern.

"Could be that we're not the only ones interested in Amir's movements," came Peter's honest reply. "But I guess we are going to find out in a moment."

Ten minutes later, KB pulled into the filling station and headed for the pumps closest to the cashier's kiosk where he would be partially screened from the road. He was scarcely out of the cab before the BMW appeared, but not before the passenger in the car had glanced directly at him as they sped past.

Peter had also dismounted on his side and had also seen the man look in their direction. It was only the briefest of glances, but the face seemed familiar.

"I think he saw us, KB," he said. "And I am far from certain, but that could have been Asif in the car – which opens up another can of worms if it was – but at least we will know for sure if it was a tail if they pick us up again once we are back on the road."

KB topped off the tank, and after paying with his credit card at the pump drove the Ford back out into the road once more heading for Glastonbury.

"I'll keep an eye out behind us," said Peter. "And you guys in the back look out for the BMW parked up in a lay-by, gateway, or anywhere else they might have pulled off."

It was Hannah that spotted the BMW. As they approached the Glastonbury by-pass they entered a large roundabout and the car had taken the exit leading to the centre of the town, the driver parking up about fifty yards down the side road.

"That's the car, I'm sure," his sister reported and a moment later this was confirmed when Peter picked the BMW up in his rear view mirror as KB entered the long straight stretch of the main road that led to the outskirts of the city of Wells.

“He’s not very bright, is he?” commented KB. “And whoever it is, their organization is none too clever either. Surely they would be using more than one chase car if this was a professional job?”

“Yes, and that’s what’s worrying me,” Bowen replied. “Certainly not one of our security services, and I think that even the Pakistani Intelligence Bureau would do a better job of following us. If they are from one of the extremist groups, they could be on some kind of mission, and we know what lengths some of them will go to in order to achieve their objectives. Anyway, I’m going to report in to my folks; can you give me an accurate location for the clothing store?”

“I probably know it best,” replied Hannah. “It’s on the Wells Business Park on the south side of the city, and the store itself – Hardiman & Jacks – is between a builders supply outlet and a supermarket. There’s a large car park to the front and access off the Park Road roundabout.”

By the time Peter had finished reporting in on his mobile, they were approaching the roundabout and the Business Park was unmistakable with the big orange lettering of the builders merchants clearly displayed on the wall of the store adjoining the road.

“As you enter the car park, drop me off and then park up,” Peter ordered KB, unbuckling his seat belt. “Don’t leave the vehicle until I rejoin you, and if anything happens, take off immediately and as fast as you can. Here’s my mobile, press the recall button and tell whoever answers the direction you are heading, hopefully they will be able to arrange some back-up.”

As he slowed to enter the Business Park, Peter opened the passenger door and jumped out before KB had a chance to come to a full halt. Accelerating away, he glanced in his rear mirror and saw Peter crouching behind one of the large brick pillars that flanked the entrance to the forecourt. A second later, the BMW swung around the corner and then was lost to KB’s view as he manoeuvred the pick-up round the parking lot, eventually finding a vacant slot the second row back from the entrance to Hardiman & Jacks.

Telling Hannah and Amir to stay put and lock their doors, KB climbed into the bed of the truck and crouching down was able to spot the BMW moving slowly round the perimeter of the parking lot. Of Peter there was no sign, and as he watched the BMW’s progress his attention was diverted to the sudden appearance of a Police car, which had entered the park and had stopped outside the clothing store.

Two officers got out of the patrol car, and after looking around briefly headed directly for the Ford. Jumping over the tailgate, KB found himself facing a Sergeant and a Constable from the Avon & Somerset Constabulary.

"Good morning, sir," volunteered the Sergeant. "Everything all right here?"

Before KB had a chance to reply, a screech of tires from the far corner of the park caught their attention, and as they watched, the BMW accelerated away at high speed and rocketed out of the entrance and back onto the highway.

"He seems to be in a hurry," added the policeman. "We'll have to keep a look out for him later on."

As if on cue, Peter appeared from behind the row of vehicles to their rear and walked forward to join them. "Good to see you, Sergeant," he said, producing his ID card for the Sergeant to examine. "I doubt if you are here solely by coincidence?"

"No, sir," came the reply. "We were about half a mile down the road monitoring traffic speed, when I got a call to get here as a matter of some urgency and apart from that I know very little, so perhaps you could let me know how we might help you?"

"You have helped us already," said Peter. "But let me give you a quick briefing." Moving out of earshot, the two spent the next five minutes in deep conversation. Briefing over, the Sergeant beckoned to his Constable and bidding them a cheerful goodbye, they climbed back into their patrol car and left.

"What did you tell him?" asked KB.

"I explained the situation with our friend here," replied Bowen, nodding at Amir, "and as I managed to get the number of the BMW, passed it on to him so that the boys in blue can keep an eye open for it. Now I had better check in with my folks and bring them up to speed. I also need to get the okay for Amir to go ahead with his plans for joining the hunt tomorrow. If they consider the risk too great in the light of what has happened here this morning, they may pull the plug on it, and we don't want you spending a fortune on kit if you won't get a chance to use it, do we, Amir?"

"Tell them I am still really keen to go hunting tomorrow," came the answer. "But I will leave it to you. In any case, I hope we can still have a look around the store now that we are here?"

"KB, you take your sister and Amir in for a browse," said Peter, "while I get onto my people, and I'll catch up with you in a minute or so."

Leaving him on his mobile, the three entered the spacious and well-lit interior of one of the West Country's largest outdoor sports outfitters, and headed for the equestrian department where Hannah and Amir were soon engrossed in examining the wealth of goods laid out on the well stacked shelves.

Nearly a quarter of an hour passed before Peter rejoined them, bringing the news that Amir's hunting trip had been sanctioned.

"That's great," enthused the Nizam's son. "Now let's get down to some serious shopping. Where do I start, Hannah?"

"Clothing section first, follow me, guys," replied the girl, and with KB and Peter trailing in their wake, the two took off to the far side of the store.

"I'm a little surprised that Amir got the go ahead," commented KB as Hannah and Amir disappeared between the rack of jackets and riding breeches.

"Me too," said Peter. "But someone further up the line decided it would be good for UK – Surpor relationships if Amir was indulged, and they are sending down another team to help us keep an eye on him tomorrow. They also did a quick check on the number plate of the BMW and it seems that it is registered to a car hire company in Wolverhampton. They have asked the Police to keep tabs on it for us if they spot it, but not to intercept. It's more important that we try to trace the driver and his companion, so the hire company's office will be watched, as by now they are probably high tailing it back to the Midlands. Thankfully even though they weren't that clever, they must have realised that they had been spotted.

"Incidentally, I put in a word for you," he continued. "I told them your help had been invaluable, and asked if we could get you issued with a sidearm, even on a temporary basis. Don't hold your breath, my suggestion wasn't exactly greeted with enthusiasm but they are looking into it. This probably means it won't happen, and even if it does it will take a while for the application to go through the system, and it would certainly mean establishing a more formal relationship between you and our organization. What do you think?"

"I'm not sure to be honest," KB replied. "But I must admit that the events of the past couple of days have been a real eye-opener. I guess I wouldn't have a problem with it, but hopefully things will quieten down now and get back to normal. Do you really think that was Asif in the BMW?"

"I can't say for certain. It was at a distance and I didn't get more than a fleeting look. The guy was definitely sporting a beard, but that doesn't really help. I also asked my office to see if they could run a double check on him, so for the time being there's not much else I can do."

By the time Amir had tried on jackets, breeches, boots and all the other gear Hannah advised him that he would need, over an hour had passed before the four left the store laden with boxes which were carefully stowed in the pick-up's cab.

"The sales assistant must have thought Christmas had come early," commented KB as the last of the boxes was loaded. "Hope there's enough room left in the back for you guys," he added as they climbed on board. "How much did that little lot set you back?"

"Nothing but the best for our boy," laughed Hannah. "Made a nasty hole in a grand, but he bought well and we were able to get a deal on the boots."

"I also managed to pick up a couple of Ordnance Survey Maps," added Peter. "They kept a full range for hikers and fishermen. We can mark them up with the route the Hunt will be following and give one to my colleagues when they arrive."

The journey back to Long Lane and the pub went without incident, and with lunchtime approaching Hannah disappeared into the kitchen to help Kathy, and KB finished bottling up for Jack in the bar. After a quick sandwich, Amir went up to his room to unpack his purchases, while Peter sat himself down in a corner of the bar with his laptop to write up a full report for his office.

The Friday lunchtime trade was brisk and both Hannah and KB were kept busy. By 2.30 p.m. the last of their customers had left, and as Jack closed up the bar, a large horsebox in the maroon and gold colours of the Somerton Livery Stables drove into the car park, announcing the arrival of Amir's mount for the following day's hunt.

The driver's door to the cab of the big Mercedes truck opened, and Carol Watson jumped down to be greeted by Hannah as they were joined by KB, Peter and Amir. Carol was a chunky blonde in her mid-forties, whose tightly curled blonde hair framed a face that was fresh complexioned and unadorned by any make-up. A pair of hazel eyes shone from under the brim of a tweed cap and the firm handshake that accompanied the introductions to Peter and Amir left the impression of a confident and straightforward businesswoman.

While KB and Peter unlatched the rear doors to the horsebox and lowered the ramp, she wasted no time in politely questioning Amir on his skills in the saddle before climbing into the lorry to lead out a handsome dappled grey gelding.

"This is Shamus," she said. "He's a touch over sixteen hands, seven years old and I bought him in Ireland eighteen months ago. Loves his hunting and he's a good steady ride with lots of stamina. Not really a speed merchant, but jumps well. I should warn you he doesn't appreciate being pushed hard into fences, so as long as you line him up and give him a chance to have a good look at the obstacle, he'll give you a really good ride. Shall we saddle him up so that you can try him out in the paddock?"

While Amir stroked the horse's neck and spoke to him gently, Hannah fetched the saddle and its blanket from the horsebox. Once in place, Amir swung himself up into the saddle, and walked the horse down to the paddock to canter Shamus around for ten minutes under the critical gaze of his owner.

"He'll do," she commented to the onlookers. "Sits well and is certainly an experienced rider. He might want to hack him out for an hour this afternoon before the light goes, but everything looks good to me, so I'll just get the paperwork for him to sign."

As she walked back to the truck, Jack appeared and welcomed her as an old friend.

"Good to see you, Carol," he greeted her. "Just came over to say I'll keep a spot for your horsebox in the car park tomorrow. Normally, we only allow the Hunt servants and their boxes in, but I'll make sure there is room for you, the rest of the followers are used to parking outside on the road."

"That would be great, Jack," she replied. "Then I can just load Shamus up with my own horse after the hunt. Hannah knows that we will take care of the grooming; it's all part of our service, so I'll just get your young visitor to sign the contract of hire for the day, and be on my way. Quite a looker your young Prince isn't he?" she added with a twinkle in her eye. "Welcome in my hayloft anytime!"

Fully aware of her reputation as being something of a man-eater, Jack could only laugh at her remark, and bidding her goodbye, returned to the pub.

Leaving Hannah and Amir to exercise their horses, and Peter keeping an eye on them from the pick-up, KB climbed the stairs to Amir's room and removing the calf length black leather riding boots from their box, returned to the bar where, after collecting his cleaning kit from the back hallway, he settled down on a table next to the fire.

Polishing the new leather to the point where it would be acceptable to any self-respecting Para or Royal Marine going on parade, would be a lengthy and arduous chore, but KB set to it with enthusiasm, confident that the end result would ensure that Amir's appearance at the meet more than matched the expectation of any self-appointed critic.

He was still hard at it an hour later when Peter returned, and seeing what his friend was up to, settled down to give him a hand.

"What are we doing here exactly?" he asked KB.

"I'm not bulling the whole boot," came the reply. "Just the foot up to the stitching around the ankle. The calf piece up to the knee is just to get a decent shine with a light polish and a good buffing."

With two of them applying the traditional spit and polish, it was not long before they were able to apply the final overall rub down with the softest of KB's cloths, and admire their handiwork.

"Not quite Household Cavalry, but certainly good enough for the Cotlington Hunt," said KB as he held the boots to the light for their final inspection.

As KB packed away his cleaning kit and wiped down the table, Jack came into the bar.

"There's a Range Rover just pulled into the car park," he announced, and before he could say any more, the back doorbell rang.

"I think we'll get that, KB," said Peter, and the two of them hurried out to investigate, as the bell rang again.

Darkness had already closed in around the pub, and as KB opened the back door to the yard, the outline of two large men stood framed starkly in the doorway.

"Good evening," volunteered the shorter of the two. "Would I find that toe-rag of an ex-Para by the name of Kris Blake here – otherwise known to his instructors on his sniper course as Casper the ghost – a course which incidentally, he would have failed miserably without my help and guidance!"

At that moment KB flicked on the switch of the outside light, and in its bright glow stood the unmistakable figure of his former Sennybridge partner – Fred Nowakowski.

"Bloody hell, Fred!" exclaimed KB, totally taken aback by the sudden appearance of his friend. "What brings you here?"

"Our boss told us that you and Mr Bowen needed a hand keeping tabs on a VIP on some kind of hunting expedition tomorrow, so we just dropped by to see if we could keep you out of trouble!"

"Good to see you guys," broke in Peter. "That was quick, I only put the request in this morning."

"You were lucky, Peter," Fred continued. "We were just being debriefed having finished another job, and when they told me you and my friend KB here were involved, I volunteered us."

"Come on through," invited KB, ushering the two newcomers through to the bar. "Can I get you a drink, or perhaps tea or coffee?"

"Coffee would be fine for both of us," replied Fred's companion. "And let me introduce myself. I'm Colin Hunter, Fred's Section Leader."

As they shook hands, Peter disappeared to the kitchen to collect a tray of coffee for all of them, giving Fred the opportunity to complete the introductions."

"Colin is a former Warrant in the Guards," he explained. "Commissioned into the Red Caps when he got pissed off with poncing around in a scarlet tunic and bearskin, and he eventually finished up with the SIB. I met him on my second tour in Helmand when I was attached to Special Ops at Camp Bastion and he persuaded me to join him in the agency when we got out. He's not a bad egg for an ex-guardsman and an MP, but doesn't like getting his boots muddy and couldn't hit the side of a barn with a shotgun at ten paces, so coupled with my superior skills and natural humility we make a good team."

"Thanks for that glowing introduction," said the tall, lanky ex-guardsman, then turning to KB added, "but I guess you know better than anyone what I have to put up with keeping this renegade Pole on the straight and narrow!"

"Know what you mean. Remind me to tell you about the beret incident when we have a moment. Our friend here morphed into a rampaging rhino when it went missing, and single-handed nearly demolished an entire barrack block at Sennybridge looking for it."

"Hey, KB, bit of an exaggeration!" protested his friend.

"Hardly," came the rejoinder. "Last time I checked my bank balance I was still paying off my share of the barrack room damages!"

At that Peter came back into the bar with the coffees, and the four sat down to agree their plans for the following day. Producing the Ordnance Survey Maps he had purchased earlier, KB marked out both with the major check points, and then marked in the route the Cotlington Hunt would follow.

"Can't be sure of one hundred percent accuracy," he said. "Hounds will sometimes lose the trail the runners lay and go off on a tangent, and if they pick up the scent of a fox, anything could happen. Nine times out of ten, the whipper-in will keep them in check but if there are a couple of old dogs amongst them that break ranks, the younger ones will follow, and then there could be hell to pay, we could finish up anywhere."

"Isn't that against the law?" questioned Colin.

"Technically yes," KB went on. "If the so-called 'hunt monitors' are around, cameras will be flashing all over the shop, a lawsuit could follow, the local press will have a field day and if it gets thrown out – which is frequently the case – most of the costs will be picked up by the taxpayer."

"Okay, I get the picture," said the big man. "I will be in charge of this operation, so I suggest we start by picking out three or four potential high spots on the map which lie along the route. Fred and I can use these as OPs, while you and Peter follow in your pick-up. I have four hand held field radios with me. They have a good five mile operating range, so we can keep in touch and between us we should be able to keep our subject covered."

"He'll be riding a grey horse, so he should be quite easy to keep tabs on," added KB. "I would suggest also that it might be an idea to give one of the radios to my sister. She'll be riding with the Hunt and has promised to stay close to the Prince."

"Excellent idea – what time does the Hunt set off tomorrow morning, and how many riders are there likely to be?"

"They normally kick-off between 10.30 and 11.00 a.m." KB answered. "On a good day the Hunt will probably get twenty to thirty odd mounted, plus a couple of dozen or so following in their cars or 4 x 4's."

"That seems fairly straightforward. If Fred and I get a reasonably early start in the morning it will give us a chance to check the OPs we have picked, but the numbers could cause us problems. Is there anything else we should know about?"

"There will probably be a Police presence tomorrow," said KB. "They usually send along a car and a couple of bobbies to make sure there is no trouble. Sometimes tempers get frayed if the 'antis' start playing silly buggers and try to obstruct the riders, but usually things are pretty civilized. What's the procedure if there is an incident involving the Nizam's son?"

"Good question. Our number one priority is to ensure his safety, but equally important is the safety of the general public which in this case includes the hunt, hunt followers and the 'antis'. Unfortunately, if extremists are involved, they will certainly not have the same concerns. We will have to be very careful in any situation, and that applies particularly to you, Peter, as you are likely to be closer to the actual scene than we are. Fred has all his sniper gear with him," Hunter continued, "so there is always the chance he will be able to neutralize any ongoing threat, but again we are making an assumption that we can get a clear line of sight to any target, and that could be problematical with that number of people milling around. Let's just hope our presence acts as a deterrent, so don't be shy about showing a high profile. Anyway, unless anyone has any other points, I think that just about wraps things up. Incidentally, is there a B&B in the village where we can doss down for the night?"

"No need for that," replied KB. "We have a double en suite vacant at the moment, so if you don't mind bunking in together, you can stay here. It's our family room with a double and two full size bunk beds, so you should have plenty of room."

"We'll certainly be happy to take you up on that," came the reply. "Perhaps we should get our gear out of the Rover?"

As the men stood up, Amir and Hannah came into the bar, and leaving Peter to make the introductions, KB went through to the family's living room to tell his mother that her family room had been let for the weekend.

Chapter Fifteen

Tally Ho!

"The hounds all join in glorious cry,
The huntsman winds his horn:
And a-hunting we will go."

Henry Fielding

A sharp overnight frost had left its mark on the Somerset Levels, covering the fields and river banks with a white carpet of ice crystals that crunched underfoot and sparkled like miniature diamonds in the bright morning sunshine. Small white clouds moved lazily across an otherwise clear blue sky, promising weather that would stay fair and ensure that the members and followers of the Cotlington Hunt enjoyed the best of days for their pursuit.

Hannah had been up at first light and was already hard at work in the stables putting the finishing touches to Winston and Shamus, guaranteeing that their turn out would do credit to herself and the second son of the Nizam of Surpor. As KB crossed the yard to summon her for breakfast, a skein of greylag geese whistled their way overhead, the big birds honking to each other as they followed the line of the Yeo westward towards the distant tower of St Mary's church at Huish Episcopi, and keeping their perfect V-formation as they climbed above the rising mist that shrouded the banks and slow moving surface of the river. In one of the car park spaces, the Range Rover stood, its engine ticking slightly as the block cooled, indicating that Fred and Colin had already returned from their recce.

As he rounded the corner of the stable block, he paused to look over the half door of the tack room to see the harnesses hanging ready from the wall brackets. The leather of the bridles had been freshly saddle soaped and the brass buckles polished until they gleamed in the overhead light. The saddles rested on their trees, stirrups buffed and the girths spotlessly white from an overnight laundering in the pub's washing machine. In the stables, Hannah was plaiting Winston's mane, whilst next door Shamus stood patiently wearing a smart dark blue rug, his mane already finished and his magnificent grey and silver tail combed out until every strand fell perfectly into place.

"They both look a picture," he complimented his sister, as she came out of Winston's stable. "I hope young Amir appreciates all your hard work."

"He did his fair share yesterday," his sister replied. "But you could tell that he is used to having others do the hard work for him, so I thought I would finish the job properly. Anyway, I'm starving, is breakfast ready?"

"Mum's done a kedgeree and when I left the others were already in the restaurant, so I expect it's on the table by now."

Back in the pub, KB and Hannah joined the others at their table, already helping themselves to the kedgeree from a large serving dish that had been placed in the centre. While the aroma that arose from the spicy blend of rice, eggs and smoked fish reminded KB that he too was ready for his breakfast, he noticed that Amir seemed to lack the appetite of his fellow diners, spooning only a small amount of the mixture onto his plate and chasing a few grains of rice around its edge with his fork.

"Not hungry, Amir?" he asked. "Or would you prefer something else?"

"No, not at all," came the reply. "This is really quite delicious, but I seem to be suffering from – as you say – butterflies in my stomach."

"Don't worry," broke in Hannah, "I was so nervous before my first hunt, I threw up on the way to the meet, but once we move off and get going, I promise you the nerves will disappear and you'll really enjoy it."

"Thank you for that reassurance and I'm sure I will," said Amir with a chuckle. "And I will do my best not to let you all down. Thank you, KB for the work you and Peter put in on my boots yesterday, they look fantastic and I only hope I can get them on without spoiling the shine!"

"Don't worry, I'll give you a hand when you go up to change," suggested Peter. "And if necessary Fred and I will carry you downstairs and hoist you aboard Shamus without your feet touching the ground, won't we, Fred?"

"That's a promise," came the reply, as Fred tucked into his second helping of kedgeree. "And I'll even give you a hand putting on your make-up if you like!"

At this they all laughed, and breakfast over, leaving Hannah and Amir to go upstairs and change, KB and the three security agents returned to the car park, where Jack was already guiding Carol Watson at the wheel of her horsebox into a parking spot he had reserved for her.

"Morning, gents," he greeted them as Carol switched off the Merc's diesel. "If you could give Carol a hand dropping the ramp, and keep an eye out for the Hunt's boxes I'd be grateful. They can park over by the garage when they arrive. I've got a lad coming down from the village to take over on the gate to let in the horses and their riders, and of course the followers, so that I can get back to the bar and get the stirrup cup ready."

"What's a stirrup cup?" Fred asked, turning to KB.

"A glass of booze the landlord hands around to all the riders before they set off. It's sometimes a glass of port or even a shot of brandy or scotch and varies pub to pub. Mother makes a mean sloe gin which is renowned for its potency, so I expect that's what most of them will be getting today."

"I've heard of sloe gin," said Peter. "Don't you pick the sloes off the hedgerows and let them soak in gin?"

"That's right. Sloes are the fruit of the blackthorn. Pick them, prick them, dump in some sugar and a touch of almond essence add the gin and let it sit. Mum usually makes about eight to ten litres which keeps the pub going for a year, so the brew they will be getting today is at least a year old, and all the better for it! I'll make sure you get to try some, but probably best after we come back from the hunt, as we don't want you falling in the river! But heads up, here comes the cavalry."

At that two more horseboxes drove into the yard, followed by a Land Rover pulling a trailer. Two men climbed down from the cab of each of the lorries, whilst a sprightly elderly man got out of the Land Rover, followed by two tracksuited youths."

"That's the Hunt Secretary, Major Brennan," said KB and turning to Colin added, "I'll take you over and introduce you."

"Good to see you home again, young Blake," came the friendly greeting.

"It's good to be back, sir," KB responded. "And thank you for your help. This is Colin Hunter who is in charge of security for the Nizam's son today."

"Pleasure to meet you, Hunter," said the Major, shaking Colin by the hand. "I suggest that I call the Master and his chaps over in a minute, and you can give us a briefing so that we are all up to speed." Turning to his tracksuited companions he added, "These lads will be laying the trail today, so it will be good for them to know what is going on as well."

Peter stood back from the group, but still within earshot, and as KB turned away to join him asked, "Aren't those guys leaving it a bit late to lay the trail?"

"Not really. They usually set off twenty minutes to half an hour before the Hunt, so that the trail is as fresh as possible."

"What kind of scent do they use?" Peter asked. "I heard once that it was aniseed, is that true?"

"Used to be, but not any longer. Now it's some kind of chemical composition. Comes as crystals, smells worse than shit and the runners drag a bag full of the stuff behind them. Hounds seem to go for it but I tell you, you don't want to get the stuff on your hands, seems to linger for ages no matter how thoroughly you wash them!"

As the first of the Hunt members rode into the yard, KB noticed a small group of walkers gathering by the gate.

"Bet you that lot over there are 'antis'," he said to his friend, as they walked back to the pub. "Look at the cameras and the wide variety of kit they are wearing – everything from anoraks, waterproof trousers and hiking boots to camo jackets, tartan trews and sneakers. Couple of youngsters with Rastafarian hair-do's there also," he added, pointing to a boy in his twenties and a girl quite a few years younger, standing slightly apart from the group, their bicycles leaning against the fence. "Bet you it won't be long before you'll be able to smell the weed from here!"

"Do you mean the girl with the coloured wool plaited into her hair and the lad with the dreadlocks and funny hat trying to look like Bob Marley?"

"That's them," agreed KB. "Don't recognize them from around here, probably cycled over for the day from Yeovil."

"I'd be worried there could be someone other than me living in all that hair," said Peter as they reached the pub. "I doubt she gets far running her fingers through it! I must say though I was always a big fan of Bob Marley's music."

Inside the pub, Peter excused himself to go upstairs to check on Amir's progress and KB joined Jack behind the bar which was already filling up with those Hunt supporters who would be following on car and foot.

Kathy was busy serving customers and Jack had laid out two large trays with sherry glasses into which he was pouring a liberal measure of her ruby red sloe gin.

"Glad you are here, Kris," his dad greeted him. "You can give me a hand passing these around in a minute."

Before he could pick up a tray, Hannah and Amir appeared in the doorway.

"What do you think – will he do?" asked the girl, as Amir stepped into the room.

As she put the finishing touches to Amir's stock, the room went quiet, and as KB remarked afterwards, "I swear there wasn't a woman in the room whose tongue wasn't hanging out!"

The young man did indeed, look a picture. His jacket and riding breeches fitted him perfectly. His dark hair curled up under the back of his hard hat, and his white shirt and stock and yellow waistcoat with his black calf length boots gleaming, completed the ensemble.

"Every inch a Prince," murmured Jack. "Looks smart enough to be one of ours!"

"Come on, Your Highness," teased Hannah. "Let's get out there and saddle up, before I get trampled underfoot by your female admirers."

Picking up a tray apiece, and with Peter leading to hold open the doors for them, KB and his father soon found themselves busy passing the stirrup cup around to the twenty plus riders who now filled the yard and car park.

As they moved through the crowd, KB noticed that the runners had already left to lay their trail, and Fred and Colin's vehicle was also missing from its parking spot. Gone also was the young Rastafarian couple, but with a Police car now parked at the entrance to the car park, KB suspected that they had taken off to enjoy a quiet smoke out of sight of the two uniformed officers who were standing beside their vehicle watching the riders.

From behind the stables Hannah and Amir now emerged on Winston and Shamus to join the crowd. The Master and his deputies now resplendent in their hunting pink jackets, parted to let them through while the hounds, now out of their box waited impatiently but obediently around the whipper-in. In another corner of the yard Carol Watson was holding court to a small posse of photographers, to whom she seemed eager to point out Amir's arrival.

The press men quickly dispersed to gather again around Amir and Hannah, to be joined by the Master for a photograph. Several more followed, including Alex, who although late arriving pressed their horses forward to make sure they appeared by Amir's side as the shutters clicked.

Spotting KB, Alex moved towards him, and taking a stirrup cup from his tray, smiled at him sweetly before leaning towards him.

"If you want to be my friend for life," she said, with a twinkle in her eye as she moved away, "see if you can arrange for me to have an Amir clone in my Christmas stocking!"

Before he could think of a suitable rejoinder, Carol rode up.

"Your man scrubs up well," she said with a snort of approval. "Damn smart turn-out, a credit to young Hannah!"

"Lot of press here," KB commented. "Wonder who tipped them off?"

"Can't imagine," came the unconvincing response. "Good publicity for my stable though."

A few minutes later, the Master called for silence and as if the attention of the press were not enough, made mention of how honoured the Cotlington were to have such an important visitor amongst their numbers. After thanking everyone for their attendance and Jack and Kathy for their hospitality, a few notes on his hunting horn gave the signal that they were moving off.

The gates to the car park now wide open, the riders streamed out onto the road, turning right away from the river and through the village, then heading west out into the surrounding countryside. In their wake, a small convoy of vehicles followed led by KB and Peter in the pick-up, with the Police car bringing up the rear.

From the same vantage point that KB and Peter had used when Hannah and Amir had ridden out two days earlier, Fred and Colin watched the cavalcade as it streamed past on a drove less than a mile from them, breaking into a canter as the riders swung north towards the distant village of Hambridge.

As the morning passed and by keeping in touch on their radios, Amir was seldom out of their sight, the Hunt reaching its farthest point just after 2 o'clock in the afternoon, then turning back towards Langport and Long Lane for a final gallop through the open fields along the river bank.

A little later, Peter's radio buzzed into life and Colin reported they had lost sight of the Hunt as they turned for home, and would be returning to the pub.

"Suggest we head in that direction also," said Peter to KB. "Can we get up onto the river bank and follow them in from there?"

"Shouldn't be a problem," KB replied. "I'll turn off onto the next drove and we should be able to get onto the towpath a couple of miles before it joins the main road again at the pub."

Good to his word, KB turned into the muddy lane, leaving the rest of the followers in their cars to retrace their tracks on the hard road. With the four wheel drive put to the test, it was some time before they reached the towpath, and when the Ford eventually climbed onto the river bank, the hunt were already some distance in front, enjoying their last full gallop through the fields below them.

From the cab of the truck both driver and passenger had a clear view to their front, and when a dark figure rose from the long grass that flanked the towpath on the field side, they both spotted the man immediately. As the huntsmen drew abreast of him, his arm came back and lobbed a small object in the direction of the galloping riders.

"Jesus Murphy!" exclaimed Peter. "If that's a grenade we're in trouble."

Expecting the worst, KB accelerated as fast as he could on the greasy surface of the river bank, but instead of the explosion they both half expected, a series of cracks like rifle shots echoed across the Levels, causing several of the riders to swerve suddenly, two of the horses rearing and dislodging their riders.

"Rook scarers!" shouted KB. "That's our friend the with the dreadlocks trying his hand at sabotage!"

By now the figure was fleeing down the towpath as fast as his feet would carry him, but within a few hundred yards KB had caught up with him, the bonnet of the Ford bearing down to within a few feet of the fugitive. At that point the would-be saboteur lost his footing on the muddy track, and as Peter swerved to avoid the flailing arms and legs, tumbled headlong down the bank falling backwards into the murky waters of the River Yeo.

"That looks like our young Rastafarian friend. I'll grab him!" Peter called out to KB. "You check on Amir and make sure he's okay"

As Peter scrambled down the bank to drag the sodden figure from the river, KB took his binoculars from the truck and scanned the riders below. The two that had been unseated were both standing up and showing no signs of serious injury, while slightly apart from the main body of the Hunt Hannah and Amir were walking Winston and Shamus slowly back towards the pub.

Satisfied that no serious harm had been done and that the Nizam's son and his sister were safe, he turned back to the Ford, as Peter appeared above the bank, his right hand firmly clenched around the jacket collar of the bedraggled youth, the water still trickling out of the sleeves and pockets of his clothes and dripping from his dreadlocks.

"I'll jump into the back with him," said Peter letting down the Ford's tailgate. "We don't want him messing up your upholstery. Let's get him back to the pub and see what he has to say for himself."

With his two passengers seated in the bed of the pick-up, KB climbed back into the cab and five minutes later pulled into The Volunteer's yard to be joined by the two uniformed policemen, who had already returned and whose car was parked up in one of the vacant spaces.

As they came to a halt, Peter jumped from the pick-up to brief the officers. As he did so, the girl who had been with the youth earlier, emerged from behind the garage where she had been waiting for his return and ran across to where he sat huddled in the bed of the truck in a growing puddle of water. Leaning over the side of the pick-up and to KB's surprise, she clipped her boyfriend soundly across the back of his head.

"Alfie, you bleddy vool," she berated him. "Tol' you not to do it, didn't I?"

"Don't make no never mind now," came the sullen reply. "I'd a bin alright if that bugger hadn't drove me into the river," he added, nodding in KB's direction. "And I've lost me bleddy 'at."

"Don't look at me," KB laughed at the girl, anxious not to receive a similar chastising. "The truth is your friend took off after he had chucked his firecrackers at the riders and missed his footing on the bank. It was lucky that we pulled him out so quickly, otherwise he could have been halfway downstream to Langport by now!"

At that they were joined by Peter and the two policemen, who were both struggling to conceal their amusement as they surveyed the sorry sight before them.

"Do you think Kathy would mind if we took him inside the pub and dried him out a bit?" asked Peter. "These officers want to question him, and they will want to have a word with Major Brennan as well."

"I'm sure that won't be a problem. She'll probably be able to find some old clothes of mine for him," KB replied.

Leaving them to head for the pub, the girl trailing in their wake, KB turned back to the yard where more riders were arriving, among them Hannah and Amir. Noticing that both appeared intact and none the worse for their outing, he first sought out the Hunt Secretary who was more than slightly agitated at the recent turn of events that had turned an otherwise highly successful outing into something of a circus at the end.

"Glad to see that you and your associate caught the blighter," he greeted KB. "Where is he now?"

"The Police took him into the pub to interview him," KB replied. "And I'm sure they will want to have a chat with you."

"Good – I'll need to ask them about bringing charges," the older man responded. "Nobody hurt, thank God, but it could have been nasty. Got to stand up for ourselves, can't have these people thinking they can get away with this sort of stuff. I'll just get old Bombardier here back in the trailer," he added, patting his horse's neck, "then I'll pop across for a word with them."

Leaving the Major to unsaddle, KB walked across to where Hannah and Amir were dismounting, to be joined by Colin and Fred who had driven into the yard a few minutes earlier.

Amir was looking flushed, but a broad grin gave KB a clear indication that he had thoroughly enjoyed himself.

"Are you guys okay?" was his first question.

"We're fine," his sister answered. "Had three really good runs and it would have been four if that idiot hadn't spoilt the gallop for home. What actually happened?"

"Yes, fill us in, KB," interjected Colin. "We were on our way back via the main road, so didn't see a thing. I figured that with only a couple of miles left to run and no signs of any potential problems we could stand down, and you and Peter seem to have had things covered."

"We spotted him in the very last mile or so. You may have noticed him in the car park before the Hunt moved off. One of those pseudo-Rastafarian types, baggy trousers, Army surplus combat jacket, knitted hat and dreadlocks that would do credit to Medusa. Jumped out of the bushes a hundred yards or so in front of us and chucked a bundle of rook scarers right into the middle of the Hunt. He then took off and fell into the river when we caught up with him. Peter dragged him out, and he's in the pub being questioned by the police right now."

"Unseated a couple of our riders," added Hannah. "But no bones broken. Winston and Shamus were fab. Never broke stride or swerved, but in fairness we had gone past where he threw the fireworks by the time they went off. No doubt one of those little shits that try to sabotage the hunts – you should have left him in the river to drown!"

"It was very exciting," said Amir. "A most exhilarating day out and a truly memorable finale. You English certainly know how to put on a show for your visitors."

"Bloody good job we were already on our way home and he was out of our sight," suggested Fred. "If he had tried his tricks a bit further back up the trail where I had tabs on him, I might have dropped him if I thought he was throwing something more sinister than a few fireworks."

"Thank God for small mercies," said Colin. "Think of the paperwork and the inevitable enquiry that would have followed. Methinks that could have been the end of a couple of promising careers. Why do you call them 'rook scarers', KB?"

"Because that's exactly what they are," KB replied. "They are pretty much out of fashion now, but farmers once bought them to scare the rooks and pigeons off their crops. They come on a string of rope which acts as a slow burning fuse, about eighteen to a string. You hang the string up vertically on a pole or from a tree, light the end and every half hour or so one goes off. Not so popular these days, most farmers now use the propane bird scarers. Connect the gun to a bottle of propane, wire it up to a 12 volt car battery, set the timer and you're in business. Mind you, the areas where they can be used are limited, too close to a village and the 'Don't spoil our rural peace and screw the farmers' brigade will be up in arms in no time."

"Where would you buy these things?" asked Colin.

"A few years ago any self-respecting village hardware store would sell them. Nowadays some Farm Supply Stores keep them, and I believe you can also buy them online."

"You obviously know all about them," commented the big man.

"Yep, in my younger days we used to nick them from any farmer who happened to have them hanging up in his workshop. Our favourite trick was to take them off the rope, tape two or three together and use a short length of string covered in paraffin wax as a quick fuse. They would blow the lid off a dustbin with ease. Mind you, the ones we got on hands on were somewhat more potent than the ones you can buy today."

"Christ, KB," came the reply. "You should have joined the IRA, not the Paras! Anyway, enough of your misspent youth, let's get back to the pub and see what's happening to our hunt saboteur."

With the bar busy with post hunt followers enjoying a drink, Kathy had allowed the Police and their charge to sit at a table in the restaurant while the latter was questioned. Alfie, as he had been identified by his girlfriend, sat slumped in his chair, now attired in a pair of KB's well-worn tracksuit bottoms and an old sweater that had also seen better days. On the table in front of him lay a congealed bundle of rook scarers and a tobacco tin which lay open containing cigarette papers, filters, a zippo lighter and a small plastic bag half filled with a dark green shredded leaf.

As KB, Colin and Fred joined the group at the table, they were followed into the room by the Hunt Secretary. Getting up from the table, Peter took them to one side.

"At the least he'll be charged with possession of a Class B drug," Peter reported. "And from the questions the officers have been asking, it looks as if they will probably have him for causing a public affray, which in layman's terms roughly translates to disturbing the peace by frightening the shit out of people. Of course, Major, if your people want to bring charges as well, that's probably another matter."

"We'll have to see what our lawyers say," answered the Hunt Secretary. "Will they want statements from us now?"

"I'll check with them, but I expect if they just take the names and addresses of the prime witnesses and catch up with you later for the written statements."

Returning a few minutes later to confirm that this was the case, armed with a notepad and pen borrowed from behind the bar, the Major left to get the required information from the riders.

"I suppose they are going to need statements from us too?" said KB.

"Absolutely," Peter confirmed. "I understand they'll be taking him in to Yeovil Police Station to charge him, and he'll probably be held in custody until the Magistrates hearing on Monday. As we'll be returning to the college early on Monday morning, we might just as well follow them in and give our statements at the Station."

"I'll come with you in case you need any support in explaining why we are all here," added Colin. "Fred can stay here as he didn't see the actual incident anyway and he can keep an eye on Amir. Seeing there were no signs of any other potential trouble today, we will probably leave tomorrow morning as the risk now seems to be relatively low."

"What are we going to do about her?" asked Fred, nodding in the direction of Alfie's girlfriend who was sitting at a corner table, huddled over a mug of coffee.

"Well technically I suppose we don't have to do anything," said Colin. "But I guess that's up to you, KB."

"We could chuck their bikes in the back of the truck and give her a ride into town," KB replied. "Wouldn't hurt if she were a sympathetic witness if she is called to give evidence, and she might respond to a bit of kindness."

Walking over to the girl, KB noticed she had been crying, tears streaked her cheeks causing heavily applied mascara that had rimmed her dark brown eyes to run.

"What's your name?" he asked, sitting down in the chair opposite her.

"Cherry," she sniffed. Not sure if that was her mispronunciation of 'Cherie' or if in fact, she had been named after the fruit, it was obvious she was not about to volunteer any more information without being pressed.

"Where do you live, Cherry?"

"Mudford, 14 Silverdale Terrace," she answered, and after a pause. "Wot's gonna 'appen to Alfie?"

"I expect the Police will take him into Yeovil Police Station and he'll probably have to stay there for a while, but in the meantime my friends and I have to go into Yeovil as well, so we'll drop you and your bikes off at your home, if you like."

"Thank you, sir," the girl replied, tears starting again. "My dad's gonna kill me. He don't like Alfie much at the best of times."

Mudford lay on the northern edge of Yeovil, the short diversion from their route into the town bringing them into the main street of the dormitory village. Red brick built semi-detached council houses flanked one side of the thoroughfare, raised a few feet above the level of the road to sit on the imaginatively named Silverdale Terrace, which could not boast the vestige of anything remotely silver to bring credence to its title, and bordered by open fields with not a dale in sight.

Opening the rusty iron gate, KB pushed the bikes up the pathway that ran up to the entrance to Number 14, as Cherry followed reluctantly behind. A barely discernible movement of the curtains in a downstairs window, indicated that their arrival had not gone unnoticed. Before they reached the green paint chipped front door, it was flung open and a balding, stout middle- aged man in shirtsleeves and braces stood menacingly in the doorway to greet them.

"What have you been up to, young lady?" came the strident request in stentorian tones that were only a few decibels short of a shout. "And where's that bloody monkey?"

This statement, the latter part clearly referring to the absence of Alfie, caused another outburst of sobbing from the girl, who vainly attempted to hide behind KB to shield herself from her father's wrath.

"And I'll want a word with you," continued the tirade, this time directed at KB, who only had a split second to step back to avoid being grabbed on the shoulder by a hand the size of a dinner plate.

"Sorry, we can't stay," KB was quick to reply. "My friends and I are on our way to the Police Station, and in any case I'm sure Cherry is quite capable of explaining to you what has happened. To be quite clear, it's not your daughter that's in trouble, so I suggest you go easy on her."

"Don't you tell me how to treat my daughter," the man spat at him, clenching his fists. "That's none of your fucking business, unless you want to make it so?"

Before KB could respond to the challenge, the gate behind them creaked open and glancing up KB's would-be assailant saw that Peter and Colin were walking up the path towards him.

Without another word, the man turned on his heels and pushing the girl in front of him, slammed the door in KB's face.

"Nice friend you've got there," said Colin, as they stood the bikes up against the wall of the council house. "I pity the lass, maybe we should just hang around for a minute or two."

The raised voices from inside the house gradually died away, and five minutes later a light shone out from an upstairs room and as they watched the window opened and Cherry leant out.

"You'd better go now," urged the girl. "I've locked meself in me room, so I'll be alright. He calmed down when I tol' him you was the Police, and he'll be okay when he sobers up. Thanks for your help, honest, I'll be alright now," she repeated, as she retreated inside and closed the window.

"Poor little cow," commented Peter as they climbed into the Ford. "Fancy growing up with that for a father. Wonder how old she is; might be worth asking the Police to check her out. In spite of her make-up I wouldn't be surprised if she were under age, though these days, the way they dress and when they're all dolled up it's hard to tell whether they are fifteen or twenty-five."

"Spoken like a man with years of experience," KB chided his friend. "Didn't have you down as a cradle snatcher, perhaps I should tell my sister you fancy much younger birds!"

"You do, young Blake, and you are doomed to a life of testicular deficiency, in other words, I'll chop your frigging balls off!" came the response.

"Sounds reasonable to me," laughed Colin from the backseat. "But enough bickering, ladies, let's get to the cop shop and discharge our public duties, then I am looking forward to a quiet night in the bar, a large steak and a good bottle of wine, what say you, Peter?"

Chapter Sixteen

Recommendation

"...no man was ever written out of reputation but by himself."
Richard Bentley 1662-1742

Sunday morning crept into the pub with a whisper and a soothing lack of urgency that teased the occupants into stealing an extra hour or so in bed before arising. Eventually it was the smell of freshly brewing coffee and frying bacon that tweaked the senses of the family and their guests as Kathy was already in the kitchen preparing their breakfast.

Next down was KB, who after greeting his mother cleaned out the hearth in the lounge bar and re-lit the log fire to warm the room through before the noon opening. Calling to Rocky, he collected his jacket and the lead and collar from where they hung on the coat pegs in the back hallway, and with the dog trotting at his heels, set off across the road and on to the towpath eastwards towards Ilchester.

A watery autumn sun struggled to emerge from the gloom in the sky above him, while to the west a grey bank of cloud loomed ominously over the horizon. As he walked, a few rain drops splattered off his storm proof jacket, prompting him to turn up the corduroy collar, and taking his cap from the pocket pulled it over his thick dark brown hair, tugging the peak down until it shielded his eyes.

"Hey, young Kris, hang on there!" a voice hailed him, and as KB turned round he saw the familiar figure of a pork pie hatted and tweed jacketed Obadiah Kernworthy walking briskly along the river bank to catch up with him, a Springer spaniel at his heels and an ancient 12 bore shotgun under his arm, broken open and with two cartridges protruding from the breech.

“Morning, Mr Kernworthy,” KB greeted the farmer, whose ruddy face broke into a broad grin as he clapped KB on the shoulder.

“Wouldn’t mind if ‘ee called me Obi,” came the reply. “Every other bugger do and it zeems only right and proper now yume out the Army and settlin’ down again. Anyways, do make I veel too bleddy old when young men like you ‘ave all growed up and keeps calling me Mister, ‘specially when I’ve knowed ‘ee since you wuz no bigger’n a tadpole.”

“Obi it is then,” KB answered with a smile, pausing for a moment as the older man extracted a well-worn briar pipe from between his teeth to re-light it in the shelter of his cupped hand.

“Got the gun with you I see?”

“Aar, thought I might get lucky wiv’ a shot at a mallard or a goose, but ‘tis a bit late in the day, but you never knows.”

Pipe successfully lit and wreathed in a cloud of aromatic blue smoke, the pair continued their walk, the two dogs scouting ahead, spaniel with his nose to the ground and Rocky bounding in front, stopping occasionally to turn and make sure that KB was following.

As they came to a bend in the river, a small dark shape detached itself from the muddy strip just above the waterline and dived into the river. The spaniel immediately stopped in its tracks and one front paw raised leant forward to sniff in the direction of the ripples of water that radiated out from the spot where the animal had disappeared.

“Did you see that, Obi?” KB asked his companion.

“Never got a good look,” admitted the farmer, “but t’wer about the zize of a mink. He’ll be up for air by and by, but ‘tis ‘ard to tell the difference ‘tween they and otters when they’m swimmin’. If I gets a good look and ‘tis a mink, I’ll ‘ave the bugger,” he continued, raising his gun to his shoulder and thumbing back the hammers, as they stood and watched. With not even a ripple to suggest that the mystery animal might be coming up for air, the would-be mink slayer eased off the hammers and broke open the shotgun as they continued their walk.

“I ‘yer you volks ‘ad a spot of bother wi’ the ‘unt yesterday,” Obi volunteered. “Cud ‘ave done wi’ me and me gun I reckon, I’d ‘ave peppered the young buggers arse vor ‘ee.”

“Perhaps just as well you didn’t,” laughed KB. “As it was he fell in the river and got a good soaking for his troubles, fortunately no one got hurt, but he’s locked up at the moment so he’s had a bit of time to reflect on his misadventure.”

"Won't make no difference, you wait and zee. He'll be up afore the beaks next week, they'll gee'un a slap on the wrists and off he'll go, thumbin' his bleddy nose at us."

"Might not be quite as simple as that," KB suggested. "The Police found marijuana on him, so he might be in more trouble than he thinks."

"Nar 'ee won't," countered the farmer. "Half the kids around these days zeem to be smokin' that wacky baccy. 'Ad a young lad workin' on my varm a couple of zummers gone, who smoked the stuff. He geed me a bit to try, and it cost me dear. Bunged it into me pipe and smoked it I did, then I jumps on the tractor to do a bit of muck spreading, and backed the bugger dru' the zide of the barn. Made a 'ell of a mess, cow shit all over the place as I hackzidentally kocked the PTO into gear, and I spread the muck all over the zide of the barn and me included. Bleddy girt hole it made in the barn cladding, and missus wudn't let I into the 'ouse 'til I hosed meself orf. Won't be smoking that stuff again, I tell 'ee. It did give I a hard on tho', " Obi admitted. "But the missus wudn't let I near her, 'cos I smelled so bad. T'wudn't have bin a dead loss if'n I'd got me leg over."

With the mental image of a manure soaked Obi making amorous advances on the homely and full figured Mrs Kernworthy firmly in his mind, KB said goodbye to his walking companion and turned for home. Twenty minutes later he was back in the pub, to be greeted by Kathy who was still in the kitchen.

"I'll make you some fresh pancakes and bring them through to the restaurant, if you want to join the others," she suggested, leaving KB to catch up with his friends who had already finished their cooked breakfast, and were engaged in serious conversation.

Hearing his name mentioned, KB stopped before entering the dining room and paused to listen to the comments that were being made.

"I'd recommend him," Peter was saying. "He's certainly an intelligent lad, doesn't panic in a crisis and so far I have found him thoroughly reliable."

"He's also magic with a rifle in his hands," broke in Fred. "Seems to have a computer in his head when he is lining up a shot from a distance and it's almost as if he rides the bullet to the target. Rumours were in Afghanistan that he had the highest kill rate of any of our snipers at one time, though he never talked about it. Likes to maintain a very low profile and keeps himself to himself, but he's a good partner to have in any tight situation, and I'd certainly vouch for him."

"I'll have a word with our people when we get back," he heard Colin say, "though I'm not sure whether they would see his gammy leg as a problem."

Hearing Kathy open the kitchen door behind him, and feeling slightly ashamed of his eavesdropping, KB walked up to the table where his friends were sitting and pulled out a chair to sit down.

"Good walk?" asked Fred, as Kathy put a plateful of pancakes and half a dozen rashers of bacon in front of him.

"Yes, great. Bumped into Obi who hasn't seen any more of Amir's countrymen lurking around in the village, or he would have certainly told me. Where is Amir incidentally?"

"Hasn't surfaced yet and we probably won't see him until lunchtime," said Peter.

"Well, he'll miss breakfast and there won't be much for lunch, as he's treating us to a meal at the hotel in Ilchester this evening, though Mum will probably make him a sandwich later on if he's hungry."

"That's his problem, not your mum's," answered Peter. "She's done enough for us already. If he wants to sleep in that's fine, but he can make do on a packet of crisps if he's starving."

"We've thoroughly enjoyed your folks' hospitality too," added Colin. "But it's time for us to make tracks. Come on, Fred, let's go and get our bags packed and I'll settle the bill."

Leaving them to their packing, KB and Peter walked over to the stables to find Hannah saddling up Winston. The sky was gradually clearing of the dark clouds that threatened rain earlier, and the sun was now breaking through, dispelling the gloom and promising a better afternoon.

"Not giving him a day off today?" asked KB, as Winston lowered his head and butted him gently in the shoulder by way of a greeting.

"Just taking him out for a gentle hack around the lanes," she said. "And I'm just waiting for Alex who is coming along. By the way, Amir asked her to join us for dinner tonight, so you might want to check with Dad and find out how many he booked the table for."

"I'll do that," her brother replied. "Tell you what, Peter, why don't I go fetch my archery kit and we'll set up a couple of straw bales in the paddock for some practice? It's been ages since I had a good session with the bow, and you can try your hand as well."

"Sounds good to me," came the response. "Show me where the straw bales are, and I'll take them over while you are getting your equipment."

Leaving Hannah to sort out the straw bales for Peter, KB returned to the pub and as he came out of his bedroom, bow and arrows in hand, Fred and Colin emerged from their room with their bags.

"We're just off," said Colin. "We've said our goodbyes to Jack and Kathy and thanks again for everything."

"Thanks for your support, and it was good meeting you and seeing my good friend Fred gainfully employed and behaving himself for a change! Let me see you off."

Outside in the car park, they were joined by Peter, and after loading their bags into the Range Rover, and a final round of handshakes, the two agency men climbed aboard and drove out onto the road, to head east towards the A303.

Down in the paddock Peter had propped a straw bale up on end, supporting it with two more laid flat on the ground, and after walking back thirty-five paces from their target, KB strung the bow.

"Didn't realise you were left handed?" commented Peter, as KB shot his first arrow at the target, which disappeared over the top to bury itself in the grassy bank some yards behind.

"I'm not normally," came the response, "but I taught myself to help strengthen the muscles in the arm that caught some of the blast from the IED. I also found that when I first started, archery helped me improve my balance, but it's a while since I have put in any practice, and it certainly shows," he added ruefully, as his second arrow glanced off the side of the straw bale.

After half an hour of taking it in turns, KB's injured arm was beginning to ache as the exercise took its toll on the wasted muscles, but his accuracy was steadily improving and five of the six arrows he had shot in his last attempt had found their mark. Peter meanwhile, having admitted that he had never picked up a bow in his life, was taking a while to find the range and elevation to score any hits and his problems became even more apparent when KB moved back another fifteen paces.

"Doesn't look as if I'll ever make a bowman," he laughed, as his final attempt at the new range saw the arrow skitter through the branches of a lone apple tree which stood slightly to one side of the target.

"I shouldn't lose any sleep over it!" returned his friend. "Can't see any of the bad guys giving you time to string a bow and launch a couple of arrows if they were coming at you! There is a belief, however, that the thought of being hit by an arrow has a psychological effect on the potential recipient. There was a story that my grandfather told me about the Canadians in the battle for Normandy, just after D-Day. It seems that a unit of the Hitler Youth SS Division under the command of Kurt Meyer, was ordered not to take prisoners and they shot a number of Canucks who had surrendered.

The following day one of the Hitler Youth positions was overrun by members of the same regiment whose lads had been executed. Among the Canucks were a number of native Indians, who it is said, stuck arrows in the corpses of the German dead and then deliberately withdrew knowing that they would be found. They say it had a profound effect on the morale of the Hitler Youth, but who is to say whether that was truth or rumour?"

"Hadn't heard that one before," said Peter. "But psychology or not, I'll stick to the Glock; kind of hard to conceal a bow and a quiver of arrows under your jacket!"

Deciding they had done enough, the two replaced the straw bales in the stack and made their way back to the pub, to find that Amir had surfaced and was sitting at the bar chatting to Jack. With the lunchtime diners departing, the door opened and Kathy entered with a tray of sandwiches. Leaving Amir and Peter to enjoy them, KB helped his father collect the empties and bottle up for the evening.

"I phoned the hotel and booked an extra place for tonight," Jack said to his son, as the last tray of glasses came out from the under counter glass washer. "I told them 7.30 for 8.00 p.m. I suggest that you take Peter and Amir with you, and your mum and I will take the two girls."

"Sounds good to me," KB replied. "I'll give the lads a heads up and call Alex to tell her you will be around just before seven thirty."

Sandwiches eaten, and the lunchtime trade over, Jack and Kathy retired to their lounge while Hannah joined the three men to resume their rivalry at the pool table. After soundly beating KB and Amir in a best of five games, Peter and his sister excused themselves to take Rocky for an afternoon walk and to their obvious chagrin, Amir asked if he could join them.

As the three disappeared into the dusk of a winter's afternoon, Rocky trotting at their heels, KB climbed the stairs to his room and after replacing his archery kit in the cupboard, took off his prosthetic leg and slid onto his bed where he had no difficulty in dozing off.

Chapter Seventeen

Make Love, Not War

"And what is better than wisdom? Woman.
And what is better than a good woman? Nothing."
Geoffrey Chaucer, 'The Canterbury Tales'

It was just gone quarter past seven when they left the pub for the short drive to the hotel in nearby Ilchester. Jack and Kathy went ahead with Hannah to collect Alex in the Defender, with KB, Peter and Amir following in the pick-up.

A heavy rain had started to fall creating rivulets of water which had already flooded the ditches and were now spreading large puddles across the road surface which danced and shimmered in the stabbing beam of the headlights. Driving through a downpour was not one of KB's favourite pastimes, so conversation was at a minimum as he concentrated on the road ahead, the silence punctuated only by the clunk-clunk of the windscreen wipers as they coped valiantly with the sheets of rain.

The hotel sat in the centre of the small town of Ilchester, which for many years had been a favourite watering hole for the naval personnel who were stationed at the nearby air base and whose numbers almost matched the population of the town itself. Pulling up outside the main entrance on the High Street, KB and Jack allowed their passengers to make a short, sharp dash to the front door before driving their vehicles through a courtyard to the small car park at the rear of the large rambling building.

In the warmth of the hotel's small bar they were greeted by the owner, Philip Worsley, a long-time friend of KB's parents, who with his wife Margaret had run their business successfully ever since Philip had resigned his

Directorship of an international shipping company based in London, and moved to Somerset with their son Angus some ten years previously.

With Angus and Margaret busy in the kitchen, Philip fussed around his guests and distributed the menus. At one of the few small tables Peter and Hannah sat with Alex, while at the bar Amir was engaged in earnest conversation with the barmaid, a striking brunette who KB estimated to be in her early thirties and who was displaying an impressive pair of bosoms in a top so tight and so low cut, they threatened to spill out every time she bent forward.

As he sat down with his friends at the table, Alex leant forward to kiss him on the cheek.

"It looks as if your friend's eyes will pop out of their sockets in a moment," she said with a chuckle, nodding in Amir's direction. "But then, from where I'm sitting they're not going to be the only things that will be popping out if she's not careful!"

"Who is the barmaid?" KB asked Philip, as the latter paused at the table to hand them their menus.

"That's Helen," came the reply. "I see your friend is getting to know her, she is an outrageous flirt but you should warn him that he won't get far, she's married to a Petty Officer from the Naval Air Station at Yeovilton, although he is at sea right now. Anyway, here are your menus, the special tonight is Roast Pheasant with Game Chips and the catch of the day is monk fish tails in a Mornay sauce. I'll come back and take your orders in a minute."

Orders taken, Philip showed them through to the dining room where over their dinner the conversation turned to Amir's home country and the customs peculiar to Surpor. Once again the young Prince proved to be a charming and interesting host, regaling them with details of some of the great feasts held in the Nizam's palace which often went on all night and where the guests were expected to eat their way through up to twenty courses.

"There are numerous curry dishes of all kinds, vegetarian, lamb and goat and always a whole roast sheep for the main course," explained the young man. "The guests are entertained with dancers and local musicians and poets also take part. These occasions are held to honour visiting government officials and VIPs and also to thank our farm people for all the hard work they do on behalf of the family. I would like it very much if you could visit me in Surpor one day, and then I would make sure we held such a feast in your honour. I would also take Hannah and Alex riding with me up into the mountains," he added, turning to the girls. "But I could not guarantee as much excitement as we had yesterday, and anyone falling into one of our fast flowing mountain rivers might not be quite as lucky as the young man you rescued from the river, Peter!"

"And I suspect that the punishment for anyone disrupting a royal hunt in Surpor might be slightly more severe than a slap on the wrist from the Magistrates here!" said Peter quietly, as they finished their desserts and got up from the table to move back to the bar.

As they settled down to enjoy liqueurs and brandies, Margaret come through from the kitchen carrying a tray of coffee, and leaving Kathy and the girls to chat amongst themselves, Jack and Philip joining KB and Peter at their table, Amir once again detached himself to continue his dalliance with the flirtatious Helen.

"Had a couple of your young Prince's countrymen staying with us last week," volunteered the hotelier, "couple of strange characters, kept themselves very much to themselves and left early in a hurry."

"Did they sign the hotel register?" asked Peter, as both he and KB sat forward at this surprising news.

"They did, but I couldn't make head or tail of their scribble."

"What kind of car was it?" came the next question.

"BMW I think. I didn't take much notice but the registration number is in the book. But here's another strange thing. They were booked in until today, but they turned up here early in the afternoon on Friday and checked out."

"Did you take an impression of a credit card, or did they use one to pay their bill when they checked out?" continued Peter.

"No. They gave me a bundle of money when they arrived, which more than covered the cost of their rooms and meals, so much so that I had to give them quite a lot of change when they left. To be honest, I would not normally let a room without a credit card on file, but we are really quiet at this time of the year, and when they gave me the cash I thought I'd might as well fill up a couple of rooms without making a fuss about it. But why all the interest? – They were certainly not our usual kind of visitors, but they didn't cause us any problems."

As Peter explained to Philip the reasons for his questions, Amir joined them, the object of his attentions having finished her shift behind the bar and who, after waving everyone a cheery good night, had departed. A moment later, Amir asked the way to the Gents. Also wishing to take advantage of a break, KB suggested that the young man followed him, and together they made their way down the corridor to the toilets, leaving Peter to check out the BMW's number in the hotel's registration book.

Once inside Amir excused himself and made his way into one of the cubicles, which he still occupied when KB returned to the bar.

Back at their table, Peter was still examining the guest register which Philip had collected for him from the Reception desk.

"I see what you mean about the entry," he commented. "Can't decipher anything meaningful in the way of names or addresses and the plate number for the BMW is a barely discernable scrawl, but I wouldn't mind betting that these are the same guys that have been tailing us ever since we arrived in Somerset. Do you have any closed circuit TV cameras in or around the hotel that might have caught them on tape?"

"Sorry, never had any cause for them here" Philip replied.

"Okay. That's a pity because we think we may know who one of them is, a guy called Asif – the Prince's personal manservant, who is supposed to be visiting relatives in the Birmingham area. To be on the safe side, and even if Asif does show up when we get back to the college tomorrow, I am going to give my people a call and suggest that they make representations to the Embassy to get him replaced immediately. They might also have been able to trace the whereabouts of the BMW, which could still be somewhere in this area if they dumped it and switched to the Nissan."

At that the door opened and Philip's son Angus came into the bar, a broad grin on his face as he walked forward to join them.

"Good to see you," said the tall freckle faced red head, as KB introduced him to Peter and they shook hands.

"You look pretty happy," said his father. "Things in the kitchen this evening must have gone particularly well!"

"Not as well as for some," came the reply. "I just took the bins out to the skip in the car park to empty them, and it would appear His Royal Highness what's-his-name has his leg over our barmaid in the back of her car!"

"Oh shit!" muttered Peter, his head in his hands. "I do apologize and rest assured I'll give the young bugger a piece of my mind when I get him alone."

"I shouldn't worry too much," Philip chuckled. "It's not as if our Helen is underage or the kind of lass that would allow herself to be taken advantage of, and although I am somewhat surprised, my bet is that she is a willing participant. Just as well her old man is away though, if this ever got to his ears, I'd probably have half the matelots from Yeovilton knocking down my door to exact retribution from your guest, so probably best to pretend it never happened."

Another ten minutes passed before Amir reappeared, not even a smug smile to betray his amorous conquest of the bodacious Helen. Leaving them, Philip returned a minute later with the bill which he placed in front of the young man, who without even glancing at it placed his credit card on the plate.

"Make sure you add on a generous tip," said Peter, a distinct note of sarcasm in his tone. "The staff here tonight have certainly provided you with services beyond the call of their expected duties."

If Amir picked up on the innuendo, he showed no signs of it, and when Philip handed him the card machine, entered a final total which made even the hotelier take a second look.

"That's very generous of you," came the comment. "And I'm glad everything was to your satisfaction, needless to say you are welcome back at anytime."

"Particularly by the bar staff," said KB quietly, as the party got to their feet and bid their goodbyes to the Worsleys.

Outside in the car park, it was Jack who suggested that they should all return to the pub for a night cap, and with no lack of support from the girls they were soon on their way.

Back at The Volunteer, and with the bar now closed for the evening, they settled down in the lounge while Jack collected a bottle of VSOP brandy and a single malt whisky from his private cupboard and put them and some glasses on the table. "Help yourselves," he invited them, "and can I get you fruit juice or anything else, Amir?"

"That's very kind of you, Mr Blake." came the reply. "But if you'll excuse me, I think I'll head upstairs and see you in the morning."

"Well thank you for a lovely evening," said Kathy. "It's a long time since I have been out for a meal, and I really enjoyed myself."

With the others also thanking him, Amir left them which gave Jack and Peter the chance to share the story of Amir's escapade with the girls. After enjoying a good chuckle amongst themselves, Jack and Kathy left after KB promised his father he would see Alex safely home.

KB was hardly surprised when ten minutes later Peter and Hannah also disappeared upstairs leaving him alone with Alex. Getting up from her chair, the girl walked over to where he was sitting on the sofa and without any invitation sat down next to him, swinging her long legs over his lap.

Without thinking, he placed his hand on her thigh as she leant across him and nestled her head into his chest. The warm proximity of her body and the slightest suggestion of her perfume aroused feelings in him that had laid dormant for far too long, and as she raised her face towards him there was only a moment's hesitation as their lips met in a long and sensuous kiss.

"You are not seriously thinking of taking me home, are you?" she whispered to him, as their lips met again. "You don't have to, you know, and I don't see why Amir and Peter should have all the fun."

Knowing that an answer was not required, he took her by the hand and switching off the lights, led her up the stairs. All was quiet on the landing and the lack of a tell-tale glimmer from underneath the doors of either his parents' or his sister's room suggested that the occupants of both had retired for the night, though he suspected that his sister had already joined Peter in his guest suite. Aware that the creaking of the floorboards of the old building would have alerted any listener as they made their way down the corridor, there was little point in attempting to conceal their progress.

Once inside his room, he switched on his bedside light and turning his back to her, undressed and removed his prosthetic leg which he propped up against his wardrobe. Sensing her movement behind him, he turned as her arms came around him as she pressed her nakedness against him, kissing him again.

Leaning on her they moved to the bedside, she threw aside the duvet to allow him to slide onto the sheet. In a fraction she was beside him kissing his chest and slowly sliding down the length of his body. "Glad to see your war wounds have not affected your other bits," she giggled from somewhere around his waist. "Now let's find out if everything is functioning properly."

Chapter Eighteen

Back to Reality

"Man's yesterday may ne'er be like his tomorrow."

P.B. Shelley 1792-1822

By 7.30 a.m. the household at The Volunteer Inn were up and busying themselves in preparation for the week ahead.

Without pausing to say good morning to his mother, who was already in the kitchen, KB and Alex left quietly by the back door, and less than ten minutes later he was dropping her off at the Baker home.

As he drove into the yard, Joe was already up and busy loading his van from the shed that backed onto the property. Waving cheerfully at KB, the builder continued to load up, apparently unconcerned at his daughter's late return from what had been to all intents and purposes, a quiet Sunday evening dinner party.

As if to banish any possible doubts her father may have had as to the reason for her overnight stay, Alex leant across to KB and gave him a long kiss on the lips.

"Alex," he said, awkwardly, "I really want to say, well you know, last night was… ."

"Fabulous," she cut in. "And I can't wait to see you again. Keep in touch and take care, my soldier boy – I'm really looking forward to you coming home at the end of term."

With that, and without a glance over her shoulder she jumped out of the cab and ran across to the front door, where she turned to wave as she went inside.

In the short drive back to the pub a whirl of confused thoughts tumbled through his brain. He had not expected Alex to make such a clearly transparent move and join him in a night of love making where the passion they had shared was so totally real and he thought, could not possibly have been a product of lust alone. Did this mean she wanted the relationship they had enjoyed in their teenage years to be re-kindled, or was he no more than a temporary outlet for a girl whose desires had always been at the high end of the hot-blooded scale?

"One step at a time," he said quietly to himself, as he turned the pick-up truck into the pub car park, but although he still harboured some misgivings about the true intentions of the brown eyed girl with the long black hair, there was a distinctly warm feeling inside him when he reflected upon the last words she had spoken.

Back inside the pub, he went through to the kitchen, where he found his mother about to carry

a tray with coffee, toast and scrambled eggs through to the dining room.

"These are for Amir," she explained. "But hang on here a minute, I want a word with you."

"What do you want for breakfast?" was the first question she asked.

"Just do me a bacon sarni, thanks, Mum. Where's Peter?"

"Down at the stables with Hannah," she replied, and turning to face him added, "they're becoming an item aren't they?"

"They certainly seem keen on each other," he admitted. "But whether they are actually in a serious relationship yet, I think it's probably too early to say."

"Well, she seems totally smitten with him," continued his mother, as she took a pack of bacon from the fridge and placed the frying pan on the stove. "I'll do a couple of extra sandwiches and you can take them down to the stables if you like. But anyway, Peter seems a really nice guy but what do you know about him?"

"He's an ex-regular Royal Marine, no family that I know of, and he works for one of our security agencies. I would trust him one hundred percent and I get the impression that he has grown as fond of my sister as she has of him."

"Is his work dangerous?" she asked, a note of concern in her voice, "I mean, it's good to see Hannah with a man in her life, but Peter strikes me as the kind of person who might have a problem settling down to an nine to five lifestyle, and I can't see her traipsing all over the world in the wake of a spy."

"I would hardly call Peter a spy, Mum," he assured her. "He does have the kind of job which could take him away from home for long spells. Obviously there is always an element of risk if you are responsible for the safety of vulnerable people, what he does is certainly a lot less dangerous than going out on patrol in Afghanistan, which he did when he was in the Marines. Anyway,

I'm sure Hannah understands that so I wouldn't worry too much, she'll make her own decision about Peter in due course."

"And what about you and Alex?" his mother persisted. "Are you two back on again? Though I must say based on that young lady's reputation in the last few years, I am far more concerned about you getting hurt than her."

"Early days yet, Mum," he answered, as she wrapped the bacon sandwiches in foil. "And I know she's been kicking her heels up since I went into the Army, but who can blame her really? After all, it was my decision to go off and leave everything I had here, and I certainly didn't expect her to hang around waiting for me, even though it might have been rather nice," he added wistfully.

"You men!" said Kathy with a grin, handing him the warm parcel. "A pair of shapely legs, a nice figure and the old 'come hither' look and you become as soft and pliable as Joe Baker's putty. Just be careful, that's all I say, and keep your friend Peter out of trouble, your father and I don't want a broken hearted daughter on our hands."

"Will do, Mum," he assured her, giving her a kiss on her cheek, and leaving her to check on Amir, he joined his sister and friend at the stables.

The new day dawned on the Somerset Levels under a heavy, overcast sky, the rain from the previous night having disappeared leaving only the suggestion of dampness in the air. The three sat on straw bales in the shelter of the stables, with Winston leaning over the half door of his loose box to nudge Hannah gently on the side of her head as she munched on her sandwich. Finishing her breakfast and brushing the crumbs off her jacket, she disappeared inside the stable to give Winston his morning groom.

Nodding for KB to follow him, Peter stood up and moved away out of earshot. "I phoned my office first thing," he said quietly. "They've taken on board our concerns over Asif and will speak to Amir's Embassy today about getting a replacement for him. Apparently, even if they can get agreement, the Embassy folk will have to run it past Amir's family, so it may well be Wednesday at the very earliest before we can get an answer. In the meantime if Asif does show up when we get back, I'll move into their cottage for a couple of nights to keep tabs on him. There is a fold down bed in our digs, so I'll move it across and bunk down on it in their living room." Taking his mobile phone out of his pocket, he stabbed the keyboard with his index finger and passed it to KB.

"Take a note of this number, KB, and put it into the directory on your mobile," he continued. "If you ever find yourself in trouble and need help when I am not around, call them up and explain the problem and tell them you are working with me. My field Operative's name is 'Jason' which they will need to know to authenticate your call, and if things are serious emphasise that it's a code red situation. There are counter terrorism specialists in all County Police forces now, and the nearest to us at college will be Plymouth. You can reckon therefore, that their reaction time is likely to be the same as the time it would take them to get a car to you, unless they have a helicopter on call, which in this part of the country is unlikely. I have also spoken to them again about getting you a side arm for the duration of my mission here and I'm hoping that will be cleared by Wednesday as well. No doubt there will be a pile of forms you will have to sign, but I have told them I would feel a lot more comfortable with you carrying one, unless they want to send us another full time Operative, which is also highly unlikely as we are stretched pretty thin on the ground right now."

"Okay, I get the picture," KB replied. "I've just promised Mum that I will take care of the bloke who seems to have embarked upon a torrid affair with her daughter, so I guess some artillery on hand wouldn't be a bad idea. I have told her incidentally, that you are a professional letch and like most Royals, have the greatest difficulty in keeping your pecker in your pants, so I'd watch out if I were you, Kathy has been known to wield a mean meat cleaver and I'd hate to see casseroled bollocks a la Bowen as our pub daily special."

"I hope you bloody didn't, you prat," laughed Peter, aiming a swipe at KB which he narrowly avoided. "And as for a torrid affair, I can assure you that is not the case and I think your sister is something very special. Time to get packed anyway," he added – changing the subject. "What time do you guys have to check in at college?"

"Half past two," KB replied. "But it wouldn't hurt to get down there a bit early and we can grab some lunch in the canteen."

"I think we'll be eating there quite a lot over the next few days," his friend responded. "Or at least until we get a replacement for Asif, assuming that we'll get one. I don't fancy him cooking for us if he is involved in some kind of attempt to harm Amir, but my bet is that we've probably seen the last of him."

Back in their rooms, both men found that Kathy had conducted a dawn raid on their dirty linen, and a pile of freshly laundered clothes sat ironed and folded on the foot of their beds.

With practice born of many years' experience both were packed in less than ten minutes, and met on the landing and shouldering their Bergens, made their way downstairs and out into the yard to load the pick-up.

"You should invest in one of those fibreglass caps for the bed of this wagon," suggested Peter, as they heaved their rucksacks into the back.

"Promised myself one as soon as I have finished my course at Tamar," said KB as he secured both their Bergens with elastic luggage straps. "I also mean to get a liner for the bed, makes it a lot easier to keep clean and prevents scratches and rusting. Let's go and grab a coffee and say our goodbyes to the folks, then we'll load up His Royal Highness and get on our way."

Back in the pub, they found that Amir had also packed and brought his suitcase downstairs, and had joined Jack, Kathy and Hannah in the lounge, where a carafe of coffee and mugs were already laid out on the sideboard.

Never being comfortable with saying his goodbyes to family, KB was relieved when at last Peter suggested they made a move, and after a profusion of thanks to his parents from both Amir and Peter, the latter making no secret of kissing his sister fondly and engulfing her in a long embrace, the three men walked to the car park.

Departure was delayed for a moment when Rocky appeared and with tail wagging, made a bold attempt to join the travellers by jumping into the back seat. With some difficulty KB extracted the dog by the collar and handed him over to Hannah who had come out to see them off. With Amir onboard and his luggage stowed next to him on the back seat, KB lost no time in reversing out of his parking space, and with a final wave to his sister who was crouched by the side of his dog holding him tight as his master left, headed the Ford back towards the M5 and then westwards to the A30 and Cornwall.

Chapter Nineteen

Asif

Basio saepe volam, cui plagem diligo solam
Many kiss the hand they would cut off

Latin Proverb

By the time they had checked in at the college Registration Desk and taken lunch in the students' canteen, two o'clock was fast approaching as they made their way back to the cottages. As they came down the driveway towards the farmhouse and its surrounding buildings, the black Nissan Pathfinder could be clearly seen parked between in front of the cottages, and a wisp of smoke from the chimneys of both indicated that their arrival had been anticipated.

"Well, I didn't expect that," muttered Peter as they drew up alongside the 4 x 4 and stopped. "Play it cool, guys," he advised. "Act as normal. There is a chance we have been mistaken about Asif, but in any case I don't want to spook him until a replacement arrives or my people confirm that he is not under suspicion. Just make sure you lock your bedroom door tonight, Amir, and at all costs avoid being on your own with him."

"I can't believe that he wishes me harm," came the reply. "His family have been known to mine for many generations and they have always been loyal servants, indeed my father himself gave his personal approval to his coming here to look after me, but I will take your advice."

"KB, would you take my gear into our digs?" Peter asked. "I need to do a quick check over Amir's cottage then I'll come over later and pick up a few things I need for the night."

"Sounds good," said KB. "I've a suggestion. Why don't I go into Callington and pick up a Chinese take-away, and you can all come over for supper? It will also avoid us being out on the roads driving around after dark."

"That makes sense," his friend responded. "Come over and join us so that I can keep tabs on Asif and that way he won't get suspicious by being left out. Let's say about 7 o'clock?"

"Fine by me, Peter, and here comes our mystery man," he added as Asif emerged from the cottage and walked over to greet them.

After unloading the Bergens and carrying them up to their respective bedrooms, KB sat down by the fire in the living room and opened the large envelope he had been given when he had checked in earlier.

The first sheet of paper that came to his notice listed the subjects he was taking on his course and the marks for the mid-term exams he had taken before the break. Glancing down the sheet he was satisfied to notice that he had scored two C's, two B grades and a B+ in wildlife management, with a comment at the foot of the page that he was making 'Steady progress – an encouraging start' against which the Principal had scrawled his signature.

Well satisfied with this, he replaced the sheet in its folder and turned his attention to the course programme which laid out the activities that would be consuming his time until the Christmas break. Along with this were briefings on the classroom lectures and outdoor tutorials for the coming week, which demanded his attention for the next two hours.

At seven o'clock he left the cottage for the short drive into Callington, where he collected their evening meal from the Chinese take away. On his return, he knocked on the door of Amir's cottage and entered to find that plates and cutlery had already been laid out on the table.

Calling Asif from the kitchen, the three men sat down at the table as KB unpacked the boxes and opened them up.

"Anyone for chopsticks?" he asked as he took them out of the carrier bag.

"Not for me," said Peter and Amir also shook his head, so with the traditional Chinese implements consigned to the fire, they spooned the food onto their plates, Asif waiting until last and then helping himself to a modest portion from each carton, before disappearing back to the kitchen.

"What's the programme for this week?" Peter asked, as he helped himself to the last of the crispy fried beef.

"It looks like revision and tutorials in class all day tomorrow," KB replied. "Then on Wednesday we are up in Gunoak Woods all day at the coppicing demo."

“We’ve been there before haven’t we?”

“Yes, a couple of times on forestry projects. We can go direct from here and we’ll need to take a packed lunch with us as there won’t be time to come back to the cottages or the college canteen.”

“I suggest that while you and Amir are at the college tomorrow I’ll take Asif into town and we can shop for Wednesday’s lunch and top up on groceries,” said Peter. “Give me a list of anything you think we need.”

“Okay, will do. And now, if you’ll excuse me, I’m going to look through my course notes and have an early night.” As KB got up and left the cottage, Peter followed him outside.

“How’s Asif behaving?” he asked his friend.

“Moody and as silent as always,” came the reply. “It was fairly obvious that he wasn’t too happy about me moving in with them, but I told him that I was under orders. Also he doesn’t know yet that he could be replaced, and I don’t intend to spring that on him until the very last moment. In fact, we’ll have to take two vehicles for the coppicing field trip on Wednesday, as I’m expecting some of my people to show up during the day, hopefully with his replacement. It could be that I will have to leave Amir in your care and come back to the cottage if I get a phone call, will that be okay?”

“No problem,” said KB. “Don’t envy you the next couple of days in the company of that miserable little sod, and if you need a break, let me know and I’ll do a swap with you for a couple of hours.”

“Thanks for that, mate,” Peter answered. “Much appreciated but hopefully on Wednesday matters will be resolved and we can all relax a bit!”

Bidding each other a good night, KB returned to his own cottage, and after an hour studying his notes and catching up with the news on the television, made good his promise to himself to get an early night.

Chapter Twenty

Coppicing

"Light thickens; and the crow
Makes wing to the rooky wood."

Wm. Shakespeare 'Macbeth'

Tuesday passed without incident, Peter returning from his shopping trip with enough ready meals to minimise reliance on Asif's skills in the kitchen, and some pre-packed sandwiches for their field trip.

Due at Gunoak Woods by nine o'clock, the next morning Peter and KB met outside the cottages just after eight.

"I had a phone call yesterday," Peter reported. "My guys will be arriving just before eleven o'clock, and they will be flying down from Salisbury Plain by chopper. I've told Tom Cousins to expect them and he has cleared them to land in the paddock behind the farmhouse so I will leave you at around ten thirty to get back and lay out a marker. I'll take Asif with me in the Nissan and you follow in your truck with Amir. We'll take the same route as before, and try to keep about a hundred metres behind me. Take this," he added, handing KB the Glock. "And hopefully by the end of the day, you'll have one of your own."

Taking the automatic from him, KB walked back to his truck, and climbing into the driver's seat leant across to place it in the glove compartment. Turning the key in the ignition, he waited a few seconds then turned it again to start the diesel and allow it to warm up. As he sat waiting, with the motor gently idling, the front door to Amir's cottage opened and the Nizam's second son emerged, closely followed by Asif, who was arguing furiously with his master and clearly not happy with the way the day was unfolding.

Opening the passenger door to the Nissan, Peter ushered the gesticulating servant into the vehicle, and with a wave to KB climbed up behind the wheel. Meanwhile Amir had reached the Ford, and at KB's insistence got into the rear seat of the cab.

"I really can't see the need for all this," he muttered petulantly. "I feel I am being treated like a prisoner right now, and Asif is very upset as he cannot understand why Peter is watching over our every move."

"Peter has his reasons," replied KB as he followed the Nissan out of the yard and onto the driveway. "And you know that we did run into some problems in Somerset which have not been explained at the moment, so better to be safe than sorry!"

"I still think Peter is overreacting," came the response, as Amir slumped back in his seat, arms folded in resignation.

At the top of the driveway, they turned right onto the narrow country lane which climbed up and around the rim of the small valley in which the farm lay, now hidden from their view by a high hedge and moss covered bank, which KB knew, true to Cornish custom, concealed a solid stone wall under its seemingly harmless exterior.

Half a mile further up the lane, a second road joined them and as KB accelerated around the corner to keep the Nissan in sight, a tractor pulled out in front of them, towing a trailer laden with large round bales of fodder.

Muttering a couple of swear words to himself, KB had no option but to follow in its wake and although the driver maintained a steady pace it was till nearly two miles further on before it stopped by a gateway into a field where a large herd of cattle waited for their morning feed.

Jumping down from the lofty cab a farmhand waved cheerily at KB before opening the gate and guiding the tractor and trailer into the field, leaving the road clear for KB to resume his pursuit of the Nissan.

The delay had frustrated KB, who accelerated as fast as the narrow lane would allow to catch up with Peter. As he rounded a bend, in front of him on the crest of a slight rise in the road, he saw that the Nissan had been pulled over to the narrow verge, where it stood stationary with both front doors open.

KB's relief at having caught up was short-lived, as it became immediately clear that they had company. Of Peter there was no sight, but Asif was standing by one of two men and pointing directly at the pick-up. Even some hundred metres or so away, he could see that both the men were wearing balaclavas and as he brought the pick-up to a halt, they started to run towards him, making no effort to hide the handguns both carried.

"Get down and stay down," he shouted to Amir, as he leant across to flip open the glove compartment and retrieve the Glock. Throwing himself across the seats he opened the driver's door and tumbled out as a sharp crack and the sound of glass shattering confirmed that their assailants had opened fire. Rolling over to lie half concealed behind the front wheel he yanked back the action of the automatic to chamber a round, as two more shots rang out one smashing the window above him and a second thumping into the door panel a foot above his head. Raising his head slightly he saw one of the attackers kneeling down to take a third shot aimed at where he lay, while the other had veered off to the left hand side of the road facing him to continue his advance in a half crouching run.

Without hesitation KB lined up the Glock and fired a shot which missed his target, ricocheting off the road surface and inches to one side of the kneeling gunman but which was close enough to spoil the man's aim, causing him to fall backwards onto his heels. Before he had a chance to recover KB's second shot caught him full in the chest, and he lurched over to lay in the road his gun spilling from his grip.

For a second KB lost sight of the second attacker, but as he eased himself forward on his elbows to widen his view, the sound of heavy footsteps running reached him. As he got carefully to his feet behind the shelter of the Ford, the dark clad figure came into view sprinting back towards the Nissan, shouting to the retreating figure of Asif as he went. Steadying himself by his vehicle and with his elbows resting on the bonnet, KB loosed off two more shots which to his frustration, did no more than to increase the speed at which the runner departed. As the man drew level with the Nissan he shouted again to Asif and the two of them disappeared over the crest of the hill and out of sight. A few seconds later, KB heard the sound of an engine being started, followed by a screech of tyres on the tarmac, indicating that their attackers had fled.

Still facing up the road in the direction from which the ambush had been sprung, KB backed up to the cab of the Ford and opened the rear door where an ashen faced Amir lay sideways down behind the front seat.

"Get up and get out of there," he shouted. "And stay right beside me." With a silent Amir following in his footsteps, KB moved forward up the road to where the first gunman lay on his side. Bending down, he picked up the fallen weapon and with his own gun pointed at the prone figure, kicked it over so that the man laid face up, a large red stain spreading across his chest. Bending down, KB pulled the balaclava off his head.

"Do you recognize him?" he snapped at Amir, who reluctantly peered from behind him to take in the swarthy features of the would-be assassin.

"No, never seen him before," came the reply.

"Right, keep behind me," KB ordered. "We are going to find Peter."

As they approached the Nissan, all was quiet and there was no sign of his friend until they came abreast of the vehicle. To one side, lying on the verge and half hidden among the grass and fallen leaves from the overhead trees lay a body, and KB knew immediately from the jacket that had been half torn off as he fell forward, that it was Peter Bowen.

"Amir, stay over by the Nissan and let me know if you see any sign of anybody coming down the road from either direction and above all don't move," he said curtly.

Moving over to where Peter lay, he saw with increasing despair that his friend had been shot in the back of the head. Kneeling down beside him, he rolled the still form over momentarily recoiling as it became evident that the head shot had removed the upper part of one side of Peter's face as the bullet exited. Gently lifting up the jacket where it now lay over the body, he saw that the ex-Royal Marine had also taken a bullet to the chest.

"Jesus fucking mercy," he muttered to himself, a mixture of rage and grief welling up inside him. "The bastards must have nailed him in the chest as he got out of the car, and then finished him off with a shot to the head."

"Is he alright?" Amir called out from where he stood.

Ignoring the question and fighting back the desire to vent his rage on the hapless Prince, KB got slowly to his feet and stood for a moment, taking deep breaths as he struggled to pull himself together.

Moving away from the verge, he took his mobile out of his pocket and with studied deliberation brought up his directory on its screen and hit the emergency number Peter had given him. Seconds later the phone was answered, no indication as to the recipient of the call, but with a curt question, "Who is calling please?"

"This is Kristian Blake. I have been instructed to call you in an emergency and to tell you this is a code red. We have been ambushed and Jason has been shot."

Before he had a chance to add anything, the voice on the other end cut in. "Hold the line please, Mr Blake, and don't ring off under any circumstances."

It seemed to KB that an eternity passed before the line crackled and he heard another voice, barely distinguishable though a loud drone in the background.

"Mr Blake, this is Jason's Section Leader. Are you still under threat?"

"I don't believe so, sir," KB replied "There is every indication that our attackers have fled."

"Good," came the response. "Please can you tell me what has happened as quickly and as accurately as possible?"

"We were on our way to Gunoak Woods near Tamar Valley College when we were ambushed," KB answered. "Jason was in the lead vehicle with Amir Khan's servant, and I was following behind in my pick-up truck with Amir. We were attacked by two gunmen about three miles from the college and two miles from our destination. Jason was shot as he got out of his vehicle and I arrived on the scene shortly afterwards, and was also attacked."

"Is the Prince safe and are you okay?" broke in the Section Leader.

"Yes, the Prince is with me now, and we are both unharmed."

"And our man?"

"He's dead I'm afraid. One shot in the back of the head and another to his chest."

"I understand," came the response. "Don't let the Prince out of your sight and stay where you are until we get there. We are inbound by helicopter and should be with you within thirty minutes. We will alert the Emergency Services, and we have a fix on you via the Nissan's tracker. If anyone comes down the road, tell them there's been an accident but above all, keep them away from the scene, do you understand?"

"Yes, sir," KB replied.

"Good man. Are you armed?" came the next question.

"I have Jason's weapon and also an automatic from of the attackers, who was killed in the cross-fire."

"Understood. Don't hesitate to defend yourself and the Prince if necessary. Is his manservant still with you?"

"Asif took off with the second gunman and both escaped" KB answered.

"So your concerns about his loyalty were well founded," said the Section Leader, and after a moment's pause added, "Is there a feasible landing site close to you?"

"I think the field to the immediate south of us is level enough."

"Mr Blake, in the back of the Nissan you will find an orange marker panel.

If you can, lay it out in the field. Keep this line open and report any further developments immediately. Just hang on, Mr Blake, I have every confidence in you and we'll be there as soon as we can."

With the phone now silent, KB walked back to the Nissan, where he found the marker panel and pegs together with two small smoke canisters in a metal box at the back. Finding a gap in the hedge, he clambered through and calling to Amir to help him, pegged out the panel and then both men retreated to the Nissan to sit and wait.

Amir got into the front passenger seat, still visibly shaken by the ordeal they had just survived. As KB got in beside him, he looked up.

"I am so sorry," he said, in a low voice. "And I apologize for doubting your suspicions about Asif. I cannot understand the people who have done these things and but for you and Peter I could be dead."

"I doubt that," KB replied bitterly. "The way it was explained to me, I believe that you would have been more valuable to them alive rather than dead. It's pretty certain that you would have been held to ransom, or used as a political tool to bring pressure on your family."

Amir lapsed into silence and KB took the gun he had picked up off the road out of his pocket to examine it more closely. Immediately he recognized it as a Beretta M9 as carried by the US Forces in Afghanistan and also the Afghanistan Army. Ejecting the magazine and sliding back the action to clear the round in the breech, he counted six rounds remaining.

Replacing the rounds in the magazine and slotting it back into the grip of the semi-automatic, he sat back to wait, his mind turning back to his friend whose body now lay a few feet away. He had seen death many times during his two tours in Helmand, and although they would remain etched into his memory, this was far more personal. Even Jacko's passing, though painful at the time, was now filed away in a dark recess that held all his recollections of that time in his life, protected by self-imposed insulation that only he could access.

As he sat, he reflected on how little he knew of the man he had called a friend. Peter had told him that there were no children from the marriage that had ended a decade ago, but where was his ex-wife now, and were there other family that would mourn his passing?

A feeling of despair and nausea engulfed him, as he realised that he would have to break the news to Hannah, whom Peter had confessed had become very special to him. Would she be able to shrug off the loss and continue her life as usual? Having seen the look on her face when she looked at his friend, KB doubted that. It was pretty clear that she shared the same feelings that Peter had admitted.

The minutes dragged by as they waited, but just as KB was beginning to wonder if they would ever be found, the distinct whop-whop of rotor blades announced the arrival of the promised help, and above them a Lynx helicopter circled. Climbing back through the hedge, KB pulled the pin on a smoke canister and threw it as far as possible away from himself as pink smoke billowed out, giving the pilot an idea of the wind direction as he brought the olive green Lynx down to a low hover over the field.

Taking up a position a few metres in front of the orange marker, KB guided the helicopter down, giving the pilot a 'thumbs up' when the skids had touched down safely on the grassy sward.

The side door slid open and two men jumped down, and crouching beneath the slowly turning rotors, ran towards him. Following KB through the gap in the hedge, both paused for a brief examination of Peter's body and while the younger of the two then walked back down the road to where the gunman lay, the other beckoned KB to follow him to the front of the Nissan, in the

front of which Amir still sat.

"Bill Hutchinson," he said turning to face KB and offering a handshake. "Sorry we are meeting under these circumstances, and this is a tragedy," he added nodding towards the verge. Taking a small wallet out of his pocket he flipped it open and passed it to KB, to examine the photo ID of the man that stood in front of him. "Now tell me exactly what happened, and if you have no objections, I'll record it while the events are still fresh in your mind. Start off where you left the farm this morning." Taking a small recorder out of his pocket, he switched it on and laid it on the bonnet of the 4 x 4.

With frequent interruptions from Hutchinson questioning some of the key incidents with linked the chain of events that unravelled as KB made his report, it was close to twenty minutes by the time he finished and the recorder switched off.

"Okay," said Peter's Section Leader, "here's what will happen now. An element from the Plymouth Anti-Terrorist squad will be here shortly, and they will do a sweep of the area to fill in any gaps, and take care of the removal of the bodies. We will get young Amir on board the helicopter and out of here, as I'm afraid his college days are over. It looks as if your vehicle sustained a fair amount of damage, is it drivable?"

"I believe so, sir," KB replied. "As you can see, one shot hit the windscreen and another the window on the driver's side, and a third one went into the door. I don't think more than three shots were fired at me, so as far as I know, there should be no damage anywhere else. By the way, here is the gun I picked up off the road. It's a Beretta; standard 10 shot magazine and one in the breech, for a total of 11 on the weapon. There are six rounds left, so if you take the three fired at me, that could mean that the other two were the ones that killed Peter."

"It would seem likely then, that you got the man that killed him. I'll need to let our forensic people examine it" said Hutchinson, as KB handed him the weapon. "If the Police can find a bullet, we may be able to get a match to confirm it was the weapon. I will also take Peter's Glock from you now."

Ejecting the magazine, and sliding back the action of the Beretta to confirm the weapon was clear of bullets, he took two plastic bags out of his pocket, placing the magazine in one and the gun in the other. Allowing KB to carry out the same safety checks on the Glock, he took it from him and placed both guns in the steel box in the luggage area. Weapons secured, he walked round to the passenger side of the Nissan where he opened the door to allow Amir to climb down.

"Your Highness," he greeted the young man soberly. "I am pleased to find you safe and sound. For your own continuing safety we are going to fly you out of here now, and by tonight you will be back in your Embassy in London. Mr Blake and I will collect your belongings from the cottage and these will be forwarded on to you within the next few days. I am sorry that your stay here has to end so abruptly, but I am sure you appreciate the situation, and to be frank, the risk to you if you were to remain here is far too great, as demonstrated by events today."

"I quite understand," replied Amir. "And I sincerely regret having been the cause of so much trouble. Peter had become a good friend to me, and you have my assurance that I will do everything possible to ensure our people assist you in finding those responsible for this act of barbarity. I feel I owe my life to him and to Kris, for which," he added, turning towards KB, "I shall be eternally grateful."

As he spoke, they heard the sound of the Ford's engine spring into life as Hutchinson's associate manoeuvred it off the road, to allow a small mini bus and a van to drive through. Six overall clad policemen climbed out of the bus and two more from the van and as Hutchinson left KB and Amir to brief them, the second agent came up to escort the Nizam's son to the helicopter. Two minutes later the twin turboshaft engines whined into life, and the pilot lifted off to gain altitude and head east.

After briefing the Police, Hutchinson returned to where KB stood and watched.

"Right, young Blake." he ordered, "I'll follow you back to the cottages in the Nissan and we'll pick up your luggage and pack up Amir and Peter's belongings. We'll leave your truck there and my people will recover it tomorrow and get it repaired for you. We'll then head out in the Nissan and after I've dropped by the Principal's office to bring him up to speed on everything, you can drive me back to my HQ in Bulford. I'd like you to stay with us for a couple of days in case there is anything more you can help us with, and after that we'll take things as they come."

Back at the cottages, the two of them wasted no time in packing up Amir and Asif's belongings, and then KB was left to pack up his own while Hutchinson sorted through Peter's. KB had never had any cause to enter Peter's room, and left the Section Leader on his own as he busied himself stowing his clothes in his Bergen.

With the luggage loaded in the back of the Nissan and the Ford left locked and parked outside the cottage, KB walked over to the farmhouse and left a set of ignition keys with Mrs Cousins, explaining to her that the vehicle would be collected the following day.

The short drive to the college was conducted in silence, and KB stayed in the Nissan while Hutchinson met with Dr Windrush. Fifteen minutes later, the Section Leader reappeared and after settling into the passenger seat, KB moved the gear shift into drive and moved out of the car park and away from the campus towards Launceston, the A30 and Exeter.

"The Principal was very understanding," Hutchinson stated, opening the conversation. "And in fact after what transpired this morning seemed quite relieved that the young Prince would no longer be part of his jurisdiction. He is going to forward the course syllabus to Amir so that he can finish it off by e-mail. I get the feeling that Amir will be awarded some kind of diploma regardless of his academic achievements, so that will probably save face all round. As far as you are concerned, I would suggest you may want to postpone making a decision on your future for a few days, but Dr Windrush did say that you would be welcome back at the college at any time to complete your studies."

As they settled down for the journey in front of them, the conversation focussed more and more on him, and as the miles slipped by KB sensed that he was undergoing a casual, but nonetheless searching interrogation.

After a short drive north up the M5 at Exeter, KB turned back on to the A30 to take them past Honiton to join the A303 and then across the Blackdown Hills to the Ilminster by-pass and on to Salisbury Plain and Bulford. Passing so close to his home, KB was tempted to suggest to his companion that they stopped for a break at The Volunteer, but on further reflection decided against it. He was not ready yet to confront his sister and break the news to her, and careful thought would be needed to ensure that he let her down as gently as he was able.

As they approached the roundabout at Sparkford, Hutchinson suggested that they pull in at the truck stop and restaurant. Although not hungry himself, he followed the man in, and while the latter ordered a burger and fries, KB was content with a large coffee.

Back on the road, and with the Nissan refuelled they continued their journey east, passing the familiar sight of Stonehenge on their left, until a few miles further on, Hutchinson instructed KB to turn off the main road and head towards Bulford Camp.

"Our offices are close to the RMP Special investigation Branch Headquarters," Hutchinson explained. "We're actually part of a national counter terrorism agency administered by the MoD. We work closely with the Military, MI5, GCHQ, the UK Border Force and the Civilian Police and report directly to the Home Office. Apart from playing an active counterterrorism role, our other functions include surveillance and close quarter protection for those identified as vulnerable and as most of our people are ex-military, you should feel right at home.

"We'll find you a room for a couple of nights. The mess serves good food and there is a comfortable bar and a pool room. We have a number of civvie personnel who will take care of your laundry and your room. They're a good team, and if you need anything they will be able to help you. When you register at reception you will be allocated a pigeon hole in the mail box in the foyer, check it frequently as although it is unlikely you'll have any incoming post, messages may be left there including your Mess bill. I would also warn you that all incoming and outgoing telephone calls are monitored and there are a couple of phones in the lobby you can use if you need to. By the way, do you have a jacket and tie with you?"

"Yes, I have a blazer, will that be okay?"

"Certainly," came the reply. "I mentioned it because you will need it if you are dining in the Mess or drinking in the bar after 1730 hours, otherwise casual wear is fine. I would also ask that you do not leave the premises for the duration of your stay with us, unless accompanied by one of our personnel. As I have already said, this shouldn't be for more than a couple of days, but you will be required to go through a thorough debrief tomorrow and I will be asking you to sign a copy of the Official Secrets Act, even though you may have signed one when you joined up."

"Then what?" asked KB.

"I will need to speak to you again, but please remember under no circumstances talk about this to anyone when you do leave, least of all the press or any other branch of the media."

"So what do I tell my family? They all knew Peter and liked him, and I can't tell them he has just disappeared off the face of the earth without arousing their suspicions, nor that I have suddenly quit college for no apparent reason!"

"Good point," Hutchinson replied. "I'll leave it to you to be as inventive as you feel may be appropriate, maybe tell them that Peter was killed in an accident that somehow involved you, and that you had no stomach to continue your course. After all, I gather you and Bowen had become quite close friends, so they might find that understandable?"

"I doubt it," KB thought to himself, as he collected his Bergen from the back of the Nissan and followed the man through to the Reception Area where he signed in at the desk, and received a set of room keys from the dark waist-coated clerk who manned it.

Ten minutes later he found himself shown into a small bedroom by a porter. The room was on the third floor looking out over the car park, and KB had been grateful for the offer of assistance in carrying his luggage up the two flights of marbled stairs.

A single bed stood against one wall of the room, the only other furnishings being a standard MoD chest of drawers, a wardrobe and a small bedside table on which a lamp stood. In one corner of the room, close to the window was a washbasin with a mirror and shelf above it upon which a glass and a box of tissues had been placed. There was no television, and no sign of any plug in or aerial jack. The only concession to comfort was a small mat placed by the side of the bed, the sole covering on an otherwise highly polished lino covered floor.

At the foot of the bed lay a pillow, pillow sheet, three folded grey blankets, two bed sheets and one small and one large towel. The porter had been quick to assure him that someone would be along shortly to make the bed up for him, and after showing him where the lavatories, showers and baths were located at the end of the corridor, left KB to unpack.

Sitting on the edge of the bed, on his own for the first time since he had risen that morning, he sat with his head in his hands for a while, trying to make sense in his own mind of the day's events which had so suddenly and violently impacted on his life. What if Peter had not given him his gun – would he have been able to defend himself and not only prevent a kidnapping but also his own murder? What if they had kicked Asif out of the cottage as soon as they had found him waiting there on their return – would he have still be able to pass the vital information on the route that they were taking to the ambushers, allowing the trap to be laid? What if the tractor had not pulled out in front of him en route to the coppicing site, causing him to lose contact with Peter – would the sight of a second vehicle close on the heels of the Nissan have deterred the ambushers, or allowed him to prevent them killing Peter?

Shaking his head, it was all too obvious that even if answers to these self-imposed questions satisfied his feeling of guilt, they were unlikely to provide any defining comfort to his mental dilemma and he recognized also that allowing these thoughts to torment him further could serve no purpose. At that moment Kristian Blake, former soldier and sniper, felt the icy coldness that had served him well in the heat and trauma of Helmand, returning to freeze his emotions and file the memories deep in the recess of his subconscious.

Checking his watch, he saw that the time was nearing four o'clock, so undressing he wrapped a towel around his waist and found the bathroom where he entered one of the cubicles and after shutting the door behind him, filled the tub, and unfastened his prosthetic leg. Checking the artificial limb carefully, he noticed that he had scuffed it badly, no doubt when he had thrown himself onto the road surface from the pick-up, but otherwise it appeared undamaged. His stump, however, was an angry red and tender to the touch, and after soaking himself in the bath and drying off, he took the tub of ointment he used for treating skin sores from his wash kit and applied it liberally to the affected area.

Back in his room, he dressed carefully, hoping that a couple of hours wear would iron out the wrinkles in his shirt from where it had been hurriedly packed in his Bergen, noticing with relief that his blazer and grey slacks had survived much better. As he fastened his tie and checked his appearance in the mirror over the washbasin, he noticed for the first time a small cut above his right eye just hidden in his hairline. The wound had started to seep blood, and as he touched it with his fingers he dislodged a small piece of glass that had become embedded in his scalp. Staunching the blood that welled up as soon as he removed it, he sat back on the bed for a moment, holding a tissue against it.

Picking up the shard he examined it closely and from the rounded shape it seemed most likely that it had come from the driver's door window when the gunman's bullet had shattered it. "Lucky again, KB," he said quietly, as he realized that three inches lower it would have been dangerously close to his eye.

Removing the tissue, he took another look in the mirror and was annoyed to see that the bleeding had not stopped. Slipping on his blazer, he grabbed a fresh tissue from the box and holding it to his forehead, locked his bedroom door behind him and returned to the Reception desk in the lobby.

The same man who had checked him in was still on duty, and seeing KB approach immediately came around the desk to meet him.

"Do we have a problem, sir?" he asked courteously.

"Nothing much," KB assured him. "But if you have a plaster, that should fix it."

Looking at the blood which had by now almost saturated the tissue, the duty clerk took him by the elbow and steered him to the door.

"I think that might need a bit more than a plaster," the man affirmed. "The Medical Centre is in the next building over and I think I should take you over to have it checked out."

In no mood to argue, KB allowed himself to be escorted across the road, where he was seated in a small waiting area while the porter crossed to a small desk and pressed a button.

"Someone will be with you in a moment, sir," he was assured. "And now if you'll excuse me I must return to my post."

Thanking the clerk for his help, a minute or so later a door opened on the opposite side of the room and a middle-aged nurse appeared and beckoned to him to follow her.

Entering a well-lit and spotlessly clean room KB sat down in the high backed chair the nurse waved him into.

"Now what have you been up to?" she asked him.

"Caught by a piece of glass from a shattered car window I think," he replied, as she bent over him and examined the wound giving KB the chance to read her name tag which identified her as a Sister.

"Not too bad," she replied. "I'll clean it up and put some adhesive sutures on it which should do the trick. May need to shave off some of your hair around it to get the sutures to stay in place, and you'll need to get it checked out again in a couple of days but in the meantime, keep it dry, so no showers unless you wear a shower cap. Are your tetanus shots up to date?"

"Yes, Sister," he confirmed, as she busied herself patching him up. "They took care of all my jabs in the Army."

"Well that looks okay," she said, stepping back to look at her handiwork and turning back to her desk she removed the surgical gloves she had been wearing and pulled a clipboard towards her.

"Now I need to take a few details so I will need your full name and address and where you are staying at the moment?"

"I'm saying across the road," he replied. "And I'm told I am likely to be there until the weekend."

"No need to say more," she said. "If you don't get a chance to drop by for us to check you out before you leave, get your GP to have a look at it for you when you get home – if that's where you're heading, or any medical centre you are close to. It's clean enough now and should be fine, but better to be safe than sorry."

"Thank you for your help, Sister," he said getting to his feet and glancing in the mirror on the wall next to him.

"Looks a lot worse than it is!" the nurse laughed, noticing his frown. "But when it heals over and your hair grows back, nobody will ever notice it."

Leaving her to tidy away her dressings, KB let himself out of the door to the Centre and paused to take in a few breaths of fresh air, before re-tracing his steps to the accommodation block and Mess.

Back inside he noticed that it was now close to half past five, and rather than returning to his room he crossed the lobby to the Mess and picking up a newspaper from the pile, settled himself into one of the leather armchairs to wait for the bar to open.

"Well, look who's here!" a voice called out from the doorway, and he looked up to see Fred Nowakowski crossing the room towards him, a broad grin on his face.

"Fred, am I glad to see you!" he exclaimed, rising from his chair to greet his friend. "I'm feeling a bit like a fish out of water right now, so you are a welcome sight!"

"I'm happy to see you still in one piece too," came the rejoinder, "although it looks as if the buggers nicked you. Colin told me you had run into some trouble and I'm sorry to hear about Peter, losing a guy like that is a real blow. Peter was really popular around here and we'll all miss him; he had a very high opinion of you too. Anyway, let me get you a beer and you can tell me all about it."

"Am I allowed to?" KB asked. "Bill Hutchinson really lay it on that I was to keep my mouth shut."

"It's okay as long as nothing goes out of this building," Fred replied. "We often talk about our past assignments among ourselves, it helps to relieve the tension sometimes and it's surprising what useful tips you can pick up from your colleagues. Mind you, we never talk about upcoming missions in case they could be compromised, but as we are usually kept in the dark until the last moment, there's little chance of that."

Returning from the bar with two pints, Fred placed them on the table between them.

"Draught beer here?" KB asked, as it was clear the dark ale that filled the glasses in front of them had not come from a bottle.

"Yep, from the brewery in Devizes. I doubt if there are many drinking establishments in the whole of the garrison area that doesn't have it on tap. Anyway, cheers," Fred added, as they raised their glasses.

Between sips of their drinks, KB recounted the events of the morning for a second time that day. Listening intently his friend said nothing until KB had finished and then sat back.

"You know why you are here, KB, don't you?" Fred said quietly.

"I take it I'm here for debriefing and to make sure I don't go shooting my mouth off when I get out from here," KB replied. "Why, is there more I should know?"

"Your debrief tomorrow morning is more of an assessment than anything else. You'll find you are up in front of a panel of three, one of whom will be Colin incidentally, and if they like what they hear, you will probably be offered a job with us.

"This was always on the cards after Colin and I spent the weekend with you, and now with Peter gone that is even more likely. I don't have to tell you how much pressure any agency connected with counterterrorist operations is under right now, and with this new Government initiative to get all the agencies working together, there is no shortage of funding and so far it is working quite well. The spooks from MI5 can be a little choosy about what information they pass on to us from time to time, and I can't say that we are one big happy family yet, but things are certainly a hundred times better than they were eighteen months ago."

"I would have thought that my tin leg would be against them recruiting me?" suggested KB.

"It certainly can't be overlooked." agreed his friend. "But with your rural background and understanding of the countryside plus your military experience, field surveillance and what they call 'Specific Target Neutralisation' or 'STN' might be considered to be well within your capabilities."

"STN sounds pretty much similar to what I was doing in Helmand first time around," said KB. "Can't see that there would be much call for that in the UK."

"Hopefully not, but our activities are not always limited to what goes on in these islands. Anyway, I thought I might give you a quiet 'heads up', forewarned is as good as forearmed I believe, and it will give you a chance to think things through. Your round I think," his friend added, as he drained the last of his pint.

Glasses replenished, their conversation returned to Amir and Asif, and KB found his friend's insistence that he could not have done anything to prevent Peter's murder considerably reassuring, but was in for another surprise when Fred turned their discussion towards his sister.

"Peter and Hannah had quite a thing going didn't they?" he asked directly, studying KB's face for any reaction.

"They certainly seemed to have grown very close in the short time they had known each other," agreed KB. "But why do you ask?"

"Before we left the pub on Sunday, Peter had drafted a hand written will, which quite simply, left his entire estate to your sister. I gather he did not have any personal possessions of any value, property or anything like that, but he did have a car, a savings account at the bank and had been paying into a private pension. There may be some compensation from the Agency, so she might find she has inherited a bit when his affairs have been settled."

"But is the will legal?" asked KB. "I'm certain Hannah knew nothing about it, and on top of the shock of losing him, it's going to come as a major surprise."

"It should be legal. He made it clear that it superseded any previous will he had made, and it was witnessed by both Colin and myself, so it will probably stand up. I know he had few – if any – near relatives, and he had been divorced for some time and there were no kids from his marriage, but I guess the ultimate decision will be up to the courts if anyone challenges it."

"It's almost as if Peter had some kind of premonition, isn't it?" KB suggested to his friend.

"I knew he wasn't at all happy with the whole Amir situation," Fred answered. "And he had made a number of recommendations to get Amir back to his own country. His arguments were based on an assessment that the risks of allowing him to stay on and complete his studies, were out of proportion to any political benefit we might have gained with the Nizam, but the powers that be rejected them. Anyway, don't mention the will thing unless anyone raises the subject with you, and in any case our legal people are bound to check things out thoroughly before notifying your sister."

With that the conversation turned to reminiscing about their Army days and in particular the sniper's course they had taken together. After another pint, dinner and an hour watching television in the lounge, KB excused himself and made his way upstairs to his room.

On a neatly made bed, a brown legal size envelope lay marked 'Confidential – to be opened only by the addressee' and on it his name written in long hand.

Opening it up, he pulled out several sheets of A4 notepaper, the top one with a letterhead displaying the agency title and logo, an owl clasping a label upon which the motto 'VIGILANCE' was inscribed.

The letter was addressed to him and under the day's date and reference, he read:

Dear Mr Blake,

First of all I would like to take this opportunity to thank you on behalf of the Agency for the help and assistance you provided Field Operative Peter Bowen, during his recent assignment to provide close quarter protection for His Highness Prince Amir Akbar Ayaz Khan of Surpor.

We are aware that FO Bowen placed considerable trust in your ability to provide him with much needed support from time to time, which was certainly justified in the actions that you took to protect the person of His Highness during this morning's incident at Tregallis Farm.

Under different circumstances the outcome could have caused considerable embarrassment both to the Agency and Her Majesty's Government, and although we are deeply saddened by the brutal murder of FO Bowen, we wish you to know that having examined your report of the incident, supported by the evidence gathered on site and the testimony of

His Highness Prince Amir, we believe you acted in an exemplary manner throughout.

In recognition of this and based on recommendations from both Mr Bowen prior to his death, and two other of our Agents, we would like to make you a provisional offer of a full time position with the Agency as a Field Operative (Grade III).

If you wish to pursue this opportunity further, I have convened a meeting of an Assessment Panel in the Library of the Main Administration Building tomorrow morning, Thursday 6th November at 0900 hours. This will be an informal meeting which will enable us to get to know you better and provide you with further details of your potential responsibilities.

In the meantime, should you decide not to pursue this, I would be grateful if you would phone the number at the top of this page and inform my secretary accordingly. Arrangements will then be made to provide you with suitable transport for your use until such time as we can repair your own vehicle.

I should add that should our meeting tomorrow conclude to our mutual satisfaction, you will be required to undertake a short medical examination and to return to this centre as soon as convenient for an initial four week indoctrination course. This may be followed at a later date by further training courses as appropriate.

Finally, please read the attached statement carefully and if you consider it to be a true and accurate account of this morning's events, please sign it at the foot of each page in the space provided, and bring it with you to the meeting or hand it to my Secretary before you depart.

Yours sincerely,

Andrew F Reynard

Head of Operations

KB noticed that the letter had been copied both to Colin Hunter and Bill Hutchinson, suggesting that these two with Andrew Reynard, could be the members of the Assessment Panel.

The sheaf of papers that accompanied the letter had been stapled together, and comprised of a typed word by word account of the statement he had given Hutchinson at the scene of the ambush. Reading the document carefully, he saw no reason to make any changes, signed it and returned it to the envelope.

Twenty minutes later he climbed into bed and settling down under the covers, lay thinking of the letter. Returning to college to complete his course was still an option, but the opportunity for full time employment in an environment that could provide both variety and a chance to employ skills he already possessed was also appealing.

He would attend the meeting the following morning and make a decision based upon the extra information it promised to provide. Rolling over onto his side, he switched off his bedside table lamp, the glare from the floodlights over the car park outside filtering through the thin curtains and filling the room with a warm orange glow. Pushing his thoughts to the back of his mind, he willed himself to sleep.

Chapter Twenty-One

The Agency

Ulula cum lupis, cum quibus esse cupis – Who keeps company with wolves, will learn to howl.

Latin Proverb

At 7.00 a.m. there was a knock on his bedroom door and the same porter who had shown him to his room the previous day entered, switched on his table lamp and put a tray with a cup of tea, a small jug of milk and two sachets of sugar on his bedside table. Thanking him, KB sat up in bed, drank the tea and strapping on his prosthetic leg made his way down the corridor to the lavatories. Returning to his room, he wet shaved and strip washed at the basin and after towelling himself vigorously, dressed in his shirt, tie and slacks and slipping on a sweater, went downstairs to the dining room for breakfast.

As he entered the room to join eight early risers already seated at tables, a wave from Fred Nowakowski across the room caught his attention and he went over to join him.

"Morning, KB," Fred greeted him. "Hope you slept well. Help yourself from the buffet on the sideboard over there, and then come back and join me."

The sideboard was laden with a variety of breakfast cereals, fruit and a number of large silver serving dishes whose contents were kept warm over spirit lamps. After collecting a tray and putting two slices of brown bread into the toaster, KB lifted the lids that covered them and helped himself to bacon, sausage, scrambled egg and added mushrooms and a grilled tomato. Collecting his toast and a mug of coffee from one of two urns, he returned to the table and sat down opposite his friend.

"Have you decided to go for the interview?" Fred enquired, as KB started into his breakfast.

"Yes, I'll see how things go, and then make my mind up," he answered, and taking the letter out of his pocket, handed it over for Fred to read.

"That's not bad," came the comment, as Fred folded up the letter and passed it back to him. "Grade One is trainee level, Two limits you to working under supervision at all times with a senior FO, but by offering to bring you in at Grade Three they are acknowledging that you are capable of working on your own.

"You'll find also that promotion to Grade Four usually follows within a year to eighteen months, which is at higher pay grade and where I am at the moment. Grade Five is Section Leader level, and is the top of the ladder for FOs, unless you move into a specialist admin role. How do you think you'll cope with the medical?"

"I don't really know what they will be expecting of me," KB admitted. "They are obviously aware that I have an artificial leg, so although I can manage a gentle jog with this new state-of-the-art limb they have fitted me with, I won't be able to go sprinting after fugitives, but they must realize that."

"As I said last night, that's why I believe they'll limit your assignments to rural areas where you would be dependent on a vehicle to get you around and where you can handle missions that involve static surveillance and covert information gathering, so I am sure that will be taken into account after the medics have put you through your paces. Anyway, the best of luck, and if you are still around on Friday afternoon, catch up with me at lunchtime in the Mess and we'll run over to Bulford rifle ranges in the afternoon. I've got an ETR booked with a couple of the other guys, and if you'd like to put in a bit of target practice, you would be more than welcome to join us. I'll book us out rifles and some ammo, and you can see if you have lost any of your sniping skills!"

"I'm on for that," answered KB. "But what are you doing around here at the moment anyway?"

"On hold for another assignment at the moment, but to keep myself occupied I'm doing a course in Arabic over at the Linguistics Centre. I'm hoping it will gain me a few brownie points and it will look good on my record. I have a pad here which is really convenient and I use the Mess facilities all the time. Anyway, I'll leave you to continue stuffing your face, and we'll catch up later."

Shortly after his friend departed, KB finished his breakfast and returning to his room, read through his statement and the letter once again, and replacing his sweater with his blazer, checked his appearance in front of the mirror. The sutures were still in place and looking clean and tidy, so after carefully running a comb through his hair, he left for the Administration Building.

Five minutes later he was collected from the Reception Area by a smart young brunette who introduced herself as Mr Reynard's secretary. Handing her the envelope with his signed statement, he then followed her upstairs where he was ushered into a spacious room whose walls were lined with bookcases in the centre of which was a large polished oak table.

Around the table were eight upright chairs, their light green leather upholstery complementing the darker shade of the carpet. In the middle of the table sat a tray with two bottles of spring water and half a dozen glass tumblers and in front of three places on one side of the table, and a single place on the other, a writing pad and pencil had been placed.

Pulling back the chair behind the single place, the secretary invited KB to sit down and after informing him that 'the others' would be arriving shortly, left him alone with his thoughts.

For a moment a feeling of nervousness gripped him. This was like waiting for a Headmaster's interview at school, or for his Senior NCO's selection board to convene. Was he about to make the right decision? Could he pass the medical? Would his artificial leg allow him to meet the challenge of working in the field for the Agency?

As he sat turning these questions over in his mind, the door opened and Colin Hunter came in.

"KB, good to see you again," the older man said, giving him a warm handshake. "So sorry to hear about Peter Bowen. I know you guys had established a really sound working relationship as well as becoming friends. I have read your statement, and if it is any consolation, I believe you acted entirely properly. The primary purpose of Peter's assignment was to protect the Prince, and with your help he achieved it. Well done incidentally, on nailing one of the ambushers. We don't deliberately go looking for trouble, but when it does present itself we expect all our Operatives to meet it head on, and that's exactly what you and Peter did."

As Colin moved around to sit in one of the chairs across from KB, the door opened again admitting Bill Hutchinson, and a short, bespectacled, balding man followed him in.

"KB, this is Andy Reynard, our Head of Operations," said Hutchinson, allowing them to shake hands. "He is in the chair for this morning's meeting, but I can promise you it will be kept at a fairly informal level. Colin and I are here to see fair play, so please relax and feel free to take off your jacket if you would feel more comfortable."

"Thank you for coming over, and we'll keep this as brief as we can," Reynard interjected, sharp grey eyes scrutinizing KB from behind his half-moon glasses, "but as you will appreciate, we need to get to know you thoroughly and I'm afraid there are bound to be a lot of questions. On that score we would encourage you to put any queries to us that you need answers to, so don't hesitate to fire away at us at any time. By the way, I understand you are generally called KB. If it's alright with you, I'll do the same?"

With that, Reynard took his place between the two Section Leaders and opening up folders that they had taken from their briefcases, the interview began.

An hour and a half passed before Reynard called for a coffee break, by the end of which KB was beginning to feel that there were no parts of his life or a single corner left in his Army career that had not been scrutinized by the three men interviewing him.

When they sat down again, KB was relieved when the Head of Operations announced that they were in the final lap, and allowed himself to relax a little when the focus of their questions turned away from himself personally and became directed towards national affairs and in particular his opinion on the current terrorist threat from extremists.

"What are your feelings towards those who ambushed you and murdered FO Bowen?" Reynard asked, looking KB straight in the eye.

Pausing for a moment to concentrate on giving a considered answer to what was quite clearly a key question, KB replied, "I recognize that I may never have the opportunity to confront these men again, but if that were to happen and they were threatening other lives, mine included, I would not hesitate to take the same action as I did in dealing with Peter's killer, assuming that I had the means at my disposal to do this."

"Would you not consider offering them the chance to surrender to you?" insisted Reynard.

"That depends on the circumstances," countered KB. "It is my belief that most of these guys are fanatics, and the behaviour of jihadists to date in any confrontation, whether or not events are going in their favour, is to shoot regardless of their own safety. Equally they will not hesitate to gun down any of those around them, whether they are innocent bystanders, hostages or the opposing security forces. They go into any situation quite prepared to die for their beliefs, so I'm certainly not going to shake them by the hand and suggest they come quietly unless I have something fairly solid that will stop an AK-47 round between me and them."

"Okay, you've made your point. You have clearly formulated your own opinion as to the ethics and morality of these people, which I will admit, is probably shared by the three of us here and most of our Field Operatives. Here's one final scenario for you. You are a Section Leader about to retire, or maybe you have been promoted. You have two FOs working for you who are both likely candidates to fill your shoes. One is keen, energetic, always willing to go the extra mile and popular with his colleagues. His weakness however, is that he is not necessarily the brightest spark in the fireplace.

"The second man is highly intelligent, but a maverick. He tends to be lazy but from time to time comes up with solutions to problems that even surprise you. He tolerates your supervision, but is a bit of a loner and not that popular with his fellow FOs. Which one do you choose?"

"I'd choose the second candidate for several reasons," responded KB. "First of all if he was still showing signs of laziness having been under my supervision for some time, it would indicate that I had not been doing my job properly, so if he were a serious contender I would have already satisfied myself that this was no longer an issue. If laziness had been a problem and he had not responded to my warnings, I would have kicked his ass out of the door a long time before.

"Secondly, mavericks are those who habitually challenge established protocols, but this is not necessarily a bad thing, and if he is highly intelligent to boot he is more likely to come up with solutions to problems that are outside the box. I would have thought that in counterterrorist operations this would be a positive. Next, even if he is a loner he is clearly intelligent enough to realize that with the added responsibility he seeks, he has no option but to adapt to working within a team environment. Finally to be a leader you do not have to be popular, the most important thing is to earn your team's respect."

"Hmm, interesting," Reynard commented. "Just one more thing before I ask you to leave us, and this does not relate to you personally. Did you know of Peter Bowen's involvement with your sister Hannah, and if so, were you aware if they had made any long term commitments to each other?"

"It was quite obvious that they were seriously attracted to each other," KB answered. "And I know that Peter had every intention of carrying on their relationship, which my sister certainly encouraged. I should point out that Hannah is a mature woman who has never involved herself in fleeting romances and has always been very careful in her choice of boyfriends. I believe that had circumstances been different, there was a very high probability that their relationship would have developed into something permanent."

"Thank you, KB," Reynard concluded. "I have no further questions, how about you Bill and Colin?"

"Nothing more from me," Hutchinson replied. "Me neither," added Colin Hunter.

"So is there anything else you would like to ask us?"

"One thing, sir," said KB, "I have been in touch with my local Army Reserve Unit, the Wessex Rifles at Exeter, and they have offered me a staff position as a Small Arms Instructor and also to form a Sniper Section. I would do this on a part time basis of course, like any Reserve soldier, and this would involve me in one or two training nights a week, perhaps two training weekends a month and an annual two week camp. Would it be possible to do this if I accepted your offer?"

"Obviously any of our Operatives are entitled to time off," Reynard commented. "And what they do in that time is, within reason, entirely up to them. However, part of this job is that you are on call 24/7 and I would hate to think you were off in the wilds for a weekend somewhere with the Reserves should we require your services at a moment's notice. You may also find that from time to time the pressure of working with us is such that when you do get the opportunity for a break, the last thing you will feel like doing is what virtually amounts to a second job. However, let me discuss that with my colleagues, and if you would leave us now and wait for us outside, I think we should be able to give you an answer very shortly."

Leaving the three men to their deliberations, KB closed the door of the library behind him and found a bench seat under a window a few yards down the corridor.

His wait was mercifully short, and barely ten minutes had passed before Colin popped his head around the door and beckoned to him to return. Once again taking his seat in front of them, Reynard cleared his throat.

"Well, KB, thank you again for your time this morning and I am pleased to say that, subject to the outcome of your medical and your successful completion of our indoctrination course, we would like to offer you a position as a Grade Three Field Operative as outlined in my letter to you. Your general responsibilities will be surveillance, the gathering of information, and if so instructed – specific target neutralisation, where your training as a sniper will serve you well.. You may also be called upon to assist with close quarter protection for VIPs, and precise details and requirements for each assignment will be provided at your pre-mission briefings.

"If you accept, as all three of us hope you will, I will make an appointment for you to attend the Medical Centre this afternoon. We already have your medical records to hand, so I am hoping that this will be no more than a formality. If all is well, you will then report to our Personnel Department on the ground floor of this building at 0830 hours tomorrow morning for all the paperwork to be completed, and you will be issued with an ID card. I am told that the repairs to your pick-up truck will be completed shortly and it should be ready for you to collect from our workshops on Saturday morning.

"Whilst on assignment, you will of course be allocated an Agency vehicle, but we will be fitting a satellite tracking device to your vehicle that will enable us to keep an eye on you even when you are off-duty, I hope that will be in order?"

"Not a problem, sir," KB replied.

"On the matter of your potential involvement with The Wessex Rifles, we do have a precedent for some of our Operatives serving with the Reserves so we are prepared to give you a qualified 'yes' to your involvement, but only under the clear understanding that your commitment to us has to be one hundred percent 24/7. In fact we must insist that you keep your Section Leader fully informed of all training activities in which the Rifles expect you to participate, and the ultimate decision as to whether or not you attend any part of their training programme must be his. Do I make myself clear?"

"Absolutely, sir," came KB's immediate response.

"Good. I will be contacting the CO of The Rifles to make him aware of the situation, and if he is still keen to have you join them, the rest is up to you. That's about it from us, and unless you have any other questions, as from now, subject to the outcome of your medical, you are formally a member of our team. We'll need you here on Monday next week when you will undertake a four week basic indoctrination course, and after the Christmas break we will review what other courses may be available to you. After that we will brief you on your first assignment should we have one for you, or you will go on standby until such need or a vacancy on a suitable course arises. Is there anything else you need to know?"

"No, I think you have covered everything and I'd certainly like to accept your offer as long as everything is okay with the medical," said KB at which they stood up from their places around the table, and after handshakes all round KB was left with Colin Hunter.

"Well done, KB, welcome on board," the Section Leader said warmly. "I've already told Andy that I'd like you on my team, so hopefully we will be working together. I'll take you over to the Medical Centre now and confirm your appointment, although you've already been there I see – did you get that in the ambush?" he added, pointing at KB's head.

"Yes, I believe so," KB replied touching his bandage. "Almost certainly a shard of glass from the side window when it shattered, and I didn't notice it until I went to wash my hair yesterday."

Calling in at the Medical Centre, KB was greeted by the same Sister who had dressed his cut for him, and noting that his appointment was at two thirty that afternoon, left Colin to return to his office, while he made his way back to the Mess.

In the lobby he crossed to one of the telephone booths and dialled the pub number. As he was connected he heard a distinct tell-tale click on the handset, indicating that the call was being recorded and a split second later Jack was on the line. Keeping his conversation as brief as possible, he told his father that he would try to get home for the weekend and would catch up with his news then, and rang off before he was led into answering any questions.

Finding that the bar had opened, he ordered a mineral water with ice and lemon and a round of roast beef and horseradish sandwiches, and then sat down in one of the armchairs with a newspaper to pass the time until his medical.

Back at the Medical Centre he was shown into a large examination room as soon as he arrived, to be greeted by the Sister and a white coated Army doctor from behind a desk, whose shoulder slides carried the crown insignia of a Major.

Once seated in front of the officer, no time was wasted in answering a questionnaire and then in a small cubicle he stripped down to his underpants and submitted himself to what was he remembered, a standard service medical. He then found himself providing blood and urine samples, and a swab for DNA testing was taken by the nurse.

"I see you are keeping yourself in good shape, Mr Blake," commented the

Doctor as he completed his routine checks. "Now jump on the treadmill and let's see how that leg of yours copes with a bit of strenuous exercise. We'll start off at a fairly normal walking pace and gradually increase the speed. Let me know when you feel things could be getting out of control."

With some reluctance, but bowing to the inevitable, KB hoisted himself onto the machine and with the Doctor standing on one side of him and the Sister on the other, the machine was turned on and the treadmill began to move slowly under his feet.

At Headley Court he had managed a slow jog on a similar machine, but that had been some months ago now and after days of practice. Focussing on keeping his balance he was managing the increases in speed well until a slight stumble threw him slightly to one side and before the Doctor could hit the stop button he was propelled backwards, and toppling over landed on the rubber foam mat behind the treadmill in an undignified heap.

Helped by the Doctor he was soon back on his feet, and after a moment to regain his equilibrium managed to walk unaided back to the desk where he sat down to regain his breath.

"No bones broken and sorry for the fall, but I was expecting you to call time long before you bailed out. I must say," the Doctor continued, "that is an impressive bit of kit you have been fitted with. First time I have seen one of the new models, and you certainly broke the speed record on the machine for prosthetic users. I am going to make my comments on my report accordingly, but overall you are a picture of fitness."

Returning to the entrance to the Centre, there was another surprise in store. Standing by an Army Land Rover stood a grey haired Warrant Officer in combats, who intercepted him as he stepped outside.

"Mr Blake?" he asked, and when KB acknowledged that he was, the man continued, "I'm Warrant Officer Greenaway, I was told I would find you here. If you would like to hop on board, I'll run you over to the indoor ranges. I have been told you need clearance on the Glock, so I'll put you through your paces!"

Opening the passenger door for KB, he waited for KB to climb in.

"Gammy leg?" asked the man, watching as KB had lifted his left leg over the high sill of the 4 x 4.

"I was with the Paras in Afghanistan and fell foul of one of the Taliban's IEDs," KB replied.

"I'm an ex-Para myself," volunteered the Warrant, as he took his seat behind the wheel. "Did ten years in the Regiment and then transferred to the

Ordinance Corps after I buggered up my back. We were doing a tactical jump at night on a winter exercise in Norway when one of my mates hit the top of my canopy and took my air, so I thundered in from about forty feet up. Could have been a lot worse if I hadn't landed in a snow bank. Of course, Ordinance is now part of the Logistics Corps, but I have no complaints. This is a good number here, and I only have fifteen months to go before I pull my pension. How about you?"

"This is a totally new venture for me," said KB. "And I'm not quite sure what to expect at the moment!"

"I don't ask what you guys get up to," chuckled Greenaway, as he parked the Land Rover in front of a low, windowless concrete building, "but I have seen an increasing number come through here in recent months. Anyway, let's get you familiar with Mr Glock's brilliant piece of kit, although I guess you have probably been introduced to the 17 already?"

"Came across them in Helmand," agreed KB. "But they were scarcer than hen's teeth when I was out there, and most of them were in the hands of senior officers and very senior NCO's. We still carried the old Browning Hi-Power, but I never found myself in a situation where I had to use mine."

"Probably just as well," commented his companion, as he unlocked the outer door to the building. "Not a bad weapon, but not a lot of stopping power, so you will see quite a difference with the Glock."

"I already have," muttered KB to himself, as he followed Greenaway into the darkened ante room of the indoor range.

Flicking on the switches from a panel inside the door, the interior of the building became swathed in light from the overhead fluorescent tubes, and the Warrant moved to a second panel and quickly punched in a series of numbers on a keypad.

"Must disable the alarm," he said to KB, "otherwise we'll have every red cap for miles turning up at the front door." Beckoning to KB to follow him, he unlocked a second door and they entered a larger room furnished with two long wooden benches and half-a-dozen plywood seated and backed stacking chairs. On the longer side of the room facing them was a half concrete block wall glassed to the ceiling, through which KB could see a firing point with four positions each one looking down its own 25 metre lane. The lanes culminated in a sand pit which sloped upwards to the low ceiling, contained by railway sleepers from behind which four targets had been mounted on upright supports.

A third of the room in which they stood had been partitioned off by another heavy concrete block wall, into which a solid metal door had been set, similar to the high level security type found in bank vaults. As KB watched the Warrant inserted yet another key into the centre of the wheel which protruded from the middle of the door, and spinning it to release the security bolts, swung the door open.

Disappearing inside, he re-emerged a few minutes later carrying a large box and several cartons of 9 mm ammunition. Opening the box, the Warrant removed a Glock pistol and laid it on one of the tables.

In a few seconds he had field stripped the weapon and laid its component parts neatly in front of KB.

"This is a Generation 4 Glock 17 pistol," he explained. "Known to the British Forces as the L131A1. The weapon is unusual in that it has a polymer frame, which gained it the nickname of the 'plastic pistol', but don't let that fool you, it's a pretty rugged piece of kit.

"The weapon is a short recoil operated, locked breech, semi-automatic and can take a variety of magazines. The standard is a 17 round mag of which you will be issued with two. There is also a 10 round mag which gives you a lighter alternative for carrying on an everyday basis – again you will get two of these – and finally a 30 round mag of which you will get one. You will also be issued with a white light attachment for night use with an optional laser sight, and I will show you how to attach and use these later. You may also have occasion to be issued with a full infrared light and laser sight which are used in conjunction with night vision opticals, but for the time being we will concentrate on the version you will be getting now. You will also be getting a standard Glock polymer holster which you can adapt to wear as a belt or shoulder harness.

"You may be interested to know, that Glock have also developed a fully automatic version of the 17, which can be fitted with a lightweight shoulder stock and a double rotary magazine. I haven't seen one yet, but I believe it is quite awesome. Anyway," he concluded, "let's get you started."

The next half hour was spent with KB stripping and re-assembling the pistol and going through the basic handling drills most of which were all too familiar.

"Okay, that's enough for now," said Greenaway. "When you have a chance, put in some practice on your own, but for the time being, you'll do. Now pick up the weapon and those ear defenders and follow me. We'll see if you can hit anything on the range."

Following the Warrant through a side door and onto the firing point, KB waited while he took two fresh figure sized paper cut-out targets and a pot of glue from a steel cabinet and followed him down to the butts where he pasted them over the targets that had been used by the previous shooters.

The targets depicted a full life size figure of a masked man in a black loose fitting uniform holding an AK-47 and charging towards the viewer. "A far cry from the old Figure 11 targets I shot during my Army days which had depicted a helmeted soldier." KB thought to himself, as Greenaway finished and stepped back to inspect his handiwork.

Back on the firing point under the eagle eye of his mentor, KB loaded four 10 round magazines and slipping them into his trouser pocket, hung his ear defenders around his neck and followed the Warrant back to the 10 metre firing point.

"Right Mr Blake," came the instructions as Greenaway took up a position slightly to the left and rear of him. "I want you to fire one magazine holding the weapon single handed from the standing position at the left hand target to your front, then reload and fire a second magazine double handed at the right hand target. On with your ear defenders, and in your own time, carry on!"

Snapping a loaded magazine into the automatic pistol's grip, KB cocked the weapon, slipped off the safety catch and leaning forward slightly with his left hand behind his back, took aim at the upper centre of the target and squeezed off his first shot. The shot hit the target slightly to the right and below his aiming point, and adjusting his aiming point to compensate, fired off the remainder of the rounds.

Ejecting the magazine he reloaded, and with his left hand now cupped around his right, crouched down and moved his sights onto the second target.

As the last shot rang out a steady voice from the Warrant to his rear instructed him, "Unload and clear the weapon." With the breech open, Greenaway confirmed that the Glock was safe and the two of them walked forward to examine the targets.

"Not bad for a first attempt," came the comment from the Warrant. "Quite a spread on the first target, but a decent group on the second. It looks as if you are over compensating slightly for muzzle rise. Don't forget the Glock has a much shorter recoil than the Browning you are used to, so the barrel will remain much closer to your aiming point after each shot, but so far, so good. Now let's go back to the 15 metre firing point and repeat the exercise. We'll do the same from 20 and 25 metres, and then do the whole run over again rapid fire against the clock."

Under Greenaway's tutelage KB found himself repeating a number of practices including several using the white light and laser sight with the range blacked out, so it was over an hour later and some 200 rounds fired before they finished the practice, and KB had stripped and cleaned the weapon.

"Well done, young man," came the comment from his Instructor, as he completed his notes. "I'm happy to say that you are safe enough to be let loose with the pistol, but be warned the 'do's and don'ts' of when you can and cannot legitimately pull the weapon on duty will be well and truly rammed home to you before you complete your course. In the meantime, I've made a note of the serial number of the weapon you used today, and once you have officially signed on tomorrow and picked up your permit and ID card, you can drop by and pick it up. Now I'll run you back to the Mess."

As he got out of the Land Rover at the entrance to the Mess, he was hailed by Colin Hunter who crossed the road to greet him.

"Hi, KB, got something here to show you," he said, patting the laptop he was carrying under his arm. "Let's grab a pint in the bar, and you can let me have your ideas."

Once settled into their chairs, and with their drinks in front of them, Colin flipped open the laptop and after a few seconds keying in data, moved the laptop across to KB.

On the black and white screen, images appeared of a large parking lot, and after several cars had arrived and left, none of which KB recognized, the familiar shape of a silver BMW came into view. After parking the vehicle in a vacant bay, the driver and a passenger got out and moved to the rear of the car, where the boot was opened and each man removed a carry-all.

Pausing to talk to each other for a few moments, KB easily recognized Asif as being the shorter of the two. Closing the boot, the taller man clapped Asif on the shoulder and turned to walk away, Asif moving off in a different direction. The picture changed to a different part of the car park, and Asif could be clearly seen climbing into a black Nissan before driving away. Another change in camera picked up his companion at the ticket counter at what appeared to be a railway station.

"The CCTV cameras were in the long term car park and the booking office at Exeter St David's Railway Station," said Colin. "We also have a shot approximately a week earlier of the guy in the BMW picking Asif up from the car park where he obviously left the Nissan prior to catching up with you guys in Somerset. We know the BMW driver bought a single ticket to Birmingham New Street. We were lucky to get our hands on the footage so quickly. After the BMW took off from the encounter with you in Wells, the Police circulated the number and one particularly bright young bobby noticed it in the station parking lot while doing a routine check for stolen vehicles, otherwise it could have been weeks before the Railway authorities reported it as abandoned. What do you make of it?"

Settling back in his chair, KB sipped his beer and after thinking for a moment, replied.

"After we spooked them in the car park at Wells, they probably realised the boys in blue would be looking out for the car on the motorways, so as Asif had to be dropped off in Exeter anyway to pick up the Nissan, the driver probably thought it wiser to ditch the BMW there and take the train back to Brum, rather than risk being picked up. They could have driven from Wells back to Ilchester to pick up their bags from the hotel where we are pretty certain they were staying, and then on to Exeter via the side roads avoiding the M5, so the risk was minimal – but one thing still puzzles me."

"So far I think you are probably right on the button," said Colin. "But what's your query?"

"What was Asif up to and where did he go from the time he was dropped off in Exeter on the Friday, and when he showed up at our cottage at college on the Monday?"

"Good point," said Colin. "Any chance he could have turned up at the cottage early, let himself in and just waited the time out until you showed up after the weekend?"

"Don't think so," KB replied. "Mrs Cousins didn't mention it, and there was no food in the cottage, as he and Peter had to go into Launceston on the Monday to buy groceries, but I suppose he could have been living off take-aways."

"It's certainly worth checking out with the Cousins," agreed Colin. "And we'll follow through with a few enquiries. We also have the identity of the guy you nailed. It seems that he has been on our radar for some time as a known extremist, but slipped off a few months ago and the indications were that he had gone to Syria. If that's the case, the so-called Islamic State boys probably trained him and somehow he got back into the UK under the wire. Anyway, that's enough shop talk, how did you get on with Warrant Greenaway in the range this afternoon?"

"He seemed quite pleased with my performance and signed me off on the Glock. I'm due to see him tomorrow afternoon to pick up the weapon, after all the other formalities have been dealt with."

“You’re due at the Admin Block at 0900 hours to complete the paperwork,” Colin reminded him. “What are your plans for the rest of the day?”

“Fred’s booked an ETR in the afternoon, so I said I’d join him for some target practice, then as soon as my truck is ready and if it’s alright with you I’ll head for home and then back here on Monday for the start of my indoctrination course?”

Taking his mobile out of his pocket, Colin keyed in a number and spoke briefly. After a lengthy response from the recipient, he ended the call and turned back to KB.

“Work on your truck is almost finished and Transport Section will drop it off for you at the Admin block tomorrow morning. On Andy’s instructions, it has been fitted with a tracker, which you can activate at any time and our Control Centre at GCHQ will have a fix on you immediately. The system will also allow you to activate a voice mode so that anything you say or any conversation going on in the cab will also be transmitted to us through a secure scrambled signal satellite link. Technically you need only use the tracker/voice recorder if you are using the vehicle for work, but my advice is at least keep the tracker on at all times. We can also contact you via the wireless system, but you will only be able to receive incoming calls from us through an earphone for obvious reasons. The vehicle has also been fitted with an upgraded standard hands-free Bluetooth system to link to your mobile for your everyday use, but don’t forget this is not a secure system and your calls can be monitored easily by anyone. Anyway, I am sure the mechanic from Transport will give you a full briefing when they hand the truck back to you tomorrow.”

“No ejector seats, smoke dispensers and machine guns behind the headlights, then?” said KB wryly.

“ ’Fraid not,” came the curt reply. “And no licence to kill indiscriminately either! Just remember above all, you can do your job best by maintaining the lowest possible profile at all times. We don’t condone any form of glory hunting and if your face ever appears on the front page of any daily tabloid, you have not only failed but you will be out through the door and down the road before you have time to wonder what hit you. Having said that, we will back you one hundred percent at all times, be open and frank with us regardless of any predicament you may find yourself in, and we will protect your ass. Start playing the loner game, and pretty soon you will find your job is much harder. One final thing, it’s fine by me if you go home for the weekend and I presume you will be breaking the news of Peter’s death to your family?”

"I must," KB replied. "I'm sure Hannah will have been trying to contact Peter, and if I don't tell her she is going to start asking all sorts of questions."

"I don't have to tell you that for the time being anyway, you won't be able to give her any of the true facts surrounding the incident," said Colin. "My advice would be to come up with a story that is believable without being over dramatic. Above all keep it simple, too much detail will only cause added speculation on her part, and that you don't need. Anyway, enough of the lecture," he concluded with a sympathetic smile, "I'm sure you'll know what to say, but I don't envy you. Let's have another beer and then I'll leave you to your own devices."

Chapter Twenty-Two

A Test of Arms

"For when the one Great Scorer comes
To write against your name,
He marks – not that you won or lost –
But how you played the game."

Grantland Rice, 1880-1954

After a quiet evening in the Mess playing pool with Fred and catching up on the news on TV, KB awoke from a slightly better night's sleep and after breakfast presented himself at the Admin block for the final stages of his enrolment as a Field Operative.

After having his fingerprints and photo taken, he found himself confronted with a number of forms to fill out after which he was interviewed by an officer from the finance section who provided him with details of his salary, expense claim procedures, life insurance cover and pension rights. Up to that point, it had not occurred to KB to ask about his remuneration, and he was pleasantly surprised to learn that his salary was significantly higher than his previous pay rate as a Sergeant in the Paras. With his pension from the Army, plus any pay he received from time he put in with The Wessex Rifles, he would be comparatively well off, and certainly earning a lot more than he would have done if had he completed his course at Tamar Valley College and had found a job in Estate Management.

The hours dragged by and it was approaching noon by the time the formalities were completed, and he was handed a black leather wallet inside which his ID card was displayed and containing his side arm's permit and vehicle pass for the Bulford complex. The photo on the card stared back at him from behind its clear plastic window, cold and expressionless, while the card itself identified the bearer as being a member of the United Kingdom's Combined Counter Terrorist Agency, Ministry of Defence, Field Section. With a slight smile, the otherwise dry and somewhat officious young clerk who had conducted the final session with KB, had told him that his Field Operative's cover name would be 'Sirius'. When he asked the clerk how names were allocated, he was told that all Agency Operatives were given names from ancient mythology, adding that that Sirius was the Greek name for the Dog Star. He also provided KB with a short list of other Agency cover names which he insisted KB memorized, emphasizing that these were Operatives with whom KB was most likely to be working with, and others would be provided on a 'need to know' basis.

There were only four cover names to be confined to his memory immediately. Colin Hunter was listed as 'Hector', Bill Hutchinson as 'Leander', Fred Nowakowski as 'Centaur' and Andrew Reynard as 'Minos'. In addition, Headquarters was to be referred to as 'Olympus' in any radio or telephone transmissions.

Feeling Rocky would approve of his Agency title, KB returned the list to the clerk and returned to the reception area, where an overall clad woman in her early late twenties crossed the foyer to greet him.

"Mr Blake?" she asked.

"That's me," KB replied.

"Hello, I'm Senior Vehicle Technician Laura Majors. I have your vehicle for you, if you could just show me your ID."

Smiling inwardly, he produced the pristine black wallet and showed it to the girl, realising that this was probably the first time of many to come when he would be required to identify himself.

As the two left the building the early gloom of the November morning on Salisbury Plain had lifted and although a chill wind still blew in from the east, as they rounded the building to enter the car park the sun broke through slanting down onto the parked vehicles.

Majors had parked his truck at the end of a line of cars and 4 x 4's, and stood slightly apart from its nearest neighbour, gleaming from what had clearly been a recent wash and polish job. Opening the driver's door the girl waved KB in behind the steering wheel, and then climbed into the passenger's seat beside him.

Forewarned by the previous afternoon's conversation with Colin Hunter,

KB was ready for the briefing, but still listened intently as the girl went through the operating procedures for the tracking device and the secure radio transmitting and receiving system. Expecting to have to press some kind of concealed button to activate the systems, KB was surprised when he was shown a small five centimetre square matt black panel that had been installed and was almost invisible, on the fascia panel to the right of the steering wheel.

"The systems are activated by thumb and finger imprints on that panel," explained the Technician. "Thumb print only for activating the tracker, and index finger for the communications system. Use your thumb and index finger print in sequence to activate both, and the same to switch the systems off."

Taking what looked like a mobile phone out of one of the breast pockets of her overalls, she continued. "Now let's go through a full sequence and I'll register your prints on the system."

Following her instructions carefully and with the systems now recognizing KB's input, the girl showed him the hidden receiver in the sun visor which would pick up and transmit any conversations within the cab, and the earphone and cable stored behind the visor's vanity mirror.

"We've made one further modification," added the girl. "If you look down at the compartment at the base of the driver's door, you will notice that half of it is now taken up with what appears to be a storage box for CD's. Again you will see a similar square panel to the one that activates the other systems. Press your thumb against it and the top cover will open. The interior has a spring loaded container which will hold your side arm, and when opened the weapon will be ejected into your hand. This enables you to store the weapon safely while you are driving, as wearing a shoulder or waist band holster is not always convenient, and this will still provide you with instant access to it. These systems are secure in so much as they are limit access to you only, but I should mention that we have the means to override them if necessary.

"The original lock on the glove compartment has also been replaced with a double drop lock, the keys for which are on your key ring. The doors locks have also been replaced, and to activate them from the remote on your key ring, you now have to press the button twice to both lock and unlock the vehicle. If you forget and only press once within thirty seconds it will set off the car alarm, and to cancel the alarm you will have to insert the key in the driver's door lock and half turn it twice to the rear. In addition to the alarm going off, if the tracker is on, it will signal at our Control Centre that someone is attempting to force an entry, and you will be called immediately on your mobile. If you fail to respond to the call, a full scale alert will be initiated and the cavalry will be on their way.

"Finally, when she is due for a service, bring her into us. We don't want any mechanic from a Ford agency getting curious and fiddling around with any of the kit we have added. Now, give me your mobile so that I can programme it into blue tooth for your everyday 'hands-off' use and then we can do a walk-around of the vehicle so you can see if we have done an acceptable job on the repairs."

A careful inspection showed no signs of any of the damage sustained in the shooting and after thanking the girl for her time and the work done by her Section, he dropped her off at the workshops and drove round to the pistol range where he found Warrant Officer Greenaway waiting for him.

"Made it through the paperwork then!" the soldier greeted him. "Let's see your permit, then you can sign out the Glock and you can be on your way."

The Warrant had already laid out the weapon on the table in the ante room next to the weapons lock-up, and with it the spare magazines, night sight and holster he had been promised. KB also noticed that two 50 round boxes of ammunition had been placed on the table.

Seeing KB's attention had been drawn to these, Greenaway added, "You are supposed to be able to account for every round you fire, including any practices on ranges away from here. Any time you are up here for briefings or training, we encourage you to drop by for a practice shoot, which will also enable me to make sure you are kept current on the weapon.

"You are expected to make yourself available for a minimum of four supervised practices a year, so don't leave these until the last moment. Now, if you'll double check the serial number on the weapon with the number I have entered on the file, you can sign off against it and we are done."

Thanking the Warrant for his help, KB replaced the weapon and magazines back in the box Greenaway had provided, picked it up with the holster and slipping the two boxes of ammunition into his jacket pocket, retraced his steps to the pick-up. Once inside the cab, he took out the automatic and a ten round magazine, and loaded it. Without cocking the weapon, he made sure the safety catch was on and opening the storage compartment in the driver's door, slotted it into the recess, pressed it down until it clicked home and re-closed the cover.

The remaining magazines and boxes of ammo he locked away in the glove compartment, and placing the holster in the now nearly empty box with the night sight, stashed it away under the back seat.

It was now approaching lunchtime and on entering the Mess he checked his pigeon hole in the mail box and was surprised to find an envelope there. Opening it, he found a hand written note from Colin Hunter notifying him that Peter's funeral would take place at Salisbury Crematorium the following Wednesday at 2.30 p.m. and that he was invited to attend.

Slipping the note inside his jacket pocket, he walked through to the bar where he found Fred and two others waiting for him.

All three rose from their table as he crossed the room to meet them, and Fred wasted no time in making the introductions.

"KB these are two good friends of mine, Angus Fraser more commonly known to us as Scotty as he has hails from north of the border. Scotty is another FO, and ex-Highland Regiment, and his claim to fame is that he has done time on the North Sea oil rigs, and this is Charlie Carstairs who is a former banker and now works between here and GCHQ on all sorts of mumbo jumbo to do with the movement of large sums of money, so when you are setting up your offshore bank account to squirrel away your ill-gotten gains, Charlie is your man."

"Good to meet you guys," responded KB, shaking hands first with the tousled haired Scotsman, who KB reckoned could not stand more than five foot six in his bare feet, and then the taller lanky ex-banker whose firm handshake indicated a physical strength that his slight frame belied. The man's greying hair indicated that he was by far the most senior of the group in age and KB put him in his early fifties.

"Let me get you a drink," Charlie suggested. "We're all on weak shandy as we are handling some lethal weaponry this afternoon, is that okay with you?"

"Fine," KB agreed. Sitting down in the vacant chair, he turned to his friend and asked, "Did you get a note about Peter's funeral?"

"Yes. We'll all be there. Peter was pretty popular around here and there is bound to be a good turn-out."

"Do you think there would be any objections if my sister attended?" KB continued. "I have to break the news to her this weekend, and I know she would never forgive me if she did not have a chance to say goodbye to him."

"Can't see that there could be any objections," said Fred. "We know he didn't have any close family and the powers that be are fully aware that she was in a relationship with Peter."

Charlie returned from the bar with KB's pint and turning to Fred asked, "What's the form for this afternoon, Fred?"

"Us two snipers are going to find out if you guys are any good with a rifle," Fred responded with a grin. "As you know, I've booked an Electric Target Range and thanks to the help of our Warrant Greenaway, have managed to borrow four Sharpshooter rifles and purloin a vast amount of ammo for a wee test of marksmanship.

"I don't know if you came across the Sharpshooter when you were in Helmand, KB, but it's quite a neat bit of kit. It fires the NATO 7.62 mm round from a ten shot mag and it's semi-automatic. Effective out to about 700 metres and the idea was to provide our lads with something that could take on the Taliban at longer ranges than the standard L85A2, which as you know, is an assault rifle at its best within around 200 metres."

"I heard about the Sharpshooter, but never saw one before I left," KB admitted. "So I'm looking forward to firing it."

"Sounds a bit like the old FN pattern rifle," commented the ex-banker.

"Pretty much," Fred agreed, "but a tad more sophisticated. This baby has optical sights and a weird kind of hand grip for firing from the standing or kneeling position, but the whole package actually works pretty well. Anyway, let's order up some sandwiches, I told Greenaway we'd meet him at the ranges at 1400 hours and you still need to change out of your jacket and slacks, KB, no point in crawling around a firing point in your Sunday best."

Lunch finished and KB now attired in jeans and a heavy sweater, the four men piled into Fred's Land Rover Discovery and headed out to the ranges where the Warrant Officer had already laid out the four rifles and was busy opening a case of ammunition.

After a briefing on handling the weapon, they loaded up two magazines apiece and settled down on the firing point to zero in their own rifle.

It was many months since KB had fired any kind of rifle and he relished the solid feel of the butt plate tucked into his shoulder and the comforting thump from the recoil as he squeezed off his rounds at the two Figure 11 targets set up 200 metres down the range.

When all four shooters had finished zeroing, Greenaway announced that they would fire a series of snap and rapid fire practices at different ranges using drop down targets out to 300 metres. By the time they had finished Greenaway had opened the second box of ammunition and announced that they would take a break and fire the final practice at 600 metres.

"Let's make the last shoot a bit more interesting," Fred suggested, as the four gathered to compare notes. "I suggest £20 each into the kitty, winner picks up £50 and we give Warrant Greenaway £30 to have a drink with us this evening, what do you say?"

"Sounds good to me," Charlie Carstairs said. "Is that okay with you guys?"

With KB and the Scotsman also in agreement, they each dug a £20 note from their wallets and handed it to Fred, as Greenaway came up to join them.

"Right gentlemen, here's the practice. Two figure 11 targets at 400 metres, two ten round magazines, ten shots at each target. To make it more interesting, you will leave your weapons on the firing point, safety catch on, magazines off. You will then take up a position twenty metres behind the firing point, and on my command run forward, adopt the prone position, load your weapon and commence firing. Targets will drop after forty-five seconds. Any questions?"

"If there is a tie, Warrant?" questioned Fred.

"Believe me, sir, there won't be," came the reply. "So if there is nothing else, lay your weapons and magazines on your firing position and join me behind the firing point."

At six hundred metres the Figure 11 targets, each depicting a life-sized armed infantryman charging towards the firers looked tiny, but the three ex-servicemen seemed unconcerned at this challenge and if the ex-banker was worried, he was not showing it.

"On my whistle, gents," said the Warrant, taking the time honoured Acme Thunderer on its lanyard from the vest pocket of his combat jacket.

As the shrill blast reverberated across the ranges the four shooters hurled themselves forward and charged the twenty metres to where their weapons lay. Although only a short sprint, KB found himself falling behind his fellow competitors, but ignoring this widening gap he concentrated on maintaining as fast a pace as his artificial leg permitted, but even so all three were lying and loading their rifles by the time he flung himself down beside them.

With one quick but deliberate movement he slotted home the magazine, cradled the weapon into his shoulder, cocked it and easing off the safety catch, took careful aim and squeezed off nine shots at the distant target, leaving one in the breech. Replacing the empty magazine he fired his final round at the left hand target and resumed firing at the right hand Figure 11. Within a split second of his last shot, the targets disappeared, and breathing a sigh of relief he removed the empty magazine, cleared his weapon and locked on the safety catch.

"Clear your weapons," the Warrant ordered. After a quick check to ensure that all four of the rifles had been made safe, he added. "Pick up your brass, and join me at the range shack where I will give you your scores."

Ten minutes later with the brass cartridge cases collected, they made their way to the Range Control hut, where regulation pull-throughs, gun oil and cleaning patches had been laid out for them to clean their rifles.

As they stripped the weapons and busied themselves, the Warrant rejoined them with a clipboard in his hand.

"Pretty impressive for a bunch of civvies," he beamed at them. "Though the results may come as a surprise to a couple of you guys who consider themselves to have some degree of expertise as snipers. I have scored you on a maximum possible of 100 on each target. In fourth place Mr Fraser, with scores of 72 and 74 for a total of 146 out of a possible 200. In third place a somewhat better score of 79 and 82 for a total of 161 from Mr Blake, second Mr Nowakowski with 81 and 83 making 164, but your winner is Mr Carstairs with a very credible 84 and 85 for a total of 169."

"You're a dark horse," said KB as Fred handed over the winnings to a surprised and delighted Carstairs.

"I must confess to having been quite a keen shot in my time," the ex-banker admitted in response. "I was a member of the Honourable Artillery Company when I was working in the City and we did a lot of shooting at Bisley. In fact, I still am a member of one of the Rifle Clubs there and occasionally spend a weekend on the ranges keeping my eye in and having a beer or two with a few of my friends who also share my hobby."

"You certainly haven't lost your touch," added KB. "But after that, I certainly need to get some practice in."

"I wouldn't beat yourself up over it," said Fred sympathetically. "After all, you haven't fired a rifle for some time, and it always takes a while to get back into the groove. Anyway, let's head back to the Mess for a beer and then I take it, you are heading out?"

"I must," KB replied. "Hannah will be wondering why Peter hasn't been in touch, so I have to break the news, though God knows what I am going to tell her. She knew that Peter was some kind of security agent and that Amir was a VIP he was looking after, and I don't know how much he would have told her, so unless I tell her something really plausible, she is bound to smell a rat. On top of that, the fact that I am now working for the Agency and I have chucked in the course at Tamar Valley College is also going to take some explaining."

"Don't envy you. Having to tell porkies to our nearest and dearest is sometimes the hardest part of the job. Please give my best to your folks and tell Hannah we are thinking of her."

Chapter Twenty-Three

The Weekend

"An ambassador is an honest man sent abroad to lie for the good of his country."

Sir Henry Wotton 1568 – 1639

Just under an hour later, KB turned the Ford Ranger onto the A303 and headed west for Somerset. Mindful of the tone of the conversations he had had both with his superiors and his colleagues about the need for caution at all times, he engaged the tracker, imagining as he did so that somewhere in a Control Centre many miles away, a small red indicator was now marking his progress homewards.

It being a late Friday afternoon, traffic was heavy, and it was over ninety minutes before he reached the Podimore Cross Roundabout and turned onto the A372 for the last lap home. Turning into the car park of The Volunteer, a mixture of cars, 4 x 4's and pick-ups indicated that a number of their regular early evening drinkers were already at the bar. As he switched off the Wildtrak's motor he was relieved to notice that the light over the stable was on, suggesting that Hannah was still busying herself bedding down Winston for the night, providing him with the opportunity to break the news of Peter's death to his parents, before having to tell his sister.

Dumping his Bergen at the foot of the stairs he went through to the kitchen, where he found Kathy prepping food in readiness for the first of their evening diners.

"Kris, wonderful to see you," she greeted him with a smile, wiping her hands on her apron and planting a motherly kiss on his cheek. "We weren't sure what time you'd be home, but your dad's got some help in the bar from a friend of yours, so that we can sit down together and you can tell us all your news once we have finished in the dining room. Hey, what have you been up to?" she added, touching the sutures that still covered the cut on his scalp.

"I need to have a quick word with you and Dad now, if that's possible," KB replied, without answering her question. "So if you can spare a moment, I'll give him a shout and we can have a chat in the living room."

"I don't like the sound of that," said his mother, a note of concern in her voice. "But as long as it doesn't take too long, you'd better go and get him."

As he went into the bar, he saw that the help for the evening was none other than Alex, who was busying herself polishing glasses. There was no sign of his father, but the cellar door was open, so he guessed that he was changing a barrel.

Dropping her cleaning cloth on the bar, Alex flung her arms around his neck and kissed him firmly on the lips, prompting an outbreak of cheering from the locals accompanied by a few ribald remarks. "Good to have you home, lover," the girl whispered in his ear, as a loud cough from Jack now standing behind them, announced his return to the bar area.

"Talk to you later, Alex," he said. "Need to have a moment with Mum and Dad if you can hold the fort here for a while?"

"No problem, Kris. Nothing serious I hope, – though you do look as if you have been in the wars?" she added, pointing to the wound.

"I'll explain to you later," he said gently, then turned to his father and added, "need you for a moment, Dad." Leaving Alex to tend the bar, the two of them joined Kathy in the living room.

"What's up, son?" Jack asked, as his mother and father settled down on the settee.

"Bad news I'm afraid," he began, but before he could go any further the door opened and Hannah burst in, still wearing her jacket, red faced and breathless from the stables, Rocky trotting at her heels.

"Saw your truck, Kris. How long have you been back?" his sister chattered excitedly "Is Peter with you? I haven't heard from him for days and I was hoping he might have come back with you for the weekend."

"Sit down, sis," he said, as gently as he could, putting his arm around her shoulder and guiding her to a place between their parents. Taking a deep breath, he knelt down in front of her and taking her hands in his, uttered the words he was dreading. "I'm so, so sorry to have to tell you that Peter was killed in an accident at the college last Wednesday."

For a second his sister just looked at him in disbelief, then snatching her hands away from his, covered her face and crumpled forward, her shoulders shaking in deep, silent sobs.

"Oh my God!" his father exclaimed. "That's terrible, what happened?"

"It was a car accident, Dad."

"What kind of accident – were you involved?"

"Not now, Jack," Kathy interrupted, holding her sobbing daughter close to her. "Why don't you and Kris get back to the bar and send Alex back here. I'm sure she won't mind keeping Hannah company until I finish in the kitchen, and once our diners have left I suggest we close early."

Leaving mother and daughter together, KB led the way back to the bar where Alex was waiting.

"I've just had to break the news to Hannah that Peter was killed in an accident at the college." he explained. "Could you keep her company while Dad and I look after things here and Kathy sorts out our diners?"

"Oh, Kris, that's awful," the girl replied. "Of course I'll do anything to help, poor Hannah, she must be devastated."

As Alex left the bar, KB felt his father's hand on his shoulder. "That wasn't easy, lad," came the sympathetic comment "No questions now, you can tell us all about it later."

The evening dragged by and he dreaded the thought of the forthcoming explanation which he knew would have to satisfy the inevitable questions that would be asked. In spite of turning away several 'drop-in' late comers looking for meals and Jack's announcement to their patrons at the bar that they would be closing early, it was still close to 10.30 p.m. by the time the last of the drinkers left and they gathered again in the living room.

As Jack set a tray of brandies down on the coffee table, Hannah broke the silence.

"Was the accident anything to do with Amir and those men that were following us in the BMW?" she asked, looking directly at her brother.

"Yes," KB replied without hesitation, already aware that an account of a straightforward car accident was not going to satisfy any of his family. "We were on our way to join a field trip in Peter's car when he noticed we were being followed again. Peter tried to lose them in the lanes around the college and we were going pretty fast around a sharp bend, when a tractor came out of a field and hit us broadside on. Peter could do nothing to avoid it and it smashed into us, sandwiching us against a stone wall.

"I was in the back of the car with Amir and apart from a few cuts and bruises we were unhurt. The tractor driver called the emergency services and it took them a while to cut us out of the wreck, and they rushed Peter to hospital, but he never regained consciousness and I believe he died before they got him there."

"And what about the guys that were following you?" asked his father.

"Didn't see them again," KB replied, inwardly ashamed at the lies that were now flowing so easily. "They certainly saw what had happened and took off. Peter's people are trying to trace them now, and I have been helping them. In fact I have to go back to their headquarters in Bulford on Monday and may have to stay there for a while until they have completed their investigations."

"And what has happened to Amir?" his father asked.

"I understand they've shipped him back to Surpor. No doubt he is now considered to be too much of a security risk."

"There hasn't been anything in the papers or on the west country TV news about this," Alex commented.

"No, and there's not likely to be," KB replied. "The security agencies are keeping everything under wraps for the time being, and I have been sworn to secrecy. In fact, I had to get special clearance to explain things to you, so please, if anyone asks, Peter was killed in a car accident and leave it at that."

"All because the family of some stupid bloody playboy Prince thought he would benefit from a college diploma in the UK," Hannah sobbed bitterly, the tears running down her cheeks. "Well I hope His Royal bloody Highness the Nizam of Surpor thinks it was all worthwhile." Rising from her seat, she strode to the door, Alex following in her wake.

"If it's alright with you, Mrs Blake, I'll stay the night with Hannah. I'll call mum and tell her I'm staying over," said Alex, turning to Kathy on her way out.

"We'd like you to stay," Kathy agreed. "And thank you. See you in the morning."

As the door closed behind them, Jack sat back in his seat with a sigh, reaching across to take his wife's hand.

"What a mess," he said, and looking at his son, "are you telling us everything, Kris?"

"As much as I can at the moment, Dad," KB replied. "You will appreciate that a full enquiry is being held and you can be sure Peter's colleagues won't let things lie, he was very highly thought of and they don't take kindly to losing one of their own."

"Well at least you are okay" said his mother. "Did you get that in the accident?" she added pointing at the bandage.

"Yep, piece of glass from the window when it shattered, but it's only a scratch and nothing to worry about."

"Hmm," his mother snorted. "Shan't stop worrying until you've finished up at Bulford and are safely back at college."

"That may not be possible, Mum," KB admitted. "Naturally the folks at the college are a bit jumpy right now with all that has happened, and they may not want me around. I also need to tell you that Peter's funeral is at the Salisbury Crematorium at half past two next Wednesday afternoon, so if you want to bring Hannah up, I can meet you there."

"We'll see what she says," said Jack. "But if you will give me a hand, Kris, we'll lock up and turn in. I have a feeling it is not going to be an easy weekend for any of us."

With his parents on their way upstairs, KB called to Rocky and with the dog at his heels ventured into the night to stretch his legs. As he walked towards the paddock a cold dank wind blew in off the Levels, causing him to turn up the collar of his jacket and fasten the top button against the chill.

Pausing at the truck, he unlocked the driver's door and activated the release on the storage compartment. The Glock automatic rose silently into view, and after pocketing it he retrieved the holster from the box under the rear seat. Securing the cab and bathed in the glow from the car park's floodlights he continued his stroll to the paddock fence, pausing by the stable door. From within, Winston gently whickered at him, the horse ambling forward to stick his head over the half door, allowing KB to stroke his nose and pat his neck.

"Your mistress is going to need all the love you can give her," he whispered, as the horse nudged him gently in the shoulder. Calling to Rocky, who emerged from the shadows, he retraced his steps to the pub and climbed the stairs to his bedroom, the dog following close behind.

Undressing, he put the Glock into its holster and hung it over the back of his chair, covering it with his jacket. Slipping between the sheets, he was about to switch off the bedside light, when there was a light knock on the door and before he could say "Come in" it opened and Alex slipped into the room.

"Just came to see if I could borrow one of your T-shirts for a nightie," she said.

"Sure, second down in the chest of drawers," he answered. "How's Hannah?"

"Totally in pieces," she said, as she selected a vest from the drawer, and moved back to perch on the edge of his bed. "She is trying to put on a brave face, and she has just fallen asleep. At the moment she is blaming Amir's presence here for Peter's death, and it's probably a good thing she has something she can focus her anger on. What a terrible thing to have happen, Kris, you and Amir were really lucky."

"We were," he agreed. "And Amir was as shocked as anybody. As you can imagine, the folks Peter was working for are going all out to find who the men were in the BMW, but I think it could take them a while."

Reaching across the bed covers, she took his hand and looking him straight in the eyes, said in a serious tone that he had seldom heard before, "You take care, Kristian Blake; I know you have to help all you can, but don't get involved more than you have to, and stay out of trouble. Now I've got you back I don't want to lose you again." Leaning across she kissed him on the lips, and giving his hand a gentle squeeze, got to her feet and left the room.

Leaning back against the pillows, the realisation that the girl seemed intent on entering a new phase in their relationship had surprised him, in spite of their lovemaking the last time they met. Up to that point this had not entered his mind, believing that this might have been no more than a one night stand, but now it raised the question whether or not something more permanent was something he was ready for. How, he wondered, would she react if she knew the true nature of his involvement with the agency? She had made it quite clear that they didn't have a future when he went off to join the Paras, and his new job could spark a similar reaction.

Switching off the bedside lamp, he rolled over and pulled the duvet cover up to his chin. Sleep did not come easy, but when it did eventually overtake him, a vision of Peter lying by the roadside flashed through his subconscious. Peter was staring at Hannah, who was cradling him in her arms and laughing hysterically, but as he tried to move towards her his legs would not work. In desperation, he shouted "No!" waking himself up and finding the cover entwined around his lower body like a net.

Now wide awake, he freed himself from the tangle of his bedclothes, and sitting up he found Rocky by the bedside, panting anxiously. Stroking the dog's head to calm him, he rearranged the duvet and settled down, but it was a long time before the picture slipped from his mind and sleep overtook him once more.

He awoke to a face full of warm doggy breath and Rocky licking his chin.

“Thanks, mate,” he chuckled as he sat up. “Don’t know what you were eating yesterday, but you could certainly use a good mouthwash!”

The illuminated dial of his bedside alarm clock showed 0720, so easing himself out of bed, he hopped over to the bedroom window and peered out into the morning gloom. The stable light was already on, and as he watched, Hannah came around the corner of the loose boxes and dumped the contents of a wheelbarrow on the manure heap, followed by Alex leading Winston out into the paddock.

After showering he carefully applied the cream he had been given to his stump to prevent chafing, and after checking his prosthetic leg, strapped it on and finished dressing. Retrieving his mobile phone from the bedside table, he checked the calendar, noting that he was due at Headley Court for a routine review in four weeks’ time. From the back of his chair, he picked up the Glock in its holster, and after adjusting the belt around his waist, put on a loose fitting sweater. Walking over to his wardrobe he opened it and examined his appearance in the full length mirror attached to one of the doors. Satisfied that there were no obvious signs of the concealed weapon, he shut the doors, and with Rocky at his heels, made his way downstairs to the kitchen to find Kathy already busying herself preparing breakfast.

“Bacon and eggs coming up,” she said, as he wished her a good morning and leant over to kiss her on the cheek. “The girls should be in from the stables in a minute, so we’ll wait for them and all eat together in the dining room.”

In the bar he found his father bottling up from the previous night. “Sleep well?” Jack asked his son. Then without waiting for an answer, he added “Is everything okay? – we heard you in the night.”

“Sorry if I woke you,” KB replied. “Rocky decided he would be more comfortable sharing the bed with me, and he took a bit of persuading to get off my chest.”

“Well you certainly told him off. Actually you didn’t wake me up, I was lying awake thinking about poor old Peter Bowen,” said Jack. “Anyway, you didn’t wake your mother, but I’m not so sure about the girls. I heard them talking a couple of times.”

As if on cue, the door opened and Kathy emerged carrying a tray with their cooked breakfasts, followed by Hannah and Alex, with the tea, toast, butter and marmalade.

Sitting themselves around one of the larger tables in the dining room, Kathy passed round the plates and the mugs of tea, as KB broke the silence.

"You guys were up early; Winston must have been surprised to be turned out at the crack of dawn."

"Hannah and I thought we might go into Taunton this morning and do a bit of shopping," Alex answered." And it won't do Winston and Barney any harm if they don't get ridden out until this afternoon."

"Good idea," said Kathy. "And I wouldn't mind coming with you."

"Tell you what," said her husband, "I have to go into the wholesalers to pick up some soft drinks, mixers and crisps, so I could do that in Taunton while you girls are in town. Perhaps we might also close the pub at lunchtime, so that we don't have to rush back, unless you want to stay and man the bar for us, Kris?"

"I was going to suggest I did the driving," KB replied.

"That would be fine. I'll stick a notice on the door. We might upset a few regulars, but I can live with that. It's a long time since we have had a break anyway, so let's all head out as soon as you girls are ready after breakfast."

"Could you run me home, Kris?" asked Alex. "I could do with a change of clothes and I must turn Barney out."

"No problem, we can pick you up again on our way through to Taunton, so no need to rush as I must take Rocky for a walk too."

Breakfast finished, the five of them got up from the table and while Kathy cleaned up in the kitchen, Alex followed KB out to the truck.

"Thanks for staying with Hannah last night," KB said, as he eased the truck out onto the road and headed towards the Bakers'. "How is she this morning?"

"Neither of us got too much sleep," replied the girl. "But this morning she seems a bit more like her old self. The trip to Taunton will do her a world of good. Change of scenery and a chance to think about something else other than Peter."

"Let's hope so," said KB as he pulled into the Bakers' yard and parked outside the back door.

"See you in about an hour's time then," she said, leaning over to kiss him on the cheek. "And if you are really good, I might let you buy me something nice!"

"Typical Alex," he thought, as he headed back to the pub, a sharp jab in his side reminding him carrying a gun in a belt holster hardly added to your comfort when driving. As he brought the vehicle to a halt in the pub car park, Rocky came bounding up to meet him, and calling him to heel, he crossed the paddock to the river bank and walked down the towpath.

A watery sun was breaking through the grey overcast sky and the heavy overnight rain had flooded areas of the fields that lay on both sides of the river, a stiff breeze rippling the surface of the water, reminding him that these same fields could soon be under two or three feet of water should the winter rains hit with a vengeance. Half an hour later they were back at the pick-up, and after checking to make sure no one was watching, KB took off the belt holster, locked it away in the glove compartment and then replaced the Glock in its cubbyhole.

Once in the pub, he slipped upstairs to his room and changing out of his jeans, pulled on a pair of light tan Bedford cords. Taking a pair of suede desert boots from the bottom of the cupboard, he pulled one on over the foot on his artificial leg, and after doing the same to his other foot, got up and walked around the room to make sure the higher cut of the footwear did not impede the action of his prosthetic limb. Satisfied that everything seemed normal, he took a checked shirt out of his chest of drawers and selected a dark green V-neck sweater to match it, then donned a light green tweed jacket.

Pleased with the image that was reflected back to him in his wardrobe mirror, he slipped his wallet and mobile phone into his jacket pockets and closing his bedroom door behind him, went downstairs to the living room to where his parents were already waiting.

"Hello," his father greeted him with a smile. "What's this then – the smart-casual country squire look?"

"Don't you listen to him," Kathy interjected. "You look just fine, and in any case, Jack, at least Kris can do the buttons up on his jacket, and I bet you would struggle to do the same!"

"Hey, that's enough of that, my girl," Jack responded good naturedly. "This is an honest landlord's beer belly and a nobly won symbol of my calling."

"I not sure about 'nobly' won," Kathy countered, smartly dressed in a two-piece grey suit and pale blue blouse for the outing. "Too many pints downed lolling over the bar and hobnobbing with the locals, and not enough exercise to work it off is more like it!"

Before Jack could respond, Hannah entered the room. Matching her brother, she had changed out of her jeans and now wore dark blue figure hugging corduroy trousers and a heavy cable knit white sweater with ankle length black boots.

"You look good, sis," KB commented.

"And you and Dad look like Tweedledee and Tweedledum," came the reply.

"I don't know what we've done to deserve this verbal abuse," Jack laughed, "but let's get going. I suggest we drop the girls off in the town centre, Kris, and then head out to the wholesalers at Norton Fitzwarren. Perhaps around one o'clock we can meet up for some lunch in the cafe in Riverside Place. We should be able to park in the Coal Orchard car park, behind the Brewhouse Theatre just round the corner, what do you say, Kathy?"

"That sounds a good plan," agreed his wife, as they left the living room and headed out to the car park.

At the Bakers' Alex came out to meet them as soon as he turned into the yard. In contrast to his sister's more conservative look, Alex had chosen a black polo necked sweater, bright red mini-skirt, black tights and calf length black leather boots. Climbing into the back seat to join Kathy and Hannah, Jack could not restrain a comment.

"Hey, Kris, three smashing looking birds on board, they'll be wasted on Taunton!"

"You boys could always take us up to London for a shopping trip if you prefer," countered his wife. "But as there is a fat chance of that ever happening, we'll have to make do with lunch on you, and" she added, "with it the best bottle of wine on the menu."

Within half an hour they were negotiating the heavy Saturday morning traffic into Taunton, and after dropping the three women off in the High Street, Kris headed out to the catering wholesalers located on the big industrial estate at Norton Fitzwarren.

Several boxes of crisps, salted peanuts and pork scratchings later, plus half a dozen flats of mixers and soft drinks, they had checked out at the cashiers and were back at the loading bay.

"Let's put everything in the cab on the back seat," KB suggested. "When we park up we can leave them locked in, and then transfer them to the back after lunch."

"If it doesn't rain," said Jack wryly. "In which case we are either going to have a soggy cargo or three pissed off women being blown around in the open!"

"If it comes down to the latter option, I'll leave it to you to make the suggestion," KB laughed. "In which case I would suspect that your career as a landlord would come to an abrupt and extremely painful end. But the sun is shining now, so fingers crossed it will stay that way."

Back in town KB drove straight to the car park and as he reversed the Ford into a vacant space, Jack said. "Looking at the time, we've got over an hour before we are due to meet up with the girls. Why don't we wander over to the livestock market, sees what's around and then have a pint at The Railway; it's ages since I've been in there, and the landlord used to be a good buddy of mine when we were lads?"

"Good idea, Dad," KB replied, as he locked the vehicle, being careful to double click the remote.

The walk to the cattle market took only a few minutes. Joining the throng of farmers around the auctioneer's ring, KB was able to pick out Obadiah Kernworthy, pipe in mouth, leaning over the barrier and watching intently as half a dozen lambs were paraded for inspection.

Sale of the lot concluded, Obi waved at the auctioneer and left his ringside vantage point, to head towards where they were standing. Nudging his father, KB nodded in Obi's direction.

"Why don't we take the old boy for a pint?" he suggested.

"Good idea," agreed his father, as they moved to intercept the farmer.

"Morning, Obi," Jack greeted him. "Good to see you."

"And you too," Obi replied, a broad grin on his face, and pocketing his pipe continued, "but what brings you and young Kris down 'yer of a Saturday mornin'?"

"We dropped Kathy, Hannah and Alex Baker off in town to do some shopping, and thought we'd drop by to see what you wealthy farmers were up to on a market day. Have you had a good sale?"

"Musn't grumble," he admitted. "Jest zold six good heavy lambs and made a bob or two, and I was about to wander over to the Railway to wet me whistle."

"Mind if we join you?" asked Jack as they walked towards the exit.

"Course not, be pleased to 'ave you along; and what be you up to these days, Kris?"

"Unfortunately I have had to finish at college for the time being," KB replied. "Do you remember Amir, that young foreign chap we had staying with us at the pub, and the guy who was with him, Peter Bowen?"

"Remember 'em well. Wodn'it that Peter bloke wot got pally with your sister?"

"It was," KB continued. "Peter was keeping an eye on Amir, but sad to say we were involved in an accident at the college, and Peter was killed."

"Bleddy 'ell," came the response, as they entered the Railway Inn. "Poor bugger. Let's 'ave us some drinks and you can tell us all about it."

Shouldering their way through the throng of farmers and stockmen who almost filled the bar to capacity, they reached the bar where Obi soon caught the eye of the bartender and ordered a pint of beer for himself and Jack, and a half for KB. Seeing the landlord at the far end of the room, Jack moved off to renew his acquaintance with his old friend.

"Well, tell us wot 'appened then," said Obi, evidently keen to give KB the chance to finish his story.

"We were on our way to a coppicing demonstration not far from the college," he explained. "Peter was driving and Amir and I were passengers. One of those big four wheel drive tractors came out of a field on a blind bend and hit us broadside on. Took a while for the emergency services to arrive and Peter died on the way to hospital."

"But you'm were alright?"

"Amir and I had a few cuts and bruises, but otherwise we were unhurt."

"You'm were bleddy lucky then," said the farmer, nodding his head. "'Ow about the tractor driver, he must have bin asleep at the wheel. Can't understand why he never saw 'ee comin'. The cabs on they big machines are way up, and if 'eed 'ad his wits about 'im 'ee shud 'ave seed 'ee over the top of the 'edge."

"The banks and hedgerows where it happened were pretty high," said KB, hoping his comment would steer Obi's practical analysis of the accident in a different direction. "And to be fair, we were going at a fair speed."

"And wos 'appened to thik Pakistani feller?" persisted Obi.

"They packed him off back to his own country," KB answered. "It was quite a challenge keeping tabs on him, and someone figured out he'd be safer off at home."

"Bleddy right," said the farmer, as the door to the bar swung open and three newcomers stepped into the room.

First through the door was none other than Nathan Samson, followed by two thick-set individuals KB had never seen before. Pausing for a moment to take stock of his surroundings, the younger Samson's gaze alighted on KB and Obi, and beckoning to his companions to follow him, he strode towards them.

"Well, if it isn't the peg leg soldier boy himself," the man sneered, his face inches away from KB's. "Let you out have they – or is this old codger here acting as your nanny?"

"Yer, tha's enough that, you cheeky young bugger," Obi broke in. "Why don't you and your mates piss off?"

"You stupid old fucker," came the instant rejoinder, and leaning across KB,

Samson shoved the farmer backwards, upsetting the tables and chairs behind him and sending drinks, empty glasses and Obi Kernworthy crashing to the floor.

Grabbing the traveller's outstretched arm, KB pivoted on his good right foot and forced the arm into the small of the assailant's back, wrapping his own free arm around the man's neck in a solid headlock.

"Stay there," he shouted at Nathan's two companions who had stepped forward to intervene. "Stay there, or I'll break his bloody arm!"

"That's enough!" came a loud warning from the landlord, who with Jack at his side had moved quickly through the crowd of startled drinkers towards them. "What's going on here?"

"That's Nathan Samson," Jack volunteered. "Big trouble, and banned from my pub along with his brother and the rest of the clan."

"Bugger knocked I over," added Obi, struggling to his feet and brushing broken glass off his trousers. "T'was a clear case of assault, landlord," he continued. "And if I were you I'd have a mind to call the Police."

"Better let him go, Kris," Jack suggested. "He's gone blue in the face and you're damn near to throttling him."

"I want you and your friends out of here, now!" the landlord ordered, as KB released his grip, leaving a choking and spluttering Nathan to fall on his knees.

"We'll bloody get you for this, you fucking Blakes," the man gasped, as he struggled to his feet.

"Best you leave now," came KB's icy response. "And give my regards to your brother."

With his two companions supporting him, and adding further muttered curses, Nathan turned on his heels and made for the door.

"Might be wise to see them right off your property," Jack suggested to the landlord and with KB, followed the retreating figures to the car park. Moments later a mud splattered Range Rover sped past them and out on to the road, a still swearing Nathan leaning from the window, two fingers extended by way of a final salute.

"Isaac may not have shown his face today, but I'm sure that's his motor," KB said to his father. "So we better be on our guard for a day or so." Turning to the landlord he added, "My apologies for the fracas, sir, but as Dad will tell you, I'm afraid there is some bad blood between me and the Samson brothers, that being the younger of the two, Nathan."

"I can't see you started anything," the man said, shaking KB's hand. "I'm

Tom Gilbert incidentally, used to play rugby with your old man in our younger days. Anyway, come on back to the bar and let's get you another drink."

Inside the staff were already sweeping up the breakages and resetting the tables and chairs, and Jack and KB found Obi back at the bar with a fresh pint in front of him.

"Are you okay?" Jack asked the farmer.

"Went down with a bit of a bump, but it's me pride that's bruised more than my arse." came the cheery reply. "You handled yourself well, young Kris," he added. "Thought you wuz goin' to kill the bugger for a moment there."

After finishing their drinks, and with the scheduled time for their meeting with the girls fast approaching, father and son made their excuses and left for the cafe. Bang on one o'clock they entered the bright and sparklingly clean restaurant, and settled for a table by one of the windows overlooking the River Tone, where ten minutes later they were joined by the three women.

"Obviously a morning well spent!" Jack commented, eying the impressive number of carrier bags that were carefully placed in a corner next to their table.

"Yes, we're nearly done," Kathy replied. "I need to make a quick trip back to Debenhams after lunch. I saw a pair of shoes there I really liked, but I need your opinion before I buy them."

"And I need to show Kris something I've seen," said Alex, putting her hand over KB's on the table, and giving it a gentle squeeze.

"Well, Kris, it seems we are not finished yet," Jack smiled at his son. "So let's get the menus and order up some food."

"So, how was your morning?" Hannah asked.

"Fine," Jack responded, looking in KB's direction. "Quick trip to the wholesalers, then we parked up here, wandered over to the market, and had a quiet drink in the Railway."

"Where we bumped into Obi Kernworthy," KB added. "Who you could say, was bowled over backwards to see us!" at which remark, Jack nearly choked trying to stifle his laughter.

"Okay you guys," said Kathy, quick to notice her husband's discomfort. "There's something going on here, what happened at The Railway?"

"Nothing, dear," Jack assured her, mopping his face with his handkerchief. "Nothing that won't keep until later."

While the girls enjoyed several plates of tapas – 'pigeon food' – Jack commented – and with he and Kris both opting for a more conventional steak sandwich, the conversation turned to a blow by blow account of the women's shopping trip, and it was some relief to their menfolk when coffees and desserts were finished.

Outside, the weather was still holding fair and after a brisk walk back to the High Street, they were soon standing outside the town's main department store.

Inside, the group gave their unanimous approval to Kathy's choice of shoes and in a shorter time than either of the men expected, they were back on the High Street.

"Now it's my turn," said Alex, taking KB firmly by the arm. "It's almost next door, so not much further to walk."

A little further up the street stood Taunton's oldest and most prestigious jeweller's shop, and it was towards this that KB found himself propelled. Pausing outside the first of the windows flanking the entrance, Alex slipped her arm around his waist and hugged him as he was confronted with an exquisite display of what were obviously, very expensive diamond engagement rings.

"Aren't they gorgeous?" she giggled, as KB stared in something close to horror at the sparkling array. To his relief and before he had a chance to consider the implications of her comment, she added, "But perhaps, not for a while yet!" and tugging at his arm, led him into the shop. No sooner were they at the counter, than a sales assistant hurried forward bearing a small velvet cushion on which a St Christopher medallion laid, attached to a gold chain.

"We've had it engraved for you, as you asked" the woman announced handing it over to Alex for inspection.

"Well, what do you think?" Alex asked anxiously, passing the medallion on its chain to KB. Turning it over, he saw that on the reverse side of the depiction of the patron saint of travellers, the engraving read:

Kris

Love

Alex

"Wow!" he exclaimed. "It's fantastic, I don't know what to say except thank you, and even that sounds pretty lame."

"Come here and bend your head down," Alex ordered, and as he leant forward she undid the clasp and fastened the chain around his neck. With her arms still around him, she whispered, "But you could give me a kiss to show me that you love me." Even with his thoughts still in a turmoil, the invitation was too much to resist and Sergeant Kristian Blake, hardened veteran soldier and at one time the British Army's most lethal sniper, felt her lips touch his and for a moment became totally lost in his feelings for the girl.

"Come on you two, give it up or book a room!" he heard his father say from behind them, and breaking apart they turned to see the clearly delighted faces of his parents smiling at them. At the same time, he noticed out of the corner of his eye, his sister Hannah slip quietly out of the shop.

"Mum, Hannah," he said, nodding towards the doorway, and without needing any further prompting, Kathy followed her daughter into the street with Jack in her wake.

"Oh my God, I am so sorry, I didn't think, I should have given it to you quietly when we were on our own," Alex said, with genuine concern in her voice. "I just popped in here earlier while your mum and Hannah were across in County Stores, as I wanted it to be a surprise. Now I've gone and upset her and probably ruined her day."

"Listen," KB replied, taking her gently by the shoulders, "Hannah will understand and she certainly knows you would not want to upset her deliberately. Mum is there with a shoulder for her to cry on, and we can make it up to her later. But for now, let's find something nice for you."

At that Jack popped his head around the door. "We're going to take Hannah back to your truck and we'll wait for you there. Can you let me have your keys?"

"Sure, Dad," KB replied. "But it is a double locking system, so you must click the remote twice to unlock the doors, otherwise you'll set off the alarm, got that?"

Nodding an acknowledgment, Jack took the keys, and hurried off in pursuit of his wife and daughter, leaving KB and Alex alone with the assistant. Knowing that they were keeping his family waiting and could not afford to linger over selecting his gift to Alex, a selection of bracelets and earrings were quickly examined, but it was the chains and lockets that obviously appealed to Alex the most.

In the end, she picked out a simple gold heart shaped circlet in the centre of which any single letter of the alphabet could be selected. The assistant quickly found one with an **A**, pointing out that engraving was possible on the wide band of the surround.

"Why don't we have '*Love Kris*' engraved" Alex suggested. "Then it will match your St Christopher."

"Tell you what," he replied, "we can't really wait to have it done now, but I'll pay for the engraving, you can drop it in next time you are in Taunton, and they can do it for you while you are shopping."

“That sounds a great idea,” agreed the girl. “I’ll probably be in town again next week, and I can get it done then.” Turning to the assistant she added, “Don’t box it up, I’ll wear it now and this time, Kris, you can do the honours.”

As he fastened it around her neck the realisation that he had completely lost control of the events of the last half hour increased from a nagging suggestion to outright certainty. Coupled with it came a feeling of guilt at the very public display of affection his childhood sweetheart had been so eager to display, and a concern that he might not entirely be ready to replicate the same level of commitment.

After a few masculine fumbles with the tricky catch of the chain, Alex finally patted the pendant in place and turned to face him.

“How does it look?” she asked, holding her arms out wide so that the ‘A’ stood out boldly on the black background of her sweater.

“It looks great,” he replied, thinking to himself that they would only have to bump into Isaac and Nathan Samson on their way back to the car park, and the fracas that was likely to ensue would make the minor upset in the pub that morning look like a Women’s Institute tea party.

Credit card severely dented by the bill the assistant presented, and with Alex clearly delighted at the outcome of their visit to the jewellers, they retraced their steps to the car park. They had only gone a few yards when his mobile rang, and taking it out of his pocket he saw the word ‘Olympus’ on the incoming call identification, the code name for the Agency Control Centre.

Pressing the receive button, he replied, “Sirius,” and a female voice answered him.

“Your tracker is indicating that someone is attempting a forced entry into your vehicle, are you close by?”

“Yes” he replied. “I’m only a few hundred yards away. My apologies, I gave the keys to my father and he must have attempted to unlock the vehicle without completing the correct procedure, I’m on my way back to the vehicle now.”

“You’d better hurry,” came the response. “We’ve alerted the Police as a precautionary measure, and they may be responding now.”

“Thanks, I’m on my way. Once again my apologies...” and before he had time to say anything more the line went dead as the caller rang off.

By now they were approaching the lane leading to the Coal Orchard parking lot, and an all too familiar sound greeted his ears – the loud and raucous sound of a car horn blaring repeatedly.

"Come on, Alex," he shouted to the girl, as he broke into the best jog he could manage. "That sounds like my car alarm," and sure enough as they rounded the side of the Brewhouse Theatre, there was the Ranger, indicator lights flashing and alarm in full cry, surrounded by his family and a small crowd of onlookers.

Close by a clearly distraught Jack Blake was to be seen gesticulating frantically to two of Somerset and Avon's finest, whose patrol car had been deliberately driven right up behind the truck, blocking any chance of any would-be car thief making a swift getaway.

"Kris, thank God you're here," exclaimed his father. "Forgot to double click the damned remote and all hell let loose. Then I tried to unlock the doors using the key, but even that wouldn't work."

"Quick, give me the keys, Dad," KB said as he reached the driver's door. With relief on Jack's face he handed the key to his son, and inserting it in the lock, KB turned it rearwards twice in a half circle as he had been shown at Bulford.

In a second the alarm and the flashing indicators clicked off and silence descended on the car park, the spectators gradually dispersing, while Kathy and Hannah held on to each other, their shoulders shaking with laughter.

KB now found himself confronted by a burly traffic Sergeant who was clearly none too happy about the recent chain of events.

"I think we need a chat, sir," the big man said beckoning for KB to follow him out of earshot of his family. "Perhaps you can explain why my fellow officer and I get an emergency call from Traffic Control instructing us to drop everything and proceed at all speed here because, we were told, a member of our National Counter Terrorist Agency could be in a spot of bother."

"I am sorry, Officer," KB replied apologetically. "My girlfriend and I had some shopping to complete, and I gave the keys of the truck to my father with instructions how to disarm the security system, but he obviously got the sequence wrong."

"I understand, sir," said the Sergeant, a note of resignation in his voice. "Didn't realize that gentlemen in your line of business had time for ordinary things like shopping, but I'd better see your identification, just to keep things in order."

Taking out his wallet KB handed over his ID card, the number being jotted down in the policeman's note book before being handed back.

"Thank you, sir," the man said, "We'll be on our way now, and if I might make a suggestion, don't leave it to the old fellow, handle the tricky task of unlocking your vehicle yourself in future."

With that, he touched his hand to the peak of his hat and returning to his car, waved cheerily at Jack, before driving off into the town centre.

"What did he say to you?" Jack asked anxiously as KB rejoined his family.

"He told me that in future I'd better handle the difficult tasking of unlocking the truck myself, rather than leaving it to the old and senile."

"Cheeky beggar," came his father's reply. "I thought I had pressed the damn button twice, but clearly not. Anyway, now we have provided half of Taunton with their morning's entertainment, perhaps we better get those boxes into the back, so that we can drive these ladies home in style. Unless of course," he added slyly, "you fair maids would enjoy an exhilarating ride home in the fresh air?"

"In your dreams," came Kathy's instant retort. "Don't you think you've caused enough upset for one day, Jack Blake? Now get those boxes off the seat pronto, or you'll be feeling my hand across your ear!"

Events in the car park proved to be something of a blessing in disguise, as the conversation during the drive back to the pub was in a much more relaxed tone, and even Hannah joined her mother in a light-hearted description of Jack's antics while attempting to switch off the car alarm.

There was a moment's concern for KB, when his father remarked, "Can't understand why the law arrived so quickly, it was almost as if someone had called them."

"Probably just in the area and heard the alarm go off." came his quick response, but nevertheless, he was left with a nagging doubt that his father had not bought his explanation completely.

Back at The Volunteer, the women disappeared inside to unpack their shopping, leaving KB and his father to unload the truck.

"Well young, Kris," his father said, once the girls were out of earshot, "only ever seen my son wearing Army dog tags around his neck before, let alone a gold chain, and the one Alex is wearing is quite stunning and far from discreet. I would say, without a doubt, young man, that Miss Alex Baker has well and truly put her brand on you!"

"Hang on, Dad," KB replied. "You know Alex and I have been fond of each other for years, and she certainly seems to have changed in the last month or so."

"That's as maybe, Kris, but you mark my words, that young lady might just be hearing wedding bells, and when Kathy and Amy get together, plans for the nuptials might well be top of their agenda. You know what women are like."

"Bloody hell, Dad," KB protested. "We're nowhere near that yet, or at least, I'm not. I won't say it's entirely out of the question, but I'm not about to be rushed into anything."

"Hmm," came the response. "Having a shrewd idea of what went on between you and the lass last time you were home, my advice would be – don't let your feelings be ruled by your dick; just remember, you're a long time married."

After stowing the supplies away in the cellar, they found the subject of Jack's advice with Kathy and Hannah in the living room, where tea and hot buttered crumpets had been laid out on the coffee table.

"Bought them from M&S," Kathy explained. "So dig in, we won't be eating again until later. And," she added, as they helped themselves from the plate, "I've asked Alex if she would like to move in for a few days, it would be nice for Hannah to have the company."

"I'd like that," agreed Hannah. "You can bring Barney down and put him in one of the spare loose boxes, and Winston will enjoy the company as well."

"I'd like that too," said Alex. "Perhaps after tea, you can run me home, Kris and I can pack a few belongings, and I'll hack Barney down before it gets too dark."

"No problem," KB answered quickly, glancing across at his father, whose subtle nod in his direction quite plainly said, 'I told you so'."

With Alex settled in one of the guest rooms, the rest of their Saturday passed quickly. The pub was full to overflowing in the evening, the locals evidently keen to make up for losing their customary lunchtime drinking session, and the restaurant wasbusy right up to the time Jack called 'last orders'."

With Hannah helping her mother in the kitchen, Alex waiting table and Jack and KB behind the bar, service ran like clockwork and as the pub emptied, leaving only Joc and Amy Baker at the bar, Kathy emerged from the kitchen smiling as she greeted her friends.

"What an evening!" she exclaimed. "And what a team. Wish it was like that every night!"

"See what I mean," Jack said quietly to his son, as she and Amy put their heads together in the corner of the bar. "I'd bet a fiver, I could tell you exactly what that conversation is about, and if you can't see your mother is serious about expanding our 'team' on a permanent basis, you've got rocks in your head."

After a late night sandwich, and doing the last rounds for his father, KB mounted the stairs to his room, noticing that a light was already shining from beneath his bedroom door. Opening it, he slipped into the room to find that his bed already had an occupant.

Lying back on the pillows, her head resting on her arms, Alex had made no effort to conceal the fact that the T-shirt she had sought as nightwear previously was no longer considered a necessity.

KB lost track of the time that followed, the girl engulfing him in a sensuality and intense passion that exceeded his wildest imagination. It was somewhere in the wee small hours of the morning that they finally drifted off to sleep, at last the haunting images of the week before slipping from his subconscious.

Sunday passed slowly. As always, Kathy's lunch menu ensured a full dining room, and after the last of the patrons departed, the five of them sat down for lunch together. While the two girls helped Kathy with the final clean-up in the kitchen, Jack and KB bottled up in preparation for what was traditionally a quiet Sunday evening, with the dining room closed. At Alex's suggestion, she, Hannah and KB took Rocky for a walk while Jack and Kathy settled down in front of the television.

Hannah was quiet during their stroll down the riverbank, until they turned around to retrace their steps back to the pub.

"Kris, tell me truthfully," she said to her brother. "Did Peter ever talk about me?"

"Quite a lot, sis," he was able to reply honestly. "I believe the guy was really in love with you, if that's any help?"

"It does, it means a lot to me," she admitted. "Before he left, we had a long talk and started to make plans, but now I'll never know..." Once again the girl's faced crumpled and before she could finish the sentence, the tears flowed.

With Alex and KB on either side of her, arms wrapped around her waist, the three walked slowly and silently back to the pub, Rocky at their heels.

Once inside, Hannah excused herself and went upstairs. Pausing for a second, the dog looked at KB and then, without further hesitation, chose to follow her.

"Will she be alright, or should I follow her?" Alex asked.

"I think so," KB replied. "Rocky is with her and sometimes the company of a four legged friend who doesn't ask questions or offer any more sympathy than a gentle nudge of the head or a wet nose pushed into the palm of your hand, can be more comfort than anything we could offer. I've seen it many times in Helmand, men who have lost their mates and whose spirits have been shattered seeking the silent companionship of a mutt. It can work wonders, so we'll leave Hannah and Rocky on their own for a while, and if she doesn't come down in half an hour or so, we can check up on her."

Joining Kathy and Jack in the living room, KB settled in the corner of the settee and Alex curled up next to him. Before long, lulled by the drone of the television, KB drifted off to sleep and when he awoke, he found himself on his own in a room darkened by the onset of a winter's night. Standing up, he stretched his legs, and felt a numbness in his stump, but by the time he had reached the door and found his way through to the kitchen, where he found his mother removing a large home-made pork pie from the 'fridge, feeling had returned.

"You can help yourselves to a slice of this later if you feel peckish," Kathy said, placing the pie on a plate next to several jars of assorted pickles. "Did you have a nice snooze?"

"Yes thanks," he replied. "Where are the girls?"

"At the stables, bedding down Winston and Barney for the night. Your dad's upstairs freshening up, so why don't you pop up and do the same?"

"Good idea," he agreed. "I could do with a quick shower," and leaving his mother to her preparations, climbed the stairs to his room.

Their Sunday evening was as quiet as they had anticipated, and it was not long after Jack had closed the bar, that they all trooped upstairs for an early night. Once again KB found that he had a willing companion by his side as he switched off the bedside light.

In contrast to the previous night their lovemaking was slow and so tender that he wondered how someone he thought he knew, could be a tigress between the sheets at one moment, and so meltingly soft and caring the next.

Once again, sleep came easily to him, and when his alarm went off at 5 a.m. it was with considerable reluctance that he dragged himself from his bed, to shower, dress and pack before setting off on his journey back to Bulford.

As he moved across to leave the room, a quiet voice from the bed called him back.

"So you're off then, Kris?" she murmured. "Take care. I'm coming up with your folks for Peter's funeral on Wednesday, so I'll see you then."

Bending over her, his kissed her full on the lips and whispering a 'Goodbye' he closed the door of his bedroom quietly behind him, and left the sanctuary of his home. Once aboard the Ranger, he was soon heading east towards the great Plain of Salisbury, the truck's headlights burning a passage for him through the morning darkness, leaving in its wake a fathom of mixed emotions to be filed away in the recess of his mind for another day.

Chapter Twenty-Four

Indoctrination

Aut disce aut discede – learn or leave

Latin Proverb

By 7.30 a.m. he was pulling into the car park behind the Mess and after checking in and collecting his room key, he picked up a brown envelope that he found in his pigeon hole, and after leaving his Bergen with the porter, made his way into the dining room.

Collecting a plate of scrambled eggs and bacon from the buffet, he spied Fred Nowakowski and Colin Hunter sitting at a table in the far corner, and walked over to them.

"Mind if I join you?" he asked, as the two men looked up from their plates as he approached.

"Please do," Colin replied. "Grab a chair and sit yourself down. How was your weekend?"

"Pretty traumatic," KB admitted. "My sister took the news of Peter's death very hard, and it's going to take her a while to get over it. She and my parents are coming up for the funeral on Wednesday together with Alex Baker, which hopefully will provide some kind of closure for Hannah, but even I didn't realise just how close she and Peter had become. She told me that before Peter left they were discussing plans for a future together, so it was obviously much more than just a 'ships that pass in the night' type of romance."

"A great shame," nodded Colin. "But from time to time shit happens in our line of work, but it's never easy. How did they take the news that you are joining us?"

"To be honest, I didn't tell them too much. If I had laid that on them in addition to everything else, I don't know what Hannah's reaction would have been, and my mother and my girlfriend would have freaked out. All I've said at this point, is that I am helping the Agency with their enquiries at the moment, but sooner or later I am going to have to tell them something as they won't expect me to be staying up here much longer."

"You'll have to tell them something soon," said his Section Leader. "And probably the sooner the better, particularly if they are coming up on Wednesday.

"I suggest you give them a call this evening and tell them that you have been offered a job with us as an Instructor. After all, with your experience in the Army, that would be fairly logical, and it could be partially true as from time to time I am sure we will be using your expertise in field operations to train others. That should put your womenfolk's minds at rest, and perhaps it is just as well anyway if they don't know too much about what you will be doing. We always advise our Operatives to tell their nearest and dearest as little as possible about what they are up to. I'll also give Bill Hutchinson and Andy Reynard the nod too, so that they are up to speed if they bump into your family on Wednesday. By the way, did you find your course programme details in your Mail Box?"

"I presume you mean this?" KB replied, holding up the envelope he had collected on his way through the lobby.

"That's the one. You'll find the first couple of weeks is mainly classroom stuff, covering the legalities of what you can and cannot do, the structure of the Agency and how it interfaces with our partners, and the theories and basics of urban and field surveillance, the latter of which should be largely old hat to you. You'll also be given an insight into the workings and ethos of the main Islamic extremist groups, and also an intelligence update on what is going on in our own backyard and some of the known characters we are keeping tabs on.

"After that there will be a couple of field exercises which should take you pretty much up to the Christmas break, after which you may or may not be put on an active service footing, depending on what's up in our nasty little world of terrorism. Alternatively if there is nothing immediate that requires your special skills, you could be sent on another course. We believe very much in one on one mentoring, so there won't be any other trainee Operatives getting in your way, so all in all – the best of luck! Your first lecture cracks off at 0900 hours, so I'll leave you to it."

Thanking him as the tall man stood up to leave, KB turned his attention back to his breakfast and his friend Fred.

"How's your course going, Fred?" he asked.

"Putting it on hold for a week or so," the latter mumbled through a mouthful of toast and marmalade. Taking a swig of coffee he continued, "I'm being sent up to the West Midlands for a while, liaising with the CID. They've been doing some background checks on the car hire firm that owns the BMW that chased us around Somerset, and apparently the company is part of quite a wide network of different businesses.

"It seems a few of them are employing some interesting characters who are on our 'watch' list, so I'm going to do some nosing around on behalf of the Agency, to see if we can make any sense out of it. Anyway, I'm not off until after the funeral on Wednesday, so we'll have a chance for a few beers and a game of snooker or two in the evening before I leave."

"What happens when you are off on assignment, do they keep the same room for you, or do you have to check out?"

"Actually, they take care of us bachelor types quite well. We each have a small suite on site with a bedroom, shower room, kitchenette and a living room, which is allocated to us permanently. As you know, most of us eat in the Mess, otherwise our social life would be a bit lean and mean, but the system works well. By the way, best of luck today, I found the legal mumbo jumbo they chuck at you quite boring, but at least they get it over and done first and as the course goes on it does tend to get more interesting."

As Fred had predicted, KB found the subject matter on the first day of his course somewhat less than stimulating and at times, hard to grasp. His tutor was a sallow complexioned and earnestly bespectacled young barrister in his early thirties who, after introducing himself as Alan Maidley, informed KB that he had majored in civil law and then gone on to study criminal law electing to pursue a career with the Metropolitan Police. Now seconded to the Agency, he was a sympathetic teacher, evidently appreciating that KB's former career with the Paras was hardly an ideal background for someone who must now gain a sound working knowledge of the legal boundaries within which he would be expected to operate.

After a lunch break, taken together in the Mess, instead of returning to the classroom he was taken to the library in the Administration block. After introducing KB to the section the lawyer selected 'The Law of Entry, Search and Seizure' by Richard Stone, Jonathan White's 'Terrorism – Homeland

Security – Part 4' and 'EU Justice and Home Affairs Law' by Professor Steve Peers, with a suggestion he concentrated on the chapters concerning immigration, asylum, EU border controls and anti-terrorist sanctions in the latter.

After checking the books out with the librarian, they returned to their classroom and after what seemed to be an exceptionally long afternoon, Maidley called a close to the session, advising KB that the following Monday he would be required to undertake a short test of the subjects for which he was now being tutored before progressing to the next stage in his indoctrination.

Back in the Mess, he stacked the books by his bed and with half past four showing on his bedside clock, decided that now would be as good a time as ever to make the calls to his father and Alex to break the news of his new appointment, and if questioned – which he knew would be inevitable – to give them a plausible description of his responsibilities as an Instructor.

Picking up the wall mounted handset at the end of the hallway, he dialled the pub number, hoping he would catch his father, but it was Kathy who answered the phone.

"Is Dad around?" he asked, after answering the usual questions of – "Did you have a good trip back?" and "Are they looking after you?"

"He's down in the stables giving Hannah a hand," Kathy replied. "We don't like leaving her on her own too much, and Alex had to go home for a few hours, so he's helping her bed down Winston and Barney. Anyway," she added, "can I help?"

"I just wanted to tell you, Mum, the people here have offered me a full time job with them, and I thought I had better break the news before we meet up Wednesday."

"Oh my God," came the instant response. "Whatever would they do that for? – And in any case, they must know about your leg, how could you possibly be of use to them?"

"Thanks, Mum," he replied, a note of bitterness creeping into his answer. "But strange though it may seem, I do have a lot of skills I was taught while I was in the Army that they obviously believe could be useful in training their new recruits."

"Well I sincerely hope they will not be expecting you to do the kind of job Peter was doing, if so why would you want to put yourself in danger again? Don't you think you've done more than enough for this country of ours already?"

"It's nothing like that, Mum," he lied. "I'll be training other people to do some of the things I have done in the past, and I certainly won't be in the firing line."

"Well, you'd better not be," his mother sniffed on the other end of the line, then adding "have you accepted their offer?"

"Here goes," he thought to himself, stand by for another ear bashing. "It's really good money, Mum, up to six weeks paid leave every year, an excellent benefits package and I could be home most weekends. At the moment, my skills as an Instructor are being assessed." Hoping that this statement would allay her worries further, he continued, "And if all goes well, I should know by the time you come up for Peter's funeral."

"It sounds to me as if you've made up your mind already," his mother said with some resignation.

"Mum," he replied, "this job is right up my street. I'll be out in the open air most of the time, doing something I know I do well, and as I've said before, the money is really good."

"We'll see what your father has to say, and you'd better tell Alex. That girl has been wandering around here with stars in her eyes ever since you left, but she won't be too pleased if she thinks you are putting yourself in harm's way again, after what happened to you in the Army."

"I'm going to phone her now, Mum. So see you on Wednesday, and love to everyone," he said, hanging up.

Pausing for a moment to gather his thoughts, he took a deep breath and dialled Alex's mobile number. Somewhat to his relief, it rang through to her answering service, allowing him to leave a message.

"Hi, Alex," he recorded. "Just ringing to tell you that the folks here have made me a job offer as an Instructor, which is a really good one. I've spoken to Mum and she has all the details, so no doubt you will hear all about it. I won't be answering my mobile for a day or two as they are running some assessments on me at the moment, but see you on Wednesday. Love you." he added before ringing off.

Back in the Mess, he found Fred propping up the bar.

"You look as if you've just gone through the mangle," his friend laughed, as he ordered them their pints. "Was the first day with your legal eagle that bad?"

"No worries on that score," he replied. "I've just broken the news to my mother that I could be working for the Agency, and as I rather expected, she is none too pleased."

"No surprises there then. Have you told Alex?"

"No, couldn't get through to her, but I left a message and as she is staying at the pub as company for Hannah at the moment, I am sure there will be a full family council meeting in my absence this evening."

"I suspect Alex is the one who is going to give you the most grief," advised his friend. "Struck me as a young lady – a very attractive young lady I must say – who knows exactly what she wants out of life, and from what you tell me, I suspect you are right at the top of her 'want list' right now. I think she sees herself as the glamorous wife of a gallant war hero, pushing you to new heights above and beyond your normal social circles, with you at her beck and call."

"That's a bit hard, Fred," he answered ruefully. "I thought I saw a totally different side to her this last trip home, more like the old Alex I knew in my teens."

"Well, I may be wrong and for your sake, I hope I am – if of course, things with you and her stay on course after she realises that she has the Agency as competition for your attention in the future. But come on, time for a quiet game of snooker before supper, let's see if you are any better with a cue than a rifle!"

After dinner and two more frames of snooker KB excused himself, and retrieving his mobile phone from the porter, climbed aboard his pick-up and drove a few miles down the road to the boundaries of the Bulford complex. Plugging in the phone to his Bluetooth system, he switched it on and as anticipated, saw he had a text message. It was from Alex and simply read: 'wtf r u thnkng this bettr be a 9 to 5 job luv u 2 alx'

"Not as bad as it might have been," he thought to himself, as he headed back to the Mess, where he found Fred had left for the evening and after an hour of watching television, he opted for an early night and retired to his room.

The following morning, he was down for breakfast early and already seated when he was joined both by Fred and Colin.

"How did yesterday go?" asked his Section Leader, as he sat himself opposite KB.

"Okay I think, though I didn't realize there were so many 'do's' and 'don'ts', mainly 'don'ts'," he replied.

"Unfortunately you have to be able to show a working knowledge of them," Coin said sympathetically. "But don't get yourself too bogged down in the legal niceties, inevitably somewhere along the line you'll find you have to make a split second decision which might well be breaking the rules technically, but providing there is a sound reason for taking any reasonable action you feel appropriate, you will usually have our backing one hundred percent. Is Alan Maidley your tutor?"

"Yes, that's the guy. Seems very knowledgeable and he is certainly being very patient with me."

"Good man," agreed Colin. "Bit of a strange bird though, our Alan. His father was Project Manager for a British Telecommunications company working on a long term contract in Islamabad when he met and married his mother who came from a very wealthy and influential local family. She was of course a Muslim but after some initial opposition from her family it seems to have worked out well. Alan was born in Pakistan and holds dual nationality and also speaks fluent Urdu. Sadly when Alan was still only very young, his mother was killed in the crossfire between the Police and one of the early dissident groups and Alan was with her at the time of the shooting. Shortly afterwards, the lad was brought back to the UK by his father and educated here. If he carries any scars, he doesn't show them, in fact you could say that still waters run deep with our young lawyer friend. I do know however, that if you ever get yourself into any bother, Alan is a good guy to have in your corner. By the way, do you have a suit with you?"

" 'Fraid not, why do you ask?" KB replied.

"Some of Peter's colleagues will be acting as pallbearers for his funeral tomorrow, and we wondered if you would join us?"

"Of course I will," came the immediate response. "I'll ask my folks to bring a suit up for me tomorrow; what are the arrangements?"

"We are meeting in the motel at Solstice Park, just down the road, at 1300 hours, and then making our way down to the crematorium in Salisbury. We need to be there at least twenty minutes before the hearse arrives, so that should give us plenty of time. Andy has also booked a room with a bar for us at the motel after the service, so we can see Peter off properly and of course, your folks are welcome. Have you ever been a pallbearer before?"

"Unfortunately, on several occasions," KB admitted.

"You know the score then," Colin continued. "And by the way, no flowers, but we are suggesting that those who want to can make a donation in Peter's name to the Royal Marines Charitable Trust Fund, and there will be a collection box in the foyer at the crematorium. Incidentally, is your sister aware that she had been named by Peter as his sole beneficiary?"

"I haven't told her anything," said KB. "To be honest, she was so upset when I broke the news to her I didn't think it would be appropriate. In any case, it's not certain yet, is it?"

"Technically no, but realistically it does seem likely. I understand that a notice will be published in the papers calling for any interested party to register a claim against his estate, which will take a while."

"If that's the case, I think it would be best not to say anything to her for the time being," KB added. "After all, isn't there an ex-wife somewhere?"

"No trace of her so far," came the reply. "But I take your point. I'll tell Andy to keep things under wraps for the time being. Anyway, must leave you guys to it," the big man added, finishing his last slice of toast and draining his coffee cup. "If I don't see you before, catch up with you at the Holiday Inn. By the way, shouldn't you call Kathy right away if she has to dig out your togs for tomorrow?"

"Yep, I'll call her from the lobby on my way to my class," agreed KB.

At The Volunteer this time Jack answered the phone, and after asking him to relay the message to Kathy concerning the need for his suit, a white shirt, black tie and shoes, he suggested that they meet at half past twelve, to give himself a chance to change before the other pallbearers arrived.

"Where's this motel?" his father asked.

"Easy to find, Dad." he replied. "Go past Stonehenge and straight on through the next big roundabout you come to, keeping on the A303, and the motel is located on the Solstice Park about a kilometre further on. You turn off left where it is signposted, loop back over the A303 and you can't miss it."

"Sounds fairly simple," said Jack. "Alex is borrowing her dad's car and has kindly offered to drive, as the Land Rover isn't exactly built for long distance comfort, but if it's alright with you we thought we could all travel down together to the crematorium in your truck?"

"That was my plan, Dad. We are going back to the Holiday Inn afterwards anyway, for Peter's wake, so I am sure you will be able to leave Joe's car parked there."

"Sounds good, son. Made up your mind about the job yet?"

"Almost certainly going to take it, Dad," he replied. "But plenty of time to talk about it tomorrow; must dash now or I'll be late for a class."

After ringing off, he collected his notes from the previous day from his room and made his way to the Administration Building to meet his tutor. Warning him that he would be absent the following afternoon, KB was surprised that Maidley was already aware that he would not be present for the scheduled lectures, appreciating that the lawyer's status within the organization was probably such that he was kept fully appraised of most of the Agency's activities.

After another day attempting to absorb as much as possible of the constant stream of information fed to him by his earnest tutor, and after a second trip to the library to sign out yet more books, the man suggested that he spent Wednesday morning revising rather than attending class, a suggestion KB welcomed.

Feeling mentally exhausted after his day, it was a relief to return to the Mess where once more he found Fred all too willing to help him wind down.

"I'm knackered, Fred," he admitted. "Not used to working out the old grey matter at this level of intensity, even college gave you more time to think things through. Thankfully, Maidley has given me tomorrow morning off to 'revise', so the pressure will be off for a few hours."

"Tell you what," his friend replied, "why don't you ditch the books and join me for a work out at the gym, then after breakfast I've got some time booked on the pistol range? You can always catch up on the revision later."

"That sounds a better idea, in fact I was thinking of staying here over the weekend rather than making the trip home again, so I can revise before the exam on Monday."

"Probably a good plan," said Fred. "This place will be pretty quiet, but don't forget to tell the porter you'll be staying over. Incidentally, the Mess doesn't cater for lunches or evening meals on Sunday, so you'll have to fend for yourself."

Wednesday dawned grey and cold and when his alarm went off at quarter past six, it took quite an effort to get up and don his tracksuit. A slow drizzle greeted him as he walked over to the gym where Fred was already warming up. Concentrating on building up the strength in his arms and upper body, he worked himself hard for an hour, and after showering and changing the two met again for breakfast in the Mess.

At the indoor range, they found Warrant Greenaway waiting for them, with the targets already set up.

"Good to see you, gents," he greeted them warmly. "Didn't expect to see you again so soon; more often than not I have to drag you folks in to keep current with your practices."

"My friend here seems to think he has something to prove," Fred laughed in reply. "So let's see who has the edge with the Glock!"

Three quarters of an hour later and after five practices, Fred was ahead in three and KB in two. After the final practice, a twenty shot timed shoot at 25 metres, Greenaway declared in KB's favour, so with honours even, they turned their attention to stripping and cleaning their weapons.

"Some nice shooting this morning, gentlemen," commented Greenaway. "Well above our basic standard requirements; wouldn't want to be on the receiving end in a fire-fight with either of you!"

Back in the Mess there was time for a quick coffee, before Fred left to get changed. Checking out at the porter's desk, KB made his way out to the car park and deciding that it would be best to be early at The Holiday Inn, climbed into the Wildtrak's driving seat and headed south for the A303.

At the motel, he explained to an efficient and smartly dressed receptionist that he was part of the group gathering later in the afternoon for Peter Bowen's wake, who confirmed that it would be quite in order for his family to leave a vehicle in the parking lot while attending the cremation service in Salisbury.

On the spur of the moment, he asked what their day rate would be for a room, thinking that this would make it easier for him to change into his suit when his family arrived, and also provide some privacy for his mother and the girls if they needed it prior to the wake.

"Of course, sir," she replied to his query. "We have a special corporate rate for all members of the Agency, and I can let you have a room until six o'clock this evening for £40.00."

Thanking her, he handed over his credit card, filled out a day occupancy registration form, and received the keys to a ground floor suite.

"Leave the card open," he told the girl, "I may want to charge lunch and drinks to the room."

"No problem," she replied, handing the card back to him. "We'll close it when you return the keys later."

Thanking her for her help, he made his way to the bar and after ordering a large orange juice, took a seat by the window overlooking the car park.

Twenty minutes later and earlier than he had expected, he recognized the Bakers' Vauxhall Insignia with Alex behind the wheel as it pulled into the car park, and downing the last of his drink, went out to meet them.

"You made it in good time," he greeted his father, who was first to get out of the car.

"No wonder," Jack replied. "That girl should be driving Formula One. She certainly doesn't worry too much about official speed limits!"

"Got you here in one piece, didn't I?" came the response from the driver's side. "If you want to get your suitcase, Kris, I'll just pop the boot open."

Walking around to the back, he paused to open the rear passenger door for his mother, before pulling the case from the cavernous trunk.

"I don't think I forgot anything," said his mother, as the five of them made their way back to the hotel. "Where are you going to change?"

"I've booked a day room," he replied. "Much easier than trying to change in the gents' toilets, and thought it might be useful if you and the girls want to freshen up after we get back from Salisbury."

Apart from her initial greeting, KB became acutely aware that Alex was saying very little as they walked towards reception, and Hannah had not spoken at all.

Both girls were dressed in black, and Kathy had chosen a light grey two piece, while Jack had been persuaded to eschew his usual tweed jacket for a grey suit, blue shirt and black tie. Somewhat relieved, he noticed Alex had chosen to wear her pendant, giving him hope he was not entirely out of favour.

Seeing them settled back in the bar, and with a round of drinks ordered, KB found the day room and quickly changed, noticing with some satisfaction that his suit, which had not been worn for some years, still fitted him well even if it were a little tight across the shoulders.

Back at their table, he found his mother and the girls talking quietly among themselves, while Jack stared silently out of the window.

"How about some food?" he ventured, picking up a menu. "We've got plenty of time before the others arrive, so is anyone hungry?"

"I could certainly eat something," agreed his father. "It's been a long time since breakfast as we were all up and about early this morning."

"I'm not really hungry," Hannah admitted, her brother noticing how pale she was looking, a slight puffiness around her eyes suggesting that the morning had not been without its trauma.

"Nor me," said Kathy. "Perhaps we could find something light?"

"Why don't we go for the sharing platter?" Alex suggested. "It seems to have quite a number of things on it."

"Fine by me," KB agreed. "We could add a couple of portions of chips, and if you want something more substantial, Dad, go ahead."

"I think I'll try their bacon baguette," Jack said, with some relief. "Don't go much for those olives and hot chicken wings and stuff, and a baguette would suit me fine."

"And contribute another inch to your waistline," Kathy added wryly.

Returning to the bar, KB placed their order, and while they waited for it to be served, it was Jack who raised the question he knew would be coming.

"Tell us about this job then. What exactly will you be doing, and what kind of a deal is it, that's assuming of course, you have already accepted their offer?"

"I have accepted it," he admitted. "Subject to my passing the assessment tests I am doing at the moment. As I told you briefly on the phone, I'll be putting into practice a lot of what I learnt in the Army, as an Instructor to trainees at the Agency.

"This means I will be teaching them the skills they need to conduct what the Agency calls 'covert surveillance' which basically means keeping an eye on suspects in the field, without them knowing they are being watched. It's all about concealment and observation, which was a key part of my sniper training, so I am well qualified for the job."

"Will you be doing any of the things Peter was doing?" his sister was quick to ask.

"Not likely," he replied. "Most of my time I will be working outside, teaching the trainees camouflage and concealment, giving them advice on what they should be looking for and supervising field exercises from time to time, when we put everything I have taught them to the test."

"Well that doesn't sound too dangerous," said his mother, with some relief. "Will you be away a lot?"

"When courses are running here at Bulford I should be home almost every weekend," he continued glibly. "If we are running a field exercise, I could be away for a week or so at a time, as they won't always be run locally, in fact, they could take place almost anywhere in the UK and even occasionally abroad with some of the Agencies we work with in other countries."

"How about salary?" his father cut in.

"Over thirty-five grand a year for starters, plus all expenses, a good pension, life insurance and salary increases as I rise in seniority. Pretty much the equivalent of what a Staff Sergeant gets if I had still been in the Army, so it's not at all bad."

"That's pretty good, Kath," Jack admitted.

"I suppose all this makes me feel a bit better," his mother replied. "What do you think, Alex?"

"I think Kris and I need to have a chat on our own," the girl answered, as their food arrived at the table.

Not long after they had finished their meal, Fred appeared at the entrance to the restaurant and beckoned KB to follow him. In the lobby the pallbearers were gathered and at Reynard's suggestion they moved into the lounge for a briefing.

Apart from Fred, KB and the Head of Operations, Colin Hunter, Bill Hutchinson, Charlie Carstairs and Scotty completed the group.

"Colin, you and Charlie are the tallest so you two will pair off at the rear." said Reynard. "Fred, you and KB will be in the middle, and Bill and myself will be at the front. Scotty, you are the shortest of us, so you will lead us in and make sure the coffin does not slip. It's only a short distance from where the hearse will arrive to the chapel and there are no steps, so it should be an easy carry. The coffin will be draped with the Union flag, and Peter's green beret and campaign medals will be placed on top. After the service, KB you will walk forward and remove the beret and medals and you and I Colin will remove the flag. I will hold it at the fly and Colin, will fold it from the hoist. Once folded, KB will place the beret and medals on top of it, and as it is highly unlikely Peter will have any relatives or designated next of kin present, I think it would be appropriate if I presented it to your sister, KB, what do you think?"

"I think she would be very pleased," KB replied, momentarily at a loss to find the right words.

"One other thing," the man continued. "The Royal Marines are sending a bugler to sound last post, and after the blessing and as we leave the chapel, the Royal Marines march past will be played through the audio system. The chaplain at the crematorium is familiar with handling these occasions for the military, so we are in good hands. If there are no questions, I suggest you take a comfort break if needed, and then we will gather in the car park before moving off for Salisbury."

Back in the restaurant, KB signed off his tab and while Kathy, Hannah and Alex left to 'powder their noses', he took the opportunity to mention to his father that Reynard intended to give the flag to Hannah.

"You'd better warn her," Jack advised him. "I think she'll be keeping her emotions pretty well in check, but it wouldn't be fair not to tell her."

As they emerged into the car park, they found the pallbearers waiting for them, and KB wasted no time in introducing his family to his new colleagues.

As it turned out, his warning to Hannah of what to expect at the service became unnecessary when, after shaking her warmly by the hand, Andy Reynard put a hand on her shoulder and took her aside. Out of earshot from the rest of them, he spoke to her quietly and KB was relieved to see her nod her head several times.

"Time to make a move," he said as he and Hannah rejoined them. "I'll take Colin and Bill with me, Scotty and Charlie with Fred and KB you can bring up the rear." Handing KB a slip of paper he added, "Here's the post code of the crematorium, KB, plug it into your sat-nav if you lose us, so we'll see you there."

As they turned onto the A338 it was Hannah who broke the silence.

"Why is Mr Reynard giving me a flag, Kris?" she asked her brother.

"At the funerals of serving or former members of the Armed Forces, it is tradition that the coffin is draped with the Union flag, which is often handed to the next of kin as a memento," he replied. "And this is often accompanied by that person's medals and in this case, Peter's green beret, which is treasured by Royal Marines as much as the maroon beret is by the Paras."

"Yes, but I'm not Peter's next of kin," she replied. "So why me?"

"We all knew how you and Peter felt about each other, and as Peter does not have any family, Andy Reynard and Bill Hutchinson, who were his superiors, thought it would be appropriate."

"Well I think it's a very nice gesture," Kathy broke in. "And I'm sure Peter would have wanted you to have something to remember him by."

"And there may be more to come," KB thought to himself, little knowing just how much and how true that would turn out to be.

Chapter Twenty-Five

Gift Horse

"I could manage that horse," replied he, "Better than others do."
Alexander the Great on seeing Bucephalus (Plutarch)

The funeral had gone as well as any such occasion could. KB had not been surprised at the number of people who attended the service. Even in the relatively short time he had been associated with the Agency he had come to realise what a well-liked and respected man Peter had been.

Andy Reynard's eulogy had emphasized the professionalism of the man, but also underlying Peter's compassion and concern for others. Hannah had played her part stoically and it was not until the final notes of the Last Post had faded away that she allowed herself a moment to dry her eyes, her father's arm firmly around her shoulders. Lifted by the buoyant strains of 'A life on the Ocean Wave' as they left, the sombre mood was lightened by a relaxed reception back at the hotel, which KB felt certain Peter would have appreciated most of all.

Before they departed for their return journey back to Somerset, KB had a brief opportunity to explain that he would not be home for the weekend, and with Alex showing no signs of wanting to pursue the conversation on his future, it was with mixed emotions that he waved them off from the car park.

As Fred had predicted, the Mess was quiet enough over the weekend to allow KB to catch up on his revision, enabling him to pass his first test paper with moderate success the following Monday. During the week further work in the classroom followed, with an in-depth study of the current known status of various terrorist factions believed to be operating within the United Kingdom. With Fred away on his assignment in the Midlands however, his off duty hours were spent in further studies with no distractions except for visits from Colin

Hunter, who joined him from time to time for an update on his progress, and to pass on some useful hints on how to tackle some of the more onerous sections of his training.

After phoning Kathy to tell her to expect him, it was with some relief and anticipation of a quiet weekend at home that not long after checking out from the Mess in Bulford, he was turning the Ranger into the car park at The Volunteer Inn.

As he climbed down from the cab, his sister came round the corner of the stables and beckoned to him excitedly.

Dropping his Bergen by the side of the truck, he caught up with her by the loose boxes, both interior lights shining out into the darkness of the winter evening. From one, Winston peered out over the half door, while Hannah stood in front of the other.

"Look what landed on my doorstep yesterday," she greeted her brother, and stepping up KB found himself looking into the dark brown eyes of one of the most striking horses he had ever seen.

"Isn't he handsome!" she enthused. "He's a six year old Anglo-Arabian thoroughbred, just over 16 hands, registered with papers and everything."

"Good grief, sis, he's a beauty." he exclaimed. "He must have cost you a fortune!"

"Not a penny, Kris," the girl went on. "He arrived yesterday. He's a gift from Amir, and he says he's mine for keeps, and I can do anything I want with him. I've only ridden him once this morning, and he goes like the wind. Haven't jumped him yet, but if he is any good, I'm going to see if he'll make it as a three-day eventer. I'll show you Amir's letter when I come up to the house."

"What does Winston make of him?" he asked, moving across to stroke the muzzle of the other horse. "Must feel his nose has been put out of joint."

"I've been making an extra fuss of him," she assured. "Anyway, he's got used to having Barney around, so the company will be nice for him. I must admit I haven't turned them out together yet, but I'm hoping they'll get on."

"I hope so," he replied. "See you later. Oh, by the way, how's Alex?"

"She's okay. A tad pissed off with you for taking a job with the Agency, but if she's genuinely fond of you, she'll get over it. She went home after the funeral, and collected Barney after this new fella arrived yesterday morning. I think she's a tiny bit envious, but I'm going to involve her in anything I do with him. I don't want her to feel left out, I'd hate to lose her as a friend."

“Me too,” he said to himself, as he left his sister to her work and walked back to the pub.

After taking his Bergen up to his room and unpacking, as expected he found his mother in the kitchen preparing vegetables for the evening meals, and after she willingly accepted his offer of help, he found himself standing at the sink next to her peeling potatoes.

“Hannah seems really happy tonight,” he said as he dropped his first potato into a saucepan of water.

“Yes, and isn’t it great!” Kathy replied. “That horse couldn’t have arrived at a better time. It’s given her something new to focus on and really helped her. Your dad’s a bit worried about the expense of keeping another one, but I’m sure we’ll manage.”

“I’ll tell Dad that I’ll chip in,” KB said without hesitation. “After all, I’m earning good money and my outgoings are minimal, so I’d be pleased to help.”

“I’m sure that will be appreciated, but I shouldn’t rush in too quickly,” his mother warned. “If you and Alex do decide to make a go of things, you’re going to need every penny you earn, and as much as I’m fond of the girl, that one won’t be cheap to keep.”

“Too early to say that yet, Mum,” he answered. “And in any case, I gather I’m not altogether in her good books right now.”

“Well, I’m sure she’ll be in tonight, so you can have a nice quiet chat with her then,” she added. “And when you’ve finished those spuds I’ll put the kettle on and we’ll have a cuppa and a quick snack together in the lounge, just to tide us over until we close later. Your dad’s in there already, snoring his head off last time I looked in on him.”

With the last potato peeled, in their private lounge KB found his father fully awake from his nap and catching up on the news in the local paper.

“Home safely then?” he commented, looking up as KB joined him in one of the easy chairs. “What have you been up to this last week?”

“Just background stuff, Dad,” he replied. “Everybody who is part of the Agency goes through the same indoctrination – who the bad guys are, and what they are up to, and the tell-tale signs of any activity our agents need to spot when they are on field assignments.”

“So when do you start your proper job?” Jack asked.

“I’ll have finished my training by Christmas, so will probably have my first bunch of recruits under my wing in the New Year.”

“So you’ll be home for the Christmas holiday then?”

"Certainly looks like it, and to be honest, by then I'll probably need a break, so I'm really looking forward to it."

Just then the door to the lounge opened and Kathy came in, carrying a tray of sandwiches, a sponge cake and mugs of tea.

"Hannah's on her way in," she said, as she set the tray down on the coffee table. "What was that I heard you say you were looking forward to?"

"Kris was just saying that he's expecting to be home over Christmas," Jack interjected. "Which means it will be the first time we have had the family together for a year or two."

"We'll have to push the boat out then," said Kathy, as she handed a mug of tea and a plate to KB.

"What's the pub schedule over the holiday, Dad?" KB asked.

"Busy as usual," came the reply. "Open all day on Christmas Eve, fully booked for Christmas Day lunches but once the punters have departed we will be closed for the rest of the day. We're opening at noon for drinks only on Boxing Day and I'm closing again in the afternoon with a self-service buffet in the evening, but having you around will be a great help."

"Don't forget we have the meet here on Boxing Day also, Dad," said Hannah as she joined them. "And if my big brother is going to be at home, I thought he might like to ride Winston for me while I give my new boy his first public airing."

Nearly choking over the mouthful of tea he was in the process of swallowing, KB managed to splutter, "Hang on a moment, sis, you know me and horses. We're best friends as long as I'm not riding them, but once I'm in the saddle, that relationship seems to change!"

"Don't be daft," came the rejoinder. "Or would your leg be a problem?"

Being only too aware of the subtle challenge in his sister's remark, he paused briefly before replying.

"I don't think so. Let's just say I'll think about it, and perhaps we'll give it a trial run when you ride your new steed out one day, but right now, I'm not making any promises. Anyway," he added, anxious to change the subject, "what's the new kid's name?"

"His official name, as per the register, makes him sound a real woos – Conte de Vainqueur – which suggests there may have been a French connection in his bloodline, but I can't imagine the locals swallowing that one without a snigger or two, so I'm going to re-name him. As Peter died protecting the guy who gave him to me, I'd like something that connects the horse with him, any ideas?"

Surprised at his sister's suggestion and the calm way in which she had made it, it was a moment before he answered.

"You could always call him Bootneck," he suggested, hoping his attempt at humour would not upset her.

"Oh, Kris, that's awful," came the instant response. "But why Bootneck?"

"It's one of the nicknames we in the Army bestow on the Royal Marines," he replied. "And I'm sure Peter would see the funny side of it!"

"Well I can tell you now, it won't be Bootneck," she said firmly. "You'd better come up with something better than that."

Thinking carefully he ventured, "Okay then, how about Commando?"

"And what does Commando mean?" she asked.

"It's a collective noun for a bunch of bootnecks," he replied, ducking as a sandwich came whistling across from where she sat. "No, seriously, sis," he added quickly as a second missile was about to be launched in his direction. "It's not that at all. To be a Royal Marine Commando is something quite special, not quite as special as being a Para of course, but it does mean that you've been trained to tackle almost any task that comes your way, and believe me, to be able to call yourself a Commando gains you respect in any Armed Forces, anywhere in the world."

"I really like that," Jack said. "It's a really strong name, just hope he can live up to it."

"I like it too," agreed Hannah. "Commando it is. Oh and by the way, here's the letter from Amir that came when he was delivered." Digging into the pocket of her jeans, she pulled out a crumpled envelope, from which she extracted a single sheet of paper which she handed to her brother.

"*My Dear Hannah*" he read.

"*Words cannot express my sadness at the loss of my good friend Peter Bowen and I know that you two were very close. In truth, it was due to his bravery and that of your brother, that I still have my life and I am truly mindful of the debt I owe.*

I have thought long and hard of how I can show my gratitude in some small way, and knowing that you and I share a great love of horses I hope you will accept this gift with my very best wishes. Please do with Conte de Vainqueur whatever you wish, and I am sure that whatever the future you choose for him, he will give you much enjoyment.

I hope that at some time in the future, our paths may cross again and please remember you are always welcome here at my home in Surpor.

My family join with me in offering you our deepest condolences at this time. Please give my warmest regards to Kris, Jack, Kathy and Alex.

With sincere affection,

Amir"

"That's great, sis," he said, refolding the letter and handing it back to her, noticing as he did that the brave face was beginning to crumble. With a mumbled excuse that she needed to change, his sister left him with his parents.

"Have you read the letter?" he asked, as Kathy stooped to pick up the remains of the sandwich off the carpet.

"Of course," she replied, replacing plates and mugs on the tray. "I'm leaving you to it; I still have work to do in the kitchen."

"You took a chance then, young man," his father commented, as Kathy left the room. "Your attempt at humour could have backfired, but I must say, the arrival of 'Commando' seems to be helping her get over Peter. Just as a matter of interest and between you and I, Amir certainly thinks you played more than just an onlooker's role in Peter's accident, so what's with this 'bravery' bit he mentions in his letter?"

For a split second he was tempted to tell his father the truth but heeding the words of caution he had been given, he said, "Bit of an exaggeration, Dad. Didn't do too much except keeping Amir from freaking out until they got us out of the wreck."

"Hmm," came the response from the older man. "Still not certain you are telling us everything, but no matter. Now if you would like to come and give me a hand bottling up, I would appreciate it."

A steady Friday night kept him and his father busy behind the bar, and it had just gone nine o'clock when the crowd of regulars were joined by Joe and Amy Baker with Alex, the latter greeting him with a cautious smile and a quick kiss on the cheek.

"Can we go somewhere quiet for a moment for a chat?" she asked, as he served them their drinks.

"Sure," he answered. "Dad can manage here for a moment. Let's go back to the lounge."

"How's the new job going then?" she asked, as he closed the lounge door behind them.

"A bit boring, still doing stuff in the classroom at the moment," he replied. "But I expect to get started for real after Christmas."

"Kris, I'm concerned," the serious tone of her voice suggested that she was still none too happy with his choice of employment. "I understand that you will be working for the Agency as an Instructor, but I am not convinced this is going to keep you out of the firing line. After all, Peter was supposedly just guarding a student at college and look what happened to him. I know the student was not your usual farmer's son, but who could have possibly imagined that Peter would be killed in a quiet country lane in the backwoods of Cornwall, apparently in the line of duty? I mean, what would you say if you were asked to undertake the kind of assignment he was involved with?"

"No one at the Agency is suggesting that kind of involvement," he assured her. "But I'll have a much better idea of the scope of my responsibilities in a few months' time. Alex, we've grown up together and you know how I feel about you, always have, so I'll make you a promise. If after six months I am finding that things are not working out as I had expected, I'll quit the job, and find something else – perhaps even go back to college – what do you say?"

"I suppose that's reasonable," she said. "But in the meantime, Kris, although I want to see as much of you as possible, I think we should have a clear understanding that we are both free agents. I won't be going out looking for anyone else, but at the same time, you never know what lies around the corner and that goes for both of us."

"I understand," he replied. "But I won't be looking for anyone else either."

"That's settled then," said the girl. "Now come and give me a proper kiss, before we brave the prying eyes and questions that I'm sure our parents are bursting to ask."

Ten minutes later they returned to find that Kathy and Hannah had finished in the kitchen, and had joined Amy and Joe at the bar. As Alex had predicted, they had to fend off a few none too subtle questions from their respective mothers before the conversation turned to Commando's arrival, and Hannah's plans for the thoroughbred.

"He's the right build for a Trials horse," suggested his sister. "And he's certainly got the speed. If he's got the stamina and jumps well, he might make the grade."

"Then there is the element of dressage," KB reminded his sister. "That's a tricky discipline at the best of times."

"We thought we'd ask Carol Watson for her advice," said Alex. "She was quite a star at three day events in her day, and rode at Badminton several years running. If anyone can tell us whether Commando has the makings of an eventer, she will."

“Sounds as if you have the makings of a ‘Team Commando’ here,” laughed Joe. “But you girls are going to have your hands full with his training, and exercising Winston and Barney as well.”

“We could have some help with that,” said Hannah, looking directly at KB. “When my brave brother is home for the weekends, he’s going to help us ride them out, and he has also volunteered to ride Winston for me on Boxing Day meet.”

“I don’t know about ‘volunteering’ ” KB retorted. “More like being press-ganged, and in any case I’ll need to get some practice in before then.”

“No time like the present,” Alex suggested, with a twinkle in her eye. “What say we all ride out together on Sunday morning? Traffic will be light if we want to hack them around the lanes, or we can always go for a gentle canter across the Levels.”

“What an excellent idea,” laughed his sister. “You can give me a hand sprucing up the tack tomorrow, Kris, and we’ll plan on setting off at around nine on Sunday morning.”

“Railroaded again,” his father said to him quietly, nudging him in the ribs. “I’m really beginning to worry about you.”

As he climbed into bed later that night, the full realisation of what he had committed himself to

fully dawned on him, first of all in his commitment to Alex. Six months was a long time, and who knows – he reasoned – perhaps he would have had enough of the Agency by then and he would be able to keep his promise to her?

Putting those thoughts to one side, he concentrated on the more immediate dilemma he faced. After so many years being no more than a sideline supporter of his sister’s equestrian activities, now he had agreed to get astride a horse again and become an active participant in her plans.

An accident, perhaps resulting in an injury to himself or damage to his precious artificial leg, would not endear him either to his new employers or the technicians at Headley Court who took so much care in servicing and making constant improvements to his state-of-the-art prosthetic limb. On the other hand if he were to retain any kind of respect from Alex and his sister, backing out was not an option, so offering up a silent prayer to Mother Nature in the hopes that on Sunday morning a massive storm would sweep across the Levels forcing a cancellation of the planned ride out, he switched off his bedside light and was soon fast asleep.

After taking Rocky for a walk and breakfast the following morning, Hannah was true to her word and KB found himself confined to the tack room for nearly two hours cleaning and saddle soaping all the accoutrements needed for the next day. By 11.00 a.m. he had finished the tasks his sister had allocated him, and leaving her schooling Commando in the paddock, walked back to the pub to make himself a cup of coffee.

He had just sat down in the lounge to enjoy his break, when the pub phone rang. Picking it up he was surprised when instead of someone calling to make a dinner reservation as he expected, the CO of The Wessex Rifles came on the line.

"Morning, Sergeant Blake," came Lieutenant Colonel Hazell's crisp tones. "Glad I caught you in. Three things, first of all we have had approval from the MoD to enrol you if you are still interested, with the acting rank of Staff Sergeant to become substantive after six months if all goes well. Secondly, I received a call from a Mr Andrew Reynard confirming your new civilian occupation, and I must congratulate you. Mr Reynard filled me in on the background to your recruitment, and it seems that you already have made your mark with the Agency.

"He also stressed the need for the upmost confidentiality, and apart from myself there will only be a few others aware of your position, and then on a strict 'need to know' basis. Among them will be Major Denby, our Training Major, Captain Phillips, our Adjutant and of course the RSM, all of whom you have met already. I have told Mr Reynard that we will support you in any way we can, and if you need to take advantage of any of our facilities, you only have to ask.

"Finally, we are having a Battalion get-together on the Saturday evening before Christmas. Bit of an 'open house' for our soldiers and their families with a buffet laid on and all that sort of thing, and a chance to mix and mingle. All three of the Messes will be open – Officers', Senior Ranks' and the Junior Ranks' Club, and we are putting on a few displays to entertain our guests. Officers and Senior Ranks will be in Mess Kit and the men in No.2 Dress, so if you can dig out your uniform, please feel free to wear it. Gives us a chance to show off a bit, and the womenfolk always seem to like it! Please bring a guest if you would like to invite someone, and we hope to kick things off at about 1900 hours. Lord knows what time things will end; our pre-Christmas gatherings have a reputation for being fairly lengthy affairs, but I'm usually on my way home well before midnight. How does all that sound?"

"It sounds fine, sir," he replied. "And thank you for the invitation to the open house. I believe I will be finishing at Bulford at midday on the Friday, so I'll look forward to joining you on Saturday. I would also like to bring a guest with me and look forward to seeing you then."

"Splendid," said the CO. "See you at the party, and in the meantime the best of luck with the Agency; from what Reynard has told me you have taken to it like a duck to water, so I hope it continues to go well."

Reflecting on the phone call, the pleasure he felt at the outcome was tinged with surprise. In his years in the Regular Army he had never come across an instance when the Commanding Officer of a Battalion had taken the time to speak to a Sergeant personally on such matters, usually delegating such matters to his Adjutant or the RSM. Obviously the Colonel felt his status as a member of the Agency merited such involvement, and already he found himself warming towards the Rifles.

There was of course, another problem that he would now have to confront. In his efforts to minimize the hazards to his new profession to his family and Alex, he had not mentioned his potential involvement with the Army Reserves. Perhaps, he thought to himself, he could somehow explain that a combination of both was all part of his overall job description, maximizing the employment of the skills the Army had given him. Alex of course, would be his guest at the Battalion's Christmas party, and he hoped that by giving her an opportunity to share a social event of this kind with him, he might persuade her that there was another side to his new position that they could enjoy together.

The Volunteer stayed open on Saturday afternoon, and his father was delighted when he offered to run the bar for him, giving the older man the opportunity for a much welcomed afternoon relaxing. By the time Jack came to relieve him, night was drawing in fast and he barely had time to take Rocky for a walk along the river bank in the gathering gloom. As he turned for home a shadowy figure confronted them, bringing Rocky to a halt a couple of metres to his front, the dog leaning forward to sniff the air and growl a warning to the intruder.

Cursing himself for leaving the Glock in his truck, he was relieved when the newcomer flicked a lighter to ignite a pipe of tobacco, illuminating the ruddy features of Obi Kernworthy.

"Hold on there, young Kris," came the familiar voice out of the gloom. "An' tell your bleddy dog to back orf, don't want the arse of these breeches tord out like 'ee did to thik Samson fella."

"Sorry, Obi," KB hastened to reply. "I guess we're both a bit jumpy. What brings you out at this time of night?"

"Jest checkin' on the sheep I got in the next field along. There's bin talk of sheep rustlers up to their tricks again in these parts, and I never 'ad a chance to check on 'em earlier, as I was down to Taunton market again this marnin'."

"I'll join you," said KB. "Do you have a torch with you?"

"Oh ar," replied the farmer. "Got one of these gurt big jobs along wi' me. Shines a fair old light, so we should be able to zee pretty good."

"How do these sheep stealers work, Obi?" he asked the man, as they walked back along the river bank.

"Was a time when the buggers only went about their work very late at night when all us volks were sound asleep," he said. "But just recently, any time after dark zeems to suit 'em. There's so few coppers around these days, they'm jest thumbin' their noses at us and don't zeem to give a duck's twaddle about being spotted. Mind you, wudn't like to tackle 'em on my own anyway, Police tell us there's always at least dree or four of them working a flock, plus their dogs and they done it so often, they'm got really slick at it. Big cattle truck all ready to load up, an' everything."

"Once they've got them loaded, where do they take them?"

"Oh, they'm bleddy clever," Obi continued. "I unnerstan' they'll buy a few sheep yer and there at regular markets, all legal an' above board as it twer, and then alter the paperwork so it looks like they bought the whole load proper. Then they head up north to some wholesaler who turns a blind eye to where the lambs come from, and 'ee pays 'em cash at way below the real market price. Next thing you know, lambs all butchered and before mother knows it, she's bought a piece an is servin' it up for Zunday lunch."

"Do you think that was what Nathan Samson and his mates were up to when we bumped into them at the market two weeks ago?"

"All I knows is, the buggers didn't buy any of mine, and I didn't see 'em when I were down there today, so who knows?"

Reaching the flock, Obi switched on the big hand-held torch and swept the beam slowly over the flock.

"They all zeem to be there," he said. "And to be honest, I thought they be alright; to get a wagon down yer to 'em would be difficult, and they'd 'av to drive out to the road before loading 'em up. As the only gateway is close to the village and almost opposite your pub, they'd be taking a real chance, but the sheer neck of these buggers is unbelievable and as nearly all my animals is premium lamb, they might consider the risk worth it. Anyway, let's get back, it's getting too cold for an old fella like me to be farting around out yer, and I might just take a pint off 'ee before I 'eads 'ome."

"You're more than welcome, Obi," KB replied. "And I suggest you keep that torch of yours switched on. We don't want to be slipping off the bank and into the river on a night like this."

"True enough," said the farmer, shining the light down the towpath. "Reckon' that water is cold enough to freeze yer bollocks off; I have enough trouble finding mine as it is, without they becoming frost bit."

Back in the warmth of the bar, KB saw Obi settled into a seat by the fire with a pint in front of him, and excusing himself, went upstairs to shower and change.

After he showered, he hopped over to his wardrobe, and from its inner recess removed his spare artificial leg. Seated on the bed, he strapped it onto his stump, and standing up took a couple of turns around his bedroom. It had been months since he had worn this particular prosthetic limb, and it lacked all the refinements of the new model he had grown so use to. It took a while therefore, for him to feel comfortable and become accustomed to the more stilted gait which he was now forced to adopt to avoid tripping up.

After ten minutes he was satisfied that it would suit his purpose, and replacing it with the leg that had now become his daily companion, he put it to one side. No point in risking more than he had to when he rode out the following morning, and he felt sure his spare would do just as well slotted into a stirrup.

Downstairs in the bar, he was met by Alex carrying an armful of bottled mixers from the cellar.

"Hi, Kris," she greeted him. "Dropped in early to have a chat with Hannah and as your dad tells me you're in for a busy evening, I've volunteered to give you a hand."

"Thanks for that, all help much appreciated," he said. "And by the way, we've been invited to a party."

"Where and when might that be?" she asked.

"Saturday before Christmas, an evening bash down in Exeter at the Headquarters of the local Army Reserve unit – the Wessex Rifles.

"As part of my new job I've agreed to help them train their snipers, and their Commanding Officer thought it would be nice to invite me and a guest to their pre-Christmas party. It sounds quite a lavish affair, apparently everyone is expected to dress up for the occasion, and I thought you might like to go with me?"

"I'll need a new outfit," came the quick reply. "It's ages since I've been to a posh do."

"Tell you what," he heard himself saying. "We'll drive down to Exeter in the morning, do some shopping and I'll buy you a new dress if you haven't found anything suitable by then. We can check in at a hotel and have a nice lunch, go to the party in the evening, stay the night and come home on Sunday morning, what do you say?"

"Sounds great," she said, and then putting her arm around his shoulder whispered, "even though it seems as if you are going to a lot of trouble just to have your wicked way with me!"

"The thought never occurred to me," he whispered back. "But now that you mention it... ."

Laughing as she pulled away from him, the tone of her next question was rather more serious.

"Are you all ready for tomorrow morning?"

"As ready as I'll ever be," he admitted. "I can't believe I allowed my sister to talk me into it. I think the last time I got on a horse was when you and I went for a ride together just before I left to join the Army."

"You'll be fine," she assured him, and with a twinkle in her eye added, "but if you do come a cropper, my first aid skills are second to none, particularly when it comes to giving the kiss of life."

"I bet," he thought to himself, as they turned back to the bar to serve their waiting customers.

In spite of his silent pleas to Mother Nature for a downturn in the weather, Sunday morning dawned cold but bright, with the slightest dusting of an overnight frost suggesting in racing pundits terms, that the going across the Levels and down the droves would be 'good to firm'."

Eight o'clock found him sitting on his bed strapping on his spare artificial leg, after digging out a well-worn pair of jeans and a checked flannel lumberjack shirt from his wardrobe.

Downstairs the kitchen was empty, suggesting that Kathy was planning a brunch for the family after he and the girls had returned from their ride, and seeing the lights from the stables, he guessed Hannah had beaten him to it and was already getting Commando ready for his exercise. Putting on the kettle, he made two mugs of strong tea and with Rocky following, carried them across the car park, where he found his sister mucking out her new horse's stable.

"Tea's up, sis," he called to her, opening the door to the tack room and feeling relieved that during the short walk he had managed to avoid spilling too much of the steaming brown liquid, while concentrating on keeping his balance wearing the unfamiliar prosthetic limb. Setting the mugs down on the workbench, he retrieved his hard hat from a peg on the wall where Amir had left it and put it on, fastening the chin strap.

"Can you grab a bale of straw for me and I'll be right there," she called back.

Around the back of the stables Hannah kept a small stack of straw and hay bales and as he threw back the tarpaulin that covered them, a grey rat the size of a large kitten shot out from underneath and dived between his legs in a bid for freedom. In a flash Rocky sprung forward in an attempt to seize the fleeing rodent, knocking into KB as he struggled to stay on his feet and tipping him backwards into the straw.

"What the hell are you up to?" Hannah laughed, as she came around the corner of the loose boxes to see him lying on his back and with his legs in the air, the dog leaning over him frantically licking his face by way of an apology.

"Rocky tripped me," he said, as he struggled to lever himself up on the straw bales. "It's this bloody leg, I thought I'd be clever and use my spare one just in case I came off Winston and damaged my high-tech one on this ride I stupidly allowed myself to get talked into."

Detecting the note of bitterness in her brother's last remark, she helped him to his feet and dusted the straw off him. "You don't have to do this if you don't want to," she said sympathetically, but just then the clip-clop of hooves across the car park announced Barney's arrival and a moment later they were joined by Alex.

"A bit late to back out now, sis" he replied. "So let's get this show on the road."

Hannah had already saddled up Winston, who she now led out of his stable across to the mounting block, and which KB climbed, swinging his good right leg over the horse's back and landing in the saddle in an effective if somewhat inelegant movement.

Lifting his artificial leg up he allowed Hannah to slot the foot into the stirrup and she checked the girth for any last minute adjustment.

"Looks pretty good, Kris," she commented. "How does it feel?"

"A tad strange and bloody uncomfortable," he replied. "I'd far sooner be standing on the tailgate of a Herc waiting for the green light, but as strapping on a 'chute is out of the question – let's get on with it."

With Hannah leading the way on Commando, the three horse cavalcade moved out across the park, and as they got level with the back door of the pub, Jack and Kathy emerged.

"Had to see this," Jack called to them. "Cheer up, Kris, don't look so bloody miserable, this could be the first of many!"

"Or the last!" he called back, waving to them as they turned out of the yard onto the road.

"Which way are we heading?" asked Alex, as she drew level with Hannah.

"Up onto the towpath and along by the River to Stodgell's Drove, across East Moor towards Kingsbury and then back," came the reply.

"That's the same route as Hannah took Amir," KB thought to himself, happy to let the girls go on ahead as he brought up the rear, Rocky loping along at their heels.

The trip out to Kinsgbury was uneventful. Once on the Moor, Hannah let Alex move into the lead and the three of them broke into a gentle canter. The grey of the morning was lifting as they approached the village, the sun breaking through and dispelling the gloom of the November morning with bright shafts of sunlight that shimmered off the surface of the wide expanses of water that were a constant feature of the Levels at this time of year. A hundred or so metres to their left a flock of plovers took off in a flurry of spray, looping and wheeling around them as they climbed away.

To his surprise KB found that he was enjoying himself, gaining confidence with every stride that Winston took, so much so that he urged the horse forward to close the gap that had opened up between himself and the two girls in front of him.

With the tower of Kingsbury church looming in front of them, Hannah and Alex reined in their mounts, allowing him to catch up with them. As they rested their horses, Alex took a small flask from her jacket pocket and unscrewing the top, took a swig then handed it to Hannah.

"Dutch courage for the return trip," Alex said, smiling as she passed the flask to KB. "Although I must say you're doing really well, Kris. Maybe you missed your vocation and should have enlisted in the cavalry!"

"A definite 'no' to that," he replied. "Wouldn't have made it as a donkey-walloper."

Just then the first peal of bells rang out from the church tower, echoing across the Levels as they had for hundreds of years. As if in reply, and at a pause in the change, the bells of the Long Sutton church could be heard faintly in the distance.

"It sounds as if they're talking to each other," said Alex as they sat listening.

"It also means we should be heading back," added Hannah. "If we are to be home in time for the brunch Mum is preparing for us, we'd better get going. I'm going to give my new boy here a bit of a gallop, so you don't have to try to keep up, Kris – just take it easy and we'll see you at home."

"In half an hour or so!" laughed Alex, as she wheeled Barney around to follow her friend.

"Come on, Winston, old son," he muttered to his mount. "We're not taking that lying down," and digging in his heels, he urged the big hunter forward.

Eager to accept the challenge the horse broke into a headlong gallop, the speed of which almost unseated him as they thundered in pursuit. Gritting his teeth, he soon caught the rhythm of Winston's powerful strides and within half a mile had drawn level with Alex and Barney. Whooping like an Apache Indian he gradually pulled ahead of the girl, but in spite of their efforts, he and Winston were not able to make any ground on the fast disappearing figure of his sister. Easing the horse up gradually, he allowed Alex to catch up with him and moments later they joined Hannah who had reined in the thoroughbred and was waiting for them.

"Crickey, don't know about a three day eventer, but if that horse can jump as well as he gallops he's got to be a natural as a National Hunt chaser," exclaimed Alex as Barney stood head down, blowing hard from his exertions. "And if you brush up your riding skills, Kris, you could be in the saddle," she added. "Just imagine, you could make history, the first one legged National Hunt jump jockey!"

"Not in a thousand years," he was quick to answer. "An occasional ride out like this on Winston, and maybe, I say again maybe, the annual Boxing Day Hunt, but there is no way I am being conned into getting on board that streak of lightning for a trip round Wincanton or Cheltenham. Anyway, I am sure if Hannah can develop his jumping skills, there will be a few point-to-points she will want to ride in, eh, sis?"

"We'll see," she replied. "But let's walk them home to cool off – they've all had a pretty good work-out."

Back at the stables the three horses were rubbed down and leaving them on nets of hay, their riders joined Kathy and Jack for the promised brunch. After fresh grapefruit, Kathy gave them the option of a full English or steak and eggs, an American tradition which was frequently asked for when transatlantic visitors stayed over at the pub during the summer months, and one of KB's favourites.

After brunch, KB climbed the stairs to his room to shower and change the artificial leg he had worn for their ride for the more advanced prosthetic. Sitting on the edge of his bed, he was checking his stump for any signs of chafing, when his bedroom door opened and Alex slipped into the room.

Before he could say a word, the girl started to undress.

"Your jaw has dropped about six inches," she laughed at him. "But, lover boy, I have to tell you that bouncing up and down in the saddle makes me feel as horny as hell, so if you think your riding for the day is over, you can think again! It's back in the saddle for you, my lad, and I can promise you this is going to be far more exciting than any gallop we had this morning, and don't you dare pass the finishing post before I do, or you're in big trouble!"

Tossing her discarded bra onto the floor, she stepped out of her panties, and pushed him back onto the bed, the next half hour proving the truth of every word she had spoken.

Chapter Twenty-Six

The Festive Season

"At Christmas play and make good cheer,
For Christmas comes but once a year."

Thomas Tusser 1524-1580

In the weeks leading up to the Christmas break, back at the Agency he found himself spending less and less time in the classroom and more time in the field. For KB working in a rural environment was never a problem and he thoroughly enjoyed the variety of tests and assignments he was given. Even an assignment covertly observing an Army training exercise in the wilds of Northumberland's Otterburn ranges in the bitter cold of early December did nothing to suppress his enthusiasm.

It was, however, in the urban jungles of Bristol and Birmingham he struggled. Static surveillance was boring but tolerable, but moving around the darkened streets of some of the less fashionable areas of those great cities was frequently unnerving and left him feeling vulnerable and exposed. In the country his disability provided him with less of a physical challenge where he could rely on easy access to a vehicle, but following suspects through back alleys and winding side streets on foot brought home the realisation that he could not expect to be as agile as any of his targets, and it showed in his course assessments.

It was following one of these week long exercises, that he found himself in front of Andrew Reynard. Half expecting to be thrown off the course having lost two of the three suspects he had been tasked with trailing, he was not surprised at the stern demeanour of the Chief of Operations when he was shown into his office.

"Sit down, KB," said the Director of Operations, in whose hands KB's future now lay. "Let me get straight to the point. When we employed you, it was recognized that there would be limitations to the areas in which we could best use your talents, and your last two assessments have certainly confirmed that. You are obviously in your element working in the countryside, and in that respect your mentors have given you some of the highest ratings I have ever seen on any of the courses run here since I took over.

"The downside is that in an urban environment you are like a fish out of water, and although your static surveillance skills are quite satisfactory, unfortunately that only accounts for about a third of the time you could be spending on this type of assignment.

"Quite frankly, once you are on the move you become quickly disorientated and your mentors tell me that even in a crowd you unfortunately stick out like a sore thumb, so you could be something of a liability in an urban scenario.

"However, again on the plus side, I note you have been putting in plenty of time on the pistol and rifle ranges and you are undoubtedly a superb marksman, so all in all I have decided that we would be wise to keep you, even though the counter terrorist activities that we are usually engaged with tend to be focussed on the larger areas of population. I will, however, be putting a note in your file to the effect that your primary assignments should be in rural environments in which you clearly excel; are you prepared to accept that?"

KB had willingly given his consent, and was about to leave when Reynard added,

"I see you have booked out over the Christmas holiday, so please give my regards to your family. To give you an update on Peter Bowen's will, as you know, we have been advertising for any claimants against his estate to come forward, and our legal people have been contacted by his ex-wife. It appears she has re-married and is currently living in Australia, and it seems a relative saw our notice in a newspaper and notified her. As your sister was not married to Peter and had known him for only a relatively short time, the ex-wife could have a strong claim. It seems certain that the distribution of Peter's estate will now be down to a Probate Court, and I'll give you a 'heads up' if that becomes the case, so that Hannah can also submit a claim if she so wishes."

Thanking Reynard for his consideration and relieved that his new career was not about to come to an abrupt end, he left feeling relieved that his forte for merging with his background in open countryside had been recognized and that hanging around in bus shelters or on street corners might not feature quite so prominently in his future activities.

A few days later he was delighted when Fred Nowakowski appeared in the Mess one evening, having completed his assignment in the West Midlands.

"Good to see you back, Fred," he greeted his friend. "My skills on the pool table have definitely gone a bit rusty in your absence. What can I get you to drink?"

Setting two pints down on the table in front of them, Fred asked,

"So how is the indoctrination going? You're still here so I guess things can't be too bad."

"Reckon I'm only here by the skin of my teeth," KB admitted ruefully. "Things were going really well until they let me loose on the streets of Birmingham, then everything went to rat shit. It seems that I haven't lost my expertise for crawling around in the weeds unnoticed, or – to coin a phrase – 'floating around unseen in the woods at night like Casper the freaking ghost', but once I'm rubbing shoulders with a bunch of commuters or skulking around in some dingy backstreet, I might as well walk around with a bloody great neon sign on my back advertising my presence!"

"So has Reynard had words with you?" his friend asked.

"Yep. Very civilized, but the end result was that my future activities will be mainly restricted to working outside urban areas, which actually suits me well, but probably limits my usefulness to the Agency."

"I shouldn't worry too much about that," said Fred. "We're so damn short on the ground at the moment I'm sure there will be plenty of work for you. Anyway, whatever you do will be a lot better than the stuff I've been up to my eyes in since I last saw you."

"How did that go?" KB asked.

"Reams and reams of data the CID boys put together, all stemming from the one car hire company the BMW came from. In fact there are about thirty companies across the UK who are all interlinked through shareholdings or directorships and it's virtually impossible to determine who is pulling the strings or who sits at the centre of the spider's web. The only common link we have uncovered to date is an organization called Dar al-Amn – literal translation is 'The House of Safety' or a place where Muslims are free to follow their own religion and live subject to their own laws without interference. They're an Islamic fundamentalist organization, a registered charity and apparently one hundred percent legit. Their ultimate objective is to create a self-governing Islamist enclave within the UK with elected leaders, sending their own representatives to Parliament. Their main offices are in London and they're supported by charitable donations from the majority of those thirty companies I mentioned, plus some of the local Muslim communities in our major cities.

"They are very subtle in the way they promote themselves. They insist they are a democratic foundation, willing to work within our overall legal framework whose only wish is to live in peace and harmony with their Christian neighbours. There is certainly no evidence to suggest that they preach or condone any kind of hatred or violence, and to date the hierarchy have tended to regard them as a somewhat harmless if quirky, political anomaly.

"Anyway, my full report will be on Andy's desk in the morning and I've no doubt Charlie Carstairs will also be examining the data in detail, but I have a shrewd suspicion that now they are on our radar we shall be keeping a closer eye on them in future."

"So, no whisper or trace of the whereabouts of Asif, then?"

"Not a hint," added Fred. "Disappeared off the face of the earth to all intents and purposes. His mug shot has now been circulated though, so if he does show up anywhere, there is a chance he could be nabbed. He has no known relatives in Birmingham by the way, so his claim that he was going to spend the weekend with them was a load of bullshit, and so far he hasn't turned up in Surpor or Pakistan, although even if he did, there's no guarantee we would know about it. Anyway, enough shop talk, let's have another pint and some dinner, then I'll take a couple of quid off you on the pool table."

The weeks passed quickly in the run up to Christmas culminating in his final assessment, in front of his full interview board. Apart from the concerns expressed over his shortcomings in the urban exercises, his mentors had generally given him an above average rating in all of the other areas that the indoctrination course had covered, and his position as a qualified Field Operative was confirmed.

Fred had already departed early for the Christmas break, taking part of his annual leave so that he could spend a full two weeks with relatives in Poland. KB had also been able to negotiate three days extra over and above the two days Christmas holiday, so with the weekends he was looking forward to a nine day break.

Signing out after lunch, he stopped off at the pistol range on his way out of the Garrison and delivered a Christmas card and a bottle of single malt whisky to Warrant Greenaway. This, he felt, was the least he could do to show his appreciation for the extra time the man had spent coaching him to a level where his skills on the ranges had been sharpened to a new edge. Clearly delighted with his gift, the Warrant wished him well, and following a further brief stop to fill up with diesel, he set off for Somerset and Christmas in the pub.

He was not surprised to find that The Volunteer was already dressed in full Christmas regalia as he pulled into the car park. Jack had strung coloured lights around the building, and a fully illuminated Christmas tree stood on the patio by the rear porch. Dropping his rucksack in the hall, he walked through to the bar where he found Kathy putting the finishing touches to a second smaller Christmas tree which stood by the entrance to the restaurant.

Garlands of holly and ivy had been hung from the oak beams and a large wreath interwoven with silver and gold baubles hung above the open stone fireplace. More coloured lights framed the bar and every table in the restaurant boasted a centrepiece of fir cones surrounding a pair of red candles.

"Looking great, Mum," he said, giving her a big hug and a kiss.

"We've made a special effort this year," she replied. "So I hope it will be appreciated."

"Good to have you home, son," his father greeted him, as he joined them. "It looks as if we are in for a busy one, so we can use all the help we can get."

"You know I'm not here tomorrow, Dad?" KB reminded him. "I'm taking Alex down to the Rifles' Christmas party in Exeter, so we'll be away most of the day and I've booked a hotel so we will be staying overnight."

"I hadn't forgotten," said Jack with a grin. "Got some extra help coming in from the village over the weekend and for most of the week, so we'll be okay, and Alex is coming in tonight to give a hand if we need it."

"That sounds good, Dad. I hope we can get away around ten o'clock tomorrow morning, as I have some Christmas presents to get, and I expect Alex will want to do some shopping too."

"I'm sure she will," added his mother. "But I do know she has already bought herself a new dress, so you won't have to worry about that, but I'm sure she'll find something else for you to spend your money on!"

"Probably," he replied. "But I'll have to buy her something for Christmas anyway, so I was fully expecting it. Anyway, I need to get upstairs and dig out my Mess kit. I might need to borrow that ironing board, as everything has been hung up in a valise and it's been months since it saw the light of day, so it will certainly need a good airing and almost certainly the dress shirt will need an iron on it."

"You'd better get to it then," said Kathy. "I'll put the ironing board up for you in the living room."

Upstairs in his room, he took the suit bag from his wardrobe and unzipped it, hoping that the moths had not found a way in, always a potential hazard in a building as old as The Volunteer Inn.

Taking out the scarlet tunic with its maroon lapels and cuffs, the black waistcoat and overalls, he checked them carefully and with relief, found no tell-tale signs that moths had been busy. Next he retrieved the black leather George boots he wore with the Mess kit from the bottom of the wardrobe, noticing that they would need some enthusiastic bulling to restore them to an acceptable level of shine, and took his maroon beret off the shelf. Finally, he found his dress shirt in the chest of drawers with its black bow tie, and folding these together with the overalls over his arm, went downstairs to the living room where the iron and ironing board were waiting.

By the time he had finished ironing, polished his boots and given his tunic and beret a good working over with the clothes brush, an hour and a half had slipped by. Taking down his suitcase from the top of the wardrobe, he packed it with his beret, the dress shirt and tie, white braces for his overalls, black socks and a change of shirt and underwear for Sunday morning, leaving the last minute items to be packed before they left. His boots were carefully put into a carrier bag and then placed in the bottom of the valise, which now hung with his Mess kit on the outside of the wardrobe. Mentally checking that he had everything ready, he crossed to his chest of drawers and took out the small box containing a miniature of his Operational Service Medal with its Afghanistan clasp and oak leaf from his Mention in Dispatches, to be pinned on his Mess Kit tunic. Opening it up, he checked to make sure the contents were still intact, remembering to add a pair of Parachute Wings cuff links and the studs for his dress shirt.

Satisfied that he had done everything he could in preparation for the weekend, he had a quick shower and after changing into jeans and a sweater, joined his father and Alex in the bar where they were already busy serving the early arrivals for the evening.

"Hi, Kris," the girl welcomed him with a quick kiss on the cheek. "All set for tomorrow?"

"Just about," he replied. "If it's alright with you, I thought we might head out at around ten o'clock, to give us plenty of time to get down there, have a look around the shops and have a bite of lunch somewhere nice? I've booked us a room in a hotel overlooking Cathedral Green and we'll get a cab out to Wessex Barracks and back. On Sunday morning we can have a leisurely breakfast at the hotel and still be back here around noon."

"Got it all planned then," came the response. "Really looking forward to it; all those handsome young men in their uniforms. I hope you can keep up with me!"

"I'm sure I can," he replied firmly, as they both turned their attention back to the pub's waiting customers.

The evening turned out to be as busy as Jack had predicted, but with the three of them behind the bar, they soon settled into an easy routine, which enabled Alex to break away from time to time and help out Hannah waiting on tables. At half past nine Amy and Joe Baker came in for a drink, and by ten o'clock Kathy had finished the last of the meals, and was able to join them at the bar.

By eleven the remaining few drinkers had left, followed soon after by the Bakers, Alex agreeing with KB that a fairly early night would be wise if they were to be away by ten the following morning.

"I've asked Amy if they would all like to have a late lunch with us on Christmas Day," announced Kathy, as they settled down in the lounge over a light supper. "And she seemed more than happy to accept. I thought I'd roast a goose and a nice sirloin of beef also for those who prefer it, and I've warned her we won't be eating until around five. They'll be plenty of choice of starters and desserts left over from our punters' Christmas lunches, so it won't be too much extra trouble."

"It sounds like a lot of extra work to me," said Jack. "But if you are sure, Kath, we can make quite a party of it."

With that, his sister and their parents went upstairs, leaving KB to walk Rocky around the yard and lock up for the night.

Outside all was still and quiet, as the chill of a clear frosty night settled over the village. Checking that the horses were snug and secure in their stables, he opened the driver's door to the pick-up and took the Glock out of its compartment.

Re-locking the vehicle he retraced his steps to the pub, Rocky at his heels, and after switching out the lights, secured the back door and climbed the stairs to his room.

At seven a.m. his alarm went off, and by seven thirty he had showered and dressed, packing the last of his overnight gear into his suitcase. Taking the Glock out of his jacket pocket, he buried it under the shirts in his chest of drawers and putting on a heavy knit roll-neck sweater he went downstairs and finding the kitchen was empty, called to Rocky. Putting on his heavy winter jacket he took a torch off the shelf in the utility room and with the dog at his heels, ventured out into the dark of the morning.

Overnight sub-zero temperatures had left a white dusting of hoarfrost covering the car park, and his breath hung heavy in the cold air. Picking his way carefully across the slippery surface, he switched on the torch and crossed the road to join the towpath. The black water of the River Yeo moved sluggishly to join the River Parrett, and as he shone the light on to its surface small plates of ice were reflected in its beam, nudging each other like dodgem cars as the current carried them downstream.

"Must have been a cold one last night, old boy," he said to the dog, as he turned up the collar of his jacket against a mild but bitingly cold nor-westerly breeze. "Could be in for some snow," he added using his countryman's instinct to smell and sense the slight dampness in the air, and as if signifying his agreement, the dog elected to stay trotting close by him rather than embarking on one of its more usual forays a way ahead of him.

Back in the yard, the lights from the stables were on and he found Hannah busy mucking out.

"Shouldn't Alex be helping you with that?" he asked, noticing that in addition to Winston and Commando, Barney was also in residence.

"She usually does," his sister replied. "In fact she's pretty good helping out, and with two horses of mine to exercise now she certainly does her bit. But I did suggest she gave things a miss this morning, knowing that you two were off for the day. Have a great time by the way. Alex is certainly looking forward to it, and I'm not entirely sure whether that's because of the social event itself, or the prospect of having some of the Army's fittest young men vying for her attention."

"She did say as much to me!" KB admitted.

"Well, that's our Alex and you'll never change her," Hannah said. "Just keep an eye on her – a good halter might help, but I doubt if she'd appreciate that!"

"Me neither!" KB laughed. "Can I give you a hand here?"

"Good Lord no," came the reply. "You're obviously all changed and ready to go, and I can't have you picking her ladyship up smelling of the stables, so see you up at the house in a while for breakfast."

With his offer of help firmly declined, he left his sister to her work and joined his mother in the kitchen.

"Breakfast will be in about ten minutes. If you could lay a table up for me in the dining room, that would help," she said. "It's porridge and then egg and bacon butties, which should tide you over until lunchtime. You might want to take a carton of clotted cream out of the fridge and grab a jar of honey from the pantry. Your father always likes a spoonful of each on his porridge, he says it makes it edible."

"It's no wonder he's getting a belly on him," commented his son. "He should take more exercise."

"I'll leave you to tell him that!" Kathy replied, as KB left for the dining room, honey and cream in hand.

Breakfast over, KB helped his father change a couple of barrels and finish bottling up, then carried his suitcase out to the truck, stowing it on the floor in the rear of the cab, and hanging the valise from one of the hooks thoughtfully provided by the Ford Motor Company for such eventualities. He then de-activated the tracking device, confident that the watchers monitoring their screens back in Bulford would not have the slightest interest in his movements during the next few days.

Checking his watch, he saw that it was just past nine thirty, so after returning to the pub to say goodbye to his family, he fired up the Wildtrak and headed up the road to collect Alex. Parking in the yard, there was no sign of anyone around, so walking up to the back porch, he rang the doorbell and Amy answered it.

"Come on in, Kris," she welcomed him. "Alex is upstairs at the moment getting ready. Have you got time for a quick coffee?"

"Thank you, that would be nice," he replied as he followed her through to the farmhouse kitchen, warmed by the presence of a large Aga range.

"Sit yourself down and have some shortbread," she said, opening a tin and putting it in front of him. Selecting a slice, he took a bite of the butter and sugar flavoured biscuit.

"This is good shortbread, Amy," he said, as she brought his mug of coffee to the table.

"Well thank you, Kris," she replied, smiling with pleasure at the compliment, "I made a fresh batch yesterday, and it turned out rather well. It's a favourite of Joe's and he always likes taking a couple of slices with him to have with his tea break when he is working on site."

Just then a large orange marmalade cat which had been sleeping in front of the Aga, got up, stretched and walked slowly over to where he sat. Sitting down on the floor in front of him, the cat fixed him with an unwavering stare, yawned and then advanced a further two steps to rub itself against his leg.

"You're a fine fellow," KB said, bending down to scratch his ears.

"That's Archie," said Amy. "We've had him quite a while now and he's not as agile as he used to be, but watch him, if he likes you he'll try to get up on your lap by clawing his way up your leg, which can be extremely painful."

Right on cue, the cat stretched, extended his claws and half leapt onto KB's trouser leg.

"There, I told you!" Amy exclaimed. "Knock him off, Kris, before he scratches your leg to pieces."

"No chance!" KB replied, laughing. "He's climbing up my artificial leg and he'll have a job making any impression on that!"

"Kris, I'm so sorry," Amy said, swooping on the cat and retrieving it from KB's lap, just as Alex came through the kitchen door.

"What's going on here?" she asked, as her mother shot past her to drop the cat in the hallway and close the door behind it.

"I was just demonstrating to your mum the advantages of having a tin leg when being subjected to a cat attack!" KB replied, still laughing.

"It sounds as if Archie's been up to his tricks again, but at least it means he likes you," said Alex. "Consider yourself lucky that you weren't wearing tights – I've lost count of the number of pairs Archie has ruined for me."

"Fortunately I gave up wearing tights when I joined the Paras. Generally we leave that sort of thing to the female element of Her Majesty's Forces," he replied. "Though I believe the practice is not unknown among the officers of certain cavalry regiments where I understand they favour the more traditional stockings and suspenders."

"Kristian Blake," the girl rebuked him. "Sometimes I don't know whether you are telling me the truth or just teasing me, so enough of your nonsense, my stuff is in the hall so you can put it in the truck for me and we'll be on our way."

The second suitcase was soon in the back of the Ford and after saying their goodbyes to Amy and a quick run to the M5, they headed south to Exeter, spurred on by a medley of music which at Alex's insistence blared forth from the sound system as she sat beside him, feet up on the dashboard, giving a final coat of varnish to her already scarlet nails.

It was just past eleven fifteen when KB pulled the Ford onto the narrow road that skirted Cathedral Green in the centre of the city, and drew up outside the main entrance to the hotel. Immediately a doorman appeared assuring KB he would take care of their luggage and park the pick-up. Carefully briefing the man on the necessity to press the remote locking device on the key ring twice to secure the vehicle, KB and Alex followed him to Reception where KB registered and ordered a taxi to pick them up at seven fifteen that evening, with a return for half past midnight.

Upstairs they found they had been given a large and airy bedroom with double windows overlooking the Green and the cathedral. The room was furnished with a king sized double bed, two armchairs, a dressing table, two chests of drawers and a large wardrobe. A flat screen TV sat on a table in the corner, under which an electric kettle, mugs and three china jars had been set, together with several small packets of assorted biscuits. A Christmas Market was in full swing on the Green and as he stood at the window watching the shoppers scurrying between the rows of stalls, Alex emerged from the en-suite with a large smile on her face.

"There's a large Jacuzzi bath tub in there, Kris," she exclaimed. "With plenty of room for two, so we'll have to try it out later!"

Just then there was a knock on the door, and a bellboy came in with their luggage. Before leaving he went to great pains to explain to them the workings of the various gadgets, including the controls for the Jacuzzi, and after thanking him and accepting his tip, he left them to unpack and hang their evening wear in the wardrobe.

Outside the city centre was teeming with pre-Christmas shoppers, and it was nearly three hours later that they found their way back to the hotel, loaded down with an impressive number of carrier bags.

KB had found Alex's help in selecting Christmas presents for his family invaluable, and as a result had purchased a blouse for Kathy, a smart check shirt for Jack and a crew necked sweater for Hannah. Alex had found gifts for Amy and Joe, and having assured KB that she had already managed to find an outfit for the evening, after much deliberation and return visits to two shops, KB had bought her a pair of white high heeled shoes decorated with small gold buckles and a gold evening bag with a matching belt. These she assured him, would be lovely advance Christmas presents and would go well with her dress.

Back in the hotel they enjoyed a late lunch in the Bistro next to the Reception area and after a quick look around the Christmas market on the Green, went upstairs to their room.

As Alex followed him into the room, she slipped the 'Do not Disturb' notice onto the door handle and sitting on the bed, kicked off her shoes and lay back with her head on the pillows.

"That was a fantastic morning's shopping, Kris," she said, leaning over to give him a long kiss, as he lay down beside her. "But we must have walked a fair way, so I suggest a nice snooze for a couple of hours, then a bath and we'll be all refreshed and ready for the evening."

"That sounds like a great plan to me," he replied, but once they had undressed and climbed under the sheets, he was not at all surprised that the promised nap was delayed for some time.

When he awoke the room was in darkness, illuminated only by the glow of the streetlights outside. Panicking for a moment that they had overslept he switched on the bedside light and to his relief it showed just past five o'clock. Getting up, he hopped through to the bathroom, steadying himself against the wall as he went, and turning on the taps he watched as the Jacuzzi slowly filled. Over the wash basin he found a sachet of bubble bath gel which he emptied into the steaming water, and when it reached a satisfactory level he tested it for temperature, and returned to the bedroom.

Alex was still fast asleep, her face framed by her long black hair which covered the pillow on which she lay. Bending over, he kissed her on the cheek and watched as she awoke and stretched her arms above her head.

"Time to get up, sleepy head," he whispered. "The bath is run and all ready, so see you in a minute."

Back in the bathroom, he switched on the water jets in the Jacuzzi and as a layer of bubbles started to form on the surface of the tub, he eased himself into the water. Lying back, he closed his eyes as the warm water foamed around him, feeling the tension in his muscles relax as it soothed and massaged his body.

A few minutes later he sensed her presence in the bathroom, and opening his eyes he sat up as she lowered her lithe naked frame into the water, her back to him.

As she lay against his chest, he put his arms around her. Is this, he wondered, what love is all about – or are we no more than two people making the most of a moment that may or may not ever be repeated? For a split second a picture of Isaac Samson flashed through his mind taunting him with images that made him feel distinctly uneasy, but before he could dwell on those thoughts, she giggled and breaking from his embrace, leant forward.

"Come on, lover boy," she said, tossing him a flannel over her shoulder. "Earn your keep and wash my back for me!"

After doing as he was bid and having scrubbed himself clean he left the girl in the bath and towelled himself off. After a quick wet shave in the wash basin, he hopped back to the bedroom, and after putting on clean underpants, took his boots and overalls out of the wardrobe and attached the braces. After thinking through the slight problem that now confronted him, he decided that his best option was to pull the tight fitting overalls over his artificial leg first, then pull the sock over the foot, and finally fit the boot to the foot. That done, he then pulled the trousers over his right leg and finally attached the prosthetic limb to his stump.

The system worked well, and standing up he was able to pull the overalls up and over his buttocks. His white dress shirt then went on next, and tucking in the shirt tails he buttoned up the flies, noticing with some concern that the fit around his waist was a little snugger than when he had last worn his Mess kit, an indication that Kathy's home cooking was having an effect on his waistline.

With cuff links and shirt studs in place, he next turned his attention to tying the black bow tie, and after several attempts at ensuring a neat knot that stayed satisfactorily in a horizontal position, he buttoned up the waistcoat and slipped on the jacket.

Opening the wardrobe door he examined himself in the full length mirror, and was reclosing it when Alex came in from the bathroom, clad in one of the hotel's bathrobes and vigorously drying her hair.

"Wow, Kris!" she exclaimed in surprise. "You look very smart I must say! Do all you soldiers dress up like that for special occasions?"

"It is a tradition for officers and senior NCOs," he admitted. "But we don't all dress the same, in fact tonight you'll probably see a number of different styles and colours."

"One thing's certain," she replied. "They won't be any sexier than you, but instead of lolling around here and waiting for me, why don't you go down to the bar and have a drink, and I'll be with you in about half an hour?"

"Good idea," he said, checking his watch. "We've still got plenty of time, so no need to hurry."

Picking out a hair dryer from one of the drawers in the dressing table, she sat down in front of the mirror. Crossing over to where she sat, he put his hands on her shoulders and bent over to kiss her on the cheek.

"See you downstairs in a while then," he said, and picking up his wallet from his bedside table, he slipped it into the inside pocket of his tunic. On his way out, he retrieved his beret from his suitcase, and left her to get ready while he made his way down to the bar.

The hotel bar was quite small and illuminated solely by wall lights shielded by rose coloured lampshades which bathed the room in a warm glow. Of the eight or nine tables, six were already occupied, so he took a stool at the bar and ordered a whisky.

"Your preference, sir?" asked the barman as he replaced the glass he had been polishing in the overhead rack.

"Black Grouse if you've got it," he said, noting the man's eyebrows rise slightly. "Perhaps," KB thought to himself, "he's surprised that a mere sergeant should express a preference for a particular branded whisky," but hours behind their own bar at The Volunteer had given KB an opportunity to sample most proprietary scotches, and Black Grouse was his favourite.

"And with it, sir?" the barman asked, placing the glass in front of him.

"Just a dash of water thank you," he replied, and a moment later a small crystal jug was placed next to his glass.

The minutes slipped by and he was on his second scotch by the time Alex made her entry. Up to that point conversation from the occupied tables had been quite lively, but as she walked towards him for a second or two it died away completely, and KB could see why.

Alex looked stunning. Her long black hair hung loosely almost to her waist, and the simple white cocktail dress she wore clung to her figure showing every curve to perfection. A narrow neckline plunged to her waist emphasized by his gold chain. The dress was gathered at the shoulders leaving her arms bare, the gold belt and evening handbag matching the sparkle of the tiny gold buckles on the high heeled shoes he had bought her.

Fully aware that she was the centre of attention, she giggled slightly as she climbed onto the bar stool next to him.

"Will I do, kind sir?" she said, as her dark brown eyes searched his face for a reaction.

"Alex," he said. "You look absolutely gorgeous, and that dress is fantastic, wherever did you find it?"

“Leaning towards him, in a low voice she confided, “I bought it online, but that’s our secret. Now are you going to buy me a drink?”

“In that outfit, nothing less than a glass of champagne will do,” he smiled at her, and with the barman now practically climbing over the bar in his eagerness to serve them, Alex was soon sipping on a tall fluted glass of the pale golden fizz.

A little later their taxi arrived and after a ten minute journey, pulled through the gates of Wessex Barracks. Other vehicles were already unloading their passengers at the front entrance and after checking with the driver to make sure that they would be collected for the return trip later that evening, KB and Alex joined the queue as it moved forward into the large drill hall.

Camouflage nets with strings of coloured lights intertwined had been suspended to lower the ceiling and at one end of the hall the stage was flanked by two Christmas trees, the brightly lit stage itself laid out to accommodate an orchestra. As they moved forward Lieutenant Colonel Hazell and RSM Doble approached to greet each couple in turn.

“Sergeant Blake, a pleasure to see you again; so glad you could join us,” welcomed the Commanding Officer. “And who is this charming young lady?”

“May I present Miss Alexis Baker,” replied KB formally, noticing that the Colonel had cupped her proffered hand in both of his and was obviously in no hurry to let go.

“Welcome, Sergeant Blake,” interjected the Regimental Sergeant Major. “You’ll find the Senior Ranks Mess on the left just down the corridor over there,” he added pointing to the far side of the hall. “Please make yourself at home, and I’ll be joining you shortly.”

“Who are the men in dark green?” Alex asked, as he steered her through the throng of men with their wives and girlfriends.

“They’re the officers and senior NCO’s of the Rifles,” he answered. “And the lads in the khaki service dress are the Riflemen and junior NCO’s.”

“I haven’t seen too many red uniforms like yours,” she continued.

“I doubt if you will see any others exactly like mine,” he replied. “But there will be one or two from other branches of the Army. Just let me know when you see one and I’ll tell you the name of their Regiment or Corps.”

“I doubt if I’ll bother,” she said. “Unless there is some dishy bloke wearing one!”

A few yards down the corridor a dark oak door with a brass sign fixed to it bearing the legend ‘Senior Ranks Mess’ greeted them, and pushing it open they entered the hallowed enclave of those men and women who quite rightly laid claim to being the backbone of the British Army.

They had not taken more than three steps inside when a broad shouldered Warrant Officer stepped forward and without bidding shook KB warmly by the hand.

"You must be Sergeant Blake," he said. "Our soon to be Small Arms Instructor. I was told to keep an eye out for you, and please come on in and meet some of your new colleagues. I'm Toby Snaith, by the way, for my sins Chairman of the Mess Committee, and this is?" he asked, turning to Alex.

"Alex Baker," KB replied, as the Warrant shook her hand and with his hand on her shoulder added, "follow me both of you, come and let me introduce you to some of the lads and their womenfolk. By the way, Sergeant Blake, what do we call you?"

"I was always known by my initials 'KB' in the Paras. Much shorter and easier than Kristian, and as we had two other Chris's in my Battalion, it avoided any confusion."

"KB it is then," agreed Snaith. "Now let's do some more hand shaking and I'll get you some of our punch. It's an excellent brew and packs quite a kick, so I hope you're not driving!"

Introductions over, KB and Alex found themselves cornered by a couple KB guessed would be in their early forties. The tall red headed Sergeant had introduced himself as Ralph Hawken from D Company in Truro, and his only slightly shorter wife, as Merryn. The jovial Cornishman wasted no time in quizzing KB on his experiences in Afghanistan, but before he was able to provide more than a brief outline, the door opened and the RSM walked in, immediately calling for silence.

"Listen up, Ladies and Gents," the man called out, in only a few decibels below parade ground volume. "Most of you know the score but for our first timers, we will be leaving shortly and going upstairs to the Officers' Mess as their guests, after which they will join us back here. We will then all go down to the Junior Ranks for a quick visit and then the band will start playing for us in the main hall. Downstairs in the basement, the miniature range has been converted into a disco for those of you who enjoy less formal surroundings. All the Messes will be open to all until midnight, and a buffet supper will be served from 2100 hours, so finish your drinks and follow me."

"Is he always as loud as that?" Alex said quietly to KB. Overhearing her, Ralph Hawken laughed.

"Most of the time," he replied. "He certainly knows how to get your attention, and woe betide anyone who steps out of line and thinks he can get away with it!"

"Well, I think he's rather scary," she added.

"He's meant to be," said KB, as they joined the group leaving for their visit to the Officers' Mess.

Upstairs they were met by stewards carrying trays of red and white wine and others laden with canapés.

As they sipped their drinks and took in their surroundings, a fair haired officer approached them wearing a high collared black tunic with red collar and cuffs, bordered by heavy silver piping.

"Hello," he said, shaking KB by the hand. "Nice to see a bit of colour amongst all this Rifle green! I'm Captain Hugo Wellsbury, Duke's Own Yeomanry. Like yourselves I'm a guest here, and you are?"

"Sergeant Blake, sir," KB replied. "Until recently with the Parachute Regiment and shortly to join the Rifles here as their Small Arms Instructor, and this is Alex Baker."

"Hello, Alex," Wellsbury said. "If I may say so, you are a delight to behold. Your Sergeant here is a very lucky man! Now, can I get you anything from the bar? I'm not sure just how drinkable that wine is, so if you would prefer something else, I would be more than happy to oblige."

"No thank you, sir," KB answered. "We're fine."

"Then I shall leave you to it," he said. "In the hopes that our paths will cross again before the night is out," he added, giving Alex a meaningful look, and waving cheerily he disappeared towards the bar.

"He was really nice," Alex said. "And that uniform is very sexy. What is the Yeomanry, Kris?"

"In the old days they were volunteer cavalry," KB replied. "Farmers, farmer's sons, virtually anyone who lived in the country and could ride, and usually their officers were the squires and landed gentry. Now they are armoured regiments, equipped with tanks."

"So do they wear suspenders and stockings?" she giggled.

"I wouldn't know for sure," he teased her. "But if you get the chance, you'd better ask the gallant Captain."

"I don't suppose I'll see him again. You wouldn't know if there's a ladies' room around here anywhere, Kris?"

"Just down the corridor on the left hand side," said a female voice behind them, and turning Kris found himself facing a small, petite girl wearing the scarlet and gold of the Adjutant General's Corps, the pips on her epaulettes showing she was a Lieutenant.

Short cropped auburn hair framed her elfin-like features and KB found himself looking into the greenest eyes he had ever seen.

"Thank you so much," Alex replied. "See you in a minute, Kris. Stay here and don't move, or I'll never find you again."

With Alex out of earshot, the new arrival took a step towards him and looking quickly around her, took him by the arm and steered him away from the other couples nearby.

"Welcome, KB," she said, "or as this is the first time we've met, I should really call you Sirius. My Agency cover name is Calypso. Don't look so surprised, your mouth is open and people will be wondering what I've just said to you! I'm Lieutenant Danica Janes, while we're both doing our Army Reserve stuff I'm the Assistant Adjutant to the Rifles, but if we bump into each other in the field, I prefer to be called Dani."

"I'm sorry," KB replied, still taken aback. "But I certainly wasn't expecting that."

"I'm sure you weren't," she continued. "I was in Bulford last Friday and Bill Hutchinson briefed me and told me you were joining the Battalion and gave me clearance to make myself known when you showed up. As Assistant Adj, I've been in charge of the guest list, so when I saw your name on it, I thought I'd look out for you."

"I'm glad you did," he said. "And if we get the chance, I look forward to working with you, are you in Field Ops?"

"Yes," Dani answered. "Joined the Agency when it was just a fledgling organization eighteen months ago and was in communications to begin with. Got fed up after a while listening in to non-stop chat and asked for a transfer. In due course I qualified as an FO and I must admit life now is far more interesting. Incidentally," she went on, "I saw the Honourable Hands-up-your-skirt Hugo zero in on your lady friend, and if you don't mind – a word of warning, he's a real babe magnet, and he knows it. His father is John Wellsbury, Viscount something-or-other and the family own a sizeable chunk of Dorset and have estates in Hampshire and Wiltshire, so money is no object, and Hugo knows how to flash it about.

"In fairness, Triple H – as we call him behind his back – is a good officer, ex-Hussars and now with the Dorset Squadron of the Yeomanry, but at the moment he's on temporary posting to the Squadron who have a detachment here in Wessex Barracks, so he was able to wangle an invitation for tonight although he should really be at their own Christmas party.

"Knowing Triple H, he probably thought there was a better chance of sweeping some young maiden off her feet here than back in Dorchester, where I suspect his reputation probably limits his hunting ground, so be warned, I'll bet that's not the last you'll see of him this evening. Anyway, Sergeant Blake, I must circulate, but here's hoping we get a chance to work together."

"Thank you, ma'am," KB said with a grin, clicking his heels together and bowing slightly in mock formality as she rejoined the crowd, thinking to himself as he watched her go, that no matter how hard they tried, the designers of Mess Dress for women seldom managed to make it look in the slightest way feminine. Moreover he surmised, there was no doubt that in spite of the air of cool professionalism Miss Danica Janes exuded, under the tunic and ankle length black skirt, she was definitely all woman.

Ten minutes passed before Alex returned, looking slightly flushed and carrying a glass that clearly was not the house wine they had been served with earlier.

"You were a long time," he reproached her mildly. "And what's that you're drinking?"

"Sorry I took so long," she said, looking away from him. "But on my way back I bumped into Hugo and he poured me a glass of champagne."

Noticing the familiarity in which she now referred to him, and with Dani's warning still fresh in his mind, he guessed that the Captain had almost certainly not come across Alex by accident and that it had been well planned ambush, rather than merely a chance encounter.

Fortunately the opportunity for any further immediate advances from Triple H were temporarily curtailed, when the RSM called for silence, and in stentorian tones, thanked the officers for their hospitality and invited them to the Senior Ranks' Mess.

Inside the Mess the wine had been replaced with punch, and the canapés with cocktail sausages on sticks, a variety of thin sandwiches cut into quarters and curried hard-boiled egg halves. Spying Ralph Hawken and his wife standing on their own, KB and Alex crossed to meet them, and at Ralph's suggestion, he and KB left the girls to chat, while they circulated amongst their guests.

Recognizing Captain Phillips, the Adjutant who KB believed was one of the major influences in securing his appointment to The Wessex Rifles, KB eased his way through the crowd towards him.

"Hello, Sergeant Blake, nice to see you here," the Captain greeted him. "Are you enjoying our little Christmas party so far?"

"Very much so," he replied. "I just wanted to thank you for your help and to let you know that I hope to start parading with you early in the New Year."

"That's good news, Blake. The CO informs me that you have a new job, which sounds as if it might be right up your street, and if we can help at all, please don't hesitate to ask. We must all pull together in these troubled times. Have you finished your training yet?"

"Yes, sir," KB said. "I passed the indoctrination course and after Christmas it looks as if I may be doing some instructing for my new bosses, unless they have an assignment for me."

"I see you've met the Ice Maiden!" the Adjutant continued with a smile.

"Pardon, sir?" KB answered in surprise.

"Lieutenant Janes, my Assistant. I saw you two chatting up in our Mess, and as you are both in the same line of business I assume you were talking shop. In fact it was unlikely to be anything else as her nickname is well deserved! Let's just say that many have tried, and I suspect none have succeeded!"

With that, and wishing him all the best for Christmas, Phillips excused himself and headed towards the RSM who was holding court to a small gathering of officers at the end of the bar.

Even though the Junior Ranks Mess was double the size of the Officers' and Senior Ranks', it was so crowded it became almost impossible to move, and after several complaints from Alex, KB was relieved when it was announced that the band had now started playing in the Drill Hall and that the buffet was open.

The crowd thinned out quickly, and he was about to suggest to Alex that they moved on when he was confronted by two Corporals in khaki Service Dress with the black buttons and wide black belt fastened by a silver clasp depicting the bugle badge of the Rifle Regiments.

The shorter of the two boasted the ruddy complexion of a countryman who spent most of his life in the outdoors, and whose chubby face and impressive waistline suggested that he probably had difficulty in passing the annual fitness test. His taller and thinner companion sported a near shaven head and barely discernible eyebrows, above a hawked nose that would have done credit to a bird of prey.

Trying to look serious and in a respectful tone, the former was first to speak.

"Excuse me, Sergeant," he said. "Are you the new Small Arms Instructor we've heard rumours about?"

"That could be me," KB replied. "And who are you, Corporal?"

"Johnny Newcombe, Sergeant and this is my mate Bert Dingle. We're both members of the Battalion Rifle Team and it's said you will be coaching us?"

"That could also be true," KB answered. "What is your speciality?"

This time it was Dingle who spoke up. "We both shoot the rifle in competition. Johnny is the long range specialist with the sniper rifle and I also fire the GPMG. We also heard you were going to form a sniper section, and hope that we can join it."

"If you are both good shots, then that's entirely possible," KB said. "What do you guys do in your civilian jobs?"

"I drive a wagon for the Devon County Council," Newcombe volunteered.

"And he's also a dab hand with a shotgun," broke in his companion. "So if you ever want a pheasant or two, Johnny's your man, providing you're not too fussy where it came from! I work for the Council as well, mainly grass cutting during the summer and doing other maintenance work at this time of year."

"I get the picture," said KB. "Make sure you are there for the first rifle practice I organise and I'll see you get the chance to try out for the sniper section."

"Thank you, Sergeant," they chorused, leaving KB to pay his respects to the Mess President and lead Alex back to the hall.

The lively strains of the Salamanca Band in full orchestra mode already filled the air as they arrived at the edge of the dance floor, where already a dozen or more couples were being whirled around by their partners, while others lined up by the buffet at the far end of the hall.

"Come on, Kris," Alex said, grabbing him by both arms and leading him forward. "Enough Army stuff for the evening, let's see how we do on the dance floor."

It only took a few minutes of attempting a quick step, for KB to realize that trying to slide his artificial leg over the floor in some kind of unison with his good leg and in time to the music, was far more difficult that he had expected, and was more than relieved when the music changed tempo and Alex suggested they attempted to copy the moves of the other dancers.

"Come on, Kris," she demanded, as he watched dumbfounded as the couples twisted and jerked their hips. "It's called twerking, and it's easy – just watch!"

Within a few minutes of attempting to follow her provocative thrusting and swivelling as her body rose and fell in time to the beat, he was aware that the attention of a number of spectators and their fellow dancers had focussed on his partner.

"Get with it, Kris," she encouraged him. "Stop hopping around and flapping your arms like a penguin, get down and dirty – it's fun!"

"Hang on, Alex!" he exclaimed. "If the looks on the faces of these folks is anything to go by, you're about to get locked up for making obscene gestures in public!" But just as he was about to protest further the music ended and before the band could re-start he grabbed her by the arm and hustled her off the floor, not without several wolf whistles and enthusiastic applause from the onlookers.

"For goodness sake, Kris," she complained. "It's only a bit of fun, you old stick-in-the-mud. You'd better make it up to me with a large drink and a plate of food, as I'm famished."

"Of course I will," he replied, thankful that she had accepted his reluctance to continue dancing. "Why don't you make your way back to the Mess while I organise the food and I'll join you there in a minute."

Joining the queue at the buffet, it soon became obvious this was going to take some considerable time as they moved forward at a snail's pace. In fact it was nearly fifteen minutes before it was his turn to be served and another five before he left with two plates laden with cold beef and ham, salad and bread rolls.

In the Senior Ranks' Mess, there was no sign of Alex. Looking around, he saw Ralph and Merryn Hawken at a table in the corner and crossed the room to where they were sat enjoying their supper.

"You haven't seen Alex around, have you?" he asked them. "I was supposed to join her here, but she seems to have gone missing."

"She hasn't come since we've been here," Ralph answered. "But why don't you leave your food on the table here and see if you can find her? There are a lot of folk around but she shouldn't have gone far."

Thanking the man, KB retraced his steps to the Junior Ranks' Mess but still there was no sign of the girl. Reluctantly he climbed the stairs to the Officers' Mess, uncomfortable at the thought of entering the preserve of the commissioned ranks uninvited, but on opening the door and taking a quick look around the room, he could still see no sign of her.

If he had hoped to leave unnoticed, this was not to be, and Danica Janes beckoned him to join her at the bar.

"Let me guess, you've lost your girlfriend?" she greeted him sympathetically. "Don't say I didn't warn you!"

"Do I take it then she's been in here?" he asked, already knowing the answer.

"She has indeed," came the reply, "Stuck her nose around the door and before you could say 'Happy Christmas', Triple H pounced, almost force fed her a glass of champers and disappeared with her on his arm. My guess is that you will find them in the basement enjoying the subdued lights and intimate atmosphere of the disco, so you'd better buck up and track her down before he advances to the next stage of the notorious Hugo seduction process."

"Dare I ask what that is?" he said.

"Something along the lines of 'Come outside and let me show you my Jag' if he is sticking to his usual routine, and if she isn't in the disco, it's a black two seat sports convertible and you'll find it in the officers' parking section."

"It sounds as if you know all about it," he said, a slight note of sarcasm in his voice.

"Let's just say I've been there, but certainly haven't done it and wouldn't be seen wearing the T-shirt," she smiled at him sweetly. "Now get cracking and rescue your lady, though she strikes me that in this kind of situation she is unlikely to consider herself a damsel in distress!"

Knowing full well that she was right, he found his way down to the basement and following the familiar sounds of a disco in full cry, pushed his way into the dimly lit interior. Immediately he recognized the track being played as Adele's 'Someone Like You' and those on the floor were taking full advantage of the slow tempo, the girls with their arms around their partner's necks, bodies pressed close together as they swayed to the rhythm.

Alex had her back to him, but as he hesitated before approaching her, Hugo Wellsbury looked up and saw him standing by the door. A smile crossed the man's face and he leant forward and whispered something in her ear.

Turning to face him, she broke free from his embrace and still holding his hand, walked over to where KB stood.

"Are you looking for me?" she asked him curtly.

"And why shouldn't I be?" he asked her with equal bitterness. "I was getting something to eat for us, and you were supposed to meet me in the Mess, remember?"

"Well, I waited for you there, and when you didn't show up, Hugo kindly looked after me and after your performance on the dance floor, I thought the chance for a visit to the disco with someone who knows how to put one foot in front of the other in time to music without looking like a constipated parrot was too good to miss."

"I meant for you to wait for me in the Senior Ranks'," he snapped back. "And if you consider shuffling around down here dancing, I'm just as capable of managing that as anyone. Anyway, when you've finished your 'dance', I'll be waiting for you upstairs and I am sure Captain Wellsbury will escort you to the right Mess this time."

"Don't worry, Sergeant Blake," smirked the officer, "I promise to take care of her, and all in good time, I will return her to you safe and sound."

Back in the Senior Ranks' Mess he found the Hawkens' still sitting at their table, and rejoining them, picked up his knife and fork deciding that there was point in wasting good food.

"Didn't find her then?" volunteered Ralph.

"Oh I found her alright," he replied. "Wrapped around the neck of a Yeomanry officer in the disco."

"Never went much on those Yo-Yos," said the Cornishman. "We had a joint exercise with them on Bovington tank ranges last summer, and although I didn't have much to do with them, by all accounts some of their officers were a proper bunch of Ruperts. They seem to think that riding around with their heads sticking out of the turret of 50 tons of slow moving target makes them something special, but give me a spade and a patch of ground to dig a hole in any day!"

As Hugo Wellsbury's interpretation of "all in good time" was appearing more and more likely to be the rest of the evening, KB consoled himself with a few drinks at the bar talking shop with his fellow NCOs and swopping yarns with those of them who had also done tours of duty in Afghanistan.

He was beginning to feel more relaxed and less concerned about the potential threat posed by Wellsbury, when Danica Janes came into the Mess.

"I reckoned you'd still be on your own," she said, "and I thought you might like some company, how about a large dry white wine and soda? Then if you're not about to leap up and go girl-friend chasing around the Armouries again, you can tell me all about yourself."

"I'll do that, as long as you do the same," he replied. "Let me get the drinks and we'll find a table."

Time passed quickly as they chatted about their respective pasts. KB found that he could talk about his injuries quite openly, reckoning that Dani with her military background probably understood better than most, and would not interpret his frankness as sympathy seeking. Dani herself, he learned, came from a family with a Royal Navy background whose father had finished his career as a Chief Petty Officer in the Fleet Air Arm. She had secured a place in a Grammar School, gone on to Bristol University where she had spent her spare time in the University OTC and after gaining her degree, had applied for a short service commission and passed out at Sandhurst.

"Must have been a bit of a disappointment to your old man that you didn't choose the Navy," he commented at which she laughed.

"It was more of a shock when I chose to go for a commission," she said. "As I was the first ever in our family to become an Army officer, and although I'm no longer a regular, Dad still wonders why I didn't make an honest career out of being a Wren!"

"And what do your folks think of your job with the Agency?" he found himself asking.

"To be honest, I don't give them too much detail. Mum would go bananas if she thought I was doing anything other than sitting behind a desk."

"Me too," he agreed. "Mine believes my activities are restricted to being an Instructor, but I guess one day there's always a chance the truth will out, as they say. Anyway, at the moment all is going well and me being home for Christmas is helping."

"Do you manage to fit in a family gathering amongst all the activities at the pub?" she asked.

"Christmas Day we'll all be sitting down together, and Alex and her parents are joining us. It's the day after I'm not looking forward to," he admitted. "My sister has two horses and has persuaded me to ride one of them in the local Hunt which always meets at the pub on Boxing Day. It's been a while since I've ridden, so I'm approaching the whole thing with a certain amount of trepidation."

"It sounds as if you should have been in the cavalry, not the Paras!" Dani laughed. "But talking of our dashing horsemen, it looks as if our favourite Yeoman and your missing girlfriend are about to catch up with you!"

"That was some dance you must have had," KB said, standing up as Hugo and Alex came across to the table.

"Oh for goodness sake!" Alex answered him petulantly. "It was just a bit of fun, and Hugo has been a perfect gentleman."

"As no doubt, you would expect of me," added Wellsbury, at which Dani coughed loudly. "And in any case," he went on, ignoring her, "I see you have been enjoying some charming company yourself, although Sergeant, as you well know, the service does not look too kindly on non-commissioned ranks consorting with officers!

"An exchange of pleasantries perhaps, on social occasions such as these, but lengthy and intimate conversations, tut, tut, not good form. However, be that as it may, I regret I must leave you, and to you my dear," he said turning to Alex and taking her hand and giving her a less than subtle wink, "may I say what a pleasure it has been making your acquaintance, and I hope our paths may cross again before too long."

"He's got a bloody nerve," KB muttered, as the man disappeared into the corridor, prompting Dani to rise from her seat.

"I must be making a move too," she said, giving KB a gentle squeeze on the arm as she moved past him. "And I'm sure you two have a lot to talk about. Have a great Christmas, and I look forward to working with you in the New Year, Sergeant Blake."

"Thank you, Ma'am, and all the best for Christmas to you too," he said, as she turned and left them.

"Have you had anything to eat?" he asked as they sat down, hoping to avoid a silence that was threatening. "I'm afraid they've cleared away the plate I got for your earlier, but I can see if the buffet is still open?"

"I had some food upstairs," Alex answered. "Hugo got the steward to bring us a tray, but I'd love another drink if they still have some of that punch left."

Fighting back the urge to comment on her preference for her choice of a dinner companion, he found that there was still plenty of the potent brew left, and satisfying himself with half a pint of draught beer, returned to the table.

"Please don't go all silent on me, Kris," she said as they sipped their drinks. "I thought you were off somewhere chatting to your Army buddies when you weren't in the Mess, and Hugo was so nice and I was having so much fun I didn't realise the time had gone by so quickly. He does have a nice car though," she giggled.

"So he tried the 'Let me show you my Jag' line, did he?" KB replied, a note of bitterness in his voice.

Taken aback, the girl took a moment and then retorted, "And who told you about the Jag? I bet it was that green eyed witch you were chatting up!"

"Yes it was Lieutenant Janes as a matter of fact," he admitted. "She thought

I should be aware of Captain Wellsbury's reputation as a woman chaser when you went missing on me."

"I bet she did," Alex snorted. "And if I bump into her again, I'll tell her to mind her own bloody business, the skinny little cow. Anyway, if she knows about the Jag, it only means she's been there herself, so she's a right one to talk!"

"Actually, if you are interested, her nickname around here is 'the ice maiden'," he replied "So I suspect Hugo's invitation fell on deaf ears."

"Hugo would have been shit out of luck anyway," she giggled again. "It's a lovely car, but there's absolutely no room in the back and there's a very large gear lever that would certainly get in the way. "And," she added mischievously, "as I never fancied hanging a leg out of a car window least of all in the middle of winter, I can assure you, my darling, you had absolutely nothing to worry about!"

In spite of himself, KB found himself laughing, and clearly relieved at breaking the tension she leant across the table and put her hand on his. "Tell you what though, Kris," she said in a more serious tone, "If you want to give it a try, why don't we go for a gentle stroll around the dance floor, and if you promise not to break into your penguin mode, I'll promise not to get cross with you again!"

Inwardly marvelling at the subtle way in which she had quietly managed to manoeuvre him into a position where he felt guilty for doubting that her disappearance with Wellsbury was no more than harmless fun, they finished their drinks and returned to the Drill Hall. The dance floor was crowded and a slow waltz filled the air, and he was happy to find that once having joined the slow moving couples he only had to shuffle around in time to the music. Before they had taken a few steps, she slid her arms around his neck and nestled her head against his chest.

"I'm sorry," she murmured, "I've been a bitch, haven't I?"

"Probably my fault for not making it clear where you should wait for me while I was at the buffet," he answered, holding her tightly to him, "so I won't punish you by treading on your toes."

"Just give me a good spanking later!" she whispered in his ear, but before he could find any words to answer her, the music stopped, and on the stage Colonel Hazell stepped forward to the microphone.

"Ladies and gentlemen," he announced. "First of all may I say how delighted I am that so many of you have been with us this evening and I hope you have all enjoyed yourselves as much as I have. I am sure you would wish to join me in thanking Captain Phillips and his staff, and Regimental Sergeant Major Doble and all our NCOs and men who have put so much of their time and effort into organizing this event, and of course, our cooks for putting on such a splendid buffet. Finally a big thank you to our own Salamanca Band for entertaining us with such a faultless and varied repertoire, which judging by your performance on the dance floor has been much appreciated."

Without further bidding, applause accompanied by foot stamping, whistles and cheers echoed around the room. Holding up his hands for silence, the Colonel continued.

"It is now approaching midnight, ladies and gentlemen and the band will shortly be standing down, but the disco will remain open for another hour. As I see you are already all on your feet, the band will now give us what I am sure will be a lively rendition of Auld Lang Syne followed by the National Anthem, and to close their part of the evening, they will be joined by the Bugles to play us out with our Regimental March Past. Thank you, and please carry on."

Small, tight circles were quickly formed and arms linked for a rousing chorus of the Robbie Burns classic which made the National Anthem that followed somewhat subdued by comparison. The mood changed again, however, when the strident blast of silver bugles rang out throughout the hall and the band swung into the quick tempo of 'Mechanised Infantry', many of the revellers jumping up and down and waving their arms above their heads in time to the beat.

"Don't tell me they march to this," Alex gasped as she followed them. "Not ideal for wearers of high heels!"

"The Rifles have always marched at this speed," KB explained, as the last notes died away. "In the days when armies were drawn up in lines facing each other across the battlefield, the Light Infantry and Rifle Regiments were usually deployed as skirmishers on the flanks of the line infantry regiments, and they had to move quickly to wherever the generals decided they were needed."

"Well, Kris Blake," she replied. "This evening has certainly been different, and the lesson you have dished out in military traditions has been a blast! What's next on the agenda, time for home?"

"Almost," he said. "By the time we have said our goodbyes and thank you to the Colonel and the RSM, our cab should be here – so let's see if we can find them."

Farewells discharged, they made their way towards the main entrance and as they stepped into the cold fresh air, Alex swayed slightly and grabbed his arm.

"Ooops!" she chuckled. "A tad too much punch perhaps. Hang on to me, Krissy baby; don't want to do a face plant in front of all your mates!" Putting her arm around his shoulders, KB held her firmly around the waist and guided her towards their waiting taxi as she gave a regal wave to the onlookers. Opening the back door he eased her gently onto the seat making sure it was fully closed before going around the back of the vehicle to get in at the other side.

As he slid in beside her she leant towards him and gently keeled over, her head in his lap, and almost immediately dozed off.

"I see your lady friend has had a good evening!" said the cabbie, as he turned the taxi out onto the street.

"A little too good, I'm afraid," KB agreed.

Back at the hotel, it took help from the night porter to get Alex to their room, where KB laid her gently on the bed.

"You wouldn't be able to find me a basin or a bucket, would you?" he asked the young man, as he swung her legs up onto the covers and slipped off her shoes.

"I'm sure I can, sir," he replied with a grin. "I'll be back in a moment."

True to his word, a few minutes later there was a knock at the door, and as he opened it the lad passed him a small red plastic pail.

Thanking him, and handing him a fiver for his trouble, which the porter acknowledged, and after adding a cheery "Good night, and good luck, sir!" KB closed and locked the door, and turned his attention to the bed where Miss Alex Baker was now sound asleep. Sitting down beside her, he gently slipped the dress off her shoulders and rolling her onto her side, unzipped it and with some difficulty tugged the garment down over her hips and legs until he was able to remove it completely and fold it over the back of a chair. Wondering if Hugo Wellsbury had discovered that Alex was bra-less, he dismissed the thought and turned his attention to removing her tights.

"Woss going on?" she mumbled as the last garment was removed.

"Don't worry," he assured her. "You're back in the hotel and in bed, so go back to sleep."

Pulling the duvet over her, he undressed and went to the bathroom, leaving both the light over the basin, and the bedside lamp at her side switched on. As he slid in beside her, she rolled over, her right arm coming across his chest, tucking her head under his chin.

For the next three hours he drifted in and out of sleep, always conscious of the girl beside him and awakening every time she moved. It was just past four in the morning, when he woke from a shallow sleep to find her sitting up beside him, holding her head.

"Are you alright?" he asked, already knowing the answer.

"No I'm not," came the reply. "There's a hammer in my head thumping so hard, it feels as if it is going to drop off. Must go to the loo," she added, swinging her legs out of the bed and feeling her way slowly towards the bathroom.

Some time passed before she returned, only to sit on the bed again, making no attempt to climb back under the covers.

"Don't want to lie down," she said. "The room's going round and round and it's making me feel dizzy."

"Stay where you are and I'll make us a cup of tea," he said, fastening on his artificial leg, and after collecting the kettle from the corner table, he filled it and found the tea bags and milk he needed for their brew in the china jars. As he waited, he opened one of the packets of biscuits and with the kettle boiled and tea made, carried a mug across to place it together with the biscuits on her bedside table.

"See if that helps," he said, collecting his own mug and returning to his side of the bed. "But if it makes it worse, you'll find a red bucket by your bedside".

"You're too kind," she answered him mournfully, as she sat sipping her tea. "Can I go somewhere and die quietly?"

"A few hours ago, I might have said 'yes' to that," he replied with a chuckle. "But I've decided to keep you, so drink your tea and try to get some sleep!"

The remainder of the night passed without incident, and when he awoke his bedside alarm clock was showing a few minutes after eight thirty. Getting up without disturbing the slumbering girl, he showered, shaved, and was halfway through getting dressed before she stirred and sat up in bed.

"God!" she said. "Is it that time already?"

"It is if you want some breakfast," he answered. "How's the head?"

"The throbbing seems to have stopped, but there still seems to a dull ache just behind my eyeballs. Did I disgrace myself last night? – I don't remember much after we left the building."

“You made an impressive exit,” he teased. “After trying to snog the Colonel, you threw up over the bonnet of the Honourable Hugo’s Jaguar, collapsed in a heap in the car park and had to be carried to the taxi shouting to everyone that cavalry officers wore suspenders and stockings. Apart from that, no one would have known you were there!”

“Oh Lord!” she exclaimed, “Did I really?”

“No, not really,” he laughed. “But you came bloody close!”

“Finish dressing and get out of here, you lying bastard!” she shouted at him, picking up one of her shoes and throwing it at him, which he narrowly avoided as it bounced off the wardrobe. “And when I’ve forgiven you, I’ll meet you downstairs in the dining room!”

KB was not surprised that he had a fairly long wait before Alex joined him, and while he helped himself to a full plate of fried eggs, bacon, and sausages from the breakfast bar, she settled for a small serving of scrambled eggs and toast. It was evident that even the latter was proving to be a challenge as she picked at it without enthusiasm, eventually managing to clear barely half of it before declaring that she could manage no more.

Refraining from making any further comments about her fragile state of health, back in their room KB helped her pack, and after checking out at the front desk loaded their luggage into the Ranger and with Alex safely on board, headed out of the city.

With traffic light, KB decided against taking the M5 north, and instead took the A30 to Honiton and then onto the A303 across the Blackdown Hills towards Ilminster. A warmer day with a darkly menacing overcast sky had brought heavy rain with it and a strong nor-westerly wind buffeted the truck as they dropped down to Horton Cross and the Ilminster by-pass.

Alex had curled up on her seat and the warmth of the heater had lulled her into a sound sleep, the lack of any need to make conversation allowing him to concentrate on driving, as the wipers strived valiantly to keep the windscreen clear of the steady downpour and occasional torrents that swept over the bonnet as he drove through inches deep water that ran across the road.

By the time they reached Podimore Cross and turned off onto the A372 towards Long Sutton and home, the rain had eased off but as he crossed the River Yeo into Long Lane he noticed that it had risen by several feet and was already forming deep muddy puddles on either side of the bridge.

As he turned into the Bakers’ yard, Alex awoke and yawning, stretched her arms over her head.

"Wake up, sleepy head," he said, as she looked around her.

"Home already?" she murmured in reply.

"Yep, and it's a shitty day out there, so I suggest you make a dive for it, and I'll bring in your case."

Taking his advice, as soon as he drew to a halt Alex got out of the cab and turning up the collar of her jacket ran to the front door, leaving KB to follow in her wake carrying her suitcase.

In the kitchen, Joe was sitting at the table, a mug of coffee in front of him, while Amy stood at the sink peeling potatoes.

"Did you have a good time?" she asked, as she came forward to greet them, wiping her hands on her apron.

"Judging by her somewhat pale complexion, I should say that was an unqualified 'yes'" chuckled Joe. "I see all the signs of a monumental hangover, unless I'm very much mistaken."

"Oh God, don't you start as well," came the quick response. "Kris has already given me enough grief, so if you don't mind, I think I'll just go upstairs for a lie-down."

"I'll bring your bag up for you," KB said, following her up the stairs, and leaving it inside the door to her room.

"Thanks for everything, Kris," she said, turning to give him a kiss. "I'm going to get my head down for a couple of hours, but I'll catch up with you later."

Downstairs Amy had returned to preparing their Sunday roast and Joe was reading his Sunday newspaper.

"Can I get you a coffee, Kris?" she asked as he came into the kitchen.

"Thanks, Mrs Baker, but I'd best get back. I know we've got a full dining room for lunch, so I'm sure Dad can use my help behind the bar."

"Off you go then. Say hello to your folks from us, and we may drop in this evening for a drink," she said and with that he left them, minutes later turning the truck into the car park of The Volunteer.

Inside the pub, he took his suitcase, valise and bags of Christmas shopping straight up to his room, coming downstairs to be greeted by an enthusiastic Rocky, whose tail wags and short barks showed how pleased he was to see him home.

Both Kathy and Hannah were busy in the kitchen, roast joints of beef and pork, and a turkey crown already resting on the sideboard. Carrots and cabbage were cooking in the steamers while Kathy poured cheese sauce over a large dish of cauliflower, to be returned to the oven to join trays of roast potatoes and parsnip.

"Hey, the wanderer returns!" his sister called out as she stirred a pan of gravy on the stove. "How did it go?"

"I suppose you could call it a success," he called back. "That's if the size of Alex's hangover this morning is anything to go by! Otherwise suffice to say, the evening had its moments."

"It sounds to me as if things did not go exactly as expected," added his mother. "And you can tell us all about it after lunch. Our first bookings are due in about twenty minutes, and you'll find your dad in the bar, and I know he'll be glad to see you."

KB found his father pulling through a new barrel, and the older man's smile confirmed Kathy's sentiments.

"Didn't think you were going to make it, son," he said. "I take it that you enjoyed yourselves?"

"Alex certainly did," KB answered. "And she's at home right now sleeping off the after effects of a tad too much punch coupled with copious amounts of champagne lavished on her by an over attentive Yeomanry Officer!"

"To which, no doubt, she responded accordingly," commented his father wryly.

"Once the dust had settled, I suppose there was no harm done," KB replied. "But at one stage I must admit I thought she'd done a runner on me!"

"Catch a tiger by the tail and there's always a chance you'll get mauled," his father added. "So the trick is to know when to let go, but I'm sure you knew that already! Anyway, I'll be opening up in a minute, so you can help me stack away these last few bottles and then we're just about set to handle what looks like a sizeable invasion."

As Jack had predicted, the influx of their customers was impressive and it was three hours later before the doors were closed for what remained of the afternoon.

It was no surprise to KB that as the family sat down to their late lunch, his mother and sister focussed their conversation almost entirely on the Rifles' Christmas party. In response KB described everything as best he could without going into too much detail about Alex's dalliance with Hugo Wellsbury, only an occasional knowing look from his father suggesting that there was one listener at least who suspected that there was more than he was prepared to tell.

Lunch over, Jack settled himself down in front of the fire in their living room for his afternoon nap, and with Kathy putting away the last of the dishes before joining her husband, KB followed his sister down to the stables.

"How's Commando behaving, sis?" he asked, as they rounded the corner of the tack room.

"He's a bit of a handful," the girl admitted. "But we've started to build up a good relationship and I'm sure he is going to be a winner, though I wouldn't like to say at what just yet! I have started to jump him over low fences and he seems to enjoy it, but it will be really interesting to see how he behaves on Boxing Day. I haven't forgotten that this will be a big day for you as well," she added with a grin. "So I thought we should get in a few long rides around the lanes over the next day or so to get you ready!"

"Thanks for that," KB said ruefully. "I rather hoped you might have had a change of mind."

"No chance, brother dear," came the response, and recognizing that he had little in the way of expectation that her decision might change in his favour, he helped her bed the horses down before taking Rocky for a walk.

The threatened 'long rides' turned out to be something of a success, and although by no means convinced that the quantum step up to becoming an active participant in the Boxing Day meet would be a pleasurable experience, he resigned himself to the fact that there was no way out.

Alex had not accompanied her parents to the pub that evening, which hardly surprised him, but in the busy run up to Christmas Day he found himself working alongside her in the pub, and with the Rifles' party not mentioned again, their relationship quickly returned to an easy going normality punctuated by moments of close intimacy in the confines of his room, whenever they were able to escape the confines of what Kathy insisted on referring to as 'our team'.

Christmas Day arrived and went, with a moment of parcel opening around their own private Christmas tree in the lounge, and the Bakers joining them for their family lunch after which both Hannah and Alex joined him for his afternoon walk down the river bank with Rocky. The spell of wet and windy weather had blown itself out, and sunshine broke through the clouds as they strolled down the towpath.

"Looks as if it's going to be fine tomorrow," Hannah said. "So it shouldn't be too soft underfoot."

"I wonder if the 'antis' will be out in force. We don't want a repeat of last time," Alex added, "although we haven't got His Royal Highness and his entourage to contend with."

"I wish Amir and Peter were going to be here," Hannah replied quietly, looking up at the sky and biting her lip.

Noticing the tears welling up in her eyes, KB put his arm around her shoulder and pulled her close to him.

"Bet you do," he said. "And I still miss the old bugger too, you know."

"Oh shit," Alex exclaimed, coming around to her other side and putting her arm around Hannah's waist. "Sorry, Han, opened my big mouth again without thinking."

"Don't worry," came the response. "When I go out tomorrow, I know Peter will be right there with me."

"Well at least he won't have the dubious pleasure of having to gallop alongside you with his arms being pulled out of their sockets, the cheeks of his arse bruised, and his bollocks on fire whilst praying that the day will come to a swift and dignified conclusion," KB ventured, hoping that his attempt to inject some humour would help his sister and at which, to his relief, both girls laughed.

"Thanks, bro', what would I do without your sense of humour to liven things up?" Hannah said, still chuckling. "Now let's get back, I'm freezing and a nice cup of tea would go down a treat."

Boxing Day dawned bright and sunny with just a hint of overnight frost. By ten o'clock the car park was already filling with riders and their horses, and KB felt a growing unease in the pit of his stomach as he helped Hannah saddle Winston and Commando. Winston stood placidly, taking it all in his stride but the younger horse was already showing signs of excitement, pawing the ground and snorting as the Hunt and its followers grew in number.

Alex had already saddled Barney and was chatting to Carol Watson as KB emerged from behind the stables astride Winston.

"Hey, Kris," Carol called out. "Never thought I'd see you on a horse again, what brought this about?"

"I've been roped in to help Hannah out," he replied. "So I'm not exactly a willing conscript!"

"Alex has just been telling me about the new horse," she continued. "It sounds as if it has a lot of potential, but I gather he's quite a handful."

"Judge for yourself," Alex broke in, as Hannah appeared on Commando who was unashamedly showing off, picking up his forelegs and tossing his head in the air as she struggled to keep him in check.

"He certainly is a good looker," said Carol admiringly, as Hannah joined them, her face already red with the effort of keeping Commando under control.

"Do-ee want a hand there?" called out a familiar voice, and KB glanced down to see Obadiah Kernworthy standing a few yards away.

"Thanks, Obi," Hannah said. "If you could grab him by the bridle and help me quieten him down, that would be a great help."

With Obi holding the horse's head firmly, and the chances of any serious misbehaviour greatly reduced, the riders were able to sit back and relax as Jack and Kathy handed round the stirrup cup. The Boxing Day event had attracted an unusually large numbers of riders and hunt followers, but nowhere amongst them could KB see signs of any protestors.

"Don't zee any of the volk that caused all the fuss last time," Obi commented, as if reading KB's thoughts.

"Bigger fish to fry than us," said Carol. "My bet is that they will be concentrating their efforts at the larger meets today, but you can bet that there will be one or two out there keeping an eye on things."

With a few brief notes on the huntsman's horn signifying it was time to move off, KB moved Winston in behind Alex and Hannah as they left the yard and turned left and up onto the towpath heading west towards Langport and the Levels, where the hounds were quick to pick up the scent leading the field out towards Muchelney.

Before they reached the hamlet and its abbey, they cut across the fields to Thorney and over the River Parrett to West Moor and on towards Hambridge. The pace picked up as they ran parallel with the old Westport Canal and just after crossing the B3168, the ground dipped sharply towards a narrow four foot wide drainage ditch flanked on either side by a low bank topped with a stand of reed. KB headed Winston towards a small stone bridge which traversed the ditch, but many of the riders chose to jump the natural obstacle, with Hannah and Alex among the leaders.

As KB slowed to cross the bridge, he watched Hannah urge Commando forward to follow Alex and Barney who had already cleared the ditch in an easy jump. To his surprise Commando checked his stride short of the ditch and slithered to a sudden halt, throwing Hannah forward and over his head, to land in a twisted bunch of arms and legs on the far side. Realizing she had landed awkwardly, he rode Winston to where she lay unmoving and cursing his prosthetic leg, he dismounted awkwardly and knelt down beside her.

In a moment Alex was by his side, and as he bent over his sister, her eyelids fluttered and then closed again.

"Don't try to move her; she must have banged her head when she hit the ground. We need an ambulance," he added, concern showing in his voice.

"I've just phoned for one," came a reassuring answer from Major Brennan, the Hunt Secretary who had joined them. "If they send one out from the Ilminster station, it should be here shortly. I'll walk up to the road to guide them in."

"Where's Commando?" came a murmur from Hannah, opening her eyes and blinking at them.

"Don't worry, Carol's got him, just lie still, the ambulance is on its way," said Alex, holding her friend's hand.

Barely ten minutes passed before they heard the sound of the approaching ambulance's siren and moments later two green overall-clad paramedics were kneeling over Hannah talking to her.

"Looks like a slight concussion and probably a broken collar bone," the senior paramedic informed KB, as they lifted Hannah gently onto the stretcher. "We'll take her into A&E at Yeovil General, and she should be fine."

"I'm her brother. Is it alright if I come with you in the ambulance?" KB asked, and after getting the man's approval, he turned back to Alex.

"Alex, would you be a pal? Hack Winston back to the pub for me and tell Mum and Dad what's happened? Also, would you ask Carol if she can take Commando back with her to Somerton, and I'll phone her later? If Hannah's going to be out of action for a while, she could stable Commando for us and give him some schooling."

"Of course I will, Kris," Alex replied. "Having Carol handle Commando also makes sense. We'll see you later and I hope everything goes well with Hannah."

By the time he caught up with the ambulance they had already loaded Hannah onboard, and climbing in he was pleased to see that she now appeared to be fully awake and taking in her surroundings.

"What's happened to Commando?" she asked, as he sat down beside her.

"All taken care of, sis," he replied. "Carol Watson is going to look after him for a while until you are back on your feet, and in the meantime Alex and I can take care of Winston."

"I feel like a prime idiot," his sister said. "And my bloody shoulder is hurting like crazy."

"Try to relax and keep the mask on," interjected the paramedic, and turning to KB added. "She refused morphine, but the oxygen should help. Just keep talking to her; we don't want her losing consciousness."

Once in the hospital, Hannah was whisked away leaving KB to sit in the waiting room. An hour passed before a tall, fair haired woman appeared, whose brisk manner and the stethoscope around her neck immediately identified her as a doctor.

"Mr Blake," she called out, and when he stood up, beckoned for him to follow her to a small side room, where she shut the door behind them.

"Hello, Mr Blake," she said, shaking his hand. "I'm Doctor Jan Haydon, and I've been looking after your wife." Before he had a chance to correct her mistake, she continued, "I'm pleased to say that apart from a slight concussion and as we suspected, a broken collar bone, no serious injuries have been sustained. We've strapped her up and we'll keep her in overnight under observation. All being well you will be able to collect her tomorrow but she'll need to take it easy for a while. Lots of bed rest and keep her away from the horses. I also had obstetrics check her over and the baby seems fine, but we would suggest she comes in for a scan in the next three to four weeks so that we can make sure everything is as it should be. You look surprised?"

"Err, yes," he stuttered, trying to find the right words. "You see, I'm Hannah's brother, not her – err – partner, I mean husband – or whatever, but it doesn't matter as long as she's okay."

"I'm so sorry," said the embarrassed doctor. "My apologies if I've let Hannah's secret out of the bag, and I do hope she won't mind. Anyway, I see she has more visitors waiting outside, and as soon as we've moved her upstairs into a ward, the nurse will come and fetch you."

As she left, Jack and Kathy came through the door, the worry lines etched on Jack's face and Kathy clearly upset.

"It's alright, Mum," KB said, giving her a hug. "And don't look so worried, Dad, they're going to keep her in overnight for observation and she has broken her collar bone, but otherwise nothing serious, and it looks as if we'll be able to bring her home tomorrow."

"Thank God for that," his mother replied with a sigh. "We were so worried when Alex told us, and your father must have broken half a dozen speed records to get here."

"There is something else," KB added. "But Hannah can tell you about it herself."

"I didn't see that coming," was Jack's first comment as they left the hospital some time later. "I knew she was smitten with that Bowen fella, but I didn't realize it had – well – gone that far."

"If it's any consolation, Dad, I knew Peter pretty well, and I can tell you that he was equally smitten," KB assured him. "In fact if things had turned out differently I believe they would have certainly got married."

"Well I think it's perfectly marvellous that we are going to be grandparents," Kathy said emphatically. "So don't you go getting all pious and 'holier than thou' on me, Jack Blake. When I think of what you and I got up to in the back of that old van of yours before we got married all I can say is, that we were damn lucky to get away with it. As it was Kris showed up almost nine months to the day after we got married, and if I remember rightly, the most I saw of our honeymoon in Newquay was the ceiling of our room in the Cliff Top Hotel – so don't blame your daughter for taking after you!"

"I'm only thinking of Hannah," said Jack defensively. "It won't be easy for her, raising a kid as a single mum, and what bloke is going to take her on if she meets someone else?"

"Raising children is never easy, even with both parents involved," argued Kathy. "And Hannah

will get all the support she needs from all of us, and if there ever is another man in her life, we'll cross that bridge when we come to it."

"What about the horses?" Jack persisted. "She's got two of them now, and they're not going to take care of themselves?"

"You let me worry about that," KB broke in. "I'll fix things with Carol Watson to look after Commando until Hannah's back on her feet again, and we've got enough friends in the village to take care of Winston, as well as helping you and Mum out in the pub, so let's get home I'm starving and could use a stiff drink!"

"And I've got a buffet to lay out for this evening," added Kathy, "so we need to get a move on."

In the aftermath of Christmas, the days that followed were strangely quiet. Carol Watson had been more than happy to keep Commando at her livery stables for a while, and promised KB she would make sure the training regime that Hannah had initiated for the horse would be continued. Alex had agreed to look after Winston, with help from one of Obi Kernworthy's young labourers who the farmer had promised, was 'good around animals'."

As much as the family had tried to keep it to themselves, the news of Hannah's pregnancy rapidly spread around the village, and after her release from hospital KB's sister had been overwhelmed at the number of their neighbours wishing her well.

Alex in particular seemed delighted at the prospect of becoming what she termed 'an honorary aunt', and in true Alex fashion sprung another surprise on KB as they walked by the river that Sunday afternoon.

"I have a feeling," she said to him, as she put her arm around his waist and pulled him close to her, "that I am going to get awful broody with Hannah having a baby, and it would be nice to have another little Blake for him or her to grow up with. Sooo," she continued, before he had a chance to say anything, "I think we should get engaged, what do you think?"

"Bloody hell, Alex!" he exclaimed. "First of all, I never thought of you as being the broody type, and secondly I thought you weren't prepared to make any commitments until we saw how my job was working out! So what brought this about?"

"A lady is entitled to change her mind," she replied primly. "And I've realized in the past few days you are far too good a catch to let go, Kristian Blake, so what do you say? Perhaps an announcement on New Year's Eve and a spring wedding? Oh, and by the way, I've decided that I love you – very much."

"What can I say?" he found himself answering. "Except I love you too, so let's do it!"

The next moment he found her arms around his neck, and as their lips met and she pressed her body close to his, any doubts he had disappeared in that moment.

"Pity it's so bloody cold," she giggled in his ear, "as it appears that down by the river something's stirring and I'd love to take full advantage of it – if I didn't think there would be a serious danger of frostbite. So let's head back to the pub and see if we can steal our way up to your room without disturbing your folks. Just one other thing," she added. "I know you go back to work tomorrow, but not a word of this to anyone until New Year's Eve, let's make it our secret and surprise everyone."

It was much later that evening as he was helping Jack behind the bar, when his mobile phone rang.

"Hi, KB, Colin here," came the familiar voice. "Hope you had a great Christmas, but just to let you know, the boss has called a meeting for tomorrow morning in the main conference room at 0830 hours. Apparently it's important and you'll be front and centre. So be there and don't be late!"

Chapter Twenty-Seven

Into the Field

"I see you stand like greyhounds in the slip,
Straining upon the start. The game's afoot."

Wm. Shakespeare. 'Henry V'

By half past seven the following morning, KB was turning the Wildtrak into the staff parking lot at Bulford, and after checking in with the porter in the Mess and dumping his Bergen in his room, went downstairs to the dining room where the breakfast buffet was already busy.

Taking a tray he helped himself to scrambled eggs, bacon and toast and headed for a vacant table by the window. As he sat down the sound of female laughter rose above the low buzz of male conversation, and he looked up to see Danica Janes crossing the room and heading towards his table followed by Colin Hunter.

The formal uniform of the Adjutant General's Corps had been replaced by a dark green short sleeved shirt and matching trousers, drawn at the waist by a leather belt. As he got up to greet her, he noticed the logo of the Exmoor National Park embroidered above the left chest pocket, with the title 'PARK RANGER' picked out in yellow capitals on the shoulder epaulettes. A pair of stout hiking boots completed her outfit.

"Hi, KB, good to see you back," his Section Leader welcomed him. "I understand you two have met, so no introductions necessary."

"In rather different surroundings last time!" the girl said, with some enthusiasm. "How did Christmas and the Boxing Day Hunt go?"

"Christmas Day was great, but the Boxing Day Hunt didn't exactly go as planned," he replied. "It's a long story and I'll tell you about it later."

"And it certainly looks as if you will have plenty of time," added Colin, "as it appears you two are going to be seeing a fair amount of each other in the immediate future, but I'll leave it to Andy to fill in the details at the meeting. Let's get breakfast done with, and we'll make our way over to the conference centre."

In the large, brightly lit room several people were already seated as Andy Reynard's secretary distributed briefing notes. Behind a raised dais, a screen took up most of the end wall, flanked by a large scale ordinance map on one side, and a detailed drawing of a building complex and its surrounds on the other.

Walking forward to examine the map more closely, KB recognized the area it covered as a section of the north Devon and Somerset coastline, stretching from Lynton and Lynmouth in the west to Porlock and Minehead in the east. The southern extremities included North Molton and the town of Dulverton, a large blue topped map pin drawing attention to the latter. A similar map pin, this time red topped had been placed in the top centre of the map on the Somerset side of the county border with Devon, under which the legend 'Langaller Estate' was clearly depicted.

"That's why we are here," said Dani, pointing at the red pin and turning towards the second map added, "and that is a blow-up of the Langaller Manor lay-out."

Before KB had a chance to move across for a closer look, the door opened and more attendees entered, among them Fred Nowakowski, Bill Hutchinson and Charlie Carstairs, with the Head of Operations, Andrew Reynard bringing up the rear.

Acknowledging Fred's wave, KB took a seat in the front with Dani on his left, Colin electing to seat himself immediately behind them.

Checking his watch as he mounted the dais, Reynard turned to face his audience.

"Good morning, ladies and gentlemen," he began. "Thank you for your promptness and although we are slightly ahead of schedule, as everyone appears to be here, let's make a start as we have a long morning in front of us.

"First of all some formalities, as most of you know, I am Andrew Reynard, Head of Operations for the Agency, and you will understand if I limit remaining introductions to the reason why you are here, rather than naming you individually. Please just raise your hand when I refer to you, then we'll all know who you are representing in any discussions that follow this briefing.

"We have amongst us this morning colleagues from GCHQ, MI5, the Police Counterterrorist unit, Armed Forces Liaison, the UK Border Force and the Home Office, as well as several of our own Field Operatives and their Section Leaders.

"I have also asked one of our financial investigation team to join us. The finance team have played a major role in unravelling some of the background data that has enabled us to carry out an assessment of the situation we have been reviewing, and prompted us to initiate further action. Finally, I would like to extend a special welcome to the gentleman standing at the back of the room, who many of you will recognize as a senior member of the British Council of Muslims.

"As we all appreciate, the overwhelming number of British Muslims totally abhor the actions of Islamist extremist groups and are entirely supportive of our Government's measures to limit and eventually, we all hope, put an end to the acts of violence perpetrated by this very small minority, so it is entirely appropriate that he should be with us today to be kept appraised of every step as it develops.

"Every one of you has received a briefing document which you may wish to refer to during this meeting, but I would ask you not to make notes and to leave the document behind when you leave. Your departments will be receiving detailed minutes of the meeting in due course, so at this stage the less paperwork in circulation, the better.

"The centre of our attention this morning, is Langaller Manor, the hub of what was once a large estate located in the northern sector of the Exmoor National Park and for generations the home of the Foxton-Wills family, who made a considerable fortune out of the wool trade dating back to the early 17th century.

"Unfortunately in the 1930's the family found its financial resources severely depleted and at the outbreak of World War Two were quite happy to see the Manor House requisitioned by the Army as a convalescence home for wounded servicemen. After the war, the Manor was handed back to the family who shortly afterwards, sold it off and for the next three decades it functioned as a small private school.

"Although the adjacent Langaller Farm was run moderately successfully by tenant farmers, some five years ago the educational institution was acquired by a larger Devon based public school. Shortly afterwards the Manor House and the one remaining farm were sold to an organization known as Dar al-Amn roughly translated as ‘The House of Safety’. The stated purpose of al-Amn was to establish a Madrasah or Islamic School there, with a special curriculum for those students intending to become Imams.

“What marks the Dar al-Amn School out from a number of similar establishments in the UK is that it appears to be aimed primarily at the sons of members of the wealthier Muslim community willing and able to pay relatively high school fees. It is therefore in effect, a higher educational institution limiting its intake to students of age fifteen years and upwards to eighteen, or even into their early twenties if studying to become Imams.

“We also believe that from time to time scholarships are awarded to the less wealthy sector of the Muslim community, on the recommendation of their own local Imam. As with many of our own conventional public schools, the Dar al-Amn Academy, as it is now officially known, is a registered charity and as such entitled to certain tax advantages.

“Shortly after Langaller was acquired by the al-Amn group, a planning application was made for some major alterations and additions to the existing Manor House and its buildings, which eventually received planning approval, albeit in the face of some opposition from local residents and the Exmoor National Parks Authority.

“These objections were, however, eventually overcome when agreements were reached with several nearby villages to improve or provide facilities such as community and recreational centres. This may suggest to some of you a form of ‘back-door incentive’ but as some of you will be aware, it is no more than a number of our major supermarket chains have done to ingratiate themselves in areas where they wished to establish new outlets.

“The alterations and extensions to the Manor commenced immediately after planning approval was granted, and the first alarm bells rang when it was noted by local trades’ people that none of the major construction contracts were awarded to local businesses, and even supplies of heavy building materials such as bulk concrete were coming from companies largely based in the Midlands.

“After an initial outcry, this was explained by the fact that nearly all these companies had connections with the al-Amn organization, either as supporters of their political agenda or by Directorships, and eventually the vociferous complaints quietly dissipated.”

Pausing to take a sip of water, Reynard took off his glasses and after polishing them on a handkerchief, replaced them on his nose and continued.

"You will find a fairly detailed break-down of this organization's political objectives in your briefing notes, but to summarize, al-Amn's aim is to establish a self-governing Islamic enclave within the United Kingdom subject to Sharia Law, this to be achieved by legal and democratic means.

"Fairly extensive research by some of our colleagues here today, has not put up any red flags which might indicate that they are anything other than what they purport to be, but with an obvious potential for subversive activities beneath this otherwise legitimate surface, we decided to maintain a watching brief on them about eighteen months ago which coincided with their first batch of students graduating from the Academy.

"Since then, some of these graduates have gone on to universities and others have simply pursued careers in several different sectors, predominantly teaching at secondary school level, the legal and accounting professions. That is of course, in addition to those who have gone on to enter their mosques as Imams.

"However, in recent months no less than eight cases have come to our attention of attempts being made by teachers to radicalize their students, university students attempting to do the same among their fellow undergraduates and likewise Imams selecting members of their congregation for a similar purpose. In six of those cases the individuals concerned have all attended, or have links to the Dar al-Amn Academy. In every instance, this has been brought to our notice by members of the British Muslim community and channelled through to us by our friend here today, for which we are extremely grateful.

"Another major factor that has caused us concern is the apparent disappearance off our radar of a number of these graduates, and as recently as two weeks ago another former student of the Academy was identified as a casualty of an American strike against a stronghold of the so- called Islamic State, suggesting that some of them may have left the UK to join that organization.

"In light of this, we recently upped our surveillance of Langaller to a higher level with drone over-flights, satellite imagery and with an agent on the ground, and I would now like to call upon the Field Operative charged with this assignment to give you a report."

With that Reynard beckoned Dani forward, and with no hesitation and every sign of outward confidence, she took his place on the dais.

"Since commencing this assignment," she commenced, her voice clear and precise, "I have been working as a Ranger with the Exmoor National Parks authority, ostensibly to assist with their annual deer count and cull. This has been with the full knowledge and consent of their Executive, whose Chairman has seen to it that although my true purpose remains known to only a few, I have received their full cooperation.

"This has given me the flexibility to move about the park at will, and the drone flights that our Head of Operations referred to have enabled me to provide the Park Authority with the most accurate deer count they have probably ever had, to the amazement of my fellow Rangers." A ripple of subdued laughter ran through the audience, as she continued.

"I should state right from the outset, that to date I have not been able to gain access to the compound which now houses the Academy, nor would I have any credible reason for attempting this overtly. The Langaller Estate boundary is marked by a low dry-stone wall and within that, the compound itself is surrounded by a ten foot high wire fence, supposedly erected to keep deer out. Having driven around its perimeter there is no possible way a stray deer could find its way in, let alone give me an excuse to enter.

"I have, however, set up an observation post overlooking the Manor House and most of the grounds immediately surrounding it and can confirm the following.

"To all outward appearances the Academy is exactly as would be expected. Students have been observed taking full advantage of a number of sports facilities, and physical training in groups appears to be an integral part of everyday life, and in all winds and weathers. Traffic in and out is almost entirely limited during the daytime to what would be considered normal deliveries of supplies, although there are regular incoming and outgoing flights by helicopter, using the main playing field as a landing site.

"On such occasions two or three passengers have been observed visiting the Academy, and the same number leaving. Two different helicopters have been logged, and it has been established that they belong to a West Midlands based charter company.

"No night-time traffic by road or air has been noted, although in fairness and for obvious reasons I have not been able to monitor the Academy on a 24/7 basis. I have spent several nights maintaining a watch on the Manor, but there was no movement in or out on any of these.

"With regards to the compound itself, allow me to take you through the complex, building by building, by means of these aerial photos and satellite images. The buildings can also be seen on the map behind me if you need to take a closer look later. Lights please."

The lights dimmed and an aerial photo came up on the screen behind her. Picking up a laser pointer a small dot of red light appeared, which Danica centred on the main building.

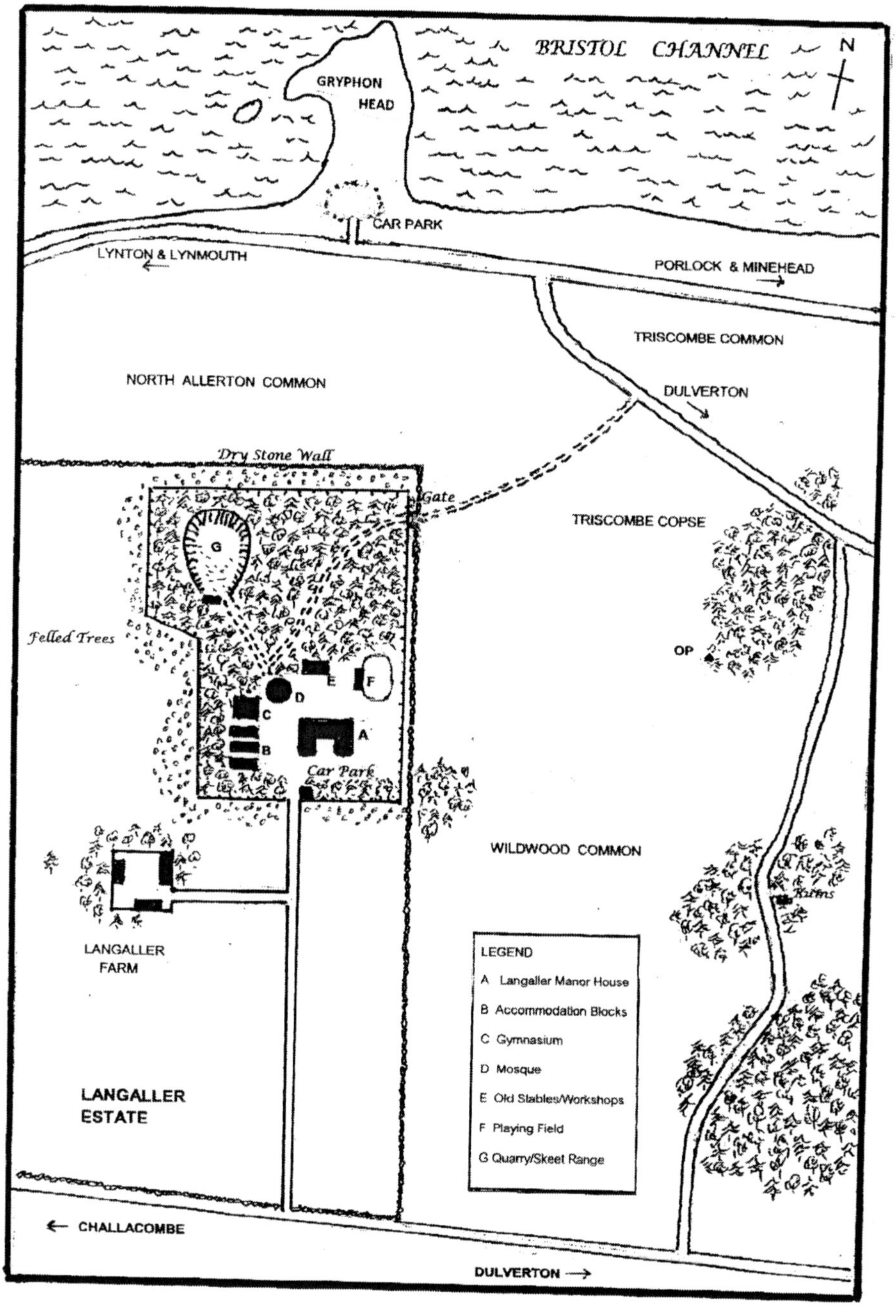

"This is the original Manor House which as far as we can gather now houses the administration centre, staff accommodation and classrooms. There are also fully fitted kitchens, a large dining hall and a library, plus several rooms which are probably used for leisure purposes. No planning permission has ever been submitted for any structural alterations. Immediately to the west of the Manor House, three new double storey accommodation blocks have been built, and according to the plans submitted they provide dormitory style sleeping quarters and ablutions for approximately eighty students in each block, plus small en-suite rooms for supervisory staff or senior students."

The laser dot moved again to the open area between the Manor House and the accommodation blocks.

"This whole area is hard surfaced and is what we would probably call a quadrangle with a gymnasium on the west boundary and on the northern edge of which is this circular building which according to the plans is the school's own mosque.

"From the centre of the building a tower or minaret extends to a height of approximately twelve metres or forty feet. No doubt it is from the top of this tower that the students are called to prayer, but it must also provide an excellent vantage point from which much of the compound can be kept under observation. To the north east of the mosque this low single storey building was the old stables, but we believe is now probably used for garages or storage. To the east of the stable block this area here is used as a playing field and you will note that it is surrounded by a 400 metre running track, and on its western edge we have an old cricket pavilion which was erected when the Manor first became a school. As I have already mentioned, the playing field is also used frequently as a helicopter landing pad.

"You will notice that the whole area inside the boundary fence is heavily wooded, although at one time and before the fence was erected, the woodland extended quite a distance out from the new perimeter. It can be seen from the tree stumps that show up quite clearly on the photo that this area has been extensively logged. Licences to fell these trees were applied for and granted, subject to the Estate establishing a new plantation. This has been planned for but not yet planted out to the south of Langaller Farm.

"One further feature of the Manor complex worthy of scrutiny, is the old quarry here in the north east corner of the fenced compound. The stone from which the original Manor House was built came from here and it was temporarily re-opened to provide materials for the new buildings. According to the official planning documents the quarry has now been equipped as a skeet range, complete with a range shack.

"There appears to be only one entrance to the compound through the main gate in the middle of the fence on the southern perimeter. You can see this is flanked by a small building which provides accommodation for the security guards, who man the gate on a round-the-clock basis. There are a number of tracks running through the woods inside the compound, but they all end at the fence with no obvious means of egress.

"You will notice, however, that in the north east corner of the dry stone walling there is a gate, so it is possible that the fence immediately behind it could be removed to provide an exit if required.

"Please note also the farmhouse and buildings here to the south east and some distance outside the compound. This is Langaller Farm, from which all the Estate's agricultural activities are run, including a horticultural section. Sheep, goats and a small beef herd are raised on Estate land, all slaughtering and butchering taking place off site at a Halal licensed abattoir.

"We know also that the farm is managed by a graduate of the Royal Agricultural College, and the background checks carried out indicate that he has no connection with the Dar al-Amn organization and comes from a sixth generation farming family with origins in North Yorkshire.

"That is about all I can tell you about the Langaller Estate as it is today," she concluded, "so lights please."

As the lights flooded the room, Andrew Reynard stepped forward as she left the dais.

"Thank you," he said nodding towards Dani's retreating form. "After our next presentation, which I understand will be relatively short, we will take a half hour break during which time coffee will be served. This will give you a chance to go through the briefing notes to prepare any questions you may have. One further factor which should be noted concerns the loss we suffered recently of one of our Field Operatives. Our man was killed by unknown assailants while providing close quarter protection for a foreign national in the UK, the latter attending college in Cornwall at the invitation of our Government.

"In conjunction with our own investigations into this matter and information provided to us by the Police, a link, albeit tenuous at present, has been established between the vehicle the assailants were known to be driving on or about the time of the incident and al-Amn, in that the hire company that owned said vehicle are active supporters of this organization.

"That in itself could be no more than coincidence, but what we have been able to establish is that this company and many others under similar ownership appear to be connected to al-Amn financially or through shareholdings and common directorships.

"The picture that is emerging is one of a network or spider's web of commercial and mutual political interests spreading to all four corners of the United Kingdom, and with Dar al-Amn at its centre. To expand on this further, I would now invite our MI5 representative to brief us on their assessment."

At Reynard's bidding a young man KB estimated to be in his early thirties got from his seat and strode to the dais.

"Having been kept in the loop by our colleagues here at the Agency," he began, "we have come to some similar conclusions. In short, we share their concerns as to the potential threat posed in the event that Dar al-Amn's agenda is far more subversive in its objectives, than those that are publicly stated.

"At Langaller there is a strong possibility that they could be using their extensive facilities not only to radicalize a broad cross-section of young men from among the British Muslim community, but also to train them in every facet of subversive operations.

"At present the Academy is graduating around eighty students a year, so in five years some four hundred will have been re-established as active members of society.

"Not only would these graduates be capable of influencing and recruiting others to their cause, but their capability to act independently as 'lone wolf' terrorists committing acts of violence similar to those we have seen recently in Europe, is of major concern. Alternatively the potential for them to operate in groups or 'cells' and to lie dormant gathering intelligence until activated to conduct widespread but co-ordinated attacks, is significant.

"With a UK based centre, the logistics of moving recruits in and out of the United Kingdom to obtain the level of training that might now be provided by the Academy is simplified considerably, and the risk to their being intercepted reduced accordingly.

"I make no apologies therefore, for underlining what to most of us here must have been obvious in terms of the potential threat posed to our national security, should our fears about the true purpose of the Academy be confirmed. Thank you for your attention."

Once more Andrew Reynard took the stand, as the man from MI5 reclaimed his seat.

"As promised, we will be breaking shortly, ladies and gentlemen, but first allow me to forestall two obvious questions before we re-convene.

"First of all, like all schools and academies, the establishment at Langaller is registered and subject to regular inspections by the appropriate authority. In this case, however, and because it is entirely funded privately by its sponsors with additional revenues coming from fee paying parents, it is not subject to scrutiny by OFSTED, although it is visited annually by an agency that deals almost exclusively with religious educational institutes. To date the reports on the Academy have resulted in it receiving very high ratings in all areas.

"Secondly, in consultation with our legal department and the Police, it has been agreed that at present we do not have sufficient hard evidence to justify applying for a warrant that would enable us to carry out a detailed examination of the Academy's facilities. Furthermore, even if we were successful in obtaining a warrant and carried out such a search, there is always a chance that we might not be successful in securing the evidence we need, and in effect all we would achieve is warning al-Amn that we have them on our radar.

"With this in mind we will be taking immediate steps to advance our covert investigations to the next level, so if and when we hit them, we hit them hard, with maximum surprise and with the object of neutralising them completely.

"In the event of the latter, we will set up a tactical command centre located at the Exmoor National Park offices in Dulverton, marked on the map with the blue pin. The Park Authority will be notified accordingly, and apart from being close to our objective – marked with the red pin – there is an added advantage in that they have their own in house communications centre to keep in touch with their Rangers by short wave radio, and we can tap into this asset.

"We will re-convene in half an hour to take your questions and discuss any other relevant matters."

Leaving the dais, Reynard headed directly towards where KB, Dani and Colin were sitting.

"I want to see all three of you in my office as soon as the meeting is over," he said. "Now the cat is out of the bag with this lot, we cannot afford to waste any time, so be prepared to get your skates on."

It was close to noon by the time the meeting broke up and they filed into Andrew's office. As they entered he was taping the large detailed map of the Langaller Estate on to the white board behind his desk.

"Grab a seat," he said as he stepped back to check his handiwork.

"Right," he said, sitting down behind his desk. "This is the plan. The problem we have been facing is to get someone into the Academy compound with a legitimate reason for being there, and without raising any suspicions. We have considered a covert insertion, but it's too risky and not practical. From what Dani has told us, apart from the fence there are signs of closed circuit infra-red TV cameras posted at regular intervals around the perimeter, and there may even be trip wires set up inside the fence.

"You will have seen from the aerial photos the extent of the logging that has been carried out around the compound which is all legal and above board, but also, not by accident we believe, makes an approach to the wire difficult without detection. We have noticed, however, that a number of old growth trees have been felled inside the compound, and as there is no record of licences being granted for these, this may provide us with the lever we need to get you, KB, inside for a good look around.

"In this respect, the course you were taking at Tamar Valley College should stand you in good stead, and your cover will be as Forestry Commission Woodlands Officer carrying out a routine logging inspection. As back-up you can also claim that you are checking for any signs of Ash die-back which is a disease causing problems in our forests at present, so if you don't already know what to look for, you'd better find out.

"You will be given an alias, your credentials are being prepared as we speak, and our Transport people will fit you out with a suitable vehicle. The Forestry Commission Western Region Supervisor has been notified and your identification will show a contact number here if anyone checks up on you. Should you run into the real local Woodlands Officer for Exmoor, tell him to contact the Supervisor direct, but we are hoping that you will be in and out before anyone starts asking questions.

"You will need to find a couple of night's accommodation in the area, but avoid pubs, large B&B's and hotels. I am sure Dani can help you find something.

"Your access will probably be through the Langaller Farm Manager, so check in with him first. You'll be on your own, but Dani will provide back-up. Don't be too pushy and maintain as low a profile as possible. Apart from reporting back as soon as you have completed your assignment, if you get the chance, text us with details of anything unusual you come across direct from the site but don't compromise your presence by doing so.

"I want you out of here and on the road to Exmoor as soon as possible, so that you can make your visit to the Academy tomorrow. Report in when you're in situ, or if there are any delays. Anything to add, Colin or Dani?"

"You have a dog don't you?" asked Colin. "I suggest you collect him on your way down and he can ride around with you. It might add to your cover. If you are seen with a dog for a companion it could be reassuring if your authenticity is suspected, after all, intelligence agents would not be expected to be seen in the field with a dog trotting at their heels!"

"I'm staying in a holiday cottage on a farm just four miles north of Dulverton on the Exford road," added Dani. "There are four cottages, and the others are all vacant at the moment, so I'll book you in, and give you the address and leave it to you to make your own way there."

"Any questions from you, KB?"

"No, sir," he replied. "Everything seems fairly straightforward, but there is one other personal matter I would like to mention."

"I'll wait for you outside," Dani volunteered, leaving the three men together.

"So what's the problem, KB?" Reynard asked.

"It's not really a problem, sir, but I thought you should know. Over the Christmas holiday, we found out that my sister Hannah is pregnant, and she's positive that the child is Peter Bowen's."

"Glad you told me," came the response, "as it will certainly strengthen your sister's claim on Peter's estate. If necessary, I believe there are some non-invasive pre-natal tests which can be conducted to establish the paternity of an unborn child, so I will inform our legal department immediately. With Peter's DNA on record here, do you think your sister would object if a test is necessary?"

"I can't honestly say, sir. But I'm sure my sister will want to do the best for the child, so I can't imagine she would refuse."

"Good, then off you go and get down to Transport to collect your vehicle. Pick up your new ID before you leave, and I believe they've got a Forestry Commission uniform for you as well. If you think of anything else, let Colin know. Good luck and all being well, I'll see you back here in a day or two."

Taking that as his cue to depart, he joined Dani who was waiting in the corridor and went downstairs leaving Colin in the office.

"If you like, I'll give you a lift down to Transport," she offered as they exited the building. "Then I'll be on my way. In case you need it, I've got a copy of the Langaller Estate map, but you should get one when you pick up your documents so we can compare notes at the farm," she added, as they climbed into her Land Rover Defender. "The farmer and his wife are good people and I usually eat with them in the evening, and I'm sure it won't be too much trouble for them to feed an extra mouth," she said, as moments later they drew up outside the Transport Section buildings.

"I'll see you later, though it could be a while, as you won't be breaking any speed records in that," she laughed, pointing at an ageing single cab Land Rover pick-up parked outside the workshops. "It must be yours. I see they've added a broad yellow stripe to it and a Forestry Commission logo to the doors – aren't you the lucky one!"

"Thanks, Dani," he replied. "Look forward to meeting you at the farm – assuming I make it!"

Waving her goodbye, he walked towards the small office that occupied a corner of the workshops as Laura Majors came out to meet him.

"Mr Blake – good to see you again," she greeted him. "Come to collect your vehicle?"

"It looks as if that's the one," he replied without enthusiasm, nodding towards the Land Rover.

"It is indeed. The best we could do for you at short notice, but appearances can be deceiving. As you can see this old girl has seen some service, but mechanically she is as sound as a bell. We've tidied her up a bit and given her a full service and check over, and although she may not be in prime showroom condition, she should be more than adequate for your needs. No extra bells and whistles on this baby though, just a tracker which transmits permanently and we've fitted a sat-nav for you, and a hands-free kit for your mobile. We've also replaced the lock on the glove compartment which was knackered, and fitted a tool box in the bed which you will find has the kind of kit in it that a Forestry Commission Woodlands Officer might use.

She's fitted with twin fuel tanks, with a change-over switch on the dash. Engine is a 2.2 diesel and both tanks are full, so you won't need to re-fuel for a while. Otherwise she's completely standard and ready to roll. If you would just like to sign her out for me," she said, handing him a clipboard, "you can be on your way."

With the release form duly completed, KB unlocked the lid on the tool box and flipped it open to find inside under a neatly folded tarpaulin, a yellow hard hat, a folding saw, a full size felling axe and a wide canvas belt with pouches containing a clasp knife, a small hatchet and a can of red fluorescent spray paint. In addition a large heavy duty torch, a 50 metre open frame measuring tape and a pair of work gloves completed the kit. All the equipment had the appearance of being well used, and odd bits of twine and a wire lay amongst an accumulation of dust and grit in the bottom of the box.

Re-locking the lid, KB climbed into the cab and checked the familiar layout finding it similar to the many that had been for so long the mainstay of the light transport fleet of the British Armed Forces. Driving a manual again having got used to the automatic gear box in his Wildtrak would be a challenge, but after practising dipping the clutch pedal and changing gear several times, he switched on the engine and cautiously engaging first, pulled away and out onto the camp road.

Back at the Admin Centre a lengthy and tedious hour was spent being briefed on the documentation and check lists he would need to carry out his logging inspection, application forms for the licence to fell trees and warning notices if regulations had been breached.

He was then provided with a detailed map of the areas logged by the Langaller Estate, with every tree stump identified by a licence number. The new plantation lay out was also shown, as were suspected areas where there was evidence of individual trees being cut down, but for which a licence had not been obtained. Finally he swapped his Agency ID for a Forestry Commission photo ID card, and signed for a set of Ordnance Survey maps for the whole of the Exmoor National Park area.

Following directions he was given, he made his way to the Agency tailor's section, and pushing open a door at the end of a long corridor he found himself in a room half filled with racks of clothing that would have done justice to a major theatre's wardrobe department.

Behind four long tables, seamstresses worked away busily at their sewing machines and in the corner a young man was putting a pile of trousers through a steam press. Looking up as KB entered, he came across to the counter to meet him.

"Kristian Blake," KB introduced himself, and showing his ID, "I believe you have some gear for me?"

"Ah yes, Mr Blake," the young man replied, checking the ledger in front of him. "The Forestry Commission working uniform, so please follow me so that I can take a few measurements."

In a small closet, the man took a tape from around his neck and measured KB's chest and waist. Kneeling down he extended the tape measure to take an inside leg measurement, and gave a slight gasp of surprise when instead of finding resistance from KB's left calf muscle the trouser leg hung loose around the prosthetic limb.

"Sorry about that, sir," he said, obviously embarrassed.

"Don't worry," KB laughed. "Fortunately the leg is the only artificial appendage below the waist!"

Standing up, and still red in the face, the lad was quick to change the subject by asking KB for his collar and shoe size.

"Collar 17, and shoe size nine, but why the need for all this?"

"You get a work shirt, trousers and safety boots in addition to the jacket," came the response. "The boots will be brand new, so you'll have to scuff them about a bit. We're going to have to make a few alterations to the clothing, so if you wouldn't mind coming back in about an hour, everything will be ready for you."

As he left the building, KB checked his watch and seeing that it was already well past one o'clock headed across to the Mess for lunch. As he entered the dining room, Fred waved to him from a table at which Colin and Bill Hutchinson were also seated and after collecting a bowl of soup, a plate of macaroni cheese, bread rolls and butter from the buffet, he walked over to join them.

"Expected you to be wearing a check shirt and whistling 'I'm a lumberjack, I'm okay' "chuckled Colin, as he sat down with them. "All set to go then?"

"Just about," he replied. "I've still got a bit of gear to pick up, then I'll be on my way."

"It should be a piece of cake," Colin continued. "But take care, always expect the unexpected, but barring any hiccups you should be in and out tomorrow, so we'll see you back here on Wednesday. Look forward to your report."

"What are you going to tell your folks?" asked Fred, as Colin and Bill excused themselves and left the two of them to finish their lunches.

"I shall tell them I'm off to Exmoor for a couple of days on a field exercise, and actually, taking Rocky with me will help. They'd never think I was off on a hazardous assignment taking the dog with me. I just hope I can get back on New Year's Eve as Alex and I are going to announce our engagement."

"I shouldn't count on that," said his friend. "Even if you are finished on Tuesday, depending on the outcome, you are bound to be involved in planning the next stage if another level of action is considered necessary, so you could find yourself tied up here for several days. If I were you, I would tell the young lady that you may have to take a rain check on the announcement."

"That will go down like a lead balloon. I foresee much foot stamping and hair tearing," he replied.

"KB, if she really is the right one for you, she will understand, and in any case she can't go through life expecting everything to go as she wants it to, particularly if you guys tie the knot. Anyway, I must leave you to it and get back to my paperwork. Alan Maidley, Charlie Carstairs and I are still trying to unravel the mysteries of the al-Amn network and it is proving to be a nightmare."

"One thing before you go," KB said to his friend. "You are fairly up to speed with all things Islamic. Won't the students at the Academy be away on a break right now?"

"Not likely," came the answer. "But it shouldn't make much difference to your visit, even if they are. Hardly surprisingly Muslims don't recognize Christmas as an official holiday, though they will probably be breaking for the celebration of Mohammed's birthday later in January, so I suspect the school will be in full session right now."

"Thanks, Fred, see you later," KB acknowledged as his friend left him to finish his lunch.

Before returning to the tailors, KB retrieved his Glock and holster from the Ford, collected his Bergen from his room and checked out with the hall porter leaving the keys of his pick-up with him for safekeeping. Slinging the rucksack in the cab of the Land Rover, he locked the weapon in the glove compartment and drove back to the Admin Building where he was greeted once again by the young man who had taken his measurements earlier.

A large brown paper parcel awaited him, with a pair of steel toed safety boots in a separate plain carrier bag.

"Shirt, trousers and heavy duty woollen socks in here," said the youth, patting the parcel and with a flourish he produced an olive green, fleece lined jacket with faux fur trimmed hood from under the counter. "And your jacket, sir. It's storm proof and should be pretty warm, and in the pocket you will find a pair of fleece lined leather gloves, which all-in-all, should set you up pretty well."

Thanking him, KB examined the jacket briefly, noting that the legend 'FORESTRY COMMISSION' had been stencilled in large yellow letters on the back. Putting the jacket and parcel under his arm, and with the carrier bag firmly gripped in his hand, he retraced his steps to where he had parked the Land Rover, and stowing his new acquisitions on top of the Bergen, climbed aboard and headed away from Bulford towards Somerset.

Although as Laura Majors had promised the Land Rover ran sweetly enough, Dani's comment that he wouldn't be breaking any speed records proved equally correct and it was nearing six o'clock by the time he pulled off onto the side road that would take him to Long Lane. Reckoning that it would be better to confront Alex and explain to her in person that he was unlikely to be home for New Year's Eve, he drove past The Volunteer and went straight to the Bakers' house.

It was Amy who answered his knock on the door, and she seemed unduly surprised and more than a little flustered to see him.

"Come on in, Kris," she said, leading him through to the kitchen, where Joe was already seated at the table, a mug of tea in front of him, reading the paper.

"I can't stop, Mrs Baker," KB explained, "I just dropped by to see if Alex was around. We were hoping to get together on New Year's Eve and I may not be able to make it."

There was a moment's silence as Joe folded his paper, while Amy stood by, nervously wiping her hands on her apron.

"She's out at the moment, Kris," Amy began, "and I'm not sure when she will be back, but I … ."

"Kris needs to be told," said Joe, interrupting her. "He's going to find out soon enough. The truth is, lad," he continued turning to face KB, "she had a phone call yesterday, and she's gone away for a few days."

"Not an emergency in the family or anything like that, I hope?" KB asked.

"Hardly," came the wry response. "I gather the call was from some posh Army bloke she met when you took her down to that party in Exeter, and within a couple of hours of his calling her, he appeared at our doorstep and he's taken her off to Paris for New Year's Eve."

"I'm so sorry, Kris," Amy said, the worried look on her face saying it all. "It all happened so fast, I couldn't stop her. She didn't say anything about it until ten minutes before he arrived in his fancy sports car, and I didn't have a chance to call Joe."

"I promise you, Kris," Joe added, "I would have tried to stop her going if I could have got back in time, but I tell you, she's going to get a real flea in her ear from me when she gets home."

A red mist clouded his vision and it felt as if a black shroud had engulfed him. As his senses recovered from the shock everything became crystal clear, but it seemed an eternity before he could find any words to say.

"I understand," he eventually mumbled, as much to himself as to her parents. "It's just that – well – I guess it doesn't matter now, but Alex and I were supposed to be announcing our engagement on New Year's Eve, however now it seems she has had a better offer," he added bitterly.

"Perhaps it's all perfectly innocent?" Amy suggested hopefully, at the same time looking as if she was about to burst into tears.

"I'm afraid 'perfectly innocent' is not in the vocabulary of Captain Hugo Wellsbury, Mrs Baker," he replied bluntly. "If indeed it is Wellsbury who has taken your daughter off to Paris, and to be frank, I don't believe it could be anyone else. Anyway, thank you for being so honest with me, and please tell Alex I dropped by. You'd better give her this as well," he added, removing the St Christopher medallion she had given him from around his neck and laying it on the table. "I don't think I'll need Alex's kind of protection on my travels, with or without St Chris's blessing!"

With no further words spoken, he left them in the kitchen and a few minutes later turned into the car park of The Volunteer.

He found both his parents in their living room, and Kathy's pleasure at seeing her son again soon turned to anger when he told them about the outcome of his meeting with the Bakers.

"Whatever's got into her?" Kathy demanded. "She must be crazy to go off on a whim with a man she hardly knows!"

"Undoubtedly the lure of Paris and having a wealthy young buck paying court to her," Jack suggested. "But we all know Alex. To be frank, I always thought she was a class one gold digger and certainly a premier league opportunist, and in my opinion, son, you are well out of it; you would never have had a moment's peace married to that one! But what brings you back so soon?" he added.

"We've got an exercise on Exmoor for a couple of days, Dad," KB replied. "So I thought I'd drop by and pick up Rocky. Give him a chance to run around with me in the open air, and he'll be good company."

"Good idea, son," agreed his father. "He could do with some exercise as he won't be going out with Hannah for a while. She came home this morning and is upstairs in bed, so go up and say hello to her before you leave."

"Not staying for supper then?" asked Kathy.

"No, Mum, this is a flying visit. I have to be in Dulverton by eight o' clock at the latest, so I have to get going."

He found his sister propped up in her bed and after a brief chat and a report on the Alex saga, he said his goodbyes, and with Rocky settled in the cab of the Land Rover beside him, he plugged the address of the farm into the sat-nav.

The journey west gave him ample time for reflection, and with his anger at Alex's betrayal diminishing as the miles slipped by, the cabinet in his mind was opened once again and the folder marked 'Alexis Baker' was filed and the drawer slammed shut. There were, his reason told him, more immediate matters to hand that would demand his total concentration and he could not allow any emotive or painful thoughts to distract him from his purpose.

Chapter Twenty-Eight

Reconnaissance

Vipera in verpecula est – Look before you leap, for snakes among sweet flowers do creep.

Latin proverb

At a quarter to eight he was pulling into the farmyard where he drew up next to the Exmoor National Park Land Rover. Pleased with the time he had made, he was unloading his Bergen when the door of one of the cottages in front of him opened and Dani came out, to be greeted by an enthusiastic Rocky who had decided in an instant that here was a new friend to be made.

"Hello again," she said, bending to make a fuss of the dog. "I was beginning to worry about you."

"Yes, sorry I'm a bit late," he answered her. "My stop off to collect Rocky from home took a little longer than I expected, for reasons I'll explain later."

"Oh dear," she commented. "Nothing too serious I hope?"

"Let's just say that Hugo Wellsbury has raised his handsome head again," he said, "and leave it at that for the time being."

"I think I probably understand already," Dani replied, with a shake of her head. "But let me show you to your cottage, which is right here next to mine. Our hosts have already eaten, but the good lady of the house is keeping a couple of bowls of stew warm for us, which we can eat over in mine while we go through our plans for tomorrow."

He found his lodgings warm and comfortable and after stowing his gear in the single bedroom, he fed Rocky from one of the tins of dog food he had brought with him and then joined Dani in the living room of her cottage where the promised stew, a loaf of home baked bread, and a dish of farmhouse butter was already laid out on the table. A log fire burned in the grate, and with a sigh of contentment Rocky settled himself down on the hearth rug, while KB and Dani took their seats for supper.

"Man, this is good," he said as he tucked into the steaming bowl of food. "I was getting hungry."

"I take it that the reappearance of Triple H in your life has not spoiled your appetite then?" the girl asked innocently.

"Actually, not as much as I thought it would. The bugger turned up this morning at my girlfriend's house and seemingly, has whisked her off to Paris for New Year's Eve where I'm pretty certain, the festivities will not necessarily be confined to a gentle saunter down the Champs Elysee and a rendition of Auld Lang Syne around the Eiffel Tower at midnight."

"You've got that right," she answered. "It would be a fair assumption that somewhere along the line there will be a fireworks display. I just hope the young lady likes her sex kinky. From what I've been told – not from first-hand experience I can promise you – I believe our Hugo belongs to the 'whips and chains' fraternity, which is not entirely unusual amongst the ranks of our hallowed aristocracy, and from their history the Wellsbury bloodline is no exception – founder members of the Hellfire Club and all that associated debauchery."

"You've done your research well," he laughed.

"Amazing what you can find on the internet," she replied. "But eat up. There's an apple and blackberry crumble to follow with as much cream as you can manage to help it on its way."

Half an hour later, dishes washed and returned to the farmhouse, and with a mug of coffee each to hand, Dani spread her map of the Langaller Estate out on the table and they sat down to look at it again in detail.

"What time are you planning to visit?" she asked him. "Are you going to call cold, or try to make an appointment?"

"I thought I'd phone the Farm Manager first thing, and hopefully agree a time for my visit for sometime tomorrow morning," he replied.

"Probably a good idea. I've met the guy a couple of times and he seems a pretty decent sort, but if you allow him the courtesy of a call, he's less likely to go all bolshie on you. His name is Adam Firth, by the way, married with a couple of kids and in his mid-thirties. He seems to have a strictly 'business-only' relationship with the Academy and his bosses, and hasn't offered any information on the set-up there in the conversations we've had. In fact everything seems to be kept very much at arm's length as far as he's concerned."

Pointing at the map, she added, "I've been using Triscombe Copse here as a good vantage point to keep the place under observation.

"It's on high ground overlooking the compound and you can see a lot of what is going on from there. However, the trees screen some of it but there is nowhere else in the area where you can get a better view of the Manor House and the buildings. I'm usually there for most of the morning but this afternoon I'm due to help some of my Park Ranger colleagues cull a couple of deer from a herd we've been tracking over on Challacombe Common, and I should be around to help them. If all goes according to plan, however, you should have finished your inspection by then."

"I should hope so, but if I am delayed, I'll give you a shout on your mobile. Have you got Firth's number?" he asked.

Nodding an affirmative, she took her own mobile out of her shirt pocket, and after dialling up her directory she passed it to him to copy the number into his own phone.

"I don't think there is anything else I can help you with," she said, "so it's all up to you from here in. In fact, as it promises to be a long day tomorrow, I'm going to turn in. I've got some provisions in, so if you want to come over for a coffee and some breakfast at around 8 o'clock, you're welcome."

"Thanks, I didn't have a chance to pick up any groceries myself so I'll take you up on that," he replied. I'm going to turn in myself, so please compliment the chef on a great supper, which was much appreciated, and I'll see you in the morning."

Outside in the yard, while Rocky investigated his new surroundings, he unlocked the cab of the Land Rover and took the Glock and its holster out of the glove compartment. Calling to the dog he went inside his cottage shivering slightly as the cold night air invaded the living room. Checking the radiator on the wall under the window, he found it only slightly warm to the touch. Deciding that he would catch up on the news before turning in, he put a match to the fire and as the kindling caught and licked around the logs that had been laid in, he sat back in the comfort of the settee and switched on the television.

It was sometime later when he awoke to find that Rocky had joined him on the sofa and was fast asleep, his head in KB's lap. The logs in the fire had burnt down to a few glowing embers, and easing himself out of the chair, he turned off the TV. Unlatching the front door Rocky trotted out into the darkness, returning a few minutes later with no inclination to stay out in the cold any longer than necessary. The sky above was clear of cloud and the stars twinkled brightly in the thin night air. A full moon illuminated the farm building in its silver beams and already a layer of frost had collected on the bonnet and windscreen of the Land Rover. Shutting the door after the dog, he pushed the bolt across to lock it and went upstairs to bed, the dog at his heels.

Sleep came easily and when his alarm awoke him at 7 o'clock he wasted no time in getting showered and dressed. Slipping the tan shirt he had been issued with over a white T-Shirt, he then put one of the heavy duty socks on his right foot, and the other over the foot of his artificial limb. Next came the tan trousers followed by the heavy work boots, and finally he adjusted the strap until the holster sat snugly over his left shoulder. After removing the magazine of the Glock he cleared the weapon and checked the action before re-loading it and sliding it home. Taking the Forestry Commission jacket out of his Bergen, he tried it on for size and found it a comfortable fit. Examining his reflection in the mirror, he zipped it up and noticed with satisfaction that there was no tell-tale bulge to suggest he was carrying a weapon. Placing the Agency mobile phone he had been given into a jacket pocket, he put his own into the left chest pocket of his shirt and buttoned down the flap to secure it.

Downstairs he took some of the wood ash from the fireplace and added a daub of soot from the chimney breast, dampened the mixture under the kitchen tap and rubbed it sparingly into the pristine rawhide leather of his boots. Drying off the surface of the boots with a handful of paper kitchen towel and washing his hands, he inspected his handiwork.

"That doesn't look too bad," he said to a curious Rocky, who had been standing watching his master's strange behaviour. "Now let's go next door and join the ice maiden for breakfast!"

The lights were on downstairs in the neighbouring cottage and before he had time to knock, Dani opened the door to greet him.

"Come on in, KB. Toast is on its way and the kettle's on, so sit yourself down. The uniform looks pretty neat incidentally, and I like the jacket, it looks a darn sight warmer than the one the National Parks folk give their Rangers."

As she spoke, he slipped it off and hung it over the back of the kitchen chair before sitting down.

"I see you are carrying then," she added, nodding at the shoulder holster. "And as far as I know they don't body search their visitors, so you should be okay. To be frank, I don't know whether I would go in there armed to the teeth, it's going to be awkward if you're hanging around in a warm office for any length of time and they invite you to take your jacket off – that would certainly blow your cover! Also if it does turn out that they are manning a mini fortress in there, it's hardly likely you would be able to fight your way out."

"No, but at least I'd make sure they remembered my visit," KB answered wryly.

"KB, you're thinking like a soldier," the girl said reprovingly. "You're supposed to be an ordinary working civilian doing a straightforward job. This is first and foremost a recce, not a search and destroy mission, so don't charge in looking for trouble. Whether or not you take your side-arm is your call, but I know what I'd do."

"You're probably right," he admitted ruefully. "I'll leave it locked in the glove compartment."

"That makes more sense," she agreed. "Now here's your coffee, instant I'm afraid and help yourself to toast. There's plenty more if you want, and a jar of homemade raspberry jam to go with the farmhouse butter. There's also Marmite, if that's what turns your crank. I'm a Marmite fiend myself, but it's not to everyone's taste."

Breakfast turned out to be an unhurried affair, and KB was surprised at how relaxed he felt in her company. When the conversation turned to his service with the Paras and in particular his last tour in Afghanistan, he found recalling the details of the IED incident much easier than he had at any time before, nor were there any undue or over sympathetic comments from his listener.

It had gone half past eight when they rose from the table, and while Dani washed the plates at the sink, he put in the call to the Langaller Farm Manager.

The tones of the voice that answered him were level and measured, with just the slightest suggestion of a northern accent.

"It is short notice, but I'll do my best to accommodate you," came the response to KB's request for a visit. "Unfortunately I have to be in Dunster myself this morning for a couple of hours, but I suggest you do your preliminary inspection of the planned plantation location and the logged area outside the perimeter of the Manor grounds on your own first, and by the time you've finished I should be back and we can take a look at the wooded area inside together. My bosses are a little sensitive to strangers wandering around the estate," he added, "so I'll phone and warn them that you'll be working in the area this morning, and make an appointment to visit the grounds later, will that suit you?"

"That sounds excellent," KB answered. "I'll drop by the farm and wait for you there after I've finished."

"It sounds as if that went well," said Dani, as he rang off.

"Well, he can't see me himself until this afternoon, so I won't be able to get inside the compound until then, but in the meantime he suggests that I might like to do an inspection of everything outside the perimeter this morning on my own."

"If that's the case," she replied, "there's no point in me going up to Triscombe Copse to keep an eye on the compound if all you will be doing is wandering around the outer area for half a day, so why don't you follow me up there now and you can see for yourself what kind of an OP it makes?"

"Good idea, as soon as you are ready we will be on our way."

Ten minutes later they locked up their cottages, and with Rocky sitting beside him in the cab of the Land Rover, he followed Dani's Defender out of the farmyard and was soon climbing west up Winsford Hill. Once through Simonsbath, Dani turned north towards the coast and shortly afterwards branched right onto a narrow but unfenced country road. Five minutes later they entered a small wood, and slowing down he followed the Defender off the road onto a track which led them into a small clearing.

Turning his pick-up around so that it was facing back towards the road, he unlocked the glove compartment and took out his binoculars. Opening the driver's door he dismounted, followed by an enthusiastic Rocky who quickly set about exploring his new surroundings. Looking around he saw that the trees had completely screened the vehicles from the road, and calling the dog to heel he crossed to where Dani was spreading an Ordinance Survey map on the bonnet of her vehicle.

"That took us over half an hour without meeting any farm traffic to slow us down," she said, "so normally I'd allow at least forty minutes to reach here from our lodgings. This is the way we came," she added, tracing the route with her finger on the map. "And here is where we are now, about fifty metres in from the road and a hundred metres or so from the west side of the wood which overlooks the Manor. There is quite a lot of heavy undergrowth to get through until we reach the OP, so follow me."

The heavy undergrowth she described proved to be something of an understatement, and frequently bending double to duck under the lower boughs of the stands of beech and ash, whilst weaving his way through the thick clumps of hazel and hawthorn, he was glad when she signalled him to pause before she crouched and crept forward towards the open edge of the copse.

Just as the undergrowth ended, a low lateral mound rose from the turf, behind which Dani now lay prone. To provide overhead cover she had woven a small camouflage net into the brush, through which the morning sunlight struggled, moist tendrils of mist rising as its warmth melted the frosted grass beneath.

Lying down beside her, he eased himself forward and raising himself on his elbows looked out on the scene below.

Above seven hundred metres slightly to his left and in front of him, the Manor House of the Langaller Estate could be clearly seen with the sports field and its pavilion to the right of it and the circular mosque with its tall turreted minaret behind. Several runners were lapping a six lane track which encircled the playing field, and other figures could be seen moving around the open area which surrounded the house itself. Tall old growth trees rose in profusion throughout the whole of the compound which, as Dani had described at the briefing, was encircled by a high wire fence, topped with what looked like razor wire.

"Behind the Manor House are the accommodation blocks," said Dani. "And the mosque screens the gymnasium. Unfortunately, because of the tree cover we only have a clear view of about a quarter of the whole fenced area and I have tried several other places, but I can promise you this is the best vantage point by far."

"I'm certain it is," he reassured her. "It gives us a pretty good view of the main buildings, but I can see now why the folks at Bulford were so keen for someone to get inside. It would be hard to establish any kind of a case for a search warrant with evidence based solely on observation from this distance, but you did a good job of finding this spot. We'll make a sniper of you yet!"

"No thanks," she replied firmly. "I'll limit my marksmanship to taking out the occasional ageing or infirm red deer."

"What's this mound in front of us?" he asked. "It looks pretty solid."

"It is," she said. "I've removed some of the turf and it's all stone underneath. It looks like a fairly primitive dry stone wall constructed many years ago. I wouldn't be surprised if at one time, pigs were allowed to root around in the wood, and the wall could have been built to pen them in."

"Or it might even have been some kind of a fortified outpost," he suggested. "Perhaps a patrol base in Roman times, and it certainly would have been an ideal spot for that."

"I might have known you would have found some kind of military explanation," she laughed. "But before we get too bogged down in a history lesson, I'm going to make a move to catch up with my Ranger friends, and you should be off doing your stuff as a Woodlands Officer. When you leave here turn right and at the T-junction turn right again. The main entrance to the farm and the Manor is about half a kilometre down on the right hand side. You can't miss it, and the best of luck. I'll see you back at the cottages later."

With that the girl crawled out of the hide, leaving KB to make a final assessment of the effectiveness of the OP before he too returned to his Land Rover and with Rocky sitting beside him was soon on the road and heading for the farm.

As he drove into the farmyard, the door to the farmhouse opened and a blonde haired woman in her early thirties came out to greet him. Two border collies followed her, and as he brought his vehicle to a standstill one trotted forward to jump up and put his paws on the passenger door, as Rocky looked down on him through the window.

"Hello," she said, as he got down from the cab. "You must be the Forestry Commission chap. Adam told me to keep an eye out for you, I'm Jane Firth, Adam's wife. Can I offer you a coffee?"

"That's very kind of you, Mrs Firth," he replied, "but I've got a fair amount of ground to cover this morning, so if you don't mind I'll pass on the coffee but I'll certainly check in with you later."

"Adam should be back around lunchtime," she continued, "so perhaps you'd like to join us for lunch? He did ask me to tell you that he has phoned the Estate Office and they are expecting you, but apparently you won't be able to do your inspection of the Manor grounds until later on this afternoon, so you might as well have some lunch with us and a chat with Adam rather than just hang about waiting. In fact it will be good to have some company, we don't get many visitors here and the folks over at the Manor tend to keep themselves to themselves."

"Thank you for the invitation," said KB. "I'd certainly like to take you up on it. Did Mr Firth say what time we would be visiting the Manor?"

"I gather it won't be until around three thirty, will that be alright?"

"It will be fine. Thanks again for the offer of lunch. I'll be off on my rounds and see you later, it will probably be sometime after noon before I'm finished."

Back in the cab he took out his own mobile and rang Dani. His call went through to her answering service, so he left a message saying that he was likely to be late back. Deciding that his first priority would be to do a reconnaissance around the outer perimeter to get an idea of the extent and effectiveness of the compound fencing, he drove back out of the farm, and took the hard track back to the road. Bearing left he followed the line of the wall to where it headed north and driving off the road, skirted the corner of the wall and turned onto Wildwood Common.

As he accelerated on the soft turf, he felt the rear of the vehicle slide, so engaging four wheel

drive and a low gear, he drove forward up a slight slope towards the compound.

From the cab of the Land Rover the minaret was clear rising just above the tree line, and from the enclosed gallery that topped it a watcher examined his progress through a pair of powerful binoculars. Picking up a telephone handset the hooded figure punched a number into the keyboard mounted on the wall beside him and spoke a few sentences rapidly to the listeners in the Manor House below. Replacing the handset, the man resumed his surveillance, aware that already other watchers and listeners had been alerted throughout the compound.

Oblivious to the interest that his visit had awakened, KB continued to drive north parallel to the wall. As he came level with the fence he saw he was screened by a small stand of trees which stood outside the east perimeter of the compound. Driving into their cover he stopped and leaving the engine running, jumped from the cab and crossed to the wall, levering himself up until he was sitting on top of the stones.

Between the wall and the fence a twenty metre area had been cleared of trees, the stumps still visible, each marked in red paint with a four figure number indicating that they had been felled under licence. The fence itself was a formidable obstacle as Dani had described in her briefing, topped with coils of razor wire and with CCTV cameras raised above it at intervals aligned so that they pointed along its length. Set back from the wire a series of tall steel masts each carried a cluster of floodlights and lower down attached to the same structures, small black boxes suggested that sound sensors could also be part of the Langaller Manor security systems.

Wondering whether the primary purpose of these devices was to keep students in or intruders out, and estimating that the cost of installation must have set the owners of the Estate back many thousands of pounds, KB retraced his steps to the Land Rover. Once back behind the wheel he continued to drive north until he reached a five bar gate set into it, away from which a track led to join the road just north of Triscombe Copse.

Dismounting from his Land Rover he walked over to the gate, noticing as he did so that it was padlocked, and that the hinges had been recently oiled. As he leant over to take a closer look at the fence behind he saw that the middle panel of this section had been attached to those flanking it by different fittings, indicating that this particular piece could be removed quickly to provide access to the gate and the track beyond. No tell-tale tyre marks disturbed the turf to suggest that at any time recently this had been the case, but the discovery left him wondering if this was the only part of the perimeter where such access existed.

Satisfied that he had seen all he wanted to see on this side of the Estate he turned back to drive south again past the main entrance to the Estate and continued his recce on the west perimeter of the compound. With no wall here to obstruct his access to the fence he was able to walk to within a few metres of it to examine its construction more closely. Stopping at times along the length of the wire, he let Rocky out to run through the tree stumps while clipboard in hand, he made a show of inspecting the stumps and noting their numbers, but nowhere could he find any evidence of further panels in the fence that might be removed easily or quickly.

Checking his watch, he saw it was now half past twelve, so with Rocky on board he headed back to the farm. As he drew into the yard he noticed a Jeep Cherokee had been parked in a lean-to next to the farmhouse, and after parking his own vehicle and locking the Glock and its holster in the glove compartment, he left the dog in the cab, and walked up the pathway to the porch. A few seconds after he had given two large raps on the door, it opened and he found himself facing a lightly bearded, slim built man who stood a good four inches taller than KB, and who extended a large hand to shake KB's vigorously.

"Come in, come in, Mr Blake," he welcomed KB warmly. "Sorry I wasn't here to meet you earlier, but we had a Commoner's meeting over in Dunster, and although most of the Estate land is privately owned, we still retain grazing rights on North Allerton and Wildwood Common, so I felt obliged to attend. Anyway, please come through and don't mind the dogs they're both quite friendly."

KB followed the big man through the hallway to the kitchen where Jane Firth was busy mashing potatoes while other pots simmered on a large range, the warmth from which was a welcome respite from the cold December day outside. Two children were already seated at the large kitchen table, a girl who KB guessed was approaching her teens and a boy some two or three years her junior.

"Take off your jacket and grab a seat, Mr Blake," the farmer invited him. "I gather you have already met Jane? This is Molly my daughter and Josh my son home for the Christmas holidays. Hope you don't mind eating in the kitchen, but we don't stand on ceremony here so make yourself at home."

"Please call me, Kris," KB responded. "And many thanks for the invitation to lunch. This certainly beats a sandwich and a flask of coffee in the cab of my truck!"

"Well at least it's not blowing a storm out there," Adam continued. "I can tell you, being so close to the coast we certainly feel it when one of those Atlantic gales hits us. I gather we could be in for some rain and high winds over the next couple of days, so you chose the best day for your visit. On that score, what exactly brings you here?"

"Just a routine inspection to make sure all the felling licences are in order," KB said. "And to see how the plantation is coming on. Also, we are on the look-out for any signs of Ash die-back disease which has hit some parts of the country pretty hard, but so far we seem to have avoided it in our area."

"I think you'll find all the licences in order outside the Manor grounds, but they may have taken down the odd tree inside. I can't say for sure, as I have no cause to go wandering around inside, and to be frank, I don't think it would be appreciated if I did. My remit is to manage the farm, and to be fair, my bosses give me a pretty free hand to run things here as I please, so I don't go out of my way to poke my nose into their business. As far as the plantation goes, we have a suitable area marked out but planting hasn't started yet, and I'm waiting for the go-ahead, so you might want to give them a nudge if and when you meet them later."

"I didn't see any farm workers around this morning," KB said. "Do they expect you to manage on your own?"

"That's a bit of a sore point, to be frank," the farmer replied. "I could certainly use some full-time help, but at present the arrangement is that they send students down from the Manor when I ask for a hand with anything, but I can't always get them when I need them, and it's not the best way to operate."

Before KB could comment further, Jane opened one of the oven doors on the range and took out a large pie dish, placing it on the table and following it with dishes of mashed potato, cabbage and carrots.

"I hope you like steak and kidney," she said, cutting into the crust and handing him a plate with a generous portion of pie. "Help yourself to vegetables and please tuck in while everything is hot."

"Thank you, this looks fantastic," he replied. "I must admit this is a particular favourite of mine."

"So are you from a farming background?" Adam asked, as Jane joined them at the table.

"No, I grew up in a village where my parents still keep the local pub. Decided to join the Army when I was old enough and after I got out I did a forestry and estate management course at Tamar Valley College and that led me to where I am today."

"I couldn't help noticing that you walk a little stiffly, was that why you left the Army?"

"It was indeed," KB admitted. "My last tour in Afghanistan I got caught in an IED blast which put an end to my soldiering days."

"Did it blow your legs off?" Josh asked innocently.

"Not both of them, and I was lucky it was only one, but now I've got a pretty neat artificial one instead, and I can do most things except perhaps, play football."

"Can I see it?" the boy continued, and getting down from his chair came across to where KB was already rolling up his trouser leg, to which the lad added, "Wow, that's pretty cool."

"That's enough, Josh. I'm so sorry," said an embarrassed Adam. "Please excuse my son's curiosity and I didn't mean to pry, but working for the Forestry Commission must be very different from the stuff you guys were called upon to do out there?"

"It certainly is," said KB. "But it keeps me working in the open air and I'm not chained to a desk or a workbench, which is fine for some people but to be frank, I don't think I could put up with being stuck inside all day. I suspect you must be able to identify with that!"

"I certainly do," agreed the farmer. "Even though I'm probably not your conventional Farm Manager, and as I said before, I find myself working on my own a lot of the time, which is not always ideal. We run a flock of close to two hundred ewes which means too many sleepless nights at lambing time, and Jane has to muck in and give me a hand.

"Last spring they did send a couple of lads down from the academy to help out, but by the time they had learnt enough to be really useful, the season was over. Mind you, they certainly have all the facilities they need for students over there at the Manor, so it's no wonder they have a problem finding volunteers when I need help. I guess they'd far sooner be in the gym or out on the skeet range than crawling around on their knees in the farmyard on a freezing cold March night tending to the needs of some cantankerous old ewe. I do hear though, that the life of a student over there is pretty spartan, but from what little I've seen they all seem pretty fit."

"I saw the sports field when I was driving around the perimeter this morning, but I didn't realise they had a gymnasium and a skeet range as well," replied KB innocently. "And of course, the mosque seems a pretty impressive building."

"For the size of the college it's massive," Adam replied. "I started work here about halfway through its construction. Before we began to stock up the farm I gave them a hand up there with the tractor and trailer shifting some of the top soil from the site and dumping it up at the quarry. I must say they certainly built that particular building to last. The foundations seemed to go down forever and I couldn't say exactly, but I reckon the concrete walls are at least a metre thick and well reinforced, plus they faced it with stone from the quarry, which I understand was a condition imposed by the planners."

"Sounds impressive," said KB. "Did you get to see it right through to the finish?"

"No," he admitted. "I was only up there for a few days, then I was busy buying in stock from some of the local markets, and I didn't even get an invitation to the official opening! In fact I only get up there about once a week to check in at their office, so I am looking forward to our visit this afternoon and the chance for a good look around, but as we've got an hour or so to kill before our appointment, let's go into the living room and we can continue our chat there. Oh, by the way," he added, "when we go by the mosque, have a good look at the windows. They're quite large, but they have been glazed with some kind of opaque glass. They always seem much darker than a window should be, and on the one occasion I was up there after dark, there was only the slightest glimmer of light from inside to show the lights were on."

Leaving KB to think through the farmer's comments over coffee, at a quarter past three, Adam suggested that they made a move and after thanking Jane for lunch, KB led the way to the Land Rover.

"Shall we travel together?" he asked the farmer. "If you don't mind Rocky in the cab with us, it might be easier than taking two vehicles."

“Fine by me,” came the reply. “And don’t worry about the dog. I take my two with me everywhere when I am out on the farm.”

A few minutes later, they drove up to the entrance to the Manor grounds, where a swing barrier was in place, blocking their entry. As they waited a swarthy heavily bearded man emerged from a small building set back to one side and came across to the driver’s window. He was dressed in black coveralls with the trousers tucked into ankle high boots and wore a matching black baseball cap. “If his overall appearance is intended to intimidate,” KB thought to himself, “it is certainly succeeding and hardly meets the conventional attire of a school porter.”

Adam raised his hand in recognition, but without acknowledging it the man directed his attention at KB.

“Identification?” he demanded, thrusting his hand through the window. Removing his Forestry Commission ID card from his wallet, KB handed it over and without pausing the man took it, and turning on his heels returned to the shack. Through the window of the timber clad building KB could see him hand the card to a second man, who was seated with his back to him. Giving the card a cursory glance, the man picked up the handset from a telephone on his desk and spoke into it at length, turning around as he did so to look at KB. His conversation over, the card was handed back to the gate guard, who returned it to KB.

“Drive up to the Manor House and wait in the visitor’s car park,” the man said curtly before striding over to lift the barrier. Pausing to replace the card in his wallet, KB glanced through the window of the shack again, becoming aware of a third man standing in the shadows to one side of his seated companion. Before he had time for a longer look, the gate guard called out to him and lifting the barrier, waved him through. Had KB paused for a moment longer he might have recognized the third man as he stretched across the desk to pick up the phone.

It took Asif five minutes to make his report, before he rang off and scurried away from the guardhouse into the woods.

“Pretty thorough security,” KB commented as he drove the Land Rover into a vacant spot in the car park.

“That’s nothing,” came the farmer’s wry answer. “From what I’ve seen, they patrol both sides of the perimeter wire regularly and I reckon they must have at least a dozen guards working here. The cost must be astronomical, but they always seem to have plenty of money.”

As the vehicle came to a halt, a short bespectacled thin man wearing a three quarter length black coat over white trousers, atop his head the traditional taqiyah skull cap, came out of a door of the west wing of the Manor House and walked towards them.

"This is Sadeed Muhammad," said Adam Firth quietly. "He is the head of administration and my immediate boss. As you are an infidel and an uninvited guest, he probably won't shake hands with you and your reception could be on the chilly side, so just bow politely and you'll be fine."

Dismounting from the cab, KB turned to face the man, who had stopped several feet from him.

He gave a barely discernible bow, which KB copied, to be met in turn by thin-lipped smile.

"Mr Blake I believe," Muhammad said, in a high-pitched voice. "You are here from your Forestry Commission I understand, to disturb the peace and tranquillity of our establishment?"

"I'll try not to, sir," replied KB respectfully. "This is just a routine inspection and I shouldn't be with you for too long."

"Very well," the man answered. "Mr Firth will be your guide and I would be grateful if you would pay me the courtesy of a visit in my office before you depart. Check in with Reception at the main entrance when you have finished and someone will bring you to my room. In the meantime, please try to stick to the paths and," he added, glancing at the Land Rover, "kindly leave your dog in the vehicle. We do not encourage vermin to roam freely in these grounds."

Without waiting for KB to reply, the man turned on his heels and headed back to the house.

"I did warn you not to expect the red carpet treatment!" Adam chuckled. "But we'd better get a move on; we've about an hour or so of good light left and a fair bit of ground to cover."

Walking across to the Land Rover, KB unlocked the tool box in the back and took out the work belt which he fastened around his waist and then the yellow hard hat which he put on. Unlocking the cab, he retrieved his binoculars and clipboard from the glove compartment, and after filling Rocky's bowl with water, left it on the floor for the dog.

The sky was beginning to darken with dark clouds scudding in on a strong wind which had picked up bringing with it a suggestion of rain. Skirting the mosque they headed towards the track that would eventually lead them to the quarry, KB pausing at intervals to push into the woods on either side, checking for new or unmarked tree stumps. After advancing steadily for about a quarter of an hour, the ground opened up in front of them and they found themselves at the south end of a quarry pit dug into the hillside.

At the wider northern end, the side of the quarry rose steeply for some sixty metres, gradually reducing in height as it ran south to where they now stood at the edge of the wood. To their left a wooden hut had been erected, in front of which duckboards had been laid and a skeet trap stood ready for use. The floor of the quarry was smooth and grass covered presumably with the soil that had been excavated from the footings of the mosque and then levelled and covered with turf. At the far end earth had been piled back against the quarry face to a height of twelve metres, finishing off what KB suspected was a range the use of which could encompass the safe firing of a wide variety of weapons.

"When they are shooting here, can you hear it from the farm?" he asked Adam, as they walked forward to the firing point.

"Barely at all," replied the farmer. "Only when the wind is blowing in directly from the north, and then it's no more than a slight popping sound. In fact I was working some sheep up on North Allerton Common, right on the Estate boundary, a few weeks back when they were firing and even then I could hardly hear anything. I suppose the depth of the quarry and the surrounding trees act as a natural sound screen so you wouldn't expect to hear too much."

As they went around the back of the hut, KB took a few steps into the wood and stopped to look around him. For a moment the only sound he could hear was the rustle of the wind through the upper boughs of the trees and an occasional creak as a trunk bent before a particularly strong gust. Then a slight snap of a twig breaking underfoot alerted his sniper's senses and kneeling down he peered through the gathering gloom towards the area from which the noise had come.

Nothing moved between the gaps in the trees and only a few dead leaves swirled around in the breeze, nor could he make out foreign shapes or sharp outlines that might have provided tell-tale evidence of the presence of a silent watcher. If, however, Kristian Blake had been a betting man, he would have placed a fair wager that he was being followed.

Standing up, he brushed a light covering of earth and moss from his knees and rejoined Adam Firth who he found standing under the shelter of an opalescent green canopy which extended from the side of the hut to cover the firing point and duckboards.

“I’ve seen some firing ranges in my time,” KB commented, “but for a school facility this is certainly one of the best. Overhead cover from the elements, and good strong duckboards to keep your feet dry,” he added, stamping his feet to test the strength of the boards and glancing down as he did so. Out of the corner of his eye, the slightest glint of metal caught his attention as a small round cylindrical tube rolled out from underneath to lie in the open. Taking his binoculars, he sat down on the edge of the duckboards and made a show of scanning the top of the quarry at the far end.

“Is that an ash tree up there?” he asked Adam pointing vaguely in the direction of the tree line where it disappeared from view, and offering the farmer his binoculars. As the farmer peered through the glasses, KB scooped the brass tube from where it lay and slipped it into his jacket pocket recognizing it immediately as an AK-47 cartridge case.

“Can’t be sure, but I don’t think so,” Adam said, as KB scrambled to his feet. “Hard to tell in this light, and rather than trek all the way up there now it would probably be best if we left a closer inspection until another day. I suggest we push on to the other side of the compound now, before we run out of time, what do you say?”

“Fine by me,” KB replied and on reaching the quarry entrance, Adam led off on a footpath which wove its way through the trees towards the eastern perimeter. Two hundred metres into the wood they entered a large open area which had been cleared of undergrowth. Across the centre of the clearing a three strand rope bridge had been suspended above the ground, and in the far corner a large cargo net had been hung between two trees. High in the branches of a tall beech tree opposite the net, a small platform had been built in front of which a single rope hung down.

“What’s been going on here?” Adam asked, turning to look at KB as he spoke.

“I would say they have made themselves what they probably would call a confidence building course. In the Army we might call it a Tarzan course, in this case for mini-Tarzans. You can see from the design that you could have a lot of fun here swinging from that beech tree over there into the cargo or scrambling net or crossing the rope bridge. Judging from the branches lying around, I’d say it is probably a work in progress and they are most likely planning on adding to it, but what interests me is that I see they’ve taken down at least three old growth trees and as I don’t see any sign of licence numbers painted on them, I should log and photograph them.”

"I doubt if Squire Muhammad is going to be overjoyed when you break the news that they are in trouble for felling trees without a licence," chuckled Adam. "But you carry on, what goes on inside the compound here is way outside my area of responsibility!"

Checking the stumps, KB marked each one with a large red cross using the aerosol can from his belt and finished by taking several photos of each stump with his mobile. At the last of these he retrieved the brass rifle cartridge and placed it on top of the stump, transmitting the shot to Bulford and then deleting it immediately. Satisfied that Adam had not noticed this, he replaced the cartridge in his pocket and rejoined the Farm Manager where he waited at the edge of the clearing.

"I'm about ready to call it a day," he suggested to his guide, "so let's get on back to my Rover and I can make out a ticket for the licence violation and hand it in to the office when I check out."

"Suits me," Adam agreed. "And I'm going to leave you to it. I can walk back to the farm and I should still have time to do a couple of chores before supper, and to be honest, those buggers could keep you waiting for hours." As he spoke the distant cry of an Imam reached them, carried on the chill dusk air.

"There you are," the farmer added. "Calling the faithful to prayer. It's going to be a while for sure until Muhammad gets to see you, so I hope you don't mind if I slip quietly away?"

"Not at all," KB replied, as they reached the Land Rover. "Many thanks for your help, and for the great lunch."

"Drop by and see us again when you're next in the area," Adam called out waving him goodbye, and as the figure of the farmer disappeared down the driveway, KB climbed into the cab to be greeted by an enthusiastic Rocky.

Flicking on the overhead light, he took a logging violation form out of the Forestry Commission file, and placing his hard hat on the seat beside him, started to fill out the appropriate boxes. As he wrote, the dog nudged his arm and then scrabbled furiously at the passenger door.

"Sorry, old son," he said, realizing that the dog had an urgent problem. "You must be dying for a pee, and with that lot at evening prayers I'm sure no one will notice if I let you out."

Leaning across, he opened the door, and with a short bark of appreciation the dog jumped out and immediately disappeared into the hedgerow behind his parking space. Picking up his clip-board he was about to resume his form filling when his concentration was broken by a short and violent outburst of barking from the bushes, followed by a yelp and silence.

Jumping from the driving seat, he ran towards the spot where Rocky had disappeared, and crouching low forced himself into the thick undergrowth. Suddenly aware of a dark shape moving behind him, he half turned towards it, but he never saw the blow that knocked him senseless, his body crashing forward to lie spread-eagled on the ground.

Chapter Twenty-Nine

Gryphon Head

Nescis quid serus vesper vehat – You know not what nightfall may bring.
Latin Proverb

The Atlantic storm swept up the Bristol Channel at Gale Force Eight, sweeping inland across Exmoor and bringing with it a torrent of rain which hammered through the trees and bounced off the tarmac of the Langaller Estate car park. Under the tarpaulin which had been thrown roughly over the bed of the Land Rover, KB stirred as a rivulet of rain water ran down a crease in the canvas and splashed off his face as he lay on his side, hands bound behind his back.

Only conscious at first of the thumping pain which threatened to explode from his skull, he blinked in the darkness, stifling a groan as he tried to move to ease his cramped limbs. A heavy weight lay across his lower body, but by flexing his legs and rocking his torso slightly from side to side he was able to work himself free of it.

Through the sound of the rain drumming on the tarpaulin, he heard voices getting louder as they got closer to the vehicle, and closing his eyes he waited for them to pass. Instead, the corner of the tarpaulin was thrown back and a bright light shone full in his face. There was a moment's silence and then the conversation resumed and the tarpaulin was thrown back over him.

The Land Rover tilted on its springs slightly as the door opened and someone climbed into the driver's seat. A few more sentences and an outburst of laughter, and then the door slammed shut and the engine burst into life. At the main gate, the Rover slowed and stopped and after a few more words between the driver and the gate guard, picked up speed as it left the compound.

Raising himself on his elbows, KB flexed his arms and found them securely fastened at the wrist by what felt like heavy duty nylon ties. As hard as he tried, he found it impossible to loosen them and for a moment lay still again as the truck turned left off the Estate land and onto the road. As he slumped back, he became conscious of a solid and uncomfortable lump in his side, and pressing as far down with his left hand as he was able, he felt the head of the small hatchet in its carrying pouch and still attached to his work belt.

The nylon ties bit into his wrists and he winced at the pain, but after several attempts he was able to undo the press studs which secured the leather cover over the axe head, and the hatchet fell free onto the floor.

The truck slowed again. Turning left KB guessed they must now be heading north towards the coast road. Struggling into a sitting position, he leant over and was able to retrieve the hatchet and grasping the head firmly in his left hand started to saw against the restraining ties. Thanking the Agency equipment team for ensuring the axe head was razor sharp, he momentarily regretted it when seconds later the blade cut through the tie and bit into the flesh of his wrist.

With his hands free, he was about to raise himself up to take stock of his surroundings, when the truck suddenly slowed to a halt and from beneath the cover of the tarpaulin he heard the unmistakable sound of sheep bleating as lights engulfed the vehicle. Levering himself up, he peered cautiously through the rear window of the cab to see that a flock of thirty or more sheep milled around in front of them. Further up the road, parked in front of the ruins of a long abandoned farmhouse a cattle truck waited, its tailgate down, and KB could make out the figures of two men urging animals into the back. Two others, one with a flashlight in his hands came towards them, working their way slowly through the sheep that filled the road. At their approach the door of the Land Rover opened and the driver got out.

Easing himself over, KB raised his head over the side of the truck until he was only at arm's length from the driver as he stood awaiting the on-comers. Glancing down, KB saw that the man was holding an automatic pistol in his right hand, concealed from the sight of the two men who now approached.

"Come out from behind that door and let's see you," called out the taller of the two, as they broke free of the flock and halted no more than five metres from the Rover. Even through the sound of the rain beating down and the bleating of the sheep, KB recognized the voice in an instant and in the same moment the driver stepped out from behind the door raising his pistol as he did so.

"Look out Isaac," KB shouted, at the top of his voice. "He's got a gun."

Startled by the unexpected warning coming from behind him, the driver half turned to face KB and as he did so, a shotgun blast rang out through the tumult of the storm, throwing the driver back against the side of the Land Rover, to slide to the ground.

Struggling free of the tarpaulin, KB climbed over the side of the truck to face Isaac and Nathan Samson, the latter holding a still smoking shotgun.

Ignoring them KB bent over the prone figure as it lay propped up against the side of the Land Rover, a gaping hole in its chest. There was no sign of a pulse. Asif lay dead on the ground, as KB retrieved his Glock from the man's outstretched hand.

"You've killed him Nathan," KB said, as he stood up.

"'Tis your bleddy fault, you told me he 'ad a gun," came the surly reply. "Anyway, what are you doing here, popping up out of nowhere?"

"You don't need to know," KB answered. "But I don't have to ask what you guys are up to, out here in the middle of the night loading sheep into the back of a cattle truck!"

"Smart bugger, aren't you?" snarled Isaac. "And before we decide what to do with you, you'd best hand over that pistol, or Nathan might just be tempted to give you the other barrel."

"That would be extremely foolish," KB said, calmly putting the Glock in his jacket pocket. "The way I see it at the moment, is that you owe me for warning you that this man was armed. Believe me, gentlemen, he would have killed you both without hesitation. As we speak the people I work for are hot footing it right here as fast as they can, and if you are stupid enough to think you could get away with another killing, they'd hunt you down wherever you finished up. I am telling you straight, this is something you don't want to get involved with."

As he spoke both men look to their left suddenly and as he glanced around in the same direction the distant glimmer of a vehicle's headlights could be seen approaching up the road he had so recently travelled.

"In fact, guys, that is probably them now, so why don't you get aboard that wagon of yours and get the hell out of it while you can. Providing you never show your noses this side of the Irish Sea again, I promise you I will say nothing about our little encounter here and believe me when I say I have the means to get rid of that," KB added, pointing to where Asif's body lay, "and to gain you enough time to give you a head start. So it's your call, Isaac, but you'd better make it quick they're going to be here any moment now."

"Bugger it, Isa," Nathan spluttered. "Let's get out of here."

With a glance of sheer hatred in KB's direction, Isaac grabbed his brother by the shoulder and the two ran back to the truck, shouting to their companions as they did so, who wasted no time in raising and securing the tailgate of the lorry. With the engine roaring and a crash of gears, the truck reversed out onto the road and lurching forward disappeared in a cloud of diesel fumes around the corner and out of sight.

Taking the Glock out of his jacket pocket, KB cocked the weapon and moved around to the far side of the Land Rover, where he crouched down as the full beam of the oncoming vehicle's headlights swept towards him. As it screeched to a halt, the driver killed the motor and for a handful of seconds all that could be heard was the steady ticking as the engine block cooled.

Taking a double handed grip on the weapon, KB slowly stood up from his hiding place as the door of the vehicle opened and the driver stepped onto the tarmac.

"KB this is Dani" came a clear female voice "Are you there?"

"Thank God it's you," he replied, stepping out from behind his Land Rover, to be met by a smiling Danica Janes. "I was praying it would be anybody other than a posse from Langaller, and right now you don't know how glad I am it's you."

"Lucky I found you," the girl said, the relief clearly showing in her voice. "I was worried when you didn't show up back at the cottage and put in a call to the Agency. They confirmed they hadn't heard from you either and that the tracker on the Land Rover was still showing you on the Estate. This didn't seem right so I called Adam Firth, and when he confirmed you should have been out of there some hours ago I decided to make a run over to see if I could find out what was going on. En-route here the Agency called me and told me your vehicle was moving and they guided me here, not a moment too soon by the look of things."

"I think our priority right now is to get out of here," he suggested. "Any ideas?"

"If that guy lying by the Rover is as dead as I think he is, let's get the body loaded into the back of your truck, and then follow me up the road to the car park at Gryphon Head," she said decisively. "We can park up there and you can fill me in on all the details, and we should phone a report in to the Agency and see what they say. By the way, where is your dog?"

"Rocky went missing back on the Estate," he said grimly. "And I got jumped when I went looking for him. If I get a chance, I'll go back as soon as I can and see if there's any sign of him. He's pretty street-wise, so with any luck he'll have found his way out of the compound and may have made his way back to the farm."

"Fingers crossed then," said the girl. "Let's get a move on. If they have someone on watch in the mosque tower he may have spotted the lights here even though we are pretty well screened by the wood, but just in case we need to get out of here ASAP. I'll pull in front of you and kill my headlights then we'll load up your truck."

As she parked her Land Rover, KB walked around to the back of his and after lowering the tailgate, turned on his own torch and flicked back the tarpaulin to reveal the heavy object that had lain across his legs when he first regained consciousness. Rocky's body lay stretched out in the bed of the truck, blood seeping from his mouth and head, staining the floor and joining the trickles of rain water to turn them pink as they ran over the back and onto the road.

"Shit!" he shouted into the sky, clenching his fists in rage. "Bastards!" he shouted again, as Dani ran up to him.

"What is it, Kris?" she asked him, anxiously grabbing his arm.

"There," he said, pointing at the back of the truck. "I found Rocky. Those fucking bastards must have clubbed him to death." Pausing for a moment to take a deep breath and regain his composure, he went on, "open up your Rover and I'll put him in the back. I can't leave him at the side of the road, it wouldn't be right after all he's been through."

"Of course," said the girl, leaving KB to do his bidding.

Spreading the tarpaulin out on the road side, he carefully lifted the dog and laid him gently in the middle. Folding the canvas around the body of his pet, he lifted the bundle and holding it tightly to his chest, walked over to where Dani was waiting with the back door of her Land Rover open. Placing it in the space behind the back seats, he stepped back to allow Dani to close the door, and without saying another word turned to where Asif's body lay, dragging it back to be lifted into the bed of his own vehicle.

"Okay, that's done, let's go," he said, fastening the tailgate and turning to face his companion who was rubbing her hands furiously against her already rain soaked trouser legs in an attempt to dry them.

Climbing back behind the wheel of his Rover, he became acutely aware of the dull ache which still hammered inside his head, reminding him that although forgotten in the adrenalin fuelled events of the last half hour, he still had a large gash and a lump the size of a duck egg on the back of his skull to contend with. Peering through the windscreen, he focussed on the tail lights of Dani's vehicle and was relieved when he could see both clearly without any suggestion of blurred or double vision.

Ten minutes later he drew up next to his companion in the Gryphon Head car park and crossing to her vehicle with some effort in the teeth of the gale, slumped down beside her in the passenger seat.

"Are you feeling alright?" she asked him, as she switched on the interior light. "You look a bit pale and you seemed a bit wobbly back there."

"I'm fine," he lied. "The bastards clobbered me and I've got a thumping headache, but otherwise I'm in one piece."

"Bend your head down and let me take a look," she ordered him. "Yep, there is quite an impressive lump there and a nasty open wound, which I can patch as soon as we get back. Now tell me what went on at Langaller, which I'll record on my mobile as back-up."

Even though he related the events of the past evening as briefly and as accurately as he could, it was still ten minutes before he finished and satisfied the girl's questions. With KB's mobile missing, along with his wallet and the AK-47 cartridge case, she wasted no time in placing a call through to the Agency using the secure transmission, and then rang off.

"They are getting the boss to the phone," she explained. "No doubt he'll be calling back shortly. In the meantime, where do you think your friend in the back of your truck was taking you?"

"I've been thinking about that," he admitted. "My guess is that we were bound for somewhere along this coast road where an 'accident' could be staged. In fact, when you think about it – howling gale, poor visibility, slippery roads and any number of places along here where a moment's carelessness could put you over the edge and onto the rocks below, which would make an accident look entirely believable. Add to that a high tide due in a couple of hours, a heavy swell running and bingo, most of the evidence – if not all – washed out to sea. In the meantime Asif legs it back to Langaller, not too far if he cuts across North Allerton Common, and well before any alarm is raised, he's back at the college, tucked up in bed."

"You're probably right," Dani replied. "And even if al-Amn realized that they had come onto our radar and their true activities were about to be uncovered, they could have won themselves enough time to wind down their covert activities here and send their key personnel into hiding, leaving us with egg on our faces and the Muslim world screaming 'ethnic minority persecution'. Net result, they are temporarily out of action, but when they start up again – wherever and whenever – they'd have more recruits than they know what to do with."

As she finished her sentence, her phone buzzed and switching it to speaker, Reynard's voice came through. Once again, KB delivered his report in detail emphasising that he had found evidence of weapons training activities on the skeet range and stressing the importance of the information Adam Firth had given him with regards to the construction of the mosque.

"Mr Firth reckons that besides the stone faced exterior there could be up to a metre or more of reinforced concrete behind, to say nothing of what lies underground. They also have some strange looking windows set into the walls – not the kind you would normally associate with a religious building. The minaret that tops it could also be doubling as an excellent observation post and the perimeter security is formidable to say the least."

"Added to the reception that they gave you and the photo you sent us, it certainly seems that we have major cause for concern," replied the Head of Operations. "But I understand you have more pressing problems right now?"

"Yes, sir," KB responded, and explained Asif's demise adding to it his theory as to what had been planned for him, had their journey not been interrupted by the encounter with the sheep rustlers.

"I think you are spot on, KB," Reynard answered. "So I suggest we complete their plan for them and dispose of the truck as they would have done, leaving Asif on board. Tomorrow's a public holiday which we can use to our advantage but as soon as I can I'll give the Forestry Commission a 'heads up' in case it is reported that one of their vehicles has gone off the road. I'll also contact my opposite number in the Police so that he can alert his local officers and make sure they have the appropriate press release to hand in case the media start sniffing around, in which it will state that two persons were believed to have been in the vehicle. That way, our friends at the college may be duped into thinking that Asif was unable to get out of the truck before it went over the edge, and it gives us enough of a head start to put a planned operation in place.

"If that makes sense to you, I suggest Dani stays there to get things moving with the Exmoor National Park Authority setting up our Tactical Command Post. In the meantime KB, get some rest, hire yourself some wheels in the morning and then get here to Bulford as soon as you can. If all goes well, I intend to be back inside Langaller in force at first light the day after tomorrow. If there are no further questions, I'll leave you to it, and by the way – Happy New Year – it will be midnight shortly and you certainly saw the old year out with a bang!"

With a click the phone went dead, leaving KB and Dani to dispose of his Land Rover.

"We need to make it look as much like an accident as possible," suggested Dani. "So rather than shove her off the end of Gryphon Head we need to find a spot where the road is closest to the cliff edge. I've got my map of the area here so let's take a look. That could be promising," she continued, pointing at a spot not far from where they were parked. "Less than half a mile west from here the road runs pretty close to a sheer drop. If I remember rightly, there is only a raised bank to prevent vehicles going over the top."

"Let's do a recce," KB agreed. "I'll follow you."

Just short of the point she had chosen on the map, Dani pulled off to the side of the road and KB stopped behind her. Getting out, he picked up his torch from the passenger seat and leaning forwards into the gale, they walked down the beginning of the steep decline that led to the small coastal town of Lynmouth.

Less than fifty metres from where they had left their vehicles, they found the bank bordering the road no more than half a metre high, and moving cautiously to the edge of the cliff, KB shone the light downwards to confirm that there were no major obstructions between where they stood and the rocks far below.

Leaving Dani, he walked back to his vehicle and easing it forward on the deserted road he soon picked up their chosen exit point in his headlights. Swinging the vehicle around in as wide an arc as possible, he straightened the Land Rover up so that it faced the bank head on and engaged four wheel drive.

As he opened the door to check his alignment, Dani came around from behind and shouted in his ear.

"It looks okay, KB, shall we give it a try?"

"I'll ease her up onto the bank," he shouted back, "so stand back in case she skids sideways."

Nodding her consent, Dani stood back as he let in the clutch and gunned the motor. As he moved forward the front tyres spun for a moment on the grassy edge of the bank, but with the rear wheels gripping the tarmac the Rover lifted itself steadily over the ridge. As soon as he felt the vehicle level off he came to an immediate halt and leaving the engine running he opened the glove compartment. After removing the holster, his binoculars, the set of maps and double checking that there was nothing left inside, he re-locked it and climbed down from the cab.

Taking off the work belt, he threw it in the bed of the vehicle where it lay across Asif's inert form. Leaning across the steering wheel, he let off the handbrake, and shutting the door moved around to the back, where Dani was already waiting.

"Come on then, let's give it a shove," he shouted to her, and together they pushed at the tailgate until after rocking it backwards and forwards several times, the Rover lurched forward and gaining momentum as the cliff edge dipped downwards, disappeared out of sight to fall to the rocks below.

"Let's get out of here before our luck runs out," she called to him, and together they hurried back to her Defender.

Once inside she wasted no time in heading back towards Dulverton, silent as they both reflected on the evening's events and allowed the Land Rover's heater to warm through their chilled frames.

"We were lucky no one came along," she said later, as they sped through the darkness. "But I suppose as it is New Year's Eve and a miserable night to be out running the roads, most folks will be safely indoors partying or seeing the old year out in front of the telly. Anyway, what next?"

"Back to the cottages to get out of these clothes and get our heads down for a couple of hours or so," he replied. "Do you know anywhere local we can hire a car tomorrow? As it's New Year's Day it could be difficult."

"There is a garage in town, and as they supply and service most of the Park Authority's vehicles I'm sure we can raise somebody to rent you a car. If not, you'd better take my Rover and I'll see if I can borrow another vehicle somewhere until you get back. What are you going to do about Rocky?"

"I need to find a vet who can arrange to have him cremated and if I can't find one in Dulverton I'll drop him into our local vet's surgery in Langport on my way up to Bulford."

"No need for that," she replied. "I know a good lad in Dulverton, and as a matter of fact, we've been out for a drink a couple of times. He's probably out whooping it up right now at the New Year's Eve bash in the White Lion Hotel, so even though he may be fighting a hangover in the morning, I'm pretty sure he'll help you without too many questions asked. By the way, how's your head?"

"Still throbbing," he admitted. "But no feelings of nausea or double vision, so no signs of concussion. I guess I was lucky, I half turned towards the guy that clobbered me just before he landed the blow, so it glanced off at an angle rather than hitting me full on."

"You must have a skull as thick as a rhinoceros," she laughed. "But I still think you should have it looked at, why don't we call by the A&E department at Dulverton Hospital?"

"The thick skull is mandatory for a Para – essential when we land on our heads, but no thanks," he added firmly. "I don't fancy hanging around in the waiting room with a bunch of drunken revellers. They'd only have to take one look at me in my current state to call the Police. If that were to happen we could find ourselves spending a couple of hours being questioned, even if the Agency were to vouch for me. Don't forget I lost all my ID back there along with my wallet so apart from anything else, you are going to have to help me out with hiring a car as all my cash, driver's licence and credit cards were in it."

"No problem with that, and I suppose you're right about giving A&E a miss," she said. "But you must let me have a proper look at it when we get back, and perhaps I can slap a dressing on it that will hold long enough for you to get to Bulford tomorrow without what remains of your brains spilling out and spoiling the upholstery of a hire car."

"You're all heart, aren't you?" he replied grimacing slightly as they bounced over the cattle grid leading into the farmyard, inwardly relieved that for the time being anyway, they could afford to relax in the relative safety of their temporary accommodation.

Inside his cottage, the fire had been re-laid and as he stood up from lighting it, for a moment he felt dizzy and put a hand out to steady himself against the stone chimney breast.

"Steady KB" said Dani, who had followed him in, and witnessed the moment. "Are you alright?"

"Thanks, I'm fine," he answered. "Nothing a few hours' kip won't put right."

"Why don't you go upstairs and have a shower and put on some clean clothes and I'll do the same?" she suggested. "I have a couple of cans of soup in my cottage and I'll come back in a little while and take a look at that head of yours while we get some food inside us."

"That sounds like a good idea," he said, making his way slowly upstairs after she left. In his room he undressed, and taking the Glock from the pocket dropped the blood stained Forestry jacket and trousers on the floor. Unfastening his prosthetic leg he hopped over to the shower and turned on the water, adjusting the temperature until a cloud of steam arose from the cubicle. Easing himself under the jet, the heat soon permeated his body driving out the chill from his bones.

Under his close cropped hair, his head wound stung as the water cleansed it and after a minute of allowing the water to massage his body, he towelled himself off and patted his hair dry, noticing a dark blood stain on the cloth as he finished.

Sitting on the edge of his bed, he took clean underpants and a T-Shirt from his Bergen, and after strapping on his artificial leg again, pulled on a pair of jeans. Hearing the front open, he made his was downstairs to where Dani was already in the kitchen, tipping cans of tomato soup into a saucepan.

"Sit down in the chair," she ordered, glancing over her shoulder. "I've brought my first aid kit in with me and I'll deal with that wound of yours."

Turning down the gas under the saucepan to leave it simmering on the hob, she walked across to zip open the satchel that lay on the coffee table.

Feeling her fingers probing gently around the gash, he stifled a wince, not noticing her dabbing a cotton wool pad with a yellow liquid she poured from a small brown bottle. A moment later he yelped as the tincture was applied to the wound, to which the only response he got from the administrator was a chuckle.

"Was that iodine?" he asked. "Are you some kind of sadist? I thought using that stuff went out of use years ago!"

"Don't be a big baby," came the retort. "It still does the trick, and in any case I thought you tough guys were immune to pain! Now stay still, and don't move, I've got some butterfly stitches here but I'm going to have to shave your scalp a bit to get them to stick through this matt of hair of yours. I know you wouldn't want me to make this hole any bigger, which could happen if you continue to leap around, so sit still."

"Well for fuck's sake be careful," he said. "And I hope to hell you're not related to Sweeney Todd!"

Five minutes later, she stepped back to admire her handiwork and declared the job done.

"Excellent job, though I say so myself," she declared. "So if you've done with your whingeing, let's have some supper."

Pouring the soup into two large mugs, she sat down beside him on the sofa and in the heat thrown out by the fire, and the warmth of the soup inside him, KB felt himself getting drowsy and for a moment he closed his eyes.

"Come on you," she nudged him. "It's been a long day and we've got another one coming up, so you should get yourself upstairs to bed. "I've got some paracetamol in my kit which should help ease your headache, so take a couple and try to get some sleep. I'll lock up here and give you a shout in the morning, so off you go."

Mumbling a thank-you, he got to his feet and after swigging down the pills she gave him with a glass of water from the tap over the sink, slowly made his way up the staircase.

Switching on the bedside light, he placed the Glock on the table and after a trip to the bathroom, unstrapped his leg and climbed into bed. Turning off the light, he turned on his side so that he was facing the bedroom door, drew the covers up under his chin and five minutes later was fast asleep.

Downstairs the girl washed the mugs and saucepan out, and left them on the draining board. Crossing to the front door, she checked that it was locked and then taking a pillow and a duvet out of a corner cupboard, unfolded the sofa bed.

Listening for a moment at the foot of the stairs until she could hear heavy, regular breathing from the bedroom, she crept upstairs and used the bathroom before returning to the living room.

After throwing some more logs on the fire and taking off her jacket, she took her own Glock out of its shoulder holster and placed it under the pillow. Stripping down to her panties, she climbed into bed and after a few moments reflecting on the day's events, was soon asleep.

Chapter Thirty

Preparation

"Let your plans be dark and impenetrable as night;
and when you move, fall like a thunderbolt."

Sun Tzu, 'The Art of War'

Dani had let him sleep until eight o'clock, and after a quick breakfast of coffee and toast they set off for Dulverton where a somewhat grumpy and out of sorts vet was persuaded by her to answer their knock on the door of the two storey semi he occupied next to his surgery. After explaining in detail what he wanted, KB left Rocky in his care, and after saying goodbye and ruffling the dog's fur for the last time, with a lump in his throat he rejoined Dani in the Defender and drove to the garage in search of a hire car.

Although open to serve fuel, it took a phone call and a frustrating half hour wait for the owner to turn up. Further complications followed when, without a credit card and driving licence the man refused to rent a vehicle to KB, eventually agreeing to put the agreement in Dani's name with KB listed as a driver, both of them having to sign a statement declaring that KB was the holder of a valid UK driving licence.

With only one automatic on the forecourt, KB had no choice but to take the Ford Mondeo that was available, and with documentation eventually completed it was approaching ten in the morning before he was able to head out of the town and east to Bulford.

Even though traffic was light and he was making good time, he resisted the temptation to break his journey at Long Lane, realizing also that if he did so, he would be faced with answering questions as to Rocky's whereabouts. Pressing on, he was on Salisbury Plain shortly before one and after a hassle getting through gate security due to his lack of ID, eventually pulled into the Mess car park just after the hour.

After walking across to the Admin building, he checked in with the receptionist who at his request put a call through to the Operations Office, reporting his arrival.

"Mr Reynard is in a meeting right now, but he suggests you have some lunch and come back at two," she said with a smile, so retracing his steps he entered the Mess and went straight through to the dining room.

The room was full and he immediately noticed that among the diners were several unformed senior officers from the services and a Police Chief Superintendent. As he searched the room for any sign of a familiar face, a hand clapped him on the shoulder and he turned to find himself facing Fred Nowakowski, a welcoming grin on his face.

"Welcome back," said the Pole. "You won't be surprised to hear as a result of your escapades over the past twenty-four hours, it seems you have stirred up a veritable hornet's nest! Let's grab some food and you can explain yourself before Reynard throws you to the wolves this afternoon!"

As they joined the line up by the buffet, the smell of hot food reminded him that it was a full day since he had his last full meal and when it was his turn, he allowed the chef to pile his plate high with a tuna pasta bake.

As he bent down to place the plate on his tray, Fred caught sight of the dressings on his scalp and gave out a low whistle. "Bloody hell, KB. That looks like a nasty crack on that thick skull of yours, shouldn't you be seeing the medics after lunch before anything else?"

"Reynard wants me back in the conference room at two, so there may not be time until later, but it probably looks a lot worse than it is, and at least the headache's gone."

"Did you get that at Langaller?" asked his friend, as they moved to a vacant table and sat down.

"Yep, I got jumped by a couple of their goons and if it wasn't for a bunch of sheep rustlers working under the cover of a howling gale and the fact that most of Exmoor's law-abiding natives were enjoying New Year's Eve, I could have finished up in a lot worse situation. In the end, however, it was our late lamented friend Asif who finished up feeding the fishes somewhere off Gryphon Head, not me."

"Asif – wasn't that the guy you thought you saw in the BMW and got poor old Pete whacked? How the hell did he get there?"

"It all makes sense when you think about it," said KB. "After he and his side-kick ditched the BMW at Exeter station, he must have made his way back to Langaller and stayed there until returning to our lodgings at Tamar Valley College. Unfortunately for them the plans to kidnap Amir were screwed up again when Pete decided to lead out that morning with Asif in his truck, leaving me to follow with Amir. After the shooting he took off with the villain I wasn't able to drop, and they must have gone straight back to Langaller.

"It can't be much more than an hour's run from where we were to the Estate via Bideford and Barnstaple, and given that it took at least half an hour to forty minutes before Bill arrived and we were able to sort things out, they'd have been well on their way by then."

"So what happened at Langaller?" Fred persisted.

"Somehow, and I'm still not exactly sure how, they must have been alerted that my visit under the guise of a Forestry inspection was not all it appeared to be. I suspect what happened is that when Adam Firth, the Farm Manager phoned them to arrange things, my name rang a bell and they made sure Asif was in a position to identify me when I showed up.

"After that they only had two options, to let me in accepting that after I left Tamar Valley College I had gone on to become a genuine Forestry Commission Inspector, or take me out and arrange an 'accident' to cover their tracks. Of course, once they had knocked me out and searched me and my truck, they found all the evidence they needed to confirm their worst suspicions. They also bashed poor old Rocky's head in and at some time in the next day or so, I am hoping I get to meet up with the bastard responsible."

"Hmm, wouldn't like to be in his shoes," commented his friend. "But tell me about these rustlers."

"Just a bunch of no-goods seeking to make some serious cash by moving the best part of a whole flock of sheep off the Moor. After I had been dumped in the back of my truck, Asif had probably been instructed to shove me and the wagon over the cliff edge somewhere on the Lynmouth road, and I came to just before we left the Estate. The thieves had sheep running all over the place and were loading up a cattle truck when we ran into them, by which time I had got my hands free.

"Asif got out of the cab to confront them and I saw he was carrying a gun – my Glock as it turned out – so I shouted a warning to them. One of them had a shotgun and Asif took a barrel full in the chest from close range – not a pretty sight. Anyway, they took off and a few minutes later Danica Janes turned up, alerted by the Agency who had been tracking the Rover. We phoned in to the boss and agreed that the best way out was to finish what Asif had started, but with him on board rather than me, and here I am."

"Just another day in the office," Fred remarked. "But I suppose that even if the rustlers hadn't intervened, with you free in the back of the truck and Dani hot on your heels, you would have probably been able to get away?"

"Who knows," KB replied. "Perhaps it's just as well we didn't have to put that to the test, but I

must say I'm most impressed with our Miss Janes, she certainly is as cool as a cucumber under pressure and a great one to be in a tight corner with."

"Well, you know her reputation," laughed Fred. "She's no pushover in the romance stakes but certainly is a first class agent, so best keep your pecker in your pants – you don't want to spoil a beautiful relationship! By the way, how is the bodacious Miss Baker?"

"Don't go there," he answered ruefully. "You were one hundred percent right, and currently she's with a Yeomanry officer of great wealth and doubtful morals paying for experiencing New Year's Eve festivities in Paris by the only way she knows how."

"Ouch," winced Fred. "Can't say I didn't see that one coming, but bitterness does not befit you my friend, so let's grab some pud and then get across to the meeting before the old fox starts sending out a search party for us."

At the Admin block the conference room was filling up, and Reynard was already seated at a table on the raised platform facing the audience, the familiar map of the Langaller Estate projected onto a large screen behind him. Beckoning KB to join him, he walked forward and took a vacant seat beside the Head of Operations, acutely aware that the eyes of everyone in the room were upon him.

"Glad you could make it, KB," Reynard greeted him. "How are you feeling?"

"Not too bad, sir," he replied. "Still a bit sore, but a lot better for a few hours' sleep and a hot meal."

"Before you leave, you should get that crack on your head checked by the Medics, and if there is any suggestion from them that you should not be back on duty, I'm pulling you off the operation, do I make myself clear?"

"Yes, sir, but I promise you I feel fine."

"I wouldn't have expected you to say anything else, KB, but I mean it. Anyway, the outline plan for Langaller has already been agreed and I'll brief you fully after the meeting. Fred Nowakowski will be working with you, and I understand you have already established a good working partnership with Danica Janes, so she will be part of our team as well.

"Your job now is to answer any questions this bunch may have for you. It should be quite straightforward, but you might get some flak from the Police Super. He believes that this should be an 'all police' operation, and it's up to you to convince him and the others here that this particular nut could take more than an armed response team to crack. Anyway, start off by giving us a brief run down on your mission and the outcome, and then we'll take questions."

As he spoke, the doors of the conference room closed as the last few delegates filed in, and Reynard rose to his feet to introduce KB as the Agency's Field Operative responsible for the internal reconnaissance of the Langaller compound.

Feeling distinctly nervous at addressing such a large audience KB kept his report as concise and as detailed as he was able, but it was still nearly fifteen minutes before he sat down.

As Andy Reynard had suspected, the first question came from the Police Superintendent who had made sure he was seated in the front row and directly in front of where KB now sat.

"I understand that your brief was to gain access to the Langaller Estate compound, and based on background information accrued by your Agency, secure evidence that the activities of the academy now operating have extended beyond their remit as an educational institute, am I correct?"

"Yes, sir."

"In that case, would you consider your reconnaissance a success?" the Superintendent continued.

"Yes, sir,"

"And yet, it seems that towards the end of your visit, for reasons that are not entirely clear, your cover as a Forestry Commission Inspector was blown. As a result, and if indeed there are subversive activities being conducted at Langaller, the perpetrators have been alerted, jeopardizing any chance we may have had of conducting a surprise operation, would you not agree?"

"It is not up to our Agent to make such a judgement," Andy Reynard interrupted. "And we have already conducted a full review as to how his visit under the guise of possible tree felling licence violations could have been comprised.

"As we know from subsequent events that he was probably recognized by an individual with whom our Agent had been in contact with previously, and who we had no means of knowing was part of the Langaller establishment."

"Forgive me for questioning the competence of your Operative," the Policeman replied smugly. "But isn't there also a chance that the questions he put to the Farm Manager might have also raised the latter's suspicions, which were then relayed to the security elements at the Estate?"

"It's possible, but unlikely," KB interjected. "Mr Firth was with me the whole time until shortly before I was attacked within the compound, and if he had alerted them, they had only minutes to react. In any case the information he gave me on the construction of the mosque was largely volunteered by him, rather than as a result of my direct questioning."

"To make my point," the policeman continued, "we are currently basing our assumptions on research conducted by the Agency which suggests, but does not necessarily prove, that al-Amn is using the Langaller facility for more sinister purposes than its publicly declared intent. A verbal and uncorroborated statement from the Farm Manager who is an employee of the organization, and evidence provided by your Field Operative that is based upon the sighting of what is alleged to be an AK-47 cartridge on the skeet range, the actual cartridge which he is unable to produce, though in fairness we do have a fairly low grade photo of this item."

"What about the fact that I was assaulted in the compound, doesn't that count for anything? And what about being driven away from Langaller by an armed man in the dead of night in the back of my own truck, doesn't that seem a little unusual?" KB countered.

"To be frank," the Superintendent insisted, "we only have your word that you were assaulted by an unknown assailant in the Manor House grounds and for all we know, the man you refer to could have been driving you to hospital.

"As for the fact that he was armed – with your weapon as I understand it – could have been borne out of genuine concern for both your safety, with some justification as it turns out as the individual was murdered shortly thereafter, apparently by sheep rustlers, who have now mysteriously disappeared without trace."

"What are you suggesting?" Reynard broke in, angrily.

"I am merely playing the devil's advocate here," came the reply. "I understand that your Operative had a distinguished career in the Army including two tours in Afghanistan, during the second of which, he lost a good friend and was himself seriously injured in an ambush.

"Is it not possible therefore, as much as I admire him for his service to our country, that he could be suffering from some form of post-combat stress disorder, and that his account of his mission at Langaller has been, shall we say, influenced by an understandable desire for revenge directed at people who might possibly share many of the ideals and objectives of those who he was fighting in Helmand Province?"

"Sit down and stay calm," Andy muttered to KB, placing a restraining arm on his shoulder as the latter rose to challenge the comments.

"Thank you for your frank assessment, Police Superintendent," Andy countered, "which I must admit comes as something of a surprise to myself and my colleagues in the room who work with this Operative. In response, as with all members of our team, this man has undergone the most stringent and exacting psychiatric and physical evaluation, and I resent the implication that we would retain the services of any individual without these safeguards.

"I for one, accept this man's report in its entirety and recommend we proceed on the basis of what we know, what our Field Operatives have reported to us and the action we must take to prevent this from escalating to a point where al-Amn becomes a major threat to our national security, are we agreed?"

To KB's relief, murmurs of assent came from all quarters of the room, and sitting back in this chair, he allowed himself to relax.

"Very well," the Superintendent added. "I accept your recommendation, but would add the caveat that this must be a Police led operation. We want to avoid any outward signs of excessive aggression as there is still a chance that when we get inside we may yet find that this is all a storm in a teacup. In this event our actions must be seen as both justifiable and reasonable and we must do our best to avoid alienating our entire Muslim community.

"We have already received the necessary search warrants and will proceed accordingly, with an initial straightforward approach to enter and search the Langaller premises. We will have in place a thirty man armed response team which I consider more than adequate, but should we require further assistance at any time during the operation our Team Leader will call for it on a 'needs-must' basis."

"We endorse that," called out a suited man, seated in the second row, who KB recognized from the previous meeting as being the Home Office representative. "Police led initially, but with the appropriate level of support in place from the military should it be needed. I am sure we all hope it won't come to that, after all, the Battle of Sedgemoor remains the last ever fought on English soil, and let's try to avoid having to re-write the history books!"

The muted laughter that greeted these remarks, relieved the tension and as the delegates left the conference room, Fred joined Andy and KB on the platform.

"Don't say I didn't warn you, KB," said the Head of Operations. "The Police always get a bit touchy when it comes to any situation where the military might be involved, and don't take the Super's comments personally. Anyway, here's the plan of action as it stands at the moment.

"You and Fred will draw whatever kit and supplies you need after the meeting, including your sniper kit and short wave radios.

"Admin have already been warned that you lost all your ID, wallet and cards during your escape from Langaller, KB, and have replacements ready for you now. There is no time to provide you with an Agency vehicle as well-equipped as your own pick-up, so I suggest you drive down to Dulverton in that as soon as you can get out of here today, and Fred follows you in the hire car. Can you find a bed for Fred in your cottage, not that you will be getting much sleep tonight?"

"No problem, sir," KB replied.

"Good. You will have to brief Danica when you get back, but her priority is to get the Firths' out of the Langaller Farmhouse and well away from the Estate before the balloon goes up. If she can persuade them by phone to leave of their own accord, so much the better as we want to minimise traffic in and out of the farm as much as possible. If they dig their toes in, she will have to pay them a visit and take the local bobby with her, but hopefully it won't come to that.

Danica has already reported in this morning and we've given her a 'heads up' and everything is set up at the Exmoor Park Authority offices in Dulverton for us to establish our Tactical CP there. In fact, the staff have been given an extended Christmas break with an extra day off, so we should have the place to ourselves. I will be at the Tactical CP later tonight, together with all other key personnel. A Forward CP will be set up at Langaller Farm to control the lads on the ground, which is another good reason to keep the Firths' well away from there.

"I want you and Fred in place in the Triscombe Copse OP before first light. You will provide us with any intel you think important, and to close the back door in the event that the woods to the north of the Manor House are used as an escape route.

“In a worst case scenario, and if our friends from the constabulary are thwarted in achieving their objectives or find themselves in serious jeopardy, we have a company of Royal Marines standing by who can be flown in by helicopter. We also have an air strike capability on call from the RAF which we can bring in as a last resort. Bear in mind, once the military are involved, they take over command and control completely. Any questions?”

“A couple, sir,” said KB. “I understand we will be taking our rifles. Under what circumstances are we cleared to fire?”

“Call me up at Tactical CP. I have all the top brass with me, so we’ll hold a committee meeting and get right back to you! Seriously though, KB, you know our rules of engagement. You are the guys at the sharp end and can see what’s happening at first hand, so between you and Fred, if you think direct action is warranted and for any reason you can’t get an immediate shout from me, it’s up to you. Obviously this includes a direct threat to the lives of you or any of our team, and in this respect you know I’ll back you one hundred percent in any subsequent operational post-mortems or official enquiries.”

“One other thing, sir,” KB continued. “Do we know exactly how many students there are at the Academy, and what the armed threat might be?”

“They are licensed for a maximum of three hundred and fifty. From our best estimate, based on the last school inspection, about a third will be in their late teens – seventeen to nineteen, or in the case of those training to become Imams, even older. A third will be in their mid-teens, and a third juniors from thirteen to fourteen. They have a teaching and administrative staff of over forty, plus an unknown number of security guards, so we could be talking well in excess of four hundred people on site, and as far as we can gather, mostly male. With regards to their armed capability, as you know yourself there is evidence that they have AK-47s on site, and if this is a terrorist training facility, it is entirely likely that they will have access to heavier weapons.”

“A question from me, Andy,” said Fred. “On our radios – who can we talk to?”

“Good question, use your Agency code names as your call signs when on air. Our operating wavelength will be connected to both the Tac CP and Forward CP. The Police and military will have their own communications, but their Commanders will also be on the same net as us. Don’t forget also, if something comes up you consider best for my ears only, call me up on your secure link mobiles.

“One more thing, it looks as if the weather first thing tomorrow over Exmoor will still be pretty shitty, perhaps to our advantage as we can operate in the shadow of the storm. Anything else?”

“Not from me,” confirmed KB.

“Me neither,” added Fred.

“Right then, off you go and the best of luck. Call in when you get down there tonight. The next time I’ll see you will be on Exmoor, hopefully when all this is over.”

Leaving Reynard in the conference room, the two made their way downstairs to the Reception desk, where KB found a new wallet was waiting for him containing his Agency ID card, driving licence, credit and debit cards and £200 in notes. He also signed for two new mobile phones, one for his personal use with a new number, and the second the Agency secure line handset.

Outside the building they made their way back to the Mess where KB collected the keys for his Ranger from the porter while Fred picked up an overnight bag which he had packed in readiness. In the car park, KB handed the keys to the rental car over to his friend, and the two of them then drove over to the pistol range and armoury where Warrant Officer Greenaway was waiting for them.

“Off to the wars then, gents?” he greeted them as he unlocked the security door to the weapons lock-up. “And what can I do for you today?”

“That depends,” said Fred. “We haven’t agreed yet who is going to do what. Who would you suggest draws his sniper rifle, and who acts as spotter and draws a Sharpshooter, Warrant?”

“No offence, Mr Nowakowski,” came the reply, “but with the practice Mr Blake put in with me before Christmas, I know he’s back on top of his form now, so if it were up to me I would let Mr Blake take the sniper rifle.”

“That’s fine by me,” Fred agreed. “Okay with you, KB?”

“Let’s do it,” KB answered, and ten minutes later they were leaving with the two weapons secured in carrying cases and with spare magazines and a hundred rounds of ammunition apiece all to be stowed securely in the back of the Wildtrak’s cab.

“I’ve just got to drop by the Medical Centre, then we’ll be on our way,” KB said to his friend. “Andy insisted that I get the bang on my head checked out.”

“No problem,” came the reply. “I’ll wait for you outside.”

Inside the Centre, he was greeted by the same Sister who had treated the cut on his head before and taking a quick look at it, she waved him through to the treatment room and sat him down in a chair next to her desk.

"Mr Blake isn't it?" she said, and in response to his confirmation, entered his name on her computer.

"That's right," he affirmed. "I need you to take a look at the bump on my head. The wound has been dressed, but it may need re-doing."

"This is quite a nasty wound," she said, after carefully examining it. "It looks as if it were done by some kind of blunt instrument, perhaps a pick-axe handle or a baseball bat?"

"I can't say what it was, I didn't see," he admitted.

"Were you knocked unconscious," she questioned him, as she continued to probe gently around the gash, "and if so, for how long?"

"I was stunned more than knocked clean out," he lied.

"When did this happen?" she continued.

"Around four thirty yesterday afternoon."

"Any prolonged headache or double vision?" she asked.

"No," he said. "I was fine in a couple of hours. Bit of a headache to start off, but I took a couple of paracetamols and got a good night's sleep, and I feel as right as rain today."

"I doubt that," she said. "But whoever put this dressing on knew first aid. The wound looks clean and the sutures are holding, but I still need the Doctor to take a look. He's out right now, but should be back within the hour, can you call back later?"

"Not really, I have somewhere I need to be fairly shortly and I may be tied up there for a while, could I drop by tomorrow?" he asked, mentally crossing his fingers that she would agree.

"Yes, I suppose so," KB was relieved to hear her say. "But don't try to do too much and take it easy. A couple more paracetamols tonight wouldn't hurt, and try to get plenty of rest."

"Thank you, Sister," he said, and without waiting to exchange any more pleasantries he left the Centre as quickly as he could.

With Fred parked next to the Wildtrak, KB gave him a thumbs up, and climbing into the driver's seat started up the diesel. With his friend following close behind him, they drove out of the Camp and were soon on the A303 heading west.

With only light traffic to contend with, they were well on their way when he called up Dani on his hands free.

“Hi there,” he greeted her, as she answered her mobile. “I’m on my way back and have Fred with me, and I reckon we should be at the cottage in around an hour and a half. Fred can bunk in with me tonight, and tell your good friend the farmer’s wife not to worry about food, I’ll pick up a take-away for all of us on our way through Dulverton. How are things at your end?”

“Pretty good,” came the reply. “Everything set up and the Firths are settled in at a hotel in town. I arranged to have a WPC stay with them to be on the safe side.”

“How did they take it?” he asked.

“Really well, in fact Adam didn’t seem at all surprised. His missus is a bit worried, which is understandable, but the kids are really enjoying themselves – taking it all as being a bit of an adventure.”

“Great, see you in a little while,” he replied, and rang off.

The traffic on the A303 remained light and once on the M5 they gained more time until turning off onto the A361 and then north onto the A369 to Dulverton.

Including a stop for twenty minutes at ‘The Blue Dragon’ in town to pick up a selection of Chinese dishes, it was still only just outside KB’s estimate of an hour and a half when finally they pulled into the farmyard and parked up in front of the cottages.

Chapter Thirty-One

In the Shadow of the Storm

Ne Puero Gladium – Do not give a child a sword.

Latin Proverb

With first light due at around seven a.m., by five o'clock they were up and dressed. Having breakfasted, they double checked their equipment and each packed a knapsack with flasks of coffee and sandwiches. By half past, Dani had left for the drive into Dulverton and the Tactical Command Post, leaving them with two short wave radio handsets already tuned in to the wavelength they would be using for the operation.

Leaving the hire car at the farm, they climbed aboard the Wildtrak and headed out for Triscombe Copse and the OP.

"Well, my friend'" said Fred, as they took the high road across Triscombe Common, "I wonder what this day will bring."

"For once I hope that the Police are right, and this is going to be a simple case of executing a search warrant, but something in my bones tells me that it isn't going to be that easy," KB replied.

A mile from the copse, KB doused the headlights and slowed down, the sidelights struggling to provide much more than a glimmer of illumination as they crept forward through the swirling rain.

"I doubt if anyone in the Compound is manning the lookout in the minaret yet," he commented. "But I don't want to take any chances."

In spite of their slow approach, within minutes they reached the copse and KB stopped, to allow Fred to dismount and guide him in on foot. Reaching the clearing, he swung the Ford around to face outwards, and then reversed it into the undergrowth. Unloading their kit, they removed their weapons from the carrying cases and then busied themselves covering the front of the vehicle with brushwood, until KB was satisfied that it would remain concealed to all but the closest observer.

With Fred following, he found the track leading to Dani's OP and un-strapping the groundsheets from their knapsacks, spread one on the grass, and pulled the second one over them to provide some shelter from the rain. As they lay prone in their hide, they found that the low mound in front of them provided a windbreak from the gale that still blew in from the west, and the natural overhead cover deflected some of the rain which might have otherwise have saturated them.

"Almost as snug as a bug in a rug," muttered KB, as he and Fred checked their rifles and loaded the magazines by the light of his pencil torch. Taking a small pack out the side pocket of his camouflaged jacket, he extracted two tubes of face paint, one black and one green and he and Fred took it in turns to apply it liberally to their exposed skin.

"Might as well do the job properly," he commented, as they checked each others' handiwork, "and in any case, I always feel a tad naked unless I'm wearing this stuff!"

It was an hour later before the pitch black of night began to show signs of surrendering to the dark grey of early dawn, and with it came a slight respite in the ferocity of the wind and an easing of the torrential rain which hammered down on them.

Focussing the telescopic sights of his rifle on the Manor, while Fred scanned the ground in front of them through binoculars, lights flicking on from behind the windows of the big house indicated that the occupants were beginning their day.

Picking up his handset and switching it on, KB pressed the transmit button and spoke quietly into the mouthpiece.

"Control, this is Sirius, radio check, over."

"Sirius, this is Control, loud and clear, over," came the response in the unmistakable tones of Dani Janes.

"Control, in position, objective in sight and signs of activity in and around the main building, out," he ended.

Leaving the handset on, it was a matter of seconds later before it crackled into life again.

"Control, this is Blueforce Commander, Forward CP established, moving to objective now."

"The cops are going in," commented KB. "I guess the next few minutes will decide whether or not we've got a major incident on our hands."

Through his scope KB could see a sudden flurry of activity within the compound with figures scurrying towards the woods that concealed the main entrance gate. Fixing his sight on one it became obvious immediately that the man was armed and carrying an AK-47.

Picking up his handset he radioed, "Sirius to Blueforce Commander, armed personnel entering the tree line immediately to your front, over."

"Roger, Sirius," came the response, and then, "Blueforce Commander to Control, initial access to compound refused but have secured gatehouse and two suspects detained, am proceeding in force to the Manor House..." but before the sender could complete his transmission, the distant crackle of small arms fire reached their ears. "....Am taking fire," the caller continued. "Wait, out."

A minute passed and the firing ceased, and then the confident tones of the Police response team were heard again.

"Blueforce Commander to Control. Two persons exiting Manor House and approaching my position. They have their hands in the air and do not appear to be armed. Awaiting orders, over."

Seconds later came the response, "Control to Blueforce Commander, assess risk and establish dialogue if possible, your call, over."

"Blueforce Commander to Control. Am going out to meet them, standby."

Through his scope KB watched as the Police Commander emerged from the trees and started walking slowly towards the south wing, arms extended with palms facing downwards.

"KB, zero in on the minaret, I see movement, possibly two hostiles," Fred broke in.

Shifting his scope from the Manor House, KB re-focussed on the tower and confirmed Fred's sighting.

"You're right, certainly two men, one with what looks like an SVD," he said, identifying the Russian made sniper rifle "Let me call it in."

"Sirius to Control," he radioed. "Mosque Tower is manned by armed personnel, sniper identified, permission to engage, over?"

"Control to Sirius," came the response. "Negative, do not, I repeat, do not engage. Hostiles negotiating with Blueforce Commander, maintain close watch, over."

"Roger, Control, out," he answered, but keeping his sights trained on the mosque, added to his companion, “Keep watching the gap between the woods concealing the main entrance and the Manor House in the area of the car park, Fred, and give me a shout if you spot anything.”

For a moment there was silence, and then Fred answered, “Two men in the open. Looks like a cop and he’s talking to a smallish guy, black coat, white trousers, wearing specs and one of those short-arse fez jobs on his head.”

“That sounds like Sadeed Muhammad, one of their head honchos,” said KB. “I don’t want to take my eyes off those scrotes in the tower, so let me know if anything happens.”

“Roger that,” agreed his friend. A minute or so passed and he continued, “Much bowing and scraping, and your friend Muhammad and his mate are going back inside the house.”

“What is the cop doing?” KB insisted. “Is he taking cover?”

“No,” came the response. “At the moment he’s hanging around – looks as if he’s waiting for a taxi.”

“Fucking idiot,” snorted KB. “He’s an easy target where he is, oh-oh,” he added, “We’ve got trouble; sniper taking up firing position, I’m taking the shot.”

“Steady, KB!” his friend warned. “You are not authorised...” but before he could complete the sentence the crack of KB’s sniper rifle broke through the sound of the wind and rain around them. Switching his binoculars to the tower Fred saw the figure of the would-be assassin slump forward, his weapon bouncing off the conical roof of the mosque and clattering onto the asphalt below.

In a split second, the policeman turned on his heels and started to sprint towards the safety of the trees, a fusillade of shots from the Manor House ringing out to speed him on his way. With a final desperate lunge he made the safety of the undergrowth, as covering fire from the armed response team silenced the shooters.

“Control to Sirius, Control to Sirius, send sitrep now, over,” came the urgent call on the radio, in severe tones that were clearly not those of Danica Janes.

“Sirius to Control,” he replied, feeling his heart pounding. “Hostile sniper had Blueforce Commander in his sights and was about to shoot. Hostile neutralized, out.”

From the grounds of the Estate, the sounds of firing subsided to be replaced by an ominous silence.

"Well, you did it, mate," Fred commented sympathetically. "But I bet that cluster-fuck at Tac CP are running around like chickens with their heads chopped off, and as far as that top cop is concerned you have screwed up his chance of glory so undoubtedly your name is mud right now. You've also probably buggered up any chance the brass had of parleying our way out of a fire-fight, so if I were you, I'd be prepared to drop my pants in anticipation of a right spanking."

As if prompted by Fred's observations, KB's Agency mobile rang and he was not surprised to hear Andy Reynard's voice on the other end.

"Congratulations, KB, the shit has really hit the fan at this end. You've got our Police Chief threatening to charge you with pre-meditated murder and our service representatives cheering you on. Meanwhile, I'm stuck in the middle, so any rational explanation you can give me for your action would be appreciated!"

"No problem, sir" KB replied. "As soon as negotiations ended and the al-Amn guys were out of the line of fire, the sniper took up a firing position and drew a bead on the cop. He had his finger on the trigger of his rifle and made some minor adjustments to his scope. I have seen enough similar cases to recognize the difference between a sniper simply observing and one about to shoot, so I made the decision and took the appropriate action."

"Okay, I think I get the picture, though I'm sure I'm going to be told that the Police marksmen had matters under control, so you aren't off the hook yet. I suggest that from here onwards you keep your head down and limit your activities to observing."

"Yes, sir" KB responded, as the line went dead.

"So, are you in the clear?" asked his friend.

"Not entirely, as you so accurately predicted, the top cop is not a happy bunny, but as I'm still here I suppose things could be worse."

Ten minutes passed with their radios silent and no sign of any further movement from the compound. Agreeing it was time for a coffee, they were about to unscrew their flasks, when their handsets crackled into life.

"Blueforce Commander to Control, no movement from the House so will enter and commence clearing, over."

"Control to Blueforce Commander, roger, out."

From their vantage point, KB and Fred watched as a line of dark blue uniformed police emerged from the tree line and sprinted towards the building and by KB's estimation all ten of the assault team reached the safety and cover of the south wing. Another five minutes dragged by, before the radios came to life again.

"Blueforce Commander to Control, access gained and am conducting room by room search. So far no sign of any occupants, over."

"Control to Blueforce Commander, acknowledged, proceed with caution, out."

"That's bloody strange," KB muttered. "No attempt to fire on the cops as they approached and they have made it inside, without any attempt to stop them. Something's not right, Fred, where have Sadeed and his mates gone? Keep watching the House and if there is any sign of movement, let's know about it."

KB had focussed his scope on the east wing of the Manor House when it happened. An angry flash lit up the sky followed in a split second by a series of thunderous explosions. Whole sections of the roof of the building disappeared as windows blew out and debris flew in all directions. A red glow from inside grew in intensity until flames licked the outer walls and shot skywards, while the outer wall of the east wing lurched inwards.

"Jesus Murphy, they've blown up the whole fucking building!" Fred exclaimed.

Pushing his rifle to one side, KB grabbed the radio and with his spare hand focussed his binoculars on the scene of devastation which now came into his view.

"Sirius to Control. Manor House blown, major structural damage and multiple fires."

Before Control had a chance to respond a new caller came on the net, the desperation in his voice evident.

"Control, this is Blueforce Section Leader. Blueforce Commander and his team had not, repeat had not, exited the building. I am taking heavy fire from mosque, request immediate back-up and medevac, over."

"Fat fucking chance of that," commented KB to his friend. "Unless the commandos are already airborne it could be half an hour before they get here."

As he spoke, his mobile rang again and he switched it to speaker.

"Sirius this is Minos," came the familiar voice. "What is your assessment from where you sit?"

"The Manor House is gone, sir," he answered. "I reckon they must have had it wired for explosives. It is also my guess that there is probably some kind of tunnel connecting the cellars of the Manor House to a basement in the mosque, which would explain the fact the birds had flown when the Police went in. They were probably playing for time all along, hoping to lure as many of our blokes into the building as possible before they blew it. For sure their wiring job was well concealed and I don't suppose the Police assault team spotted it?"

"Nope," came the reply. "And it has cost them dear. Any sign from your OP of survivors?"

"None so far," interjected Fred.

"Understood," continued the Head of Operations. "Continue to monitor. The Police have sent up their Reserve Sections to give some covering fire and see if they can get anyone out – is there anything you can do from your end?"

"Not much," admitted KB. "Short of keeping the minaret clear of any more shooters. If the walls of the mosque are as thick as Firth believed them to be, any fire we can lay down is going to be pretty ineffective unless they break out of there, and if they do, they could pop up anywhere if they have more tunnels leading away from it."

"Roger that. Back-up from our friends is incoming and they should be with us within twenty minutes or so. I alerted them as soon as you eliminated the sniper and I've got confirmation that they are airborne. They are going to drop off the FAC at your location en route to their LZ at Langaller Farm, and Calypso is on her way to you to guide them in. No need for me to tell you to keep on your toes."

KB just had time to say, "Thanks, sir" before the phone went dead.

"I'll watch the compound, you keep scanning the woods, Fred," he said to his friend.

Training his scope on the Compound once again he noticed immediately that the windows in the mosque that he had seen while passing the building on his inspection had disappeared, and all that remained were a series of recessed loopholes set at regular intervals around the walls.

"I hope our Marine friends bring some heavy ordinance with them," he commented to Fred. "The windows in the mosque were obviously concealing firing points, and if the walls are as thick as we think they are, it's going to take more than a bunch of gung-ho bootnecks with assault rifles to dislodge the buggers."

"Bugger that," said Fred. "I've got movement in the north east corner of the woods, just in the tree line beyond the compound fence and at twelve o'clock from the gate in the wall. Check it out."

Shifting his position, KB picked up the gate in his 'scope. Just as Fred had reported, he could see dark clad figures behind the fence, and as he watched the entire section swung open and one of the men sprang forward to kneel behind the gate and out of KB's sight.

"Fred, grab your radio and report that we have a suspected break-out. The section in the fence has been opened and it looks as if they are unlocking the gate."

As Fred contacted Control, KB continued his watch, but a full minute passed before the radio crackled into life and Fred reported back.

"We are to prevent break-out if possible, but all attempts must be made to minimize casualties," he said. "Apparently the Police have set up roadblocks on all roads leading from the Estate, any signs of vehicles?" he added, once more resuming his watch on the perimeter.

"None at the moment," KB confirmed, but as he spoke the gate was pulled open and two lines of men armed with AK-47s emerged in a crouching run, deploying to the left and right and going to ground in front of the stone wall.

"Did you see that, Fred – how many did you count?"

"Seen – estimate twenty," came Fred's reply. "Those guys are well trained, they know what they are doing. The black combats and balaclavas look familiar too."

As they watched, faint shouts of command were carried on the wind to where they lay, followed by the appearance of the blunt snout of a large 4 x 4 as it moved out of the woods and through the gateway. At the same time two more figures appeared to take up positions behind the line of escorts as they rose from concealment to flank the vehicle as it drove onto the track.

"Second vehicle coming into sight," sang out Fred. "They look like Toyota Land Cruisers. Hope they're not the special bullet proof models – shatter proof glass, self-sealing fuel tanks and run flat tyres."

"We may be about to find out," KB answered. "Give Control a sitrep and tell them we are attempting to immobilize them."

As Fred spoke into the radio, both the 4 x 4's increased their speed until the men escorting them were jogging to keep pace.

"Cleared to fire," Fred confirmed, dropping the handset and taking aim with his rifle. "You go for the tyres, I'll take the bodywork."

As they opened fire, the 4 x 4's slowed and the line of escorts wavered and stopped, the figures dropping to the ground to take cover as the snipers' bullets hammered into the vehicles above their heads.

Away to the north the distant sound of rotor blades could be heard, and KB glanced up to see the sleek outline of a helicopter rise above the cliff edge and skim the ground to flare out and settle down on Gryphon Head.

"That's their pick-up, Fred," he shouted. "Call it in and tell the cops to get to the Gryphon Head car park pronto. The Land Cruisers are moving again," he added. "And we now have the full attention of their escorts."

As the Land Cruisers moved further down the track towards their objective, the two groups had risen from cover and were now advancing towards the OP in a single extended line, weapons pointed in front of them, urged on by the shouts of their two leaders who followed in their wake.

As one group knelt to take up firing positions to cover the advance, the other sprinted forward, rapidly reducing the distance between the two snipers and their assailants. A ragged volley of shots rang out from the covering group, rounds zipping through the trees and bushes along the edge of the copse.

"That's random fire, I don't think they've located our position yet, but it won't be long – it's time to get serious. I'll take the left group, you take the right, Fred."

"Roger," came the response, as the two snipers opened fire.

As KB's group rose to continue their advance, his first shot hit his target, and as the figure crumpled and fell, for a second the advancing line wavered. Screaming at his charges, their leader fired his weapon into the air and the line moved forward again. Shifting his aim, KB squeezed the trigger and this time it was the leader who fell backwards.

On the right, several of the group had adopted a kneeling position to get a better line of sight to their target and this time their shots flicked through the branches above their heads, before three shots in quick succession from Fred rang out, a high-pitched yell suggesting that at least one of which had found its mark.

With their attackers now out of sight as they lay hidden in the moorland grass, KB turned his attention back to the two Land Cruisers which by now were half-way down the track and making steady progress towards the road. Taking careful aim at the slowly moving targets, he fired four rounds quickly at the side windows of the leading vehicle. The glass in both the front and rear windows cracked as the bullets struck, but he was unable to confirm if his rounds had actually penetrated. Satisfyingly, it lurched to a stop and before he could fire again, the following Cruiser pulled out and parked alongside, out of the sniper's view and using its companion as a shield.

“They’re withdrawing,” Fred sang out. “Legging it back to the woods.”

“Best hold our fire, Fred,” KB answered. “They’ve probably had enough.”

As the last of their fleeing attackers reached the cover of the Langaller Woods, KB re-trained his rifle on the Manor House which was still burning fiercely, black smoke rising in a column to be dispersed and twisted into oily black fingers as it climbed above the tree line into the full force of the westerly wind.

No sign of movement came from within the compound, and while Fred called in their latest report to Control, KB focused once again on the minaret.

At first he saw nothing, but then a slight movement from within the watch tower betrayed the presence of at least one lookout. As a head and shoulders bobbed into view, he squeezed off another shot and the figure immediately disappeared out of sight.

Satisfied that if he hadn’t actually hit the man he had certainly done enough to persuade him to keep his head down, he continued to scan the compound and its surroundings until a shout from Fred alerted him to a new danger.

From behind the dry stone wall and the gate, further movement could be seen within the tree line and as they watched the tell-tale trails of smoke grenades being thrown curled outwards to drop over the wall. Within seconds billowing clouds of smoke started to build, obscuring their view of the gate way.

“Fire into the smoke, Fred,” he yelled, and both snipers’ weapons spat fire in unison. At the same time, two hundred yards to the south, three black clad figures arose from behind the wall and from its cover, took aim at their position.

This time it was not the familiar crack of AK-47s that caught their attention, but the deeper crump of hand held Rocket Propelled Grenade launchers as their missiles arched into the air, to land short of their position, the explosions sending clods of earth skywards.

“Holy shit, KB, you’d better nail those suckers or we’re toast,” Fred called out, the concern showing in his voice. “And I’ve got my hands full, we’ve now got thirty plus of the buggers to my front and they’re going to try to rush us.”

“Make them pay for it,” KB answered. “They’ve still got a lot of open ground to cover, but be prepared to bug out when they get within a hundred metres of us,” he added, wondering at the same time if a hundred metres would give him enough time to reach the safety of his truck.

As he lined his sights on the RPG firers, a heavy rustling in the bushes behind them announced that they were not alone, and grabbing his Glock he rolled away from his rifle to turn and face the new threat.

"Hold off there, KB," the girl's voice rang out, as Danica Janes crashed through the last few feet of undergrowth and threw herself down between them.

"I was waiting for our friends to arrive and heard the firing and as it seemed pretty intense, I thought I'd give you a hand," she said slipping a rifle off her shoulder and slamming a magazine into it. "I've laid a panel indicating our position behind the copse if our friends show up," she added, as she took aim.

"Help Fred sort out that lot coming across the Common at us," KB said, turning his attention back to the RPGs. His next shot caught the gunner at the same time as the man fired the launcher, and as he toppled over the missile shot upwards vertically to explode back on the ground only a few yards in front of the wall. The second firer was more successful and KB watched as the missile curved towards them.

"Heads down, incoming!" he shouted, as the high explosive grenade detonated above and to the left of them.

As twigs and small branches rained down on them a string of expletives from Fred followed, and KB glanced over to see his friend clasping his hand to his thigh, blood seeping through his fingers.

Through his scope, KB could see no further signs of movement from where their assailants had launched their rockets, and switched his attention to the assault line which was now no more than three hundred metres from where they lay.

Taking aim, he again started to shoot as rapidly as he could, pausing only for seconds to reload. As he re-aimed the welcome crack of Fred's Sharpshooter once again joined the fusillade, while Dani fired steadily alongside them with the coolness and deliberation of a marksman.

Under the hail of shots that now sped towards their targets, the attackers faltered and the line broke. In the centre of the retreating group, one of the would-be assailants threw his rifle to the ground as he sped towards the safety of the woods, and as he did so he was gunned down by one of his companions who, arms waving, tried in vain to stem the tide of retreat.

As the last black clad figure reached safety and disappeared into the wood an eerie silence descended over the Common, giving Dani a chance to put down her rifle and examine Fred's wound.

"It looks like a bit of shrapnel from the grenade," she reported. "Do we have any field dressings?"

“There are some field dressings in my knapsack,” KB replied. “See if you can patch him up while I call in a sitrep.”

After a brief exchange on the radio, he checked the ground to his front and scanned the compound again. Finding all was quiet, he leant over to check Dani’s progress as she administered to his friend.

“Control says that our Marine friends are inbound and only minutes away, so we’re to hang on here at least until they arrive. How’s my wounded buddy?”

“He’s lost quite a lot of blood, but I think it missed an artery, but we still need to get him out of here as soon as possible,” said Dani, as the distant whop-whop of multiple rotors reached their ears. “Keep an eye on him. I’m going back to meet and greet.”

As she crawled backwards out of the hide, KB glanced at the rifle she had been using and picking it up, peering through its scope to scan the woods yet again. As he hefted the weapon he was surprised at its lightness, guessing it weighed no more than 5 lbs. Checking the manufacturer’s stamp he saw he was holding a Sako 85 Carbonlight which Dani had fitted with a Leica riflescope. This was certainly the rifle she used for her deer culling duties with the Park Authorities, but before he had time to examine the weapon further, the canopy of the trees shook with the downdraft from the rotor blades of a heavy lift helicopter as it touched down behind Triscombe Copse.

Replacing the rifle on the ground, he turned back to Fred, who was now propped up on one arm, a broad grin now spreading across his face.

“Sounds as if our saviours have arrived!” the Pole exclaimed. “Just as well, I hate playing gooseberry and the way she looks at you is getting embarrassing!”

“Fuck off, Fred,” he replied, temporarily at a loss for words, but before he could add a more suitable response, Dani crawled forward, accompanied by a burly combat clad and helmeted officer, in his wake three other Marines, one carrying a portable laser target designator.

“Hi,” drawled the newcomer, not waiting for an introduction. “Captain Chuck Gardner, United States Marines on exchange with your Royals, and privileged to be commanding this little rescue mission. Let’s take a look at what we have here.”

Sliding his frame alongside KB, the latter directed the American’s attention to the scene which lay before them, the Captain checking every detail on his map.

“Jeeze, they certainly made a mess of the stately home,” he commented.

"But I guess that's to be expected, their cousins across the other side of the Med have become experts at demolishing ancient monuments!"

Shifting his binoculars to scan the ground to their immediate front, KB pointed out the gap in the wall and the fence beyond it, and the two Land Cruisers that still remained stationary on the track.

"Don't worry about them," the Captain insisted. "Just concentrate on keeping the minaret clear of snipers and we'll do the rest. I'm leaving a platoon with you here, and my other two platoons should be at the farm by now. Our major problem is the mosque, so our FAC here will do his best to shake them up, with a little help from your jet jockeys.

"The weather is still crap, so a laser guided bomb drop may be too risky, but we can still call on the mother of all bunker busters. Once we've cracked the mosque the platoon here will enter and clear the woods down to the old stable block while we re-take what's left of the Manor House and catch them from the south. After my guys pull out from here, if you could check the hostiles you knocked over in your fire-fight, I'll make sure you have medevac laid on to take care of any wounded, and in the meantime we'll take your buddy here with us to get him checked out at the aid station they should be setting up now at the farm. Okay by you?"

"Yes, sir," KB replied, as Dani nodded her assent.

"Carry on the good work, I'll leave you to it," the American replied, and beckoning to the second man in his team, they pulled Fred backwards out of the OP and lifting him up between them, disappeared back into the copse.

"You'd better come over next to me," KB suggested to the young Forward Air Controller, and made room for him as he crawled over to where KB lay.

"Welcome to our party," he said wryly, as the man settled down and adjusted the black box of the LLDR on its tripod, noticing as he did so that the FAC wore the pips of a Lieutenant on the tab buttoned to the front of his combat jacket.

"Thanks," came the reply. "I'm Jim Williams, part of the Commando's Fire Support Team and," he added pointing to the third man, "This is my radio operator. Can you confirm the target for me please?"

As KB pointed out the mosque, Williams focussed his binoculars on it and after making further adjustments to the LLDR, activated it and shot a laser beam at the west wall of the rotund building.

After several attempts, he shook his head and drew back. "Can't do it," he confirmed. "This wind and the swirling rain makes it bad enough, but with the smoke from the Manor House blowing across, it would be too risky, we can't afford any blue on blue casualties, so it looks like Plan B."

Before he could question the Lieutenant on the nature of 'Plan B' the radio operator's field-set came to life, reporting all three platoons in position. As soon as the transmission ended, the officer plugged in his own headset to the radio and in flat, level tones, made his call.

"Zero, this is six one alpha, pickle unsafe, repeat pickle unsafe, over."

"Six one alpha, this is zero," came the immediate reply. "Initiate popcorn, I say again initiate popcorn, over."

"Zero, this is six one alpha, roger, out."

Without pausing, the young Marine continued, "Hawkeye, this is Fortune, did you read that? – over."

There was a brief pause, than a fainter female voice responded.

"Fortune, this is Hawkeye, confirm initiate popcorn, over."

"Hawkeye, this is Fortune, confirm initiate popcorn, I say again confirm initiate popcorn, out."

"Bloody hell – that was a lot of mumbo jumbo," commented KB as the Lieutenant took up his position by his side and resumed surveillance on the target. "Who was the bird calling herself Hawkeye?"

"A very smart 'bird'," he answered, "who happens to be a Squadron Leader and one of the RAF's best pilots. Your 'bird' is currently at the controls of 9.4 million pounds worth of Tornado GR4 flying above the cloud cover and probably circling around somewhere not too far from here."

"And popcorn," KB insisted. "Who or what is that?"

"A handy dandy missile with the co-ordinates for the mosque already programmed into it, which by now is approaching at about 40 metres above the ground at a speed of about 1,000 kilometres an hour following a terrain marking flight path guided by GPS."

"That should give the morning commuters something to think about," muttered KB.

"Don't worry about that," came the response. "She will have launched over the sea, so in fact the amount of time the missile will be in the air over the ground will be minimal, and in any case, when you hear the whistle of its jet engine, it's already long gone."

"And what kind of warhead does 'popcorn' carry?" KB asked.

"450 kilograms, which will be needed as our intelligence informs us that the walls could be up to a couple of metres thick."

"You're looking at that intelligence," replied KB, a note of sarcasm in his voice. "So it will need good penetration."

"That should be taken care of," the man answered. "An initial charge blows an opening in the wall, and the main charge that follows is on a delayed fuse to give maximum effect."

"So nothing can go wrong?"

"It shouldn't, but my only worry is the heat from the Manor House. The final line up to the target is by infrared homing, so I'm hoping it decides to stick to the co-ordinates for the mosque, otherwise we are back to square one."

At that point their attention was drawn to a popping noise from the direction of the compound, and peering through their binoculars they could see puffs of white smoke emanating from a series of brilliantly white globes of fire around the base of the mosque.

"That will help," said the Marine. "They're engaging the mosque with phosphorous mortar bombs. That should send out a welcoming heat signature for our airborne bunker buster."

A sense of something blue-grey flashed overhead and as they watched a small puff of smoke burst from the surface of the west wall of the mosque. There was a short delay, and then the sound of a second explosion tore through the air. As the smoke and dust cleared, a gaping hole in the wall could be seen, the red glow of fire in its centre.

"Wow!" KB exclaimed. "Some corn, some pop!"

"That," said the Royal Marine, "was Storm Shadow. Now let's see how quickly the lads can wrap things up."

As he spoke, his radio chattered into life and moments later a sustained burst of machine gun fire from the edge of the copse raked the dry stone wall and slashed into the tree line beyond the gate. As the gunner continued to give covering fire, a section of commandos emerged into the open and sprinted towards the stationary Land Cruisers. On reaching their objective the section went to ground after two of their number had quickly checked the vehicles, and having given a 'thumbs up' sign to indicate that no threat existed, joined their companions by the side of the track facing the area under fire.

It was now the turn of the two remaining sections to break cover and run towards their objective, crouching beneath the cover of the wall. With no fire from behind the fence to hinder their advance, they rose two at a time to charge through the open gate and disappear into the wood beyond.

With the two leading sections now safely in the cover of the trees, the third section followed them.

"I'm going to link up with the machine gunner and we'll cover you while you check out the casualties," volunteered the Lieutenant, rising to his feet.

"We'd appreciate that," KB agreed, and as the FAC and his radio operator departed, he and Dani readied themselves to leave their hide.

"Dani, you don't have to do this," he said, as he slung his knapsack on his back and picked up his rifle. "I can manage perfectly well, so perhaps you should get back to Control and give Andy an update?"

"Don't be an arsehole," came the curt response. "If you are worried that my sensitive femininity will get the better of me, and I'll collapse in a faint at the sight of a dead terrorist, forget it. I may not have been in the thick of it like you were, but I did a tour in Afghanistan with Brigade Ops at Bastion, so I know what one looks like. Don't forget you also introduced me to the mangled remains of your would-be murderer recently, so I think I can handle it."

"Fine by me," KB replied. "But don't touch any of the corpses, especially those face downwards. I can't see they had a chance to booby trap any of them, but it only takes a second to pull the pin on a grenade and stuff it under a body, and when you roll it over, the trigger releases and you're suddenly in a world of hurt."

"I understand," the girl said soberly, as she followed him out of the hide.

"We'll check out the Land Cruisers first," he said as they skirted the copse and made their way towards the track. "By the way, where did you learn to shoot like that?"

"My Grandfather was a ghillie on one of the large estates in Scotland. As a young girl I spent hours of my holidays deer stalking in the Highlands, and he taught me how shoot."

"He taught you well, I hope I can persuade you to try out for the Battalion rifle team."

"We'll see," she laughed, as they reached the truck. Shouldering his rifle, he took the Glock out of its holster and as Dani stood back, her rifle at the ready he stepped forward and wrenched open the door of the one nearest to them.

The driver lay slumped forward over the steering wheel, a drying trickle of blood glistening as it ran down from his scalp, otherwise the vehicle was empty.

"This was the lead vehicle. They were probably hoping it would attract all the attention," he said, as he shut the door again.

Moving around to the other Land Cruiser, that had been shielded by its partner, they found all four doors open and no sign of any driver or passengers inside.

"Whoever was here has done a runner," KB commented as he peered into the vehicle. "Probably got out and crawled back to the woods where the ground drops away the other side of the track. Let's face it, we wouldn't have seen them from where we were and they certainly had time."

Leaving the 4 x 4's behind them, they walked steadily back parallel to the wall scanning the ground at their feet.

The first body lay where it had fallen, arms thrown backwards, one hand still tightly grasping an AK-47, vacant brown eyes open to the grey skies above. With the muzzle of his rifle, KB carefully removed the balaclava that covered the face, and as he threw it to one side, Dani gasped.

They were looking down at the face of a youth who was certainly still in his teens. Slight wisps of black facial hair sprouted from his upper lip and chin, his peaceful repose showing no signs of the violence that had snuffed out his life.

"Oh God, Kris," the girl exclaimed. "Look at him, we've been killing kids."

As KB glanced at her, her shoulders slumped forward. Kneeling on the ground beside him, she covered her face with her hands and for a moment remained still and silent.

"Come on, lass," he said quietly, helping her to her feet, and putting an arm around her shoulder. "The sooner we get this over, the better."

"I'm okay" she replied, her frame stiffening as she stood up, shaking off his arm as she did so. "Just took me by surprise. You're right, let's get on with it."

As they turned into the wind once more, she thrust her head forward into the rain as if to drive away any further show of emotion, when the sound of a vehicle coming up the road and through the north eastern edge of Triscombe Copse caught their attention. As they watched an Army Land Rover ambulance emerged, blue lights flashing and headlights piercing the gloom.

Waving the vehicle towards them, KB watched as it left the road and cut across the Common towards them, stopping a few yards short of where they stood. Two medics in combats climbed down from the cab, and a third from the rear of the vehicle.

"Come to take over from you, sir," the Sergeant in charge called as they arrived. "Your boss wants you back at Tac HQ ASAP, so we'll handle things."

"Thanks, Sergeant," KB acknowledged with relief, and without wasting a moment, the two of them headed back to their vehicles.

Chapter Thirty-Two

Stand Down

"Apres nous le deluge – after us the deluge."
Madame de Pompadour (after the battle of Rossbach 1757)

After pulling into the car park of the Exmoor National Park Authority in Dulverton, they parked their vehicles next to each other and made their way to the main building. At the front entrance security duties were being shared by two Military Policemen, who after scrutinizing their Agency ID cards, ushered them through to the control room.

As they entered, Andy Reynard looked up from his desk set back from the rest at the far end of the room, and on seeing them, hurried forward. As he did so, the figure of the Police Superintendent loomed large on their left, but recognizing KB, he stopped and turned his back on them.

"I guess I'm still not flavour of the month," muttered KB as, Andy came up to them.

"Good to see you both in one piece," the Head of Operations greeted them, "But I'm going to leave you with Bill and Colin who will take statements from both of you over a cup of coffee in the canteen, but I suggest you get that face make-up of yours off first, KB! After that, I want you out of here and out of sight. The papers and the media are going to be full of this tomorrow, and as much as we will try to play it down, it is still going to be headline news.

"Under the circumstances it would be best if you two lie low for a day or two, in fact, keep your heads down for the rest of the week and I'll see you both back in Bulford after the weekend. If anyone from the press does catch up with you, play dumb and say nothing, understand?"

"Yes, sir. Any news on Fred?" KB asked.

"He's in reasonable shape. They've taken him up to hospital in Exeter to patch him up properly and he should be back at Bulford by the time you get there on Monday."

"And what about the Police, is their Super still blaming me for the fracas?"

"He is, but he doesn't have any supporters in the light of subsequent developments. It seems obvious that al-Amn had an agenda which they would have implemented regardless of any action you initiated. Unfortunately the Police lost good men in the Manor House when it went up, and hardly surprisingly he is looking for a scapegoat.

"It looks as if the explosion and subsequent fire has probably destroyed any records that al-Amn had stashed there, but the latest news from the Commandos is all good. They have now secured the compound and found over eighty of the younger students unscathed in the gymnasium. It looks as if they were going to be used as hostages until the RAF clobbered the mosque and with it most of their leaders, so things could have been a lot worse. Anyway, I must get back. Wait for Bill and Colin in the canteen, then I suggest you go back to your cottages. It looks as if both of you could do with a hot shower and some sleep, you look like a couple of drowned rats right now!"

It took less than an hour for them to conclude their interviews and give statements to the two Section Leaders, but it was close to 2.00 p.m. by the time they left the building and headed back to their vehicles.

"Maybe we should stop off at the supermarket?" Dani suggested. "We could be hanging around the farm for a day or two so we need some supplies."

"We'll do that," KB agreed. "But I've been thinking about what Andy said. If the press are going to be crawling all over the area, the chances are that someone who knows you from the Park Authority might give them a lead, in which case it wouldn't take them long to track us down to the farm. Why don't we head out tomorrow and stay a couple of days with my folks at the pub? Nobody around here knows me, so it's unlikely they would trace us there."

"That could work," she said. "I could leave my Land Rover at the cottages and we could drive up

together in your truck, which would minimize the chances of being spotted, but let's get going, I'm soaking wet and freezing so the sooner I get into some clean clothes and get something to eat, the better."

They made their trip to the supermarket as brief as possible, only too aware that their bedraggled state was attracting a lot of attention from their fellow shoppers.

“I’ll grab a bottle of Scotch,” KB said, as they loaded their provisions into a trolley. “Does that suit you?”

“I was practically weaned on the stuff,” she replied, with a grin. “It might be a good idea to pick up a cooked chicken from the deli counter for supper. It would enable us to dodge any awkward questions if we eat at the farm, what do you think?”

Back at the farm, at Dani’s suggestion they stored the groceries in her kitchen and then both headed upstairs in their own cottage to shower and change. As he undressed, KB took his own mobile phone out of his jacket pocket and switched it on.

There were two messages, one from Alex and a voice message from his father. Taking the latter first, he listened to the familiar tones of Jack Blake:

“Hi, Kris, this is your dad. There’s been some stuff in the lunchtime news on the telly reporting some major explosions on Exmoor with the Police and military involved. It’s all pretty vague stuff, but your mum’s worried, as we know you are in that area. Give us a call as soon as you can.”

Without hesitating, he pressed the call button, and a moment later his father came on the line.

“Kris, are you okay?” came the immediate question.

“I’m fine, Dad,” he replied. “I’ll be home tomorrow and I’m bringing a friend with me to stay for a couple of days. Tell Mum that there is nothing to worry about and I’ll explain everything when I get home.”

“If you say so,” came the reply. “And by the way, Alex was down here this morning looking for you. She was in a right old state, but I’m afraid your mother didn’t exactly give her a warm welcome.”

“Thanks, Dad,” he answered. “I’ve got a message on my phone from her, which I’m going to deal with now, but I have to go, see you tomorrow.”

As the phone went dead, he flicked to text messages.

‘So sory,’ he read. ‘Made big mstke. Hugo not vry nice prsn. Miss u and hop u can forgv me. Dont dsrve it, but plees plees. Luv, Alx.’

“Shit!” he muttered, throwing the phone onto the bed, and sitting down with his head in his hands.

Outside a gust of wind rattled the window pane as a flurry of raindrops splattered against it. As he sat, the image of her naked body lying next to a lean and tanned Hugo Wellsbury flashed into his head.

“No you fucking well don’t.” he said to himself, and picking up the mobile, deleted the message.

He next put a call through to Colin, who quickly agreed that their proposed trip to Somerset was a good idea. Un-strapping his artificial leg, he forced his attention to a careful examination of his stump, noticing a slight soreness where the protective sock had been soaked during the morning's rain, and had rubbed against the skin. Retrieving the jar of ointment from his Bergen, he left it on his bedside table to be applied after his shower.

Sometime later, refreshed and dressed in clean jeans and shirt, he picked up the wet clothes that lay in a pile on the floor where he had discarded them and went downstairs. Lighting the fire in the stove, he waited until the logs were well alight, then closing the doors and shutting down the damper, he draped the damp garments over a chair back in front of it. Taking the bottle of Scotch off the kitchen sideboard, he locked up his cottage and trotted through the rain, sheltering under the porch next door until a tracksuit bottomed and T-shirt clad Dani answered his knock.

Inside, the room was warm and inviting and setting the Scotch down on the table in front of the sofa, he noticed that she had already laid out two glasses and a small jug of water.

"I've been over to the farmhouse and told them we would be away in the morning," she said. "They know you will be checking out and I've settled your bill, but I'll hang on to my cottage for a day or two as I expect there will be one or two things I'll need to sort out here when we get back. The farmer is also going to lock my Land Rover away in the barn, in case anyone comes snooping and I've warned them not to say anything to anybody. They're good folks and I'm pretty sure we can trust them, but hopefully nobody is going to bother them."

"Thanks for taking care of things," he replied, unscrewing the bottle and pouring two generous measures into each glass. "Do you take water?"

"Just a splash," she answered, and then added, "Is everything alright? You look as if you've seen a ghost!"

"I haven't actually seen one" he admitted. "But let's just say that some of my immediate past has come back to haunt me, via a message on my mobile. It would appear that a certain young lady had discovered that our Hugo Wellsbury is not the knight in shining armour she thought he was, and she now wants me to forgive her."

"And will you?" she asked.

"No," he said bluntly. "She had her chance and blew it, and even if we did pick things up again, I have a shrewd suspicion it would only last until the next distraction came along."

"Hmmm, we'll see," came the response. "I don't know about you, but I'm starving. The chicken is in the oven keeping warm, so let's eat."

Their meal done, they sat back on the sofa and picking up the remote, Dani switched on the television.

"Let's see what the early news has picked up," she said as the screen in front of them filled.

The assault on the Langaller Estate was headlines, and both of them leant forward as the newsreader began his report.

"What the Police are describing as a 'serious incident' occurred earlier today on Exmoor, where it is reported by a number of local eyewitnesses that several large explosions occurred in the vicinity of the Langaller Estate. At the centre of this four hundred acre privately owned Estate, lies an early nineteenth century Manor House, now home to the Quran is Dar al-Amn Academy, a private school primarily for the education of young men from the Muslim community.

"It appears that the Academy was the subject of a raid by armed Police, during which the Manor House was blown up by persons at present unidentified. It is believed that the Police suffered multiple casualties during their attempt to gain entry, as a result of which Royal Marine Commandos were flown in by helicopter as reinforcements.

"At present the whole area is cordoned off and we cannot bring you any further details, but we understand a press conference will be held later today and we will bring you an update then. In the meantime, a spokesman for the British Council of Muslims has stated that they had been kept fully appraised by the Home Office of the Police operation, but declined to comment further."

As the newsreader turned to other subjects, Dani lowered the volume and sat back, sipping on her whisky.

"I suppose you would call that the tip of the iceberg," she said. "I bet those guys in Control will be scratching their heads over what to say at the press conference right now. I wonder who will be in the hot seat."

"One thing is for sure," he replied. "It won't be Andy Reynard or anyone from MI5. I reckon the rep from the Home Office will be front and centre, with the top cop and a senior officer from the services on the platform to lend their support and help field the questions. My guess is that for the time being they will try to keep the lid on things as tightly as possible, and the next thing that you will see is a statement in the House of Commons from the Home Secretary and possibly the PM, at which time the shit will really hit the fan."

"Another good reason for us to take Andy's advice and lie low," she commented. "Unless you want to make your fortune selling your story to one of the tabloids?"

"Oh yeah – and finish up facing a charge of treason or hiding in some God forsaken spot in a remote part of the globe – I don't think so."

"I could always come with you," she said wistfully, leaning against him and resting her head on his shoulder. "We could live like castaways on a desert island, white sand, blue seas, catching fish and collecting coconuts. But that wouldn't work," she added, sitting up. "I could never compete with the shapely Miss Baker."

"I didn't have you down for a romantic," he answered, replenishing their glasses. "And anyway, you don't have to compete with anyone."

Getting up, he put more logs on the fire and turning up the volume on the TV sat down beside her again.

As the flicker of the flames danced off the ceiling and the effects of the whisky crept through them, the soporific drone of the TV added to the warm atmosphere in the room, and without either attempting to fight it, they both surrendered to a soothing sleep.

An increasing chill in the room awoke him with a start. The fire had died down and a late night movie now filled the TV screen. Dani had gone to sleep on his shoulder, and somewhere in a semi-conscious moment during the evening, he had slipped his arm around her, so she now lay snuggled into him, her knees tucked up underneath him. Checking his watch, the hands showed that it was approaching midnight.

Bending down, he gently whispered in her ear, "Wake up, sleepy head, it's long past bed time."

Stirring slightly, she looked up at him, the green eyes that never failed to fascinate him, blinking slowly in the half light from the table lamp.

There was a slight pause, and then she spoke. "Kris, I don't want to be on my own tonight."

"I understand," he said, anxious not to misinterpret her words. "I'll bunk down here if we can find some bedclothes."

"You don't have to," she said, getting to her feet and taking his hand. "My bed is loads more comfortable, and I really want you close to me."

The first grey tendrils of dawn crept through the window as he awoke. Raising himself up on one arm he looked across at the girl. She lay, still fast asleep, the duvet tucked up her under her arm exposing her bare shoulder.

Leaning across, he kissed it gently and then sitting up, swung himself out of bed. Pulling on his vest and underpants, he retrieved his prosthetic limb from where it lay by the side of the bed and strapped it on. Easing himself to his feet, he went downstairs to the kitchen and put the kettle on.

Finding a small tray on the sideboard, he took two mugs from the cupboard above and dropped a tea bag into each. As he waited for the kettle to boil, he crossed to the living room and switched on the TV. The screen filled with a shot of the news conference in full swing. To his surprise, it became evident immediately that it was the Police Superintendent who was playing the leading role, and he watched intently as the man fielded the flood of questions fired at him by a room filled with the media.

His attention intensified when one reporter asked if any attempt had been made to negotiate with the occupants of the Manor House.

"My armed response team were fired upon when attempting to gain entry," the policeman answered, with studied deliberation. "Attempts were made to reason with those obstructing us," he continued. "But we were unable to bring these to a successful conclusion. My men then entered the Manor House in the course of executing their lawful warrant, and subsequently the suspects blew up the building with several of my team inside, unfortunately resulting in a number of casualties."

"No mention of my part, thank God," KB thought to himself, as he switched off the TV and returned to the kitchen. Filling the mugs with boiling water, he stirred them gently until both had turned a suitably dark brown colour, then added a splash of milk to each from a carton he took from the 'fridge.

Carrying the tray upstairs, he placed one mug on the table next to Dani, who stretched and opened her eyes as he did so.

"What's this?" she asked.

"Cup of tea," he replied, moving around to his side of the bed. "It may be a bit strong, but it's wet and warm."

"So what's next?" she asked.

"Well," he said, turning to look at her, "I'm going to take a shower and then we should have some breakfast and be on our way."

"Not yet you aren't," she said, dropping the duvet as she sat up. "You're coming back to bed. I want to hear some of those nice things you said to me last night, and if you can't remember them, you're in big trouble."

Sometime later, they faced each other across the breakfast table, both lost in their own thoughts until KB broke the silence.

"I had the TV on earlier and caught up with the press conference. No mention of us, and the top cop was playing it pretty cool, so as far as I am concerned, it seems I am off the hook, for a while anyway."

"That's good news," she said, and then after a pause added, "Kris, last night was special and I wouldn't want to say it will never happen again, and part of me wants it to, but," she said, her tone serious, "If you ever breathe a word of it to anyone, I'll never speak to you again and I mean it. The 'Ice Maiden' reputation suits my purpose well, so I don't want any rumours circulating around the Agency because you've been bolstering up your male ego by bragging of your conquest to the lads, understand?"

"I promise," he answered. "I wouldn't do that anyway, and I hope you realise that as you get to know me better, which I hope you will. I'm not another Triple H."

"I know you're not, and believe me, Kris, last night would never have happened if I thought you were."

"Or this morning?" he asked with a smile.

"More especially this morning," she answered emphatically. "Now let's get these dishes put away, pack our bags and get going. It's still a pretty gloomy day out there, but at least it's stopped raining."

As they drove through Dulverton, the town was already busy and stopping at the newsagents, KB went in to buy a paper. In the racks that displayed all the daily editions, the banner headlines ranged from 'MASSACRE OF THE INNOCENTS' in one of the tabloids, to 'RAID ON SCHOOL FOR TERROR' in another. Picking one that suggested it might provide a more factual account of the previous day's events, he paid the shop assistant and returned to the Ford.

"We seem to have pushed everything else off the front pages," he said, handing Dani the paper as he eased himself into the driver's seat.

As they drove out of town, he slowed as they passed the National Park Authority offices, which had been cordoned off with two armed policemen patrolling the car park. Several Police cars were drawn up alongside Army Land Rovers and a variety of other vehicles. Outside the cordon a bevy of reporters and cameramen clustered together and two mobile TV vans were parked on the kerb.

"Obviously they're still pretty busy," he commented. "But I didn't spot any Agency cars there, so my bet is that Andy and our team are long gone."

"One of the advantages of running a covert organization," the girl said.

"You can keep your head down and avoid the limelight, so let's get out of here."

An hour later, he pulled the Wildtrak into the car park of The Volunteer. The pub was already open and lights shone from the windows of the kitchen and the bar.

"Okay" he said as he switched off the engine, "let's face the music. Some of the questions that I know we are going to be asked will be tricky to answer, especially Rocky's absence. I'll do the talking but if you want to add anything that will help to give some assurance to my folks that we were not directly involved in the shooting, please feel free!"

Collecting their bags off the back seat, they were walking towards the back door when a familiar voice called from the direction of the stables. Turning around, the figure of Alex came running across the car park towards them.

"You go on in," he said to Dani. "Dad and Mum are expecting you, and I'll be along in a minute."

"Don't forget to duck," she replied mischievously, disappearing through the door and leaving him alone to face Alex.

"Kris, I'm so glad you're here," Alex gasped, throwing her arms around him. "Did you get my text?"

"Yes," he replied, making no attempt to return her embrace, "I gather things did not go according to plan in Paris?"

"No, nothing was right. Hugo turned out to be anything but the perfect gentleman, and I'm so sorry, I made a terrible mistake. But you're back now and I promise to make it up to you. I just want to forget everything, and I really need you to do the same. Please, Kris, say you'll forgive me?"

"I'm sorry too, but it's not as simple as that," he heard himself say. "I really thought we had something going, Alex, and the last thing I expected to hear was that you had taken off on the day we were supposed to announce our engagement."

"But I gather your weren't here either," she sniffed. "And anyway, who was that with you?"

"You met at the Rifles' party. That's Dani Janes, she's a work colleague and is spending a few days with us."

"And I'm supposed to believe that?" she snapped, turning on her heels and stalking off towards the stables.

"Believe what you like," he called after her, and shrugging his shoulders, picked up his Bergen and followed Dani into the house.

Inside the back hall, he dropped his Bergen by the stairs, and hearing voices from the living room pushed open the door to find Dani talking to Hannah.

"Hey, sis," he greeted her warmly. "Up and about again?"

"At last," she replied. "But under strict orders to take it easy, so Mum and Dad are having a field day fussing over me! But what have you been up to? Dani has been telling me that you were both involved in the Exmoor thing, and I'm looking forward to hearing more. I warn you," she added, "Mum nearly had kittens when the news broke, knowing you were up there somewhere, so thank God you phoned Dad yesterday. Since then she has calmed down a bit, but you'd better have a good story ready. How's my friend Rocky? I've missed having him around."

"I'm afraid he was a casualty," he answered quietly. "The poor old boy found himself in the wrong place at the wrong time, and I couldn't save him."

"Damn!" she exclaimed. "I'm so sorry, Kris, that's a bloody shame. It won't be the same without him hanging around the stables or trotting along by the side of me when we're riding out. I get the feeling it wasn't an accident, do you know who was responsible?"

"Sort of," he replied. "But whoever it was is either under lock and key right now, or Allah is explaining to him why he does not qualify for the one hundred virgins, or whatever the number is. But that's enough for now, I'll fill you in on the rest of the details after closing time when we can all sit down together. How's Commando?" he asked, quickly changing the subject.

"He's fine. He certainly benefitted from a few days of Carol's schooling but now he's back, I'm afraid he's not getting the amount of exercise he should. Alex is down at the stables mucking out now, but she hasn't attempted to ride him out yet. On that subject, what's up with that girl? In spite of the fact that she buggered off to Paris with that Army toff for New Year's, she shows up here yesterday all bright and breezy as if nothing happened and since then has been constantly bending my ear, going on about how much she missed you and how she can't wait to see you again!"

"I know," he said. "I've seen her already and I'm afraid she may not be so happy after our chat. However, I'm certain she'll get over it, and if she runs true to form, it won't be long before she's hanging on someone else's arm. Anyway, let me show Dani to her room, then I'll check in with Mum and Dad."

Outside in the hallway, they picked up their bags and KB led the way upstairs.

"I hope your Alex is not into witchcraft or voodoo," Dani said, as he opened the bedroom door for her. "I'd hate to wake up tomorrow morning with a dead chicken on my pillow!"

"First of all, she is not 'my' Alex, and secondly I promise you if you wake up with anything on your pillow, it won't be a dead chicken," he replied. "But I'll leave you to make yourself at home. See you downstairs in a minute."

Downstairs he found Kathy at her usual station in the kitchen, and after extricating himself from a near smothering hug, went through to the bar. As he came through the doorway, Jack looked up from pulling a pint, a welcoming grin spreading across his face.

"Good to see you, Son," he said, topping off the glass and handing it across the bar to the familiar figure of Obi Kernworthy, who waved a cheery greeting. "Give us a hand here and you can tell us all about it later."

"That I will, Dad," KB assured him. "But I shouldn't say too much in front of our customers, unless you want a horde of newspaper reporters knocking at the door. Have you told anyone that I was on Exmoor?"

"Nope," came the quick response. "I thought it best to say nothing. Anyway, you don't know how pleased I am to see you back in one piece, but now I see a friend of yours wants to chat," he added, nodding in Obi's direction. "So you had better be careful what you say, you know what a canny old fox he is."

Crossing to the counter, KB pulled himself a pint and walking around to the other side, pulled up a barstool next to the farmer.

"Well hello there, young fella', – bin away 'ave ee?" came the question.

"Yes, Obi, working away from home for a few days, but it's always good to get back."

"Where were 'ee too, then?" the man persisted.

"Over in Devon," he said, already regretting that he had been too specific.

"Don't suppose 'ee knows nowt about this yer then?" came the next question, as Obi peered at him from over his reading glasses, plumping a paper down in front of him on the bar top as he spoke.

There, staring at him was the headline that shouted 'RAID ON SCHOOL FOR TERROR'."

"Can't say I do, Obi," he lied. "To be honest I haven't had much of a chance to read up on it yet."

"Zeems it twer a right old how-de-doo up Exmoor way," the farmer insisted. "Zom volks be reckonin' twer closer to a massacree, but I can't zee it meself. I reckons if they buggers were up to no good, teaching kids to blow things up and that, they 'ad it comin' to 'em, don't 'ee agree?"

"I certainly do," he replied. "But let me buy you another pint, before Dad calls time."

"Don't mind if I do. Now tell me, wots up 'tween you and the Baker girl? Rumour 'as it round the village that she's bin off shagging some geezer over in Paree, bet you ain't too bleddy pleased 'bout that!"

"Obi," he laughed, "You ask too many questions. Here comes your pint; now I must finish mine and get back behind the bar." As he took a mouthful, he nearly choked when Obi fired one last question at him.

"Don't suppose you've come across any of they sheep rustlers in your travels, 'ave 'ee?"

"No," he lied again. "But a little bird tells me the Samson boys are back in Ireland, so you can relax your evening patrols for a while."

"And bleddy good riddance," the farmer said, a degree of finality in his voice.

After lunch, the family gathering he was dreading turned out to be a lot easier than he had expected. His parents seemed to accept his explanation, backed by Dani, that their role in the assault on Langaller Estate had been purely as observers, and that Dani was a work colleague.

"Come on, Kris," Dani said, as they exhausted their questions. "You can take me for a walk by the river and show me some of these wonderful Somerset Levels you are so proud of."

As they paused to put on their jackets in the hallway, he put his hand in his pocket and pulled out Rocky's lead. Shaking his head sadly, he hung it up on his peg and followed the girl out into the car park.

"Thanks for your support," he said, as they crossed the road to the towpath. "I think my explanation that we were merely observing would have worn a tad thin, if you hadn't been there to back me up."

"Didn't realize you were such an accomplished liar," she replied smiling at him. "But it's probably just as well. All I can say is, don't ever try to pull the wool over my eyes, you won't find me nearly as trusting. Must say, I like your parents and I think I could get on really well with Hannah. Tell me the story behind Commando, he sounds like quite a handful."

As they reached the bridge, a car sped by them. KB recognized it immediately as Joe Baker's, but it was Alex, not the builder behind the wheel.

"Not nearly as much of a handful as that one," he said, nodding in the direction of the car as it disappeared into the gathering dusk, realising as he said it that if she had seen them, she had certainly not acknowledged it.

Aftermath

"Soldier rest! Thy warfare o'er,
Dream of fighting fields no more;
Sleep the sleep that knows no breaking,
Morn of toil, nor night of waking."

Sir Walter Scott

Their remaining days had passed without incident. Alex had not graced the pub with her presence, nor did she attempt to contact him. The day before he had driven Dani back to Dulverton, promising that whatever came next, they would keep in touch. She had allowed him a hug, but turned her face away when he tried to kiss her, leaving him wondering that their closeness in the aftermath of Langaller had been no more than a fleeting moment. In town he made one stop at the vet's to collect the small earthenware urn which, with its brass plaque engraved with the single word 'Rocky', now lay on the seat beside him together with a bunch of early Cornish daffodils.

This Sunday had dawned bright but cold, but the warmth of the reception he had got from Jacko's parents when he called by to see them in their bungalow had more than compensated for the chill outside.

Now he sat in his truck outside the church where not so long ago he had attended his comrade's funeral. Getting down from the cab, he put the urn under his arm and picking up the flowers, pushed open the wicket gate and climbed the path to the churchyard. The trees that flanked it on the Bristol Channel side were bare of the leaves that had adorned them on that earlier summer day, but the rooks still cawed a raucous greeting as they wheeled above and settled on the wind-blown branches. From inside the church, the congregation were in full song and the strains of one of his favourite hymns reached his ears.

Pausing he listened as they started the penultimate verse and spoke the words with them until it ended.

Time, like an ever rolling stream
Bears all its sons away,
They fly forgotten as a dream
Dies at the opening day.

Following the path to the young soldier's grave, he knelt and unscrewing the urn, gently scattered the contents over the gravel surface. A slight gust of wind blew a small cloud of the grey ashes into the air, spiralling upwards and out of sight.

Standing up, he retraced his steps to the side of the church, where a small standpipe had been fixed to the wall. Filling the urn from the tap, he returned to the grave and placed it under the headstone, arranging the daffodils within it as best he could.

Standing up, he took his maroon beret from his jacket pocket, and placing it carefully on his head, paused for a moment.

"There you are, Jacko," he said quietly. "Now you've got your buddy Rocky by your side. Happy hunting my friends."

Stepping back from the graveside, he came to attention and saluted. Taking off his beret, he replaced it in his pocket, and walked steadily back along the path and through the gate to where the Ford stood waiting.

As he climbed behind the wheel, the secure phone buzzed. Pressing the answer switch a clear voice came through the speaker.

"Sirius, this is Olympus. Meeting 0830 tomorrow in the conference room. Come prepared to move out immediately afterwards, you have an assignment."

Acknowledging the call, he paused for a moment to let down the window, leaning out to allow the cool breeze to ruffle his hair. In that moment he heard a dog bark, the sound carried from the graveyard behind him. It was the familiar, joyous bark he had heard so often and with it the dam broke on the emotions he had held in check for too long. For the first time in many years Kristian Blake, soldier, son, lover, elite marksman and trained killer, wept like a child.

Sometime later, he eased the gear shift into drive and moved the Wildtrak slowly down the lane. Once more he purged his mind of his darkest feelings and slammed the steel door shut on his thoughts and memories.

Whatever he faced tomorrow, he would be ready – *Utrinque Paratus.*

APPENDIX

Requiem for a Countryman

(As read at L/Cpl 'Jacko' Jackson's funeral)

I am a whisper in the trees,
The rustle of the autumn leaves.
The crunch of footsteps in the snow,
The woodland glade where bluebells grow.
I am the warmth of summer days,
The distant moors, their purple haze.
My voice is in the ocean's roar,
As foam flecked waves crash on shore,
The mew of buzzard wheeling high,
The honk of wild geese flying by,
And in the dusk as darkness falls,
In the lonely barn owl's haunting calls.
I dreamed my dreams, I fought my fears,
I laughed my laughs and cried my tears,
I loved my loves, made friendships true,
And now, no longer here, I say to you,
I may not have won the course I ran,
But I lie at peace, a countryman.

GLOSSARY OF TERMS

AK-47 Russian designed Kalashnikov Assault Rifle. 7.62 mm calibre. Effective range 350m. Estimated up to 75 million manufactured and in circulation worldwide.

Apache American designed attack helicopter built for the British Army by Augusta Westland under licence from Boeing. Powered by 2 Rolls-Royce Turbo shaft engines. Crew of 2. Max Speed 330 kph, max range 475 km. Armament includes 30 mm cannon, Hellfire Missiles, rockets and air to air missiles.

BRF Brigade Reconnaissance Force.

CO Commanding Officer. Used to refer to the Lieutenant-Colonel commanding a Battalion or equivalent.

Coppicing Traditional method of woodland management.

CP Command Post.

Cpl Abbreviation for the non-commissioned rank of Corporal.

Dishka Russian made DSHK heavy machine gun, often mounted in pick-up trucks. 12.7 mm calibre, rate of fire 600 rounds per minute, effective out to 2000m.

DZ Drop Zone. A selected area where airborne troops can be dropped. Usually secured in advance of the main drop by Para pathfinders. A 'hot' DZ is one that may be under hostile observation and therefore likely to be covered by enemy fire.

End-Ex End of Exercise.

ETR Electric Target Range. Automated electrically controlled rifle range where the targets do not have to be operated manually (e.g. raised and lowered by hand).

FAC Forward Air Controller. Usually an Officer or Senior NCO who operates with front line troops to control and guide supporting air strikes against enemy positions.

FMC Force Mobile Command. Collective name for the combat elements of the Canadian Armed Forces (Navy, Army and Air Force).

GCHQ Government Communication Headquarters. Centralised facility for receiving and dispatching message by secure landline or communications satellite. Also monitors mobile telephone and radio communications and internet traffic.

GPMG General Purpose Machine Gun. Known in the British Army as the 'Gimpy', it is a belt fed medium machine gun, 7.62 mm calibre, rate of fire 750 rounds per minute, effective range out to 1800m.

GPS Global Positioning Satellite.

Herc Lockheed Martin Hercules four engine turboprop military transport. In use by over 60 countries worldwide.

HQ Headquarters.

ID Identification.

IED Improvised Explosive Device. Remotely detonated explosive devices used by the Taliban, and other terrorist organisations. In Afghanistan these are often Russian artillery shells or landmines left over from the Soviet occupation.

Int/Intel Intelligence.

Klicks Slang for kilometres.

L85A2 Standard issue British Army automatic assault rifle, an updated version of the SA80. Calibre 5.56 mm. 30 round magazine. Rate of fire 600+ rpm. Effective maximum range 400 metres.

L/Cpl Lance Corporal. Abbreviation for the lowest non-commissioned rank in the British Army.

LI Light Infantry. Now combined with the Rifle Regiments to form 'The Rifles'

Linney Cornish name for a lean-to.

LLDR Lightweight Laser Designator Rangefinder. Frequently carried by an FAC to 'illuminate' designated targets with a laser beam to enable the accurate deployment of laser guided bombs.

LZ Landing Zone. Designated area for landing helicopters.

Mag Rifle or pistol magazine.

Mastiff Six wheeled armoured personnel carrier. Based on the

American Cougar family of armoured vehicles it provides effective protection against most IEDs, land mines etc. Carries 8 personnel plus a driver and GPMG gunner. Powered by a Caterpillar diesel engine, range 600 miles, speed 65 m.p.h.

M/Cpl Master Corporal. Canadian NCO rank, equivalent to British Army Corporal.

Minimi Light machine gun. 5.56 mm calibre, up to 1,000 rounds per minute and effective out to 800m.

MoD Ministry of Defence.

MP Military Policeman.

NCO Non-Commissioned Officer. Ranks in the British Army include Lance Corporal, Corporal, Sergeant, and Warrant Officers.

OFSTED Office for Standards in Education, Children's Services and Skills.

OP Observation Post.

Para Parachute Regiment/Paratroopers.

PTO Power Take Off. Link to a tractor's transmission which drives the equipment on towed machinery (e.g. the spinners on manure spreaders).

Recce Reconnaissance.

Red Caps Military Police.

Re-hab Rehabilitation.

RMP Royal Military Police.

RN Royal Navy.

Reaper Unmanned US designed turboprop powered surveillance and strike aircraft in service with the RAF. Max speed 300 m.p.h., range 1,151 miles, operating altitude 25,000ft, service ceiling 50,000ft. Armed with Hellfire missiles and Paveway laser guided bombs.

RPG-7 Russian made hand held unguided Rocket Propelled Grenade launcher/ Anti-Tank weapon. Grenade weight 2 – 4.5 kg. Effective range 200m, maximum range 950m.

RSM Regimental Sergeant Major. Warrant Officer (First Class). Highest non-commissioned rank in a Regiment, Infantry Battalion or equivalent.

Ruperts Other ranks derogatory name for officers.

RV Rendez-vous (meeting place).

Sgt Abbreviation for the NCO rank of Sergeant.

SIB Special Investigations Branch (of the Military Police).

Sitrep Situation Report. Frequent communication between forward troops and their Command Post.

Storm Shadow Air launched turbojet powered cruise missile developed by the UK, France and Italy. 450 kg warhead it is a 'fire and forget' weapon, pre-programmed before launch. After launch it follows a low flight path (30 – 40m) guided by GPS. Final guidance to the target is assisted by infra-red thermal imaging camera located in the missile's nose. Range approx 550 – 600 km. Speed 1,000 km/h.

SVD Russian Dragonov (semi-automatic) Sniper Rifle. 7.62 mm calibre, Effective Range 800m.

TA Territorial Army. Former name for the Army Reserve.

Tac Tactical.

Utrinque Paratus "Ready for Anything" – Motto of the Parachute Regiment.

WO2 Warrant Officer (Second Class), e.g. A senior non-commissioned rank held by Company Sergeant Majors in Infantry Battalions.

Yo-yo's Army reservists, name for the Yeomanry.

Lightning Source UK Ltd.
Milton Keynes UK
UKOW02f0613210716

278852UK00001B/91/P